Rachel Lynch grew up in Cumbria and has written a million-copy bestselling crime series set in the lakes and fells of her childhood, starring Detective Kelly Porter. She previously taught History and travelled the globe with her Army Officer husband, before having children and starting a new career in personal training and sports therapy. Writing from her home in Hertfordshire is now her full-time job, and this is her first standalone psychological thriller.

Also by Rachel Lynch

The Rich

Helen Scott Royal Military Police Thrillers

The Rift
The Line

Detective Kelly Porter

Dark Game
Deep Fear
Dead End
Bitter Edge
Bold Lies
Blood Rites
Little Doubt
Lost Cause
Lying Ways
Sudden Death
Silent Bones

THE
RICH

RACHEL LYNCH

CANELO

First published in the United Kingdom in 2023 by

Canelo
Unit 9, 5th Floor
Cargo Works, 1–2 Hatfields
London SE1 9PG
United Kingdom

A CIP catalogue record for this book is available from the British Library.

Print ISBN 978 1 80436 522 9
Ebook ISBN 978 1 80436 523 6

Cover design by Julia Connolly

Cover images © Stocksy

Look for more great books at www.canelo.co

Printed and bound in Great Britain by Clays Ltd, Elcograf S.p.A.

1

Prologue

Her face was the most perfect tone of ivory, a bride's dress from long ago. Untouched, with a timeless beauty. One longed to reach out and stroke it, like the soft fabric of a doll belonging to a child. A temporary desire, thought better of.

In her stillness, she was a pristine specimen of human engineering. The clavicle – a master lever – joined her appendages, which swung at the perimeter, to her heart at the centre. Her décolletage was clean, as if recently washed and tended to: such a delicate veil of silk protecting the organs within.

She groaned. She was still alive.

A lightning bolt of fear. Something must be done. A line, once crossed, is a thing of the past. The job needed finishing. Something heavy would do it.

Searching around underneath the body prompted a fit of coughing and spluttering, jerking the woman's body back and forth.

Focus.

The night was warm and sticky. Perfect for lovers looking for a secret place to hide their trysts. But this corner of the field was dead as the blackest night, only the slow ambling river showed signs of movement. Away in the distance sat a row of thatched-roofed cottages behind the Red Hen gastropub, which was bidding goodnight to its last customers. Life floated across the field from the tastefully modernised beer garden surrounded by twinkling lights. It was a venue for weddings, for the privileged few who could afford to love so richly. It had reinvented itself from old-school watering hole to niche on-trend establishment, attracting a clientele untouched by misfortune. Enough money bought immunity from reality. But there were no guests over here, paying or otherwise, except the odd mosquito; small native ones, and distant cousins of the fat bloodsuckers that caused such misery far from these shores.

Finally, a wheel wrench. It was heavy and lethal. Hopefully.

At least her eyes were closed. It was a small mercy not to have to stare at those deep hazelnut spheres that performed magic tricks on every man they turned towards. Distant recollections of a science lesson at school. The dissection of a cow's eye. Staring, mahogany discs, asking endless questions, full of accusations of inhumanity.

Held tightly, the wrench transferred its terrifying power to the wielder.

The woman lifted an arm feebly, as if knowing what was coming next, begging the question of whether slaughtered animals did the same in their final moments. Did they plead with their executioner for clemency? We all do what it takes to survive.

The wrench came up and down, slamming into her skull. Three times.

It was over.

Two fingers to the perfect neck confirmed life extinct. Her beautiful body, preened and pampered with privilege, was empty now. The blood was surprisingly oily. A bottle of bleach, packed in haste after the accident, now performed its one meaningful task in life: to wash away inconvenient impurities. It squirted over her body, and inside the crevices that any decent forensic detective might focus on. Her clothes, the blanket she lay on, her phone and the detritus from the boot were all piled into black bags. The body itself wasn't heavy. Her pride outweighed her flesh and bones. She was easily flopped over the riverbank, hastily smothered with branches.

It was a stretch of the river Cam that, in summer, was heavily overgrown, and whiffed of sewage. The locals had a petition about it.

Oh my, not Cambridge?

It would take days before she was discovered. The killer wasn't concerned about being exposed.

Chapter 1

My iPhone alarm brings about a feeling of dread and disappointment every morning at six a.m. Jeremy is fast asleep next to me and I can smell last night's booze sweating out of every pore. Where I once propped myself up on an elbow and peered at him lovingly, I now roll over to a shell of a man whose wasted and swollen body lies motionless and loveless on his side of the bed where it dropped last night, or sometime this morning. I can almost see the cloud of chemicals escaping his oily skin via his liver and kidneys, and the very sight of him makes me gag.

I slip into my morning routine as Jeremy remains oblivious, and the sounds of my toothbrush and the shower do not wake him. The mirror only signals back to me the face of somebody he used to love, so I don't look in it.

Marriage, like a yawning canyon, echoes with isolation and desolation, and I push it to the back of my mind, where it is safe from searching questions. I'm tempted to welcome hope, in all its disguises, tricking me into believing that he'll work today, or do something useful, but I'm no longer a girl who hangs on to such folly.

Jeremy has been writing a thesis for twenty years, without putting anything down on paper. The big publishing deal, and the trappings of fame it would bring, are all illusions, stuck in Jeremy's head behind the fug of a hangover and under the cover of a duvet. I fund his habit, like a brazen enabler. Functioning alcoholism costs money.

I believed in him for half of my life.

The bathroom floor is cold underfoot, but it's what I need to wake up, that, and the sound of my children – teenagers now – downstairs, fixing themselves breakfast and chattering about YouTube or TikTok. Theirs are the sounds of life, unlike the murmurs of Jeremy's bodily functions as he rolls over and farts, putting me off breakfast.

I put my faith in make-up, as if it can save me, as well as distinct pieces of expensive jewellery, and a lovingly laid out couture suit. I rub Barbara Sturm lotion into my skin and I feel like a real woman again. There is no limit to what I would spend on camouflage cream.

Despite my presence and the noise of my efforts, Jeremy slumbers on, and I consider the wisdom of slamming the bedroom door behind me, just to interrupt his fitful rest. I decide against it. I'm not a child, and I have a job to do. But I do leave his wine glass on his bedside cabinet, knowing that it will compound his shame when he finally wakes. Sometimes the truth is left discarded for all to see, and sometimes it needs planting.

I close the door gently and make my way downstairs to the noise of my children, who lighten my step. My day will be filled with the minds of the broken and so I grab this opportunity to wrap myself in the clamour of the mundane and ordinary. I pick up the post and read my name: Doctor Alex Moore, MSc Hons, BSc Hons, PsyD… Those are the ones to ignore because they're usually trying to sell me something. I drop the letters casually on the kitchen counter and notice that there is rotten fruit in the bowl. I'm irritated, but not surprised. I pick it out and throw it away.

James is eighteen and he knows everything; in fact, he gets a new tattoo when he learns a bit more. He smiles at me through a half-eaten croissant and he lets me hug him. He smells of aftershave and weed. His body is strong and soon he will be a man. I know he dabbles with banned substances and he's been out all night with a pal. Lydia is just a year behind him and is bulimic. She sips juice and shies away from my morning kiss. Her skin is pale and her eyes sunken: her body is pleading with all of us to nourish her. Ewan is my baby, at fifteen. He's on the verge of manhood: a torrid point in life where I'll have to pull away, but I don't want to. He watches over James's shoulder and his eyes widen as he figures out a joke. He gets beaten up at school and there's not a damn thing I can do about it. His shoulders don't sit as tall as his brother's and his smile is timid. He surprises easily and so I lay my hand upon his cheek gently and say good morning.

'Morning, Mum,' Ewan says, chomping on a banana.

'Where is it?' Lydia demands angrily.

There's an altercation in full swing, and Lydia's face is suddenly like thunder. There's nothing that can animate her quite like her brothers' quest to sabotage her sulking.

It's just another day, and this pleases me.

'Mum, he's got my eyeliner,' Lydia says in a pleading voice, appealing to me to make her brothers disappear, to solve all her problems. But I smirk at James, against my better judgement. He is a path forger, a trailblazer; fearless and autonomous, and possessed of an extra-terrestrial superpower called confidence, which eludes his sister. But my job is merely to stop them killing one another. The years of instruction were lost a long time ago. They're fully formed humans now. Almost.

'Have you got her eyeliner?' I ask James.

'I only borrowed it!'

He ducks and dodges a croissant as it's launched in his direction by his sister.

'Lydia! Dear God, it's just an eyeliner!' I instantly regret losing my cool. I've diminished her in front of her brothers, but I can't take the words back. Lydia storms out of the kitchen and runs upstairs.

'Drama, drama!' James adds for good measure.

Now I am full of regret and go to the fridge to get milk for my coffee, but there is none left, just packets of food from Waitrose left untouched. The unwritten rule is that Jeremy sorts all of that out because I work full time. I add milk to the list of things I need to pick up on the way back from the office tonight, and I make my coffee black. It tastes bitter and disgusting and I crave the richness of something dairy to go in it. I skip breakfast, which is trendy these days because it's called fasting.

'You've got golf practice tonight,' I tell Ewan.

He looks forlorn. 'I'm going out,' he whines.

'You can go out after,' I tell him. 'What's this?' I distract them. They're playing cards while their phones churn away beside them.

'It's a magic trick,' says James.

'I know this, you've got the Jack behind your back,' I say.

'How did you know? Mum!'

I redeem myself. I'm Mum of the Year. Good at magic tricks.

Sun pierces the windows along the whole of the extension to the back of the house, and through the lanterns

7

straddling the roof. The rays are glorious and I turn my face to them, as if they'll help me through the day, or maybe they'll linger too long and give me skin cancer. One never knows on which side of chance one walks.

The pool man is here; I forgot it was Wednesday. Christ. I run upstairs to search for cash. Jeremy stirs and I remind him that I'm taking his car today. He needs to take mine to the carwash to be valeted, and go to the tip and get rid of the broken coat stand, which he denies having anything to do with. His blackouts are getting worse.

'I'll take the rubbish you have in your boot and sling it in the waste at work,' I tell him. He grunts.

I hate his car.

It's not that it doesn't work, or it's ugly or old. It's a beautiful car. But it's Jeremy's and it reminds me of him. There's always a bottle or two rolling around in there.

The pool man is pleased to see his cash on time, as usual. He's stripped to the waist, which is appropriate for the season but not necessarily the neighbourhood, and about twenty-five years old. He works out. His muscles are taut and his smile fresh. Something stirs inside me that has been dead for so long I can't remember the feeling. My eyes linger on his torso and they drift towards the point where his skin disappears into his shorts. I walk away. It's a little livener to get my day going.

'Lydia!' I scream through the kitchen and up the stairs.

She ignores me. The boys have disappeared. My children are constantly plugged into electronic equipment and it's a miracle I can communicate with them at all. I remember looking at my own mother and thinking her ancient because she'd never owned a pair of roller boots. Middle age assaults me with a deflationary slap. I'm no longer relevant.

I check my face one last time in the hall mirror. The hallway I rearranged just last week, which Jeremy didn't notice. The photograph of us as a family, smiling, happy and tanned, on Tony's yacht in the Bahamas, stares back at me from the table.

I grab my briefcase and then trot back to the kitchen for the shopping list.

'I'm gone!' I holler.

No reply.

'Lydia, don't forget your trip money!'

I recoil at the sound of my own screeching. It's exhausting, shaping children, and then realising that the effort was unrelenting and mostly pointless. The human brain is the most undeveloped organ in the body at birth. It's a blank canvas, ready to turn into a masterpiece or a catastrophe.

'You look lovely, Mum,' James says. He's followed me into the hall.

I blow him a kiss. His words linger in my head as I walk to Jeremy's car.

Chapter 2

'It hurts too much.'

'I know. Remember the Coke bottle, we don't need to shake it up and open it all at once. We can just let enough gas out to release a bit of tension.'

I'm sat in my battered old armchair, chosen by Jeremy and me at an auction in Berwick-Upon-Tweed, when we were Psychology students at Edinburgh University. It's a grand George II wingback, positioned opposite my clients. We patched the old thing up together, when we still believed in restoration.

My office is painted in different shades of green – a nurturing psychology trick – and framed images of waterfalls, beaches and mountains adorn the walls. I wait. Everyone has problems. Carrie's are genuine.

Clients march through my door like a tsunami of suffering, and they all want the same thing: to be fixed. It's what they pay me for, but like the trade in phoenix feathers, it's an illusion. In reality it takes hard labour and painful reconditioning. People think that's what psychologists do: solve problems. But that's not what my job is at all. In fact, I create more. And that's the point: things invariably get worse before they ever get better.

But Carrie Greenside is different.

Like most of my clients, she has plenty of money, but it can't purchase away her pain. She's tried. A bottomless squandering of resources poured into retreats, wellness gurus, pills and, finally, the only thing that was sure to wash away her malignant ruin: booze and drugs. But she's learned that even that is temporary medicine; a brief bandaging wrapped around a corrupted wound that peels off eventually.

I watch her as she takes her time to answer. She's spruced and dripping with tokens of her triumph over the shit pit she climbed out of. Her voice is measured, and I suspect she's invested heavily in that too, to metamorphose from the girl she once was. Carrie demands a phenomenal salary, working at a big-shot banking giant in London, speculating on the movement of capital. Money puzzles me. Trading in thoughts and feelings is so much easier. It's not that I don't appreciate the need for capitalism, but I don't understand it. I'd rather live on an island somewhere hot, with white sandy beaches and cocktails in cold glasses with bits of tropical fruit hung over the side, preferably served by the pool man. A place without government or rules. A world without telephones, TV, or internet shopping, which is all too noisy. I crave a simpler life, where things aren't as frenetic. Without modern distractions, most of the neurotic cases that spill into my office might simply disappear.

It's taken Carrie Greenside forty-odd years to talk about her childhood, and now she's taken the band-aid off the woman is in turmoil. The monumental discovery that her adult self is engineered by her childish past threatens to derail everything she's created: this life she's designed around rank, structure and reward. It's all unravelling and it's my job to help put it back together. I peer at my glass paperweight on the table between us, carved into the shape of the rod of Asclepius, and for a brief moment I see the snake slithering freely, shedding its skin and releasing its grasp of the staff.

I'm drifting off and it's not like me.

'What do you feel, Carrie?' I ask her.

'Fucking angry,' Carrie replies.

'Good. Anger is just an emotion, and it's one you're permitted to have,' I soothe.

My professional tone is a fine balance between being firm, thus allowing my clients to find empowerment, but also gentle, to treat the subject with compassion, and present to them the safety to progress. Or at least that's what I was taught in college. In reality, I'm only human. We healers were once seen as witches and tortured for our trickery. Five hundred years ago I would have been burned at the stake, but so too, I imagine, would Carrie.

Two scented candles, placed pretentiously on a shelf behind her, waft their perfume across the room. I let her anger sit between us. Carrie wears a Prada summer dress, her handbag is Chanel, and her breasts, heaving up and down with exertion, cost ten thousand pounds. I have other trinkets, so I'm not judging. Carrie chooses to wear her success like a shield, and it will be a miracle to prise it off her. She has reached her fifties as an unmit-igated success. She flies about as high in her thrusting career as anyone could. The trophy for such dedicated and unstinting loyalty and graft is enough money to forget its worth. But on the couch, in my office, her chest turns pink above her expensive dress. I could sneer at her exterior, and what it conceals, but I don't. My interest is what lies beneath, and Carrie has begun to tell me. She's allowed me into her gilded cage and I feel privileged. Outwardly, Carrie is the kind of woman other women want to be, and men want to possess. Inside, like most of us, she's a wreck. I'm reminded of the Potemkin village inside a well-used old copy of a psychological tome sat on my bookcase. Unlike the Empress Catherine, I'm not fooled, and neither is Carrie.

'*Doctor Moore?*'

The intercom startles both me and my client. Dora, my secretary, knows never to disturb a session, so it must be extraordinarily important. I lean over my desk and apologise to Carrie, who doesn't seem to mind. I pick up the receiver and listen to Dora.

The call is important enough for me to raise an eyebrow. I go back to Carrie. She's knocked off her thread, rightly so, but we soon get back on track. The noise of the industrial waste cart diverts my attention outside. It comes every Wednesday. It whines and groans under the weight of the detritus of businesses throughout Cambridge. Thankfully, I remembered to throw the bags in there from Jeremy's car. The thought of him reminds me that I need therapy, and I try to rewind to the present moment: somebody else's baggage.

Carrie pushes her blow-dried hair out of her eyes. She does so with the kind of grace money can buy. Her bracelets rattle and I wonder if the weight of them shackles her to her past.

Therapy requires uninterrupted moments of serenity. Silence and concentration are fundamental to my work, and interjections halt the bridging necessary to move between two places of emotional intelligence. I try to refocus.

'I'm so sorry about that, Carrie. It was unavoidable, I'm afraid. You were telling me about your anger. You've been rather put off, I fear. Could you take yourself back there?'

'All too easily, Alex,' she said. 'I'm fucking livid.'

I have a first-names policy. No one should be expected to trust a stranger when having to call them by a stuffy title. It goes against everything I'm trying to achieve.

'Good. What does your anger make you want to do?' I ask.

'Kill her,' Carrie says.

The number of potential murderers I get through my doors doesn't concern me. It's natural. Only this morning, I fantasised about poisoning Jeremy's half-drunk bottle of wine left in the fridge. It was only the shock that there was any left that stopped me doing it.

She stares at me and into my soul. 'It's amazing how powerful a woman can be when she's boiling with rage.'

Chapter 3

I swing Jeremy's car into the gravel driveway and turn off the engine. The air conditioning ceases to afford its protection and I'm ravenous and thirsty. The mercury topped thirty degrees today. England isn't built for heat-waves. My home is a Georgian-fronted haven of apparent tranquillity, and other people's problems pay for it. Misery makes money. The street is leafy and shaded and affords some escape from the heat. It's private and secluded, though a stone's throw away from the centre of Cambridge. Desirable real estate. I sit and contemplate what awaits me. I want to clean the inside of my head with a cool cloth.

It had been Jeremy who interrupted my session with Carrie. Dora is easily swayed by him. When sober, Jeremy is warm and persuasive. But I rarely get to witness him abstinent anymore. It's gone five o'clock and I know he'll be steadily on his way to a stupor by now, having done nothing all day apart from google successful psychologists and pretend to research his thesis. I know his passwords on my Mac computer, and I see how much work he does in a day. I know what he watches.

As I drove home, I passed hundreds of people sitting on the banks of the river Cam, drinking beer or wine, having picnics, laughing and carefree, safe in their joy. We used to do things like that: an afternoon drink, a punt on the river, or a bike ride with the kids. I wonder what Carrie Greenside will be doing tonight in her childless mansion. Her freedom to take lovers, swim naked, and book holidays in exotic places taunts me.

My breakthrough with Carrie today comforts me a little. She released some of her rage. The belief that endless talking about problems somehow repairs them is now old school, and cutting-edge trauma work is all about re-visiting and re-feeling. It's tough, but Carrie has what it takes. I take a minute to consider the horrific abuse Carrie suffered as a child, and maybe that's what I need to do: calm down before I go inside; destress and declutter all the information from my job. I concentrate on the seven-year-old girl, terrified and brutalised. Carrie's father, violent and damaged himself, took his wrath out on his daughter, as her mother stood by and watched. The wounds are deep. Children from such backgrounds often rise to the top of their fields, but equally they also end up under bridges injecting heroin. Carrie is a woman of extremes; highly emotionally intelligent, clever and inquisitive, but infected with crippling vulnerability. She doesn't just want to know how to get better, she wants to understand the process and take ownership of it. And for that, I admire her.

My moment of purging doesn't work. I still feel burdened by the suffering of others.

I don't want to go inside the house. It might fall down, even though it's made of stone. The children are likely off with friends, or at various clubs until dinner time, so for now it could be just Jeremy and me. I want a cool glass of rosé in the garden, alone. A dive in the pool. But suddenly the thought of water makes me feel as though I'm swimming underneath the surface. At the bottom is the mortgage, the kids' school fees, the family cars and the Waitrose delivery: all of it threatening to drown me in a blurry watery grave. My body feels tired and I force myself out of the car. The fierce heat of the day has withered the grand peonies in the pretty pots outside the door, and they beg me for water, screaming their need, like everything else in my life. They're lucky I don't swipe their heads off.

The reason for Jeremy's rude interruption, however, was legitimate, and we have something serious to talk about. The police want to ask some questions about a friend of ours who's gone off the grid. Monika is married to a good friend of ours, and they live just a few miles from here. It's not the first time she's taken off, and I'm not in the least bit surprised, so at first, I didn't understand why he'd made it official this time, until Jeremy told me it was his idea to call the police. My only explanation for this is that the drama Monika has managed to create is likely something that will enable Jeremy to imbibe more numbing gel tonight.

The police must investigate, to a point. Monika is an adult and is entitled to drop out of reality occasionally. After all, that's all anyone is after when they watch a movie or surf the internet mindlessly. Missing is an adjective and subject to interpretation.

I drag my files out of the car, along with the shopping, and waft my hair at my neck. My body is sticky and I need a shower. I'm put off diving into the pool because I don't know what I'll find underneath the surface. The air is muggy, and the temperature is twenty-eight degrees. After the relief of Jeremy's air-conditioned car, my body is engulfed by a fresh layer of sweat. The heatwave is due to last all week.

I slam the car door with my foot and see that Jeremy has had mine cleaned. It's negligible encouragement. I go around the back of the house and see evidence that the children have been in the pool. Discarded towels, toys they say they're too old to enjoy, empty glasses and turned over lounge chairs litter the space.

The kitchen door is open.

Jeremy is sat at the bar, looking forlorn. At least he's dressed. And we have something to talk about tonight: where Monika might be. The sight of him makes my clothes feel too tight, and I brace myself for a spikey exchange. In here, I'm no doctor.

'Long day?' he asks.

I nod. There are dirty pots in the sink, and the dishwasher hasn't been on. I throw open windows in a futile attempt to get more air in. My wedding rings are too tight.

'Kids out?'

It's his turn to nod. Years ago, an empty house would have been our opportunity to run upstairs and get naked, jumping on each other like deprived lunatics, tearing at each other's bodies and finding each other's mouths hungrily. There was a time I found him surprisingly hypnotic, and rampantly beddable, but now the thought of intimacy with him fills me with physical aversion. It's a self-preservation response that I counsel my married clients in, but I don't practise myself. The chancellor advises austerity, but he still skis in Verbier every year.

I walk to the fridge and unpack food and milk. There's a scrap of wine left in the bottom of a bottle and I pour it into a glass and drain it, glad I didn't poison it after all.

'Another one chilling?' I ask him.

'There's some outside, I'll get it,' he says.

Jeremy goes to the pool house, where we have an outdoor kitchen, mainly for parties, which we no longer have. When he comes back, I'm sat at the breakfast bar, scrolling through my phone, seeking mindless connection where there is none. I've turned into a teenager without the tight skin and years of potential ahead of me. An amateur psychologist would say that Jeremy and I are experiencing a mid-life crisis, but this is infinitely more disappointing and enduring.

He tops up my glass and we sit in silence, the point of what we intended to talk about forgotten.

'Did you take Ewan to the range?' I ask.

What I'm really seeking is confirmation of whether he was in fact sober enough to drive his son. It's immature and I feel petulant. It's been a long day.

'Yeah, I dropped him at a pal's after. We put his new bike in the boot so he can cycle home later.'

Even bikes are enablers for Jeremy's drinking habits.

'How's Lydia?'

It's a daily question. Our options are limited. Lydia isn't responding well to counselling, but ethically neither I nor Jeremy can treat our own daughter. One might think that doctors of clinical psychology would make decent parents. Not so. Maybe we're all screwed *because* we're psychologists, like James likes to tease me. It's clever and humorous when he says it, though.

I gulp my wine.

'Did you talk to her?'

He bristles. His hands tremble, and it's not the first time I've noticed it. I'm attacking him. I have no filter.

'It's not that easy. If she doesn't want to talk, then I can't force her,' he says, defensively. His words are slurring slightly.

Jeremy has never practised psychology, though he's fully qualified to do so, but he has plenty to say on the subject, mainly hidden in secret documents on my computer, which he thinks will one day be sold for millions, and which he believes are protected with passwords.

I watch him refill his glass and it puts me off my own. I cover it with my hand when he goes to do so.

'Did you at least try?' I can't let it go. He's glaring at me.

'I had other things on my mind today, like Tony and Monika.'

Ah, that's what we were supposed to be talking about. Guilt washes over me, but not too much. It's not just Monika who is missing; we're all shadows.

'Sorry, how is Tony? Did Monika just wander off again?'

He drains another glass. He'll blame it on his nerves.

'God, Jeremy, steady on. How much have you had?'

'Don't you dare moralise to me! You've no idea how utterly dejecting it is to be married to a successful high-flying and decorated psychologist and have to pick up the pieces at home.'

It comes out of nowhere. My mouth opens but no words come out. I thought we were supposed to be talking about Tony and Monika. His eyes are red and he glares at me with loathing. I don't feel fear, just pity.

I don't want any more wine, and I look in the fridge for inspiration for dinner. There is leftover lamb from Sunday's BBQ.

Tony and Monika came over.

For a few hours, over several bottles of booze, and in and out of the pool, we put a band-aid over our lives, like all parties do, and we smiled and chatted about summer holidays, and skiing next year.

Now Monika is AWOL, and I feel an idiot for not spotting something. I remember that the police want to talk to me, but I know it's a waste of time. Monika follows her own agenda.

The Thorpes' marriage is volatile and sometimes everybody needs a breather. With no children, they often take themselves off, separately, for a break. They met on a cruise, along the Danube River. Monika is a Latvian ex-model, who scooped our friend coming out of a messy divorce. Tony went away with a broken heart and returned with a new wife. One who happens to be young and beautiful. It also turns out that she is capricious and flighty.

'There's probably some perfectly ordinary explanation for a fallout.' I skip over his explosive anger from moments ago. It's the booze talking, not the man I married.

I look in a cupboard and find tortilla wraps, deciding that fajitas will be a good dinner tonight, with the lamb. I distract myself by chopping vegetables and salad. Jeremy sits at the kitchen bar, brooding. My hands are grateful for the occupation.

I'm relieved to hear the front door slam. It's Ewan.

'Hey, buddy. What the hell?' Jeremy says. He puts down his glass, which has been stuck to his hand, and rushes to his son. Ewan's face is sweaty and bruised. His chest heaves up and down and he's shaking.

'What happened?' I stop what I'm doing, putting down the knife, and I go to him. Ewan tries to speak but he can't. I understand enough to know that he's been attacked again, and his new bike has been stolen.

'Do you know them?' Jeremy bellows.

'Jeremy...' He ignores me. Ewan is desperate to get away, his face burning with shame.

'Jesus Christ! That bastard Brandon Stand!' Jeremy shouts. Ewan flinches and his eyes widen.

'It's all right, Dad! It doesn't matter!'

'It does matter! I'm sick of it! I'm phoning the head-master,' he slurs.

Brandon Stand is the son of the headmaster of Ewan's school, which sets me back almost twenty grand a year. It also means that Ewan's tormentor is untouchable.

'No! Dad! Please don't.'

I hold Ewan close and he lets me. I smell his fear, and his pain. He's living in hell and I can do nothing about it. I examine his face. What I thought were bruises wipe away in my hand. It's mud.

'We've got to phone the school, Ewan,' I tell him. His face crumples and he begs me not to make a fuss. Jeremy is still ranting in the background, but he's gone back to his wine.

'For God's sake, Jeremy!'

I feel an elastic band snap in my head, and so does Ewan, who leaves the room. I could punch my husband. I know we'll need the plastic sheet on Ewan's bed tonight.

'You need to ball your fist up and punch him straight in the face!' Jeremy shouts after his son.

'He's gone.'

Lydia walks in from outside, removing her headphones. I had no idea she was there. Neither did Jeremy.

'Hi, Mum. What's going on?'

She wears a bikini and has been sunbathing. She looks like she might snap. I hold out my arms and give her a hug. I imagine crushing a meringue for Eton mess.

'Hey, beautiful. How was your day?'

'Was that Ewan? Is he all right?' Her brow knits.

'Same stuff.'

'Oh. Will you call the police?' she asks.

'Yes. I must. They'll have to log it. They took his bike. Maybe you could talk him into giving a statement?'

'I will, Mum,' she says, going to the stairs.

'Have you eaten?'

'Yeah, I ate already, I had a big lunch,' Lydia lies. As she disappears, I see how bony her back has become. I can pick out every single muscle group in her body, because it looks as though they are sat just under the surface, protected only by a paper-thin layer of silk. I'm no longer interested in finding Monika. I want to find out where my own children have gone, and who took them apart, and how.

I turn back to Jeremy. But he's gone. Outside, on his phone.

Chapter 4

Carrie Greenside sat in her home office, which was carved out of bespoke black walnut. Her job consisted of electronic meetings with other desk-strapped executives from all over the world, so whether she was in the office or here, the outcome was still the same. The journey into London was for days when she fancied a change of scenery, and a teriyaki salmon salad from her favourite deli close to Canary Wharf. When the heat was this incessant, though, it was madness to fight for a place on the tube and choose an armpit to sniff as one hung on to the ceiling straps. Here, she had her pool, the Waitrose delivery and her early retirement plan to dream of.

A quick scroll through the news this morning reminded her that it was exam time again. With no kids to pass on her generational trauma to − a phrase she'd learned only recently, but liked − she forgot the timetabling of such trifling matters. However, it usually had the effect of reminding her of her own woeful state school education. Experts droned on about the importance of good schooling, but Carrie disagreed. She'd never give a job to a graduate who sailed smoothly from prep school to Eton, and who'd emerged from the oiled cogs of the Oxbridge churner. Those kids knew everything from books, and nothing from life. She preferred fighters, like herself. Hunger came from having nothing to eat, not from reading about it in a classroom. She preferred a character that had been hewn from granite, battled the weather and withstood the hardship of deficit.

She spoke into her mic and peered at her computer screen. The faces staring back at her were generational products of the class system in America that everyone denied existed. None of them communicated risk or combat to her and she was bored listening to them vie for her approval. The New York office, five hours behind GMT, had to fit around her schedule, like everyone else. She sipped a glass of ice-cold water with mint and lime and peered out of the window, wishing she'd taken the meeting in the garden, under her cool awning, which spread across the back of the garden from the house.

She'd been doing yoga and her mat was still laid on the neatly cut grass outside in the sunlight, waiting for her to unwind after leaning over her desk for an hour. She sat in her exercise clothes, ready for the gym and a punishing session with her personal trainer. The thought of burpees and cable swings was unappetising, but she knew it was good for her, and she'd feel better after.

'Trent, stop waffling,' she barked into the screen.

The attendees of the meeting all wore suits and pressed white shirts, and they were all men.

'I want the results by ten o'clock tonight, GMT. Get on it.'

She closed the laptop and got up from her chair to stretch. Now she could go out into the garden and enjoy the sun before she drove to the gym. She took her drink with her and closed the office door with a final click that symbolised the end of her working day. Outside, the sun wrapped her skin in a loving blanket of heat, and she breathed deeply. She finished her drink and sat back on the fur-lined garden chair, which matched the set of ten around the huge carved teak table.

Other people's gardens might ring with the sound of kids playing, but not hers. The thought of them terrified her. They were noisy and messy, and you couldn't control them. She cast an eye over the shrubbery and was satisfied that the gardener had done his job, even in this heat. The grass was burning brown and it disappointed her. It looked so much cleaner when it was green. She walked over to the shadier part of the vast garden, taking clippers with her, and chose five white hydrangeas. She carried them back to the table and arranged them in a purple glass vase, which she'd already filled with water. As she leaned over, the clippers slipped and fell from her grasp. She jerked, trying to save them from hitting her bare foot, but sliced her finger instead, along the thumb line.

'Shit!'

She sucked the digit and the dark metallic taste of her own blood dismayed her. She had no recollection of where she stored plasters or dressings for such an occurrence. She went inside to the vast kitchen, lovingly restored and modernised by a local company quite recently, and searched in drawers, where she guessed one might absentmindedly throw such sundries, and found a box of plasters, wrapping one around her thumb. It smarted.

She blamed her lack of concentration, and perhaps even her shortness with Trent in New York, on her session with Alex earlier today. It always put her off balance. But the doctor's work intrigued her. And she was safe inside her small office, which was like a cocoon of healing, with its photos of serenity and zen colour themes. It was one of the only things that checked her cynicism, and it amused her.

She surprised herself every time she stepped foot into the doctor's office, with Alex sitting on her ghastly old-fashioned chair, staring at her with her warm eyes and hopeful smile. The woman was a bloody genius. She'd managed to make her feel functional, useful even, though she'd almost walked out on her several times. Alex made her face uncomfortable truths, but she also left her daring to believe that she wasn't some kind of freak. It had taken some getting used to.

She'd been given Doctor Alex's number as someone recommended for insomnia. She was damn expensive and so Carrie assumed she was at least half decent. The chat about insomnia had lasted about three minutes, before the good doctor began dragging out her bowels and turning her inside out, eviscerating her demons. Five years later, they were getting somewhere. Alex Moore, an average-looking middle-aged woman who needed Botox, had hijacked everything she'd ever known, and all she'd built, and torn it down. It was like getting a sandblasting of the soul, and Carrie was addicted to it. Obsession with her wellbeing had replaced substance abuse, and that had to count for something. Before meeting Alex Moore, Carrie had sneered at emotion as something only the weak indulged in. Only money defined worth. Carrie's bonus last year had been two million. But she was slowly learning that one was allowed to feel, and it wasn't too bad.

She'd learned much about herself. There were only three ways to deal with a problem: accept it, ignore it, or deal with it. Carrie wasn't in the business of ignoring things, nor did she accept much. Most of the time she was known for confronting stuff head on. But the meeting she'd just ended sat with her. It was about more redund-ancies. It was her job to fire people, because no one else had her balls. Or at least that was her reputation. It was a convenient wall behind which to hide, but Alex Moore was slowly taking that apart, brick by brick. Inside the confines of a shrink's office, that was all well and good, but outside, Carrie still needed her armour.

She checked her thumb and, happy that the bleeding had stopped, she redressed it and examined her body in the full-length mirror in the hall, checking her gym kit hugged all the right places. She took a water bottle from the fridge and tutted as she spotted blood on the white marble counter top, rubbing it with her finger. A notification on her phone told her that Grace Bridge had uploaded a new YouTube video. Carrie's curiosity got the better of her and she had a spare five minutes before her session, so she opened it.

Her personal trainer had over one hundred thousand followers. Like a messiah, Grace paraded herself in front of the camera, seducing the watcher. Carrie didn't hear what she said, but noticed instead the girl's movements – her body bending this way and that, but more, smiling into the gaping abyss of social media, laughing and touting messages of superiority. Grace styled herself as an influ-encer, a modern Mecca of perfection and pain. Dishing out advice for the unworthy to follow. She wore matching Lycra sets endorsed by famous nutrition and fitness brands, probably paying her thousands.

Good girl, Carrie thought. A true entrepreneur, thanks to her wealthy parents. Carrie knew the signs, and the background to the videos was a dead giveaway. A personal trainer couldn't afford a penthouse suite overlooking King's College. Even if she sold illusions.

The internet offered that thing that had eluded the masses for millennia: free advice. But with it came a bombardment of brainwashing for the inexperienced. And this was the real cost. Grace's followers worshipped at the altar of self-improvement without the hassle of time and tariff, and they got exactly what they desired: something for nothing. Anybody could style themselves as an authority, with enough technical knowledge and arrogance. Expertise was everywhere. The problem with logging on to perfection, though, instead of working for it, was that it was only fleetingly rewarding. The rest of the time, life remained disappointing. Even to Grace herself, who seemed always afraid of her own shadow. Carrie had seen the twenty-one-year-old girl up close and personal, and her internet image didn't match her reality. The way she wrung her hands and picked the raw skin around her fingers told of a haunted soul. She was hiding something.

She watched as Grace made a wholesome super salad, and beamed into the camera, promising the layperson the elusive secret to longevity. The salad looked delicious, but who had the time? Watching other people look after themselves was so much more satisfying than being responsible for it yourself. Grace picked up a bottle of dressing and held the logo near the camera. Carrie smiled. She too had started her career in sales.

Carrie left her house and went around the side, through the garage, to her convertible Mercedes, and locked up via a new control system on the wall. The garage door opened and she got into the car, starting it up. It purred. The evening sun shone through the windscreen and she put down her visor, as well as pressing a button to release the roof. It slid down effortlessly. She shot a backwards glance at the house, momentarily panicking that it might be broken into again. She shivered but told herself not to be paranoid.

She pulled away.

Chapter 5

Grace Bridge drained a bottle of water. She was sent gallons of the stuff from one of her endorsement deals. She shared them with the staff.

The gym floor was busy. She had no time to eat.

Outside of her clients at the gym, her YouTube channel took up all her time. It had begun as a way out of her own head; an escape to another existence where she could be anybody she pleased. Now, it had grown into something that she felt responsible for. Thousands of people looked to her to inspire them with content that could be viewed quickly, regularly, and without judgement. It was the first time she'd wandered from the path forged for her by her birth. Last week, she'd reached her first ever half a million views, and it seemed that the more public exposure she received, the safer and more put-together she felt. She sought centeredness in revealing parts of herself that she could still control. Demonstrating she was in command almost convinced her that she was, and the likes and comments section galvanised the myth.

Her health advice was a philosophy that she found easy to dish out to her clients but didn't pay attention to herself. She was too busy. Those who paid her to get fit were really after something entirely different. All anyone cared about was looking better, not *being* better. Training clients was really a transactional relationship between owner and buyer. Nothing real was exchanged. It was a business of trickery. And a booming business it was. The clientele parading through the doors at the gym, from the most affluent postcodes in Cambridge, had stacks of money for pastimes and fancies. They also had time, and plenty of it. Most of it spent on social media, looking for more ways to look better. She'd pressed send on her latest video and already it had over five hundred views in half an hour. The creeping feeling that she got when she hadn't posted or checked her engagement for a while stilled after each upload, and her anxiety lessened.

People flocked to the gym in the hot weather to escape the furnace, and their frayed nerves, and she looked around for somebody she might know, scouting for business in the few minutes she had before her next client turned up. Training was about sales. Every month, the gym posted the last four weeks' stats: who'd sold the most sessions, who'd increased their sales the most, and star of the month. Gyms were like any other business: they sold stuff to make money; if they didn't, they went under. Grace targeted the ladies who lunched, and their fat Chanel handbags full of credit cards. In return, she sold endorphins and self-esteem. They were easily spotted because they looked just like her mother: seeking validation.

She noticed Orlando, the pale and overweight gym manager who'd never picked up a weight in his life but had a management degree. He was hired to make profit. He was in animated conversation with another PT as she walked past, and they stopped talking to acknowledge her. Her t-shirt was a little tight but it advertised a logo she was obligated to wear. It felt clingy against her tiny frame. But she'd worked hard to earn it. Her hair was tied up in a business-like fashion.

Grace's sales figures were healthy and Orlando never had much cause to talk to her, except to congratulate her on another sale. He'd jumped on the back of her YouTube success and the gym sponsored her content. She didn't need the money, but that's not why she did it.

'Grace, have you got a minute?' he asked. She looked up at one of the many clocks on the high walls of the gym and glanced over at the front desk. There was no sign of her client.

'I've got a seven-thirty, but she's not here yet,' she said.

'Good. Look, Ignacio needs to push himself forward a bit, you know?' he said. Her colleague glared at Orlando. She didn't say anything.

'He needs to talk more, he's too quiet. Customers don't feel pressured by him. Show him how you talk to the customers, will you? Thanks.'

Orlando strode off and Ignacio turned to her. He was one of the good guys; friendly and highly capable. He was Spanish and, unfortunately for him, too good-looking to garner much male trade, but women loved him.

'Twat,' he said, with a twang of Castellano.

Grace laughed and patted him on the arm. 'I'll show you the ropes later, clearly you have no idea what you're doing,' she teased him.

Ignacio laughed and shook his head. They'd become friends and hung out whenever they were on the gym floor together. He'd featured in some of her videos and they got more hits from women, but fewer from men. His sales figures were, in fact, excellent – it was just that Orlando was greedy. And jealous. Ignacio wafted charisma with little to no effort, even when he was mopping floors, which Orlando had him do often. Still, he never stopped smiling.

She excused herself, spotting Carrie Greenside, and went to greet her.

'Good evening!' she said. Her stomach grumbled and she ignored it.

Carrie looked over Grace's shoulder at Ignacio. Grace realised that she was picking her skin around her finger-nails again and forced her hands onto her hips so she couldn't. She'd made her fingertips sore, but she pushed the nagging pain to the back of her mind.

'Let's get you warmed up,' Grace said, taking no notice of the salacious grin on Carrie's face.

Five minutes on the cross trainer would be sufficient to get Carrie's blood pumping and her joints primed, and, more importantly, take her mind off Ignacio.

'You're looking great, Carrie. Ready to work hard, as always?'

Carrie Greenside was already a fit lady, but what Grace liked about her the most was her drive. She was disciplined, hungry and committed. Unsurprisingly, she got the results she was after, and then set new goals. She was a joy to train. She exuded the kind of independence that Grace was trying to achieve and Grace listened carefully to what she had to say. But tonight, Carrie was distracted, and Grace steered her away from Ignacio towards the weights area.

'You two make such a cute couple,' Carrie said.

Grace had her client laying on her back, holding an 8kg dumbbell in each hand, chest pressing slowly up and down as Grace checked her form.

'What?' Grace asked.

'You and Enrique Iglesias over there,' Carrie said.

34

Grace laughed awkwardly.

'Oh, I hit a nerve!' Carrie said.

'No, seriously, you didn't, we're just good friends.'

'Of course you are. I see the way he looks at you. You need to open your eyes,' Carrie said.

Grace wished she'd let it go. She felt sweat form along the crease of her back. Her throat constricted. She could hear the thud of blood in her temple, as well as a conversation over the other side of the gym. She picked her nails. Then she tried to breathe through it, like her therapist told her. But Grace's attention wandered to the dumbbell, and how she'd like to take it and smash Carrie's face in with it.

'Ouch,' she whispered. Her nail was bleeding. She hid her hand behind her back. Carrie didn't notice. She was busy concentrating now. *Up… down…*

Carrie finally stopped talking and Grace encouraged her to finish the set, catching a glimpse of herself in the vast mirror that covered the back wall of the gym. Her eyes were wide and her jaw tense. She forced herself to smile and congratulate her client, and absentmindedly wiped her brow.

'It's hot tonight,' she said.

Carrie put the weights down and sat up, looking in the mirror. 'That was good!'

'I know! Ten kilogrammes for you next time,' Grace said. 'You're ready.'

Carrie got her breath back and Grace busied herself putting away the weights and finding a skipping rope, hoping to keep Carrie quiet, and her attention from wandering.

'Let's do some high intensity,' Grace said.

Carrie rolled her eyes.

'You pay me to torture you,' Grace reminded her. Carrie followed her to a clear space on the floor and Grace handed her the ropes.

'One minute, then five burpees. We'll do it four times, that should finish you off nicely,' she said.

Carrie was a fit woman, for fifty-three. But Grace pushed her harder tonight. Carrie asked too many questions about her personal life, and her YouTube channel, and the only way to shut her up was to leave her begging for breath. At least it was better than a dumbbell to the face.

Grace glanced over to Ignacio and back to her client, hoping she hadn't noticed.

'Great video, I watched it before I came out,' Carrie said. 'I think you youngsters who use the internet like that are amazing, you don't get enough credit.'

It meant a lot when somebody as successful as Carrie was in her own right, and from her own hard work, said things like that.

'Thanks, Carrie.'

'You sure do push them out, don't you? You can't have any time to yourself,' Carrie said.

There she was again, angling for details about her personal life.

'Have you always wanted to be a personal trainer? I hear it doesn't pay so well.'

'I've got my income from endorsements,' Grace said.

'Of course you have. Wise girl. They should teach blogging and tweeting at school, I reckon. But then we can't have too many millionaires, can we? Not good for the status quo.'

Grace knew Carrie well enough to spot her satirical wit when it emerged readily, as it did during most sessions.

'What's your advice, Carrie?' Grace asked.

'My advice for what?'

'Success.'

'Crikey, Grace, I was just starting to enjoy myself. Aren't you happy with your triumphant internet fame? What do you want?' Carrie smiled up at her from the floor mat she was lying on. Grace stretched her calves.

'Just to be happy and safe, I guess.'

Carrie stared at her and Grace noticed that she was quiet for a long time, which she was unaccustomed to from the business powerhouse.

'Well, money won't buy you that,' Carrie said finally.

'I already know that.'

Chapter 6

There is a young police constable sitting on my sofa with a notepad and pen, and he's trying to tell me that everything will be okay. He's about twenty-one years of age and still thinks that the police make a difference. Even my son wants to believe him.

They were far too busy to visit the house last night, so I've taken this morning off work. I'm left supposing that victims of crime who can't afford to take time off work make up the unreported crime stats each year.

'So, we'll take your statement...' The constable checks his notes. 'Ewan, and we'll sort this out for you, all right?'

I smile at him and wonder at his altruistic passion. I don't want to ruin it for him and I remind myself to behave. I've made him tea, which he sips. Jeremy is keeping out of the way because he says he's got a headache, and Ewan will feel under too much pressure with both parents breathing down his neck, but I know it's because he's ashamed of the way he looks and smells. He hit the booze last night, like an Exocet missile, and it's a good job my air defences are intact. My ability to withstand the artillery barrage comes from acute practice in the field, however, my children shouldn't have to go to war so young. They take shelter in the refuge of their rooms – teenage caves offering sound proofing from our spats – but sooner or later, they'll outgrow them and want to venture outside.

'Brandon Stand,' Ewan says bravely. I love him. His courage blinds me.

'He's the son of the headmaster of George Paget School,' I say.

The constable raises his eyebrows.

'We've reported him before.'

'I see.'

No, you don't.

'So tell me, in your own words, what happened.'

I listen as Ewan talks the constable through the litany of pain caused by his tormentor and I know nothing will ever get done.

The constable takes notes and I can tell that this is when he's most comfortable, like all police – writing down what they should be doing, rather than doing it. I've had my fair share of brushes with their lot. In my line of work occasionally I get asked to give my expert opinion on schizophrenics, or general sociopaths. 'Nutters in need', Tony calls them. My faith in the law is dubious. But I have to walk Ewan through the motions of what society says is best to make their processes function.

'The boy's already apologised, but if you want to press charges—'

'What?' I ask.

Ewan looks at me and his eyes accuse me of treachery.

'The boy was visited at his address before I was notified to drop by, and the young man, and his father, have offered an apology for the mistake, and they pass on their whole-hearted regret. Sorry, I got the note as I was walking to the door. I just read it on my phone.'

I feel the carpet sucking the life out of me with its swirling pattern and I'm aware of Ewan's knuckles turning white. I regret making him do it. I want the constable to leave. It was a mistake.

'Right, I'll just read this back to you and then we need your signature, and your mum's, and we'll open a file.'

An open file. That's what Ewan is.

He finishes his tea and thanks me; it was perfect, apparently, and just what he needed. I've been hosting his break, which he no doubt deserved, having taken off his stab vest when he came in. He has no idea that he may need it now. I might have wondered at the underbelly of Cambridge that is considered his patch, and why he might need body armour, but now I understand.

'We don't come out this way much,' he says jovially.

Not much call for it, I assume. The children of the rich fulfil other statistics. Or at least they cover their tracks well.

'You have a lovely home.'

'Thank you, officer. When will we hear from you?'

Never.

'I'll file my report and then I'm off shift until next Tuesday, so it'll be picked up by a colleague.'

My heart sinks.

He stands up and Ewan is reminded how powerless he is in the shadow of such a tall man in a uniform. We both are.

We shake hands. I walk him to the door. When I return to the sitting room, Ewan is not there. Not even a minute has passed and the doorbell rings again, jarring me. It's the young constable back, holding Ewan's mutilated bike.

'This was left on your driveway, ma'am.'

Chapter 7

My client list for Thursday afternoon stares back at me from my computer. I still haven't called Tony. I'm avoiding it. Besides, my morning has been filled with my parental shortcomings.

Ewan didn't say much when I dropped him at school to face his daily reality. The look on his face when I refused to allow him the afternoon off was full of hatred. Admittedly, the kind of loathing wielded by a child is somewhat softer than that thrown about by fully grown sociopathic adults. However, it hurt more than I ever imagined.

I take a deep breath before my first client walks into my office, and I try to prepare myself mentally. A quiet tap on the door indicates that she is here, and the tiny hesitant sound is typical of her quest for invisibility.

I want her to be comfortable and safe but I don't feel either of those things myself. There is no avoiding the fact that the office is my turf and all clients unwind in different ways. That's why it's neutral. Once inside, clients can sit on the couch, or lie down if they wish, or they can pace around too. Anything to get them relaxed enough to talk. The last thing they're interested in is my own sense of peace and so I know they won't notice if I'm out of sorts.

The girl comes in. I call her a girl, but she's a woman, it's just that she looks like a girl to me. She reminds me of Lydia, and I go gently with her.

'Morning, Grace. How are you today?'

I know she's a fitness trainer. She trains some of my clients. And Monika too, but that information is confidential. In a small overgrown suburb, such as Cambridge, which pretends to be a city, but is really a hamlet, it's impossible not to cross lives. Grace is also a social media personality, and therein lies her contradiction. Invisibility comes at the cost of diversion, and Grace's YouTube account does a sterling job of it.

Grace walks in and closes the door. She settles in her usual place and I smile at her, allowing her to adjust from the frenetic outside world. She's one of my youngest clients. I don't counsel teenagers. It's a specialist field and laden with pitfalls. Grace is barely out of that transitional phase but her birth certificate allows me to treat her. She's an irresistibly intriguing subject and of all my clients probably has the most personal wealth. She comes from old money, with parents embedded in noble heritage. But she shuns it, and all it stands for. What Grace hasn't quite worked out yet, though, is that it's her wealth that affords her self-reflection.

She crosses her legs and picks her fingers. I notice they're bleeding again. Grace is recently washed. I pick up on these things because it indicates much about a client's mental state. How they take care of their basic physical needs indicates a lot about their emotional health and Grace still wakes up every day and washes away the grime. It's important.

We chat about the weather and her YouTube channel. I don't understand much about social media but I know enough to stay away from it, mostly. I check it to monitor what the kids are watching. Lydia follows her. So does James, for very different reasons. Ewan's search history remains mostly in the realms of video games and anime. For now.

Grace has got thinner, and I know her purging continues. Her expensive watch rattles around her wrist. She wears more make-up than usual, indicating to me that she's had a rough night's sleep. She looks prettier in her videos, wholesome and healthy, not broken. I merely get the shadows in my office. I dive in.

'We were talking last week about how you were uncomfortable with your parents paying for your treatment.'

Grace takes her first long inhalation. I wait. She has large, sad eyes. But she's no fairy-tale princess, the last thing Grace Bridge needs is a handsome prince to save her.

'I don't want their money.'

'But they want to give it to you. Whether you accept it is entirely your choice.'

'I'm letting them do it for peace.'

I don't comment. It's not my job to lead, or admonish, or give my expert opinion. This isn't a trial, and I'm not a witness for the prosecution. It's not how it works. I let her think. Meanwhile, I brood about Ewan. I can't get him out of my head. Grace's parents couldn't protect her when she needed it either...

She takes a deep breath and I can tell she's loosening up. She trusts me.

'I had a client last night and she got under my skin. I'm normally really open and friendly, and I talk about anything they want to talk about, and believe me, they talk about some crap,' Grace says.

It's like a machine gun when Grace finally wakes up.

'How did she get under your skin?'

'She implied, in a really dirty and suggestive way, that I was having a relationship with another PT.'

'Dirty and suggestive?' It's the way she spits out the two words that I pick up on.

'I think she said something like "I see the way he looks at you", but it was the way she said it, the look in her eyes, and what she was implying. It made me see red.'

'What do you think she was implying?'

'That a woman should give herself to anyone who finds her attractive.'

Strong stuff.

'So, let's talk about what happened there. Rewind to before you saw red. What is the client's normal character? Do you ordinarily have a good relationship with her?'

Grace explains that she's known the client for a long time and she enjoys training her. She describes the older woman and I know she's talking about Carrie Greenside. Her acidic sense of humour comes from years of sniffing out bullshit, there's no surprise that a twenty-one-year-old girl wouldn't appreciate it.

I listen. But I've also got to concentrate. There's a difference. I have to push Ewan to the back of my mind if I'm to pull it off. I'm also compelled to forget that she's talking about Carrie.

I can't.

'So this woman might be wistful and nostalgic about her own youth, when *she* would have wanted a relationship with the PT. It could have been nothing to do with you.'

Grace nods. She understands, but that's not the point. Carrie has *hurt* her.

'Yeah, I see that. She definitely fancies him.'

'So, leaving her out of it, tell me about the anger. What did it feel like?'

'I was lifting a weight above her head and I felt like smashing it down in her face. I really wanted to hurt her.'

'And would that have made you feel better?'

Grace shakes her head and the tears come. She sobs and I push the tissues towards her, and wait.

'I just want to fucking kill him!'

I say nothing. Now we're on the money.

The curtains billow through the open windows on the breeze, though it is neither cool nor refreshing. Grace's shoulders shake. It's powerful work. Grace never used to cry. Gradually, it subsides and the sniffs get quieter.

'Oh, God, where did *that* come from?' Grace asked.

'Inside you.'

'Why?'

Because your mother and father's money can't fix you, but you haven't found anything else yet.

'Because you're allowed to feel hurt. You've been violated in the most horrible way and you seek justice. But you want retribution too, it hurt that much. This wasn't someone bumping into you at the supermarket, this was deep trauma on so many levels. It has such an impact on your physical and emotional existence, and the pain is very intense. It's real. That pain has to go somewhere, and – right or wrong – we no longer live in a society where law and order is settled on an eye-for-an-eye basis. The village elders aren't going to throw him off a cliff.'

'We're civilised?' Grace says, smiling through her tears. It's a touchingly light moment, and one grounded in maturity beyond her years. I don't normally talk so much, but my nerves are jangling too and I can see that Grace needs it. Some do. Some don't.

45

'Allegedly.'

'I hate this body.'

Her voice is full of self-loathing. I question if I'm counselling Lydia after all.

'So do you think the "dirty and suggestive" used by your client is actually your opinion of yourself?'

I'm pushing her. The tears come again. She nods, taking handfuls of tissues.

'Because what happened was your fault?'

Another nod.

The blame-shame game is my biggest paying customer. Humans are riddled with it, including me.

'Do you really think that him raping you was your fault?'

Grace looks up at me and wipes her eyes. She shakes her head.

'But that's how he made you feel because you could do nothing about it.'

'I should have…'

'Should've what?'

She takes a deep breath.

'Fought back.'

'Because that's what they do in the movies? Your brain's first instinct was to protect you, and it's cleverer than you think. If you'd have fought back against a seventeen-stone body-builder, you probably would have been severely wounded, or worse. Your primitive brain made all these assessments in a fraction of a second, before you did, and decided to freeze. To save your life.'

She looks at me like Ewan does when I've got his back, and I guess I'm a parent to some of my clients.

'What did we say about compassion?' I ask her.

'Suffer with?'

I tell all my trauma clients about the Latin translation.

'So can you give yourself compassion? Be your own best friend? You wouldn't blame her for being raped. You don't *get* raped. You *are* raped. It's done to you, you don't participate. So what would you say to your friend who feels dirty?'

'It wasn't your fault.'

It's a whisper.

'And what can you say to yourself?'

'It wasn't my fault.'

Good girl.

Chapter 8

I question my own sanity as I use a spare hour to drive across the city to Tony's address.

His house is unquestionably the most extravagant I've ever been in, apart from his skiing chalet in Zermatt. Tony likes accumulating wealth more than anything else in his life and I don't think it's my place to comment unkindly on it. He's earned it. He started out as an investment banker who chose wisely, and now he lives off his profits. He doesn't need to work, but still dabbles in consultancy. His house is a stone's throw away from King's College and I know he bought it for seventeen million.

I'm trying not to gloat that his greatest possession is missing.

Tony's success galls Jeremy and galvanises his self-image as a failure. To me, he's just my old college buddy. I knew him ordinary, and I preferred him that way.

Despite the trappings of Tony's success, he's a generous friend and likes to spread his wealth around. He hates sycophants but is unashamedly indulgent with his loyal pals. He insists on paying for holidays and weekends away, and showers us all with unnecessary gifts. Especially Ewan. It's his character. It's how he shows love.

I was unkind to Monika at first, and for that I feel remorse. I was being protective of my friend, who's seen more than his fair share of break-ups, all deserved. As a result, I put Monika on probation for a chunk of time, but we did become friends of sorts.

Monika's car is parked in the driveway and it reminds me of a long-ago argument, buried somewhere but unearthed just now. It was about Jeremy fawning over Monika in our pool house. Later we shouted at each other. I snapped. I called him pathetic. Jeremy called me past it.

'Course I'd fuck her,' he'd said.

'In your dreams. You couldn't afford it,' I'd said.

The image of Jeremy and his flab banging into Monika's taut, naked, gym-honed body, grabbing on to her tiny breasts, and professing his love for her flashes through my head in an instant and I'm only shocked out of it by my phone ringing, interrupting the bitter recollection that leaves a sour taste in my mouth.

It's Lydia's school.

'Hello.' I step into the shade of the wisteria. Here, behind high walls and gates of affluence, it is silent, and I don't want to hear my own thoughts.

'Doctor Moore, sorry to bother you. Lydia isn't well.'

'What do you mean she's not well?'

'She's been sick.'

'Is this a joke, Mrs Tower?'

Lydia's twenty-thousand-pound-per-year-school's secretary knows very well that Lydia purges herself every day. When vomit is the product of bulimia it doesn't spread a contagion. It really is just food. Emotional food. I feel my patience ebbing.

'I mean, she's been sick in class, all over the place, in front of all the students.'

'All five of them?'

'Doctor Moore, if you'd like to collect your daughter, she's being taken care of by the nurse.'

'Mrs Tower, we agreed that Lydia should stay at school and be immersed in school life as much as possible for her to get better.'

'Not when it involves the mental wellbeing of her classmates, Doctor Moore.'

I want to smash my head against Tony's stone arch. I notice that his peonies are wilting too, but it's small consolation.

'I have an important meeting I can't get out of. I'll be there in an hour.'

I hang up and hammer on the door, as if that will help still my loosening grip on life.

Tony answers. He knew I was coming, I called ahead. He wears swimming shorts and nothing else. He takes care of himself and has always been a handsome bastard. I stride straight past him and into the house.

'Come in,' he says sarcastically. He closes the door. 'Bad mood?' he asks.

'Sorry. I just came to see how you are. Have you heard anything? Is she home? I see her car's here.'

'Nothing. I'm worried this time, Alex.'

'She didn't take her car?'

He shakes his head.

'Did she give you any reason to worry? Could she have flown back home to see her mother? A break? I know you're a pain in the arse at the best of times,' I say, smiling, trying to be normal. 'Are you going to make me a cuppa?'

I walk through to the kitchen at the back of the house, recently refurbished beautifully, and peer out into the garden. I feel more at home here than in my own. It's a stunning residence. A stone testimony to fabricated perfection, but that's not the reason why. I turn to him but he's already close behind me. He reaches out his hand and rests it on my waist. I feel the warmth of an old friend and a little tension leaves my body, but then I look into his eyes. I know every inch of him, and he me. His mouth is waiting for my comfort, he's appealing to the past. The table behind him is an antique. I see myself lying on it with Tony on top of me, and I know why he refuses to get rid of it, despite Monika pleading with him to update it. I move away from him.

'No, Tony. That's all over.'

Chapter 9

George Paget School sits behind vast swathes of old trees, planted before I was born, or my great-grandparents were. The driveway languishes uphill for a quarter of a mile and I wonder if the fees are really worth it. Ewan, Lydia…

She's waiting for me with the nurse and she looks like death.

'She fainted, twice.'

'Did you call a doctor?'

'Yes, she's been checked over, Doctor Moore. Can we talk in private?'

I don't want to leave Lydia but she barely notices me.

I'm told that if she doesn't start eating properly, she'll have to be admitted to hospital. The next stage is an intervention care plan. I've heard those words before, but it wasn't about my own child. I feel sick.

The drive home is desperately lonely and long. I don't know what to say. I seemed to get through to Grace this morning, but my own daughter is a puzzle too far.

'Let's get you home and into bed, darling,' is all I can muster.

She smiles weakly at me.

'I'm sorry, Mummy.'

It pierces my heart.

I reach my hand across to her and tell her it's not her fault.

'I wish I could make your pain go away.'

I wish she were my client and not my daughter.

'Mummy?'

'Yes, darling?'

'Why is Daddy drunk all the time?'

There. The elephant has finally crept out of its tiny hiding space and it sits on me like a crushing weight.

'He scares me when he's drunk.'

I rage inside, but my lips won't move and I know I have to make a plan for our futures, to survive, for my kids to pull through.

'Let me take care of that,' is all I can say. I can't share with her all the reasons he's an alcoholic. I can't burden her or force her into a parenting role. But it's happening right in front of me. She's not stupid, none of them are. Kids see things for what they are. My knuckles turn white around the steering wheel and I taste the anger in my mouth. It wriggles around like a great serpent, trying to poison my children, who I can't protect.

I turn into our driveway and it's some relief, because at least I can move my body, for want of moving my tongue. I help her out of the car and into the house. She can barely make it upstairs and flops onto her bed and I tuck her in, not bothering to undress her. I've already chosen a doctor to call. Thankfully, Jeremy is nowhere to be seen.

I've been away from the office for too long and my diversions will make me late for my afternoon appointments. I call Dora to let her know. I look inside the fridge for inspiration, but nothing shouts out to me and I slam it shut, imagining it's Jeremy's head. My phone makes me jump.

It's the police.

He introduces himself as Detective Inspector Paul Hunt, and he's gathering information on Monika's last known whereabouts.

The officer sounds bored, but I know that's just a hazard of his job. Crime is pedestrian to them.

I tell him that I saw Monika on Sunday at our house. He tells me she was last seen on Tuesday night, by her husband, confused, possibly drunk, and walking around her garden. It sounds about right for a night in the Thorpe house, but I don't divulge that to DI Hunt; it's none of his business.

I know the police well enough to understand their agenda as toxically benign. DI Hunt digs around looking for titbits about the Thorpes' marriage.

'We had butterflied lamb.'

I'm acutely aware that the choice of cut on Sunday is irrelevant but I've slipped easily into witness mode, where one drones on about anything and everything one remembers for want of not coming across as guilty as hell.

I apologise.

'Don't worry at all, doc.' I didn't say he could call me that. 'It's completely normal. So, was everything all right between the Thorpes? Normal behaviour?'

I know where this is going. In a missing persons investigation, the spouse is always suspect number one.

'Is Monika in some kind of danger?'

'No. Just background.'

'Of course.' My guts turn over. 'The kids came and went. We drank a fair amount, I think, and Tony and Monika got a cab home.'

'Would you say they were both drunk?'

I recall the afternoon in a series of vague stills, as if taken with an underwater movie camera. I see Tony with his arm around Lydia. Fencing with Ewan, with sticks. I remember Monika being sick all over the downstairs toilet. Ewan's face when Jeremy slurred his words. Then Lydia's turn over the toilet. Tony squaring up to his wife with his fists clenched.

'Not really. A bit squiffy, I suppose.'

'Right, doc, we're just getting a picture together, nothing to worry about. Would you say that Mrs Thorpe is a big drinker, then?'

'It depends what you call a big drinker, I suppose. She likes a drink.'

'Right. Is that the last time you saw Mrs Thorpe?'

'Yes.'

'Mr Thorpe mentioned to us that his wife has taken off for periods of time before.'

'Yes, I believe she has.'

'Do you know anything about that? Where did she go? Who did she see?'

'Well, I seem to remember Tony telling me that she'd gone to Scotland, in her car, to get some space, a long time ago.'

'Her car is parked in the family home driveway, so wherever she's gone, she isn't in her car.'

My heart rate rises.

'Do you know why she needs space from time to time, doc?'

'Don't we all? I mean, marriage is not plain sailing, is it?'

'Is there something about the Thorpes' marriage that strikes you as unhappy, then?'

'Not at all, they love each other, very much. Monika just struggles to fit in, I guess.'

'What exactly do you mean?'

'It's not easy coming from a foreign country and making a life, is it? She misses home, I think.'

'Right. Well, we'll check if she took her passport. Has she ever left the country before?'

'I really can't answer that, you'll have to ask Tony.'

'We will. It's a delicate subject, but I have to ask, do you know if a third party is involved at all, doc?'

'You mean an affair? Goodness, I think not. They're relative newlyweds.'

'Thank you for your time. Of course, if you remember anything or come across more information, please get in touch.'

'Of course, I will.'

A sinking feeling spreads across my gut. Tuesday was two days ago. A long time with no phone calls or messages in today's world. Then Tony's hand on my body. The way he looked at me as if he wanted to take me right there in the hallway like he used to. As if Monika has gone for good.

Chapter 10

I settle into my wingback as my last client pokes his head around the door. It's Henry Nelson. He's in his early thirties, and he's fit and chiselled; bright-eyed, happy, good-looking and sure of himself.

On the outside.

I enjoy my appointments with Henry, and I consider this to be because he's easy to counsel. Straightforward in the sense that he's not hung up on himself. He's seeking atonement, pure and simple. He's a gentle giant. But more than that, I admire him as one of my few clients who does not herald from a cocoon of great means. The government pays for his therapy, or more specifically, the national probation service. Henry is a scrapper and he's a genuine breath of fresh air. He's a terrible liar, and this makes him an open book; one I look forward, every week, to reading.

Henry is shut out of the money club. He works hard and owns his own building company, but he pays all of his taxes, without the help of loopholes in the Cayman Islands or the Isle of Man, and he values the cost of things. He understands penalty and prize. He's not pampered and entitled, just a recovering addict who's served time for manslaughter.

I've worked for the prison service. It wasn't my thing, but I learned that criminals are uncomplicated.

'Henry, come in. It's nice to see you. Please, sit down.'

He's over six feet tall with the physique of a rugby player; not fat but constructed of solid muscle. A winger, perhaps. He's got shaggy blond hair, bleached by the sun, and friendly blue eyes. He wears his smile easily and confidently, and chooses a place on the sofa. I need to concentrate to channel my professional demeanour and check my ego, because Henry exudes charm, and sometimes he makes me feel like Eve, if my guard is down, and my garden becomes arid. I'm not a machine, though I am a highly trained academic. I sometimes wonder whether my transferrable skills are more suited to the theatre than to medicine. Keeping a healthy boundary between client and patient takes discipline, and Henry likes to peer behind barriers, I can tell.

Henry sits heavily, filling the space, and fiddles with something he's carrying. It's a rolled-up paper bag. His arms are covered in tattoos. His hands are soft.

'Lunch,' Henry says, looking at the bag. I appreciate the time he gives up every week to attend his appointments, not just because he has to, but because he comes willing to open up and do the work on himself. It also means that, for an hour or so, he's not earning.

'Past tense?'

He nods and smiles.

'There's a rubbish bin under the desk.'

Henry gets up and throws away the bag. Sessions with this likeable young man always start in the same way: awkward and staccato, until the ice melts a little and I gain his trust again, or Henry cracks a joke. It wastes about twenty minutes per hour, but that's the way some sessions go.

'How are you this week?'

It's banal but necessary. It kicks things off.

'I'm good.'

Henry sticks to his gender role stereotype of the closed-up and non-emotional heterosexual male. I wonder what's bothering him. We'll get there eventually.

I sit and wait.

I glance at his tattoos, each one representing a period in his life when he hated himself. Each was a symbol of pain, though Henry hadn't known that at the time, and he'd spent years covering them up. To sit here in my office, in a t-shirt, is a massive leap forward. It's one reason I cringe every time my son James gets another inking, because I know so many people who scar themselves on purpose to inflict damage on soft skin because they can't see the original beauty in it.

'I met someone,' Henry finally says.

'Great news, congratulations.'

Here we go. This is what's behind the guarded behaviour. Henry's sessions revolve around his sex life because that's the beast he is. His attachment problems have always been solved through sex. And after a drug session: violence. I don't believe in fight, freeze or flight as the only trauma responses in my line of work. You can add fucking to that list too.

'She's married.'

They usually are.

'To someone else, I presume?'

Henry laughs. He loosens up. I can't imagine a ring on that finger.

'So, we've talked about your attachment to unavailable women, haven't we?'

Henry nods. 'She's different.'

Again.

'How?'

59

'She wants to leave her husband.'

'Ah, and that's not part of the plan, is it? What will you do?'

He shrugs.

'I thought it's what I wanted.'

'And?'

'I changed my mind.'

He looks at his hands in shame. He's moved on already, poor woman, whoever she is.

Chapter 11

Detective Inspector Paul Hunt made his way across the field to the blue tarp. He sucked on a vape and blew great swathes of cloud behind him. He smelled of strawberry and watermelon, but he knew the exotic whiff wouldn't last long once he got under the tarp. He'd had a pair of trainers in the car, and he'd put them on hastily, to save his shoes, which were new last month. He popped his vape into the pocket of his trousers, having left his jacket in the car. The weather was sweltering and he didn't know how those suave European cops kept so pristine under their white shirts. He had sweat patches under his arms and he felt as though his head was about to explode. The air was hot, not just warm but scalding, and the sun made his skin prickle where he'd rolled his sleeves up.

It was always a bad day when he had to view a body, especially a murder victim. He was a seasoned officer, and had seen things most people only saw in movies. But when it was real, it was different. Disappointing actually. It was never as dramatic as it was on the TV. Under the tarp, there'd be a small army of forensic specialists in white suits, like spacemen huddling over the remnants of a life. Then there'd be a photographer taking stills of what was left, as well as evidence markers placed beside the signs of human existence and what it left behind: cigarettes, drinks bottles, weapons, clothes, condoms, nails and bits of hair or jewellery. There'd also be a crime scene investigator who drew their diagrams with precision, like surveyors preparing for a house sale. Then he'd walk in and be expected to work around them all and piece together a case.

There were other things he'd rather be doing on a Friday morning, however, this was his job. Hopefully, it'd be an easy one to wrap up and, being a violent murder, as he'd been told, the CPS would want signing off quickly. Nobody wanted a messy unsolved murder in the centre of Cambridge. This wasn't London. The crime didn't fit the patch, and they could do without the attention.

He slapped gloves on, covered his shoes at the entrance to the tarp, and took time to look around. It was close to the Red Hen pub, so there might be witnesses. It was also a favourite spot of dog walkers, but they came out in the daytime, and he figured without even looking at the body that she'd been dumped under the cover of night, unless they were dealing with an escaped lunatic, which sometimes happened. There was a jetty close by with gravel access from the road, so tyre tracks would be fucking impossible unless the perp drove a tank.

He went in.

His mask didn't protect him from the stench. The damn heatwave would have worked her body like a cooker and he knew from experience that she'd been here for more than just a couple of hours. Plastic suits made space for him and he observed the remains of a woman, lying on her side, discarded like trash and covered in leaves and a silky sheen of skin slip. Her abdomen was slightly green and he knew that she was dissolving from the inside.

He braced himself for the worst of it. He'd forgotten his Vicks and kicked himself for his oversight; he hadn't attended a grisly scene like this for a good while. This might very well be his last. He was due for promotion next year and episodes like this would be handled by those junior to a chief inspector. His days as field operator, digging around in the last throes of a corpse's breath, were almost over. He'd already decided to wrap this one up quickly – it might even speed up his promotion to DCI. It was usually the lover or husband, or pimp, who did it, and that's where he'd start. It shouldn't take him long.

The photographer's camera clicked and flashed and the CSI chatted to him, pointing to a wound on the cadaver's back.

'Matches with a lung puncture – she bled out, but not here. Then there's the head wounds.'

'Overkill,' Hunt whispered.

Definitely a lover.

Music from the Red Hen travelled in bursts over the field and Hunt wished he was invited to that party rather than this one. No doubt they had no idea what was going on out here across the field by the banks of the river Cam as they ate their brunches and geared up for the weekend, sipping cocktails on ice. Then he saw it.

He knelt over the body.

'All right, guv?'

'Yeah, I think I know who she is.'

It was procedure to ask family members who report their loved ones missing for distinguishing marks, and this was an unmissable one. A great serpent tattoo wriggling up her back, which made her look like a cheap whore.

Maybe he'd get this case done and dusted earlier than he thought. The state of her body, and the fact that she had a couple of days' worth of insect activity on her, given the exposure to the elements, meant that she'd remain here at least until this afternoon, perhaps this evening. And he didn't want to shoot from the hip just yet by involving the family. The priority was the crime scene, because it was obvious that the woman was a victim of homicide. He had to gather himself and get as many facts as he could before requesting identification from the next of kin. Until he was sure, and checked with the information he had, he'd hold off informing the bloke who'd reported his wife missing on Wednesday. Some rich fella, city trader, or the like, more money than sense. Enough, for sure, to buy anything he wanted, including a new wife when he got bored of the old one. That was the beauty of experience in policing: it made the open mind more streamlined.

Chapter 12

Henry Nelson's phone rang for the ninth time and he tutted because he was in the middle of a punishing workout. His muscles jumped with tension and he slammed a dumbbell down onto the gym floor to shut up his phone. He would usually ignore calls from No Caller ID because it brought back too many painful memories of the police. However, it could also be some dickhead fooling around, a cold caller, or a wrong number. Or important.

It was the police.

His guts turned over. He cursed himself for answering. His eyes closed in regret and he felt his palms go sweaty as he held the handset tighter. He sat down on a free weights bench, heavily.

'Nelson's Bespoke Kitchens?' the policewoman asked again.

'Yes, sorry. I'm in the middle of something, can I call you back?' Henry asked.

'Is it an emergency, sir? I'd just like to ask a few questions about Monika Thorpe.'

'Who?'

'Monika Thorpe. You fitted a new kitchen for Mr and Mrs Thorpe a few weeks ago?'

'Erm, yes. What's this about?'

A momentary exhalation of relief escaped him as he realised the call was about his work, rather than his past convictions. However, an uneasy feeling spread throughout his belly. He recalled Monika's face the last time he'd seen her on Tuesday evening. The pain.

'I'm just trying to gather some information for an inquiry, sir. Mrs Thorpe was reported missing on Wednesday lunchtime. We're making routine calls trying to establish her whereabouts. We have in our notes that the Thorpes were expecting you to visit on Wednesday morning to make some minor adjustments to cupboards. When was the last time you visited the house?'

Paranoia gripped Henry. Part of him mistrusted the authenticity of the call: what if it wasn't the police? What if it was a hoax? He froze. Monika was missing.

'Sir?' the voice persisted.

'Yes,' he said. He tried to think clearly, lest he make a mistake.

'I completed the kitchen at the weekend, it was a big job; it's very grand. It took four weeks.'

'Right, sir, and Monika? Mrs Thorpe?'

'Oh, yes. She was there at the weekend, then erm, I popped in on Monday.'

'And how did she seem on Monday? Her mood?'

Henry thought back to Monika moaning loudly as she was pushed up against the new marble island, her legs around Henry's back, his work trousers around his ankles.

'She was happy,' he said.

'Over the few weeks you were there, sir, did you spend much time with Mr and Mrs Thorpe? You must have become quite familiar with their routine.'

'Yes, Mr Thorpe works a lot, sometimes in London, sometimes in his office in the garden. Mrs Thorpe was in and out, I mean, I… She was busy. I don't know what she did, if she worked. I don't think she did,' he said.

'Right. And did she have visitors?'

A creeping feeling spread up Henry's spine, and a warning signal alerted him to end the conversation. The question was no longer indicative of an innocent enquiry. The tone of the policewoman's voice told him otherwise, and to be careful. This was a history-hunting exercise and he knew from experience what the police did when they were desperate to get answers. They came across as friends of the community; caring and sensitive, until they had what they wanted, then you no longer mattered, and their true agenda was revealed. All they wanted was names: poor bastards to send to prison so they could tick off their stats. A rich woman with connections to an ex-con from the wrong side of the tracks was a worthy cliché and something lawyers would cream their pants over.

'I never saw any visitors.'

A stone settled in the pit of his stomach. It was a slippery slope. He'd just taken a huge step; no, a leap, into an unknown unwelcome in his life, but it was entirely his own fault. He'd made the split-second decision to obfuscate to protect Monika's privacy, not trusting the process of any police agenda. Now, the lie would get bigger and bigger as they pestered him with more questions, which they surely would, until they finally unearthed some evidence that he'd been in her bed. It was only a matter of time before they found a stranger's DNA on her sheets and they came looking for a predator. Then a match on the database with a known criminal.

'And did you ever overhear her making plans to see friends?'

'I didn't listen. Part of my job is respecting the client's privacy,' he said.

'Of course.'

Henry knew the policewoman didn't believe him. What tradesman didn't listen to everything that happened in the house they were working in? It was what made the stories at the pub on a Friday night so interesting: the sex toys they found in drawers, the loud arguments, the fucked-up kids, and the come-ons from the ladies of the house. It was part and parcel of what he did, and the coppers knew it. They wouldn't be interested in the fact that, despite what it looked like – a tradesman having a fling with a client – he actually had feelings for her. They wouldn't care because it wouldn't fit into their plan. They'd find out soon enough that he had a record, and that he'd enjoyed a stay at Her Majesty's pleasure, and then he'd be fucked.

The rest of the conversation went by in a blur until he was finally allowed to hang up. Depression came over him in a wave and suddenly the thought of heavy weights burdened him. He gave up on his workout and walked to the changing rooms to get a shower. He dialled Monika's number five times but each time he got a dead tone. It was stupid, really. He already knew she wouldn't answer. A few people greeted him, which was normal because he knew a lot of people at the gym, including the trainers, but he didn't reply. Instead, he walked past in a daze.

'Henry? Hello.'

A hand waved across his path and he snapped out of his trance momentarily. It was Grace, and he felt bad for ignoring her.

'Hi,' he said, and tried to smile.

'Everything okay?' she asked.

He came back to his senses. Grace wore her mask of happiness easily, though Henry knew that wasn't the case inside. He saw the distress behind her eyes because he'd been there: hunted and haunted. He knew what to look for.

He looked at her and wished he was somebody else. Somebody she could really, truly trust. She was so innocent and young and he felt true pain for her, knowing what life had thrown in her path. If there was one thing so sure in this life, it was that happiness was momentary, if it existed at all. One day, he was sure, Grace would walk into the gym without her smile, and then he'd know that she'd finally succumbed to the contaminated misery of real life, blighted by reality, and infected with sorrow, despite her best efforts to fight it.

'I can see you've finished,' she said. 'Smashing it as always.'

The realisation that Grace was Monika's PT jolted him. Perhaps the police had contacted her too? He looked for signs that she knew. He wanted to ask her, but that would seem weird. They barely knew one another – officially – and just exchanged pleasantries at the gym because he was a regular. He never spoke to Monika at the gym either, they made sure to stay away from one another. It was all part of the facade that lovers create to avoid detection. Instead, he said to Grace what he said to everybody to cheer himself up.

'You've just made my day.'

Chapter 13

Saturday 11 July

Three days before Monika's disappearance

Tony ran his hand down Monika's back.

She was stretched out on a lounger and he knew that she pretended not to be affected by his touch. Her back always drove him crazy. The softness of the skin there. The muscles underneath the tanned smooth surface. He grabbed the bottle of tanning oil and poured some into his palms, rubbing in circular motions, ignoring the black viper that stared back at him, daring him to go further.

He undid her bikini top and pushed into her skin with his hands, deeper and more purposefully. They moved under her body and found the softness of her belly. A warm need spread through his groin and he gasped as his wife adjusted herself and raised her hands above her head. It was an invitation to carry on and he opened his legs wider to give his need space to grow underneath his swim shorts. Her skin was like the finest silk and nothing he could buy her would come near its perfection.

The snake sat guard over her but Tony imagined it not there as the touch of her skin pulled him closer to her. The scent of the oil drowned his senses in the softness of her body. His body. They'd fought, but it was time to make up, and he'd apologised for calling her his possession. He'd been suitably contrite when he promised he didn't mean it when he'd said he owned her.

She stiffened and Tony's hands stopped moving.

He was irritated. What more could she want when he'd already apologised?

'What? Not ready?' he asked.

She slid her hands behind her back and tied up her bikini top and Tony looked down at what was pulsating beneath his pants. How the hell was he going to get rid of it now?

'For fuck's sake,' he chuntered under his breath. Monika tutted and faced away from him.

He got up and kicked the bottle of massage oil.

Monika turned her head and he caught a glimpse of the look on her face. It was a gaze of pure condescension. Not hatred, or even disgust, just pity. He knew then that she didn't love him anymore.

'What's really changed, Monika?' he asked her.

'What do you mean?' She twisted around and the snake disappeared.

'You know what I fucking mean. Who are you shagging?'

'Tony… I—'

'Don't Tony me. You're taking me for a fool, Monika.'

'Because I don't want sex with you, I must be getting it somewhere else? Has it ever crossed your mind that I just don't want it with you?'

It cut him through his middle and he caught sight of himself in the bi-fold doors as he walked away. His wrinkled skin and sun-marked face could never be reversed. The tightness and smoothness of her back was something that couldn't be purchased or traded. He'd never be young again.

He walked away with rage rising in his gut, but, he realised, at least one of his problems had gone away. Underneath his shorts, he'd gone flaccid once more, but that only made him resent her even more.

He'd tried to buy her. Then he'd tried to enslave her. Then he'd tried to keep her.

But he wasn't going to lose her.

Chapter 14

Ewan peered inside the fridge. It was so hot, he'd come home from school and got straight into the pool. Now he was thirsty. And hungry. He looked for anything in a packet, which ensured it would have plenty of additives for flavour. Dad did the Waitrose shop online and Mum disapproved of mostly everything and brought extra home every night. But Dad's food was tastier, even though Mum said it was crap. He listened to TikTok via his AirPods and dripped water all over the kitchen floor.

Being plugged in, despite the house being empty anyway, made sure his world was quiet. It was only penetrated by the noise he allowed in. The expletives of gaming males were like silence compared to the racket of his family. He opened a can of Coke and found cold pizza, and he chomped it as he went back up to his room to play Xbox before meeting Noah.

Friday was the best night of the week. The weekend stretched before him, and Brandon Stand couldn't get inside his house.

'Lads thinking they're having fun,' was how the police put it when they called Mum back. Dad kicked off again, which made everything worse.

He was never riding another new bike again. He'd rather dump it in a bush and walk. There were six of them already in the garage, each discarded after a minor accident or vandalism by a bully.

He checked his watch as he went back upstairs with his Coke, having finished off what was left of the pizza. Satisfied, and a lot cooler, he went to his room and began gaming. He logged on and found a couple of mates to play with. Behind his headphones and mic, he was anonymous, brave and fearless. He zoned out of life and lost himself in a world of fake enemies, weapons and women. They were normally victims of crime or innocent bystanders. Occasionally, there'd be a kick-ass female who beat the others, and that was fun. He liked those types of girls. Like his mum. Like Natalie Morgan.

> Coming to the rec?

The text was from Noah.

The rec was a few old empty warehouses, surrounded by a couple of football pitches, where kids hung out. They played football, or skated, but mostly they experimented with drugs. Ewan hadn't tried any yet. But he wanted to.

A notification on the Xbox informed him that he'd been killed inside the game he was playing, and because he told the host to fuck off, he was barred for three hours. He slammed down the controller and texted Noah back telling him he'd call for him first.

He dumped his towel on top of his PC, which sat on top of a bespoke gaming centre, boasting his Xbox, Mac and PlayStation. He listened to music through his headphones, and watched others being exterminated online, unfazed by the sensory overload. He got dressed quickly, spraying some aftershave, bought for him for Christmas by his mum. He took his phone and made sure his bankcard and house key were inside the case.

He never bothered turning anything off in his room.

The house was still quiet, though he noticed that his sister's door was slightly ajar. He hadn't heard her come in. He opened the door a little and stopped when he heard retching. For some reason, she was ill all the time. He knew about girls who threw up on purpose because they talked about it at school, but he had no idea why. Why would you? He liked food. The last thing on his mind was to throw up after eating it. What a waste of time, and food.

But that was girls.

He backed out and went downstairs. His family was weird. Except him and James. As if on cue, his older brother came in the back door, through the kitchen and into the hallway. He smiled broadly. His arms looked freshly tanned as if he'd been sitting by the river Cam all day long. That's what Ewan wanted to do when he was James's age. That, and smoke weed.

'You all right, little bro?'

He always called him that. Ewan liked it. He smiled and nodded. 'Going out,' he said.

'Meeting mates?' James asked.

James was the coolest person Ewan knew. He worked out at the gym. His clothes hung off his chest and his arms underneath rippled with muscle. Ewan wanted to join a gym as soon as he was allowed. For now, his parents argued that he needed to concentrate on his studies, and golf. He fantasised about taking Brandon Stand out in one punch with a fist the size of James's.

Ewan nodded.

'You know what Dad thinks of Noah,' James warned.

'Who gives a fuck what Dad thinks,' Ewan spat.

'Woah, fella. What's up?' James asked.

Ewan walked down the stairs and James caught him in an embrace. They pretended to wrestle.

'Are you taking your bike?' James asked. Ewan shook his head.

'Walking,' he said.

'Where you meeting?'

'Noah's.'

'You going to the rec?'

Ewan said nothing.

'You know if you want to try drugs, you can do it with me. It really isn't all that big a deal. I'll show you,' James said. 'I'd rather you did it with me than with strangers, you need to know what it's all about, to stay safe, little bro.'

Ewan paused and almost took him up on it, but something inside of him wanted to meet Noah and get wasted without his family watching, not even James. He caught his brother's eye and nodded.

'What have you done?' Ewan asked.

'Which drugs?' James asked.

Ewan nodded.

'Pretty much everything. If you wanna try, just tell me, okay? Don't take any pills from strangers,' he added.

'That's like warning me of stranger danger, I'm not a kid,' Ewan said.

'I know,' James replied.

'I'm home!' They both turned to where the holler had come from and smiled at their mum.

Chapter 15

Carrie stripped off her work suit that stuck to her body mercilessly in the heat, and looked forward to getting into her pool. She'd had better Fridays. She'd let go fifty-odd staff last week, and another twenty today, and that's why she'd caught the train into London. It was shitty work but somebody had to do it. Commuters on the tube across the city stank of body odour and graft.

She downed a large glass of ice-cold water from the filtered cooler and ran upstairs, selecting a string bikini. She tossed off the work suit – like unwanted staff, and bad memories – and twisted in front of the mirror at the entrance to her dressing room, and critiqued her figure. She swished this way and that, studying herself from all angles. The light in her bedroom, and the angle of the mirror, created a clever mirage that she marvelled at, like a child at the circus. She liked most of what she saw in the reflection and praised Grace. The girl did a good job and had an amenable manner. She was uptight for her age, and sometimes lacked humour, but Carrie could forgive that for the attention she received in the gym, and thus the fun Carrie had people-watching. Grace took herself far too seriously. She had yet to work out what she was so forcefully protecting. The girl on screen was an alter-ego, a doppelganger who espoused clean living and self-care, who championed health and fitness as a guaranteed road to long life and happiness, despite her having lived a short life herself. Carrie was suspicious of self-styled gurus who were barely out of nappies. How could they possibly know adversity? Especially ones who lived in penthouse flats in the centre of Cambridge. But it was a pleasant distraction and some of Grace's tips on food, sleep and vitamins were interesting additions to her own routine.

Gyms were curious places. They were full of good-looking people with tight bodies and fragile egos: exchanging furtive glances in mirrors, and sweating in front of strangers. Ostensibly, they were hostile environments, but Carrie had learned that members were mostly desperate to talk. She'd made more friends there than anywhere else. It amused her that in the gym, covered in the tribal uniform of Lycra and sweat, no one knew who you were. You could be a lorry driver, or a teacher, or a billionaire. No one cared.

Tonight, she was having a well-earned rest. Grace recommended down days, with no exercise, to let the body recover and mend, and she uploaded videos on it. However, resting wasn't something Carrie was used to. It felt plain odd. That was the other curious thing: she took orders in the gym. The freedom of not being in charge was extraordinary. It was like shedding skin.

She checked the alarm panel in her bedroom, installed in the spring, after the break-in. Only the cleaner and the gardener had keys.

The event had left her shaken.

The house was large, with several entrances. It had plenty of land around it too, and it was isolated. Her nearest neighbours were probably three hundred yards away and they'd heard nothing that night. It made her feel vulnerable, and that made her angry. When she'd reported it to the police, she'd expected the bastards would be caught, and full charges to be brought, and for the perpetrators to go to prison. None of that happened. Not even close.

The case went nowhere. It was a reminder to Carrie that one made one's own luck in life. People always let you down in the end. Especially coppers.

She seethed a little, even now, five months later. It wasn't the stolen jewellery, or computer, or speakers – custom-made by Bose – or the shoes, or the VIP Ed Sheeran tickets. It was the fact that strangers had been in her home, and smeared their filth everywhere. For days, the house smelled of them: unclean and alien. The stench of unwashed stale air and weed made her nauseous. They'd been in her wardrobe and taken a shit in her bathroom. The smashed booze cabinet had led the police to assume it was teenagers, and they'd sucked their teeth as they announced to her that the chances of finding them, and apprehending them, was about the same odds as a rocking horse winning the Grand National.

But Carrie also knew that the reason it had riled her so much was because it reminded her of where she came from.

Apparently there'd been a spate of burglaries in Cambridge in the new year.

So she'd installed a state-of-the-art alarm system. She had cameras placed at all the entry points, monitors set up in the kitchen, main reception and her bedroom, an intercom system, as well as an electric gate to the front of the property. Yet she still didn't feel completely safe. Her demons still woke her up in the middle of the night and made her walk around checking locks and windows into the early hours.

She heard a noise, and froze.

She moved silently to the window and peered over the garden. Nothing. Was it her imagination? Her heart rate soared and she grabbed a towel from her en-suite to wrap around her body, as if that would ward off an axe murderer. Voices climbed into her head, uninvited and unwanted. They told her she wasn't safe. They told her she didn't deserve to be safe. The layer of sweat on her body, still there from her suit, cloyed around her, suffocating her. She went to the hallway outside her room and tiptoed out into the corridor, where she heard the sound again. It sounded like a door banging. She looked up at the sensor in the corner of the ceiling, overlooking the staircase. There was supposed to be a small red dot on the small plastic box, but there was none. Her heart thumped even faster.

Sweat trickled down her forehead into her eyes and she rubbed it away. She felt exposed and pulled the towel closer round her body. Her semi-nakedness made her feel weak and frail suddenly. Her bare feet padded along the wooden floor as she crept towards the stairs. She daren't breathe. She felt a cool breeze flow down the corridor and swore to herself; she'd left the windows open in one of the bedrooms when she'd come in to do her checks this morning, because it was so hot. She tried to calm down and tell herself it was a cat or even a nosy squirrel, which they got around here in summer, looking for shade and water. They flung themselves through the air off trees and into people's houses, brazen but friendly, most of the time. She admired the ballsy little fuckers.

She approached the top of the stairs and looked over the polished wooden banister. Nothing. There was another bang and she pinpointed it to the kitchen, at the rear of the property. Then she realised that she'd left her mobile phone back in her bedroom.

The policeman's voice rang in her head. *It was lucky you weren't home, ma'am, some of these thieves can be nasty, and you living alone is an attractive prospect to them.* The tokens of insolence and vulgarity, left in her bathroom, and the fact that her bed was left unkempt, chilled her to the core. She'd thrown away the sheets and the mattress.

The police had patrolled the area more in the months after that.

But now they'd stopped.

She retraced her steps to her bedroom and found her mobile on the bed. As she did so, she peered up at the security box in her bedroom and saw that there were no lights on at all. The whole system was down. Now she ran. She sprinted out of her room and downstairs, dialling 999 as she went. She made it to the front door and looked around, frantically searching for encouragement that she was safe, she was unharmed, and that she was not in mortal danger.

All of the time.

'Which emergency service do you require?'

The voice snapped her to her senses.

She remembered the system was being tested. She'd had postal notification and telephone confirmation yesterday. It would be off for ten minutes, max.

She hung up.

Lights on boxes, all over the hallway and in the kitchen, as far as she could see, came to life and she closed her eyes. Her chest heaved and her temples thumped.

She walked slowly towards the rear of the house and checked all the rooms, one by one. She saw out of a window that a door in the pool house was banging, and she paused at the kitchen sink for another glass of cold water. Her resolve was shaken and she almost went to the drinks cabinet, the one that was now broken, to search for a shot of something brown and pungent, even though she'd poured the stuff away years ago. But she didn't. The pull of escape was overwhelming. Just a small sip…

Breathe.

A police siren startled her and to her surprise, as it came closer, she realised it had stopped outside her gates. The intercom buzzed furiously. She felt a fool as she went to the gate in her bikini and towel, to tell them it was a false alarm. She recalled her mobile number being connected to her landline in emergencies and paying extra for the privilege. Now, to her surprise, it had served its purpose.

'That was quick,' she said to a worried-looking officer. He glared at her as she informed him that it had been a mistake.

'Is everything all right, miss?'

'Yes, yes, honestly, it was a mistake.' She uttered excuses and small talk and he eventually agreed to go back to his car. She watched him get in and talk to his partner and she wondered if he was telling her that the woman who'd called 999 was crazy, and that next time, if there was a next time, they might not be so keen to run red lights with blues and twos, and might instead just take their time.

She slammed the door and pushed her back up to it, and was overcome by a craving; bare, naked and brazen. It took her by complete surprise. She'd been dry for five years. She couldn't even remember what alcohol tasted like. She felt at odds with her own brain and intensely pissed off that it was betraying her like this.

'It's just fear,' she kept saying to herself. She forced herself to calm her breathing and work through exactly what scared her. It was like a ticking clock: the *tick-tock* of taunting worries, and she could only hope to silence them slowly.

But a drink would help.

'Fuck off!' she shouted at the empty house. Her voice bounced off the solitary walls.

She strode angrily into the kitchen and threw off her towel, marching to the pool house, chuntering to herself all the way, and dived in the pool.

Under the water she couldn't feel her body tremors, but she could see the mirage shimmering at the surface. Half of her brain told her that it was the sunlight, playing tricks on the water, but the other half taunted her with the distortion: an impaired mutation.

She burst through the surface and sucked the air.

She gagged. The stench was pungent and acrid, and stung her senses. No, not again. She jumped out and grabbed her towel and caught the whiff again, but stronger this time. It was coming from behind the pool house and she followed the scent, stopping when she found the source of the rot. A squirrel, she assumed from what was left of its grey fur, decayed and maggot-ridden, stared back at her and she covered her mouth.

She was losing her shit.

Chapter 16

'I can drop you at Noah's,' I tell Ewan.

He's tempted by the air conditioning in the car and it's an opportunity for me to talk with him, in the kind of way teenagers feel safe: looking straight ahead, and not into my eyes.

'You didn't drive me around when I was fifteen, Mum,' James says.

'Stop with the driving-a-wedge-between-the-siblings crap, James.'

He laughs. He takes it well. He's right. I spoil Ewan. I know. James looks tanned and this is his last summer of freedom before he has to decide if he'll go to university or *turn into a bum*, to use his dad's phrase. For what it's worth, I don't think university is what it was. All that debt, to call yourself an academic. James doesn't even know what he wants to do with his life, but what he won't do is follow the rats around the wheel and feed into the system. I can see him on a research vessel in the South China Sea, diving with whales and meeting a nubile Antipodean girl with blond hair and a penchant for tattoos. Oh, to have those choices again.

'Where's Dad?' I ask. As if I want to know.

They both shrug at me.

I grab the keys and Ewan follows me out to the car.

'Does Noah know what happened to your bike?'

Ewan nods. 'I don't want any more new bikes. I hate them.'

'Hate is a strong word.'

He glares at me.

'Sorry, I'll stop analysing.'

We get in the car and set off to Noah's, which is a ten-minute drive, but worth the effort to spend time with my youngest son.

'Why doesn't Dad like Noah?'

'Huh?'

'James told me.'

'Oh. I don't know.'

'Is it because his dad got made redundant and now they haven't got as much money as us?'

Jesus.

'Erm. I didn't know Noah's dad was made redundant. When was this?'

'Last week, by some bitch at work.'

'Nice.'

'Dad thinks he's easy-going, doesn't he? But he's actually judgemental, especially when he's drunk.'

I grip the steering wheel. *Oh, Jeremy, I always knew there'd come a time when you could no longer hide it. That day is here, and our kids are paying the price.*

'I'm sorry.' It's the second time I've had to apologise to my children today.

'It's not your fault, Mum.'

'Is Noah's family struggling?'

'Yeah. His mum and dad argue all the time. I told him that's normal.'

I look at his side profile and wonder at his perception. 'Do me and Dad argue a lot?'

'Only when he's drunk.'

'It's a mask,' I say quietly.

He looks at me. I want to drive slower to keep him in the car forever.

'What? Like a cover?'

I nod. 'Your dad feels a lot of pressure and some people, well, they look for ways to escape.'

'Run away, more like. If he wants to escape, why doesn't he just leave?'

It stings. But it's true.

'It's okay, Mum, everybody's parents split up. Noah's are going to, I think. At least that's what he thinks.'

We're there but I don't want him to leave. He opens the door and we both hear shouting from inside Noah's house. He looks at me.

Noah appears from behind the house and smiles at his friend. I don't mind the kid. He gets high, I know that, but so does James. Maybe Ewan does too, but I haven't seen the tell-tale signs like I did with my eldest.

Noah takes his headphones out of his ears and his face changes as he hears his parents from behind the privacy of their family walls. I wave.

'Hi, Noah.'

'Hi, Mrs M.'

'Bye, Mum.'

They walk away. I sit in the car for a few seconds listening to the wasteland of another marriage before driving back to my own.

At home I begin mopping up water on the kitchen floor, presumably from the boys going in and out of the pool. I've checked on Lydia; she's still asleep. She's been in bed all day. I spoke to the doctor at length.

I lean over the sink and am reminded of Tony's touch, when I stood next to his sink, in his kitchen, today. It was a brief affair, but intense. Jeremy still doesn't know. Guilt stinks on me and I suddenly need a shower.

On my way upstairs I hear a noise in the study. I peek around the door and Jeremy is working on my Mac computer.

'You working?' I regret it instantly, but to my surprise, he nods his head.

'Can I see?'

His fingers work quickly, and he hides whatever he's been doing, just like he's been hiding himself away in here all the time I've been home.

'You don't want me to see?'

'Let's have a drink, it's Friday. How was your day?'

I'm puzzled by his mood. I follow him to the kitchen, where he gets wine out of the fridge. I bristle.

'I spoke to a doctor about Lydia today.' I whisper because I'm not sure if Lydia is eavesdropping. I let it hang. He either ignores me or doesn't want to talk about the fact that if his daughter loses much more weight, she'll be hospitalised. 'Did you book an appointment for yourself?' I ask, looking at the wine he's just poured. He keeps saying he'll get a check-up, though I know he never will.

'Oh, for God's sake, Alex, leave it off, there's nothing wrong with me. So, I have the occasional glass of wine.'

'The kids have started asking.'

'What? You're turning them on me now?'

He slams another roadblock between us. His eyes are glassy, and I know there's no point pursuing it. I change the subject.

'I went to see Tony today.'

'Monika's probably off shagging someone, we all know that, don't we?' he says. He's a stranger to me.

'And is that what you told the police?'

'As a matter of fact, I did. I told them she had a string of affairs and had probably finally met someone who kept her interested. Somebody even richer than Tony.' He laughs. His words drip with resentment and envy.

'Nice.'

'Are you telling me you don't agree?' he asks.

'No, I just think you're quick to judge, that's all.'

He laughs again.

'That's rich, coming from you.' He points his finger at me as he speaks and I find him repulsive.

I want to hit him, but I steady my hands and go to the fridge to get some cranberry juice. I'm not drinking with him. I take it outside. Ewan's crumpled bike is laying on the grass. In the garage there are six more and I throw the mangled one on top of the others. Alongside them are the discarded possessions of my life with Jeremy. A baby walker, a small boat with an outboard motor, an exercise machine, skis, a basketball hoop...

I sit in the garage, on an unopened case of wine, sipping my juice. It's stuffy and the air isn't fresh in here but it's better than the lethal atmospheric circulation in my kitchen.

Chapter 17

Grace paced up and down the gym floor. She smiled sweetly when she saw a business opportunity but lateness unsettled her and so she was jumpy. It didn't fit. Like the weights being out of place, or clients lacing their trainers wrongly.

Loud, pumping music distracted her, but she still watched the clock. She didn't like to start sessions behind schedule. It ruined her plans. She walked past people plugged into their phones. Grace had never known gyms before headphones, but she imagined them to have been more sociable places. They made new members harder to connect with. That's why she'd started her YouTube channel.

Connection is the basis of mental health, she'd said into the camera tonight, after she'd grabbed a nut bar for her lunch because there was no point cooking for one.

She looked at her watch again and tried to see the missed appointment as an opportunity, perhaps, but at what point did one assume they weren't coming at all? Twenty minutes? Thirty? She could sit and plan a new video, using gym equipment. Viewers loved props. It made her look professional, and that made people trust what she said.

Monika had been late before. She was the kind of woman who came and went as she pleased. Grace watched the main door, in between putting weights back in their place and picking up discarded mats. She was sure that Monika would have a good reason, but tardiness got under her skin. It put her out of kilter and disturbed the natural order of things that kept her routine manageable. A tiny blip that threw her off course could have disastrous consequences. But that didn't seem to concern women like Monika, who acted like she took everyone for granted. That's what money did to people and Grace was determined it wouldn't happen to her.

It crossed her mind that maybe Monika's husband had something to do with it. Grace heard snippets of her clients' lives during sessions and knew enough about Tony Thorpe. Once, she'd bumped into Monika leaving the gym, and she'd caught a glimpse of him in his Aston Martin as Monika climbed in. Grace had seen them argue, and she remembered thinking that he looked like her father. Grace had also seen the way men looked at Monika, but knew the woman preferred the size of a man's wallet to anything else.

She glanced at the door again and tutted. Hard physical graft was elusive for many, perhaps Monika simply couldn't be bothered. But it was unlike her. She walked around the gym floor one more time and acknowledged familiar faces. It was a quarter past the hour, and she decided to call her client. She went to the PT office and logged on to the computer, to check if Monika had swiped her gym card. She hadn't. So she called her mobile phone. It went unanswered. So she tried the landline listed, expecting no one to answer, but it was picked up, and a man spoke.

'Hello, who is this?' she asked politely.
'Who is *this*?' he replied sternly.

'Sorry, maybe I've got the wrong number? Is this Monika Thorpe's house?'

'Yes, this is her husband, who wants to know?'

His tone made her heart beat faster. Suddenly she found herself in an awkward situation that she hadn't planned for, and it wasn't pleasant. She felt caught, and guilty for prying, and she pictured the face of the man who'd picked up Monika in the carpark.

'Oh, erm, I'm sorry to disturb you. Gosh, it's just...' Grace was acutely aware that she might be causing a fuss. She had no idea where Monika might be but what if she was wading into some marital argument? She was gripped by disloyalty. Monika might be seeing another man.

She explained who she was.

'I've heard a lot about you.'

The words dripped through the telephone like syrup.

He's just a man.

'Grace, isn't it?'

'Yes,' she replied. Her voice shook.

'Monika isn't here. In fact, she's gone.'

'Gone?'

'Yes.'

Silence.

In panic, she replaced the receiver. Her hands tremored but the rest of her body didn't move. She felt the skin on her chest heat up. Her pulse throbbed and the room swayed. Her head felt loose and empty. She slid off the chair and sat on the floor, aware that somebody else had come into the tiny airless office. Ignacio bent over her and touched her arm. She recoiled from the contact and moved an inch away from him so she couldn't smell his body. Visions of a man on top of her – sweaty from his workout; crushing the wind out of her with his bulk

– filled her head and she closed her eyes, trying to concentrate on the fact that Monika's husband told her she was simply 'gone'.

She was vaguely aware of a small group of other PTs gathering around her, and Ignacio keeping them back and asking them to give her space. She heard voices buzzing about her head and tried to focus on a chart on the wall with stars on it. People asked if she was okay, but all at once, and their voices merged into an annoying hum. She looked at them blankly.

'Grace? Who was on the phone?' Ignacio asked. She realised that she still gripped the receiver in her hand, and she hadn't replaced it after all.

She looked at Ignacio. His arm fully cradled her and a creeping feeling started in her toes and worked its way up through her body until she tensed and froze. He rubbed her back and she looked at him in horror. He was comforting her, thinking her terrified by what news she'd heard, but how could he possibly know what she was really feeling? He couldn't. Her immobility just made him want to console her even more. The warmer she felt his hand, the closer she looked into his eyes, the more she wanted to scream and retch, and lash out all at once. She was transported back to the studio – *his* home studio – when he'd come up behind her after their boxing session. Vincent had been a client for months, and she'd trusted him.

She jumped and Ignacio recoiled. His purity of soul was what she'd once seen in Vincent. She'd trusted everybody. Inner voices taunted her and made her feel scummy and rubbish. People finally stood back and looked at her oddly, *like the police had*. Like everybody had. She felt hands on her body and she knew that she had to get out of there.

Vincent's face clanged against the voice of the Crown Court judge. The defence barrister. 'Did you encourage the defendant?'

She struggled to her feet and fled, out of the door, heading for the staff toilet. She heard footsteps close behind her. She made it to the toilet in time to lift the lid, before the puke came out of her in heaves.

At first, it was lumpy and she recognised the smell of banana and spotted bulky bits of undigested porridge. Then it slowed and became liquid, hurting her stomach as it tensed and relaxed. She was done. She wiped her mouth with her hand and closed her eyes, recognising the familiar smell of shame.

She slid onto the floor and her chest rose and fell with the exertion. She sat, panting, trying to understand what had just happened. It had been spontaneous and out of her control; she hadn't even had to use her fingers to prompt the purge. But, instead of feeling empty, her body felt the opposite: satiated and full, as if replenished. She reached over to flush the handle and felt a rising tide of purification. She'd ejaculated her fear. It felt good, and she felt energised.

She stood up slowly, turning to the door, and left the cubicle. At the sink, she washed her hands and splashed cold water on her face. By the time she left the room, and found Ignacio waiting for her outside, she was composed and calm. She smiled at him.

'I'm sorry,' she said.

'Hey, don't be sorry. Are you okay? What happened?'

'Gosh, I really don't know. It's just a client... I... he said she's gone.'

'Who said?'

'Her husband.'

'Gone where?'

She told him about the phone call, and he placed his hand on her shoulder tenderly. It repulsed her and she was reminded of the galling human habit of imposing oneself upon another's personal space without invite. She moved away. But she was no longer scared. She'd sanitised herself and for a moment she felt elation and joy.

They walked back to the gym floor together and another PT held out her mobile phone for her, which she'd dropped when she ran to the toilet. It was ringing. She looked at it strangely, as if it wasn't hers. Then she answered.

It was the police.

Chapter 18

Tony Thorpe swam the entire length of his extensive pool underwater. The retractable roof over the summer house had been drawn back and the pool was open to the glorious sunshine. It felt as if he were somewhere exotic, and not Cambridge, England. He'd got into the habit of keeping Friday afternoons free of work and when the weather was like this he couldn't be arsed to do any at all.

He swam to the steps in the corner of the pool and got out of the water, retrieving his towel from the side. His wife's absence allowed him to be messy and it pleased him. He threw his towel down after drying himself off and went to a sun lounger, where he'd left *The Financial Times*. The pink pages were warm in the sunshine and he sat back, sipping a soda. Monika didn't allow sugary drinks, so he'd gone to Waitrose yesterday and bought a box full. She had no affection for Seventies music either, which he turned up on his Bluetooth speaker. She'd been twenty-six years old when they'd met, on the cruise ship along the Danube, and it had seemed distinctly romantic at the time. Back then, she'd been flattered and grateful for attention. Now, she acted as though she owned the place. He'd thought he'd loved her, at some time in their short relationship, which is why he'd been stupid enough to make her Mrs Thorpe. But in the cold light of day, he realised that he'd been well and truly – and spectacularly stereotypically – led by his dick.

Now he could breathe. He'd left cupboard doors open, dropped crumbs on the kitchen floor, left his bed unmade, and even put away her body creams. She'd been preparing her skin for the removal of the god-awful tattoo she'd had done on her back when she was eighteen and stupid. He hadn't minded it at first, as it glided across her skin, towards her arse cheeks, and every time he took her from behind, he felt in some stupid way that he was getting the better of it, as it taunted him and crawled across her divinely perfect flesh, in the shape of an enchanting serpent, which she said protected her from evil spirits. But over the short years, he'd come to loathe it. Instead of charming him, the thing eventually began to unnerve him, as if she had a great slug wriggling up her back. The procedure was going to cost the earth but it would be worth it to get the damn thing off her.

He gulped another mouthful of cold fizz and placed the can on a table, spilling some, deliciously on purpose, with no intention of wiping it up. Today's reading was positive. Investments were consistently shaken by politics, war, weather, disease, social unrest, and even harvests the other side of the globe. It was high risk and that's exactly why it paid. At fifty-five he wasn't old or necessarily ageing, but he had to take better care of himself than when he'd been twenty-five. Hence the swimming. It caused no impact on his body, he enjoyed it and he could do it alone, like everything in his life that meant anything to him: he needed no partners.

His skin was honey-coloured from hours of leisure time at home, in between Zoom and telephone calls, sitting in the sun, reading and watching his bank balance grow. He'd reached a time in his life when he could step back a touch from the nitty gritty of deal making, and cast a general eye upon speculative business.

Christ, he didn't need any more money, but it was the pursuit of it that got his juices flowing.

He checked his phone and he had a WhatsApp from Carrie.

They'd caught the same train to King's Cross for about fifteen years. They'd begun chatting, as you do, when one catches the six a.m. train and there's no one else to talk to but yawning tradesmen and nodding revellers from the previous night's fun. The Cambridge train into London wasn't a bad service and it took a good hour. It was time to either work, reflect or chat, and Carrie, he'd discovered, was a chatter. But, unlike many women he'd come across in the city, and the little mouse who'd called him from the gym, Carrie was interesting, not just ballsy. They bonded over their sense of humour, their politics and their love of money. Their conversations were mostly about investments, house renovations, holidays and their property portfolios abroad.

Like him, Carrie flew solo. They needed no company, and thrived off success and achievement, never being satisfied with gains, always searching for the next pursuit, because that's where the thrill was: the chase. He sat back, plopped his Ray-Bans over his eyes and smiled.

He read the message:

> See Logi Trading down for the weekend.

She was mostly all business. He'd managed to peep through her armour a few times and had even invited her round for BBQs, but she always made an excuse. He understood that domestic pleasantries weren't her thing. He replied.

> That's because Logi Trading has been purchased by an anonymous buyer who will be revealed in purchase documents on Monday.

He referred to a mining company in Chile, which he'd managed to procure for a tenth of what it was worth because of a recent collapse of the mine wall, and huge casualties, resulting in massive debt and litigation. Buying at a low rate enabled him to strip the mine of assets, sell them on, restructure the facility and rent the space. It was a textbook manoeuvre but came with risk, especially in countries where one had no leg to stand on should the shit hit the fan. Carrie, being likeminded and shrewd with her money, kept an eye on such things.

> Ha! Yours truly?

He sent back a smiling-face emoji. A thought occurred to him and he put down his paper. It was a beautiful afternoon and he had the house to himself. That hadn't happened for a long time and it made him feel quite giddy and frivolous.

> Come over and talk about it? I am a free man.

There was no reply for eight minutes.

> Free for the evening or free for the
> foreseeable future?

> Latter.

This time the reply came after eleven minutes.

> Okay.

Chapter 19

Three days before Monika's disappearance

'One more, *you can do it, Monika.*'

Grace encouraged her from above her head. Monika stared into Grace's crotch and pushed the bar higher. The last centimetre of effort seemed to be impossible and she stared up at her personal trainer with panic in her eyes. Hot exhaustion stripped her arms of power and for a split second she felt chained and helpless in the position, suspended in time, not moving, imprisoned in the endeavour. Tony's words to her this morning sat in the final chasm between success and failure.

'*You're nothing without me.*'

He'd begun to suspect her, and ask her where she was going when she left the house. He paid for everything: her car, her home, her clothes... her liberty. The woman he caught the train with to London took title in her assets, and that's what Tony admired in her. But those rules didn't apply to his wife. He rabbited on about how his companion on the King's Cross service scrapped for every bit of independence she'd gained. She was a triumph, a heralded champion of female capability.

Monika had never met Carrie but had heard plenty about her.

The torture of captivity welled up inside her and travelled to her arms and she made the final push.

'*Yes!*'

Grace took the weight off her and replaced it on its rack, clapping her hands together.

Monika sat up, panting, and a regular gym-goer nodded his approval. Grace waved at him and went to stop her phone camera.

'This will go live this afternoon.'

'I told my husband, and he wasn't happy about it,' Monika said.

'He should be proud. I'm demonstrating what can be achieved with hard work,' Grace told her.

'I know, but he sees it as showing off.'

'Would he see it that way if I asked him to star in one of my videos?' Grace asked.

Monika laughed. 'No, probably not, but that's different, isn't it? Men think they're the strong ones.'

'Hmm. Well my clients prove that theory wrong every day, and that's what my channel is all about, showing that women can be tough. Not hard, but resilient. Strength isn't all about masculinity, is it?' Grace asked.

'No, it isn't,' Monika agreed.

'And you don't have to enter a body-building competition to have goals,' Grace added. 'You look after yourself, Monika. Well done. We'll get thousands of views. And besides, I ignore haters, they ruin our fun. Any dodgy comments, and I block them. My channel is taken seriously.'

Monika took her weights gloves off one by one and laid them across her lap.

'You okay?' Grace asked her.

Monika thought for a brief moment about confiding in her personal trainer, but the notion passed, and she smiled and nodded.

'Have you thought more about going back to practise law?' Grace asked.

Monika paused. 'I checked. The university said it can be done, a conversion to English law, but my husband…'

Grace stood with her hands on her hips and searched her client's face.

Ignacio interrupted them. 'Hey, Grace, Orlando wants to see you after your session. Hi Monika. Working hard, I see.'

'Thank you. She's pushing me.'

He walked away and the conversation sidled naturally back on to safer topics, like the heatwave and how the air conditioning at the gym whirred under the strain. But Monika was a little quieter for the rest of their session together.

Chapter 20

'I didn't know whether to bring a bottle or not,' Carrie said, as she stood on the doorstep, empty-handed, apart from the bag slung over her shoulder. She'd dressed appropriately for a Friday afternoon in the sun: huge Prada glasses, Armani summer dress, gold Gucci sandals, a wide-brimmed Brunello Cucinelli hat, and a Christian Dior beach tote bag.

'Come in! A bottle would always be welcome, but I see you drove,' Tony said, looking behind her. 'I can always call you a cab,' he added.

She was unexpectedly hesitant to cross the threshold, as if into a wolf's lair, but she pushed the silly intrusion aside and went in, like a girl from a long ago fairy-tale, wearing red. Carrie hadn't had a mother to warn her against running into the wood alone; in fact, she'd encouraged it.

'We've got to celebrate Logi Trading's recent acquisition,' he said.

Carrie smelled the heady scent of old flowers and noticed that a vase full of white lilies wilted without water on the hall occasional table. Signs of an absent woman. The aroma took her back to a tiny alleyway in Siena, Italy, where she'd found a small trattoria, and stopped for bruschetta antipasto and red wine, many, many years ago. The heat in the air was the same, as was the cool air of the interior, but the image disappeared as she came inside. She'd never visited Tony's house before, not wanting to accept invitations and risk crossing the line between fellow commuters. And not wanting to meet his pretty, young wife.

Tonight, she'd changed her mind.

Was it her scare at home leaving her craving company? She was no longer the sort to self-sabotage or follow foolish whims, and she was under no illusion that Tony Thorpe could be a charming flirt. So why the hell was she here? Some sense of recklessness? Deep inside she knew the real answer, but she dare not vocalise it.

He'd have booze in his house. She didn't carry a bottle with her to offer because she had none. She hadn't bought it in years.

She left her doubts at the door. They didn't matter now. She was here, and Tony looked happy and relaxed, which was a blessing in their world. Both were so used to gloomy, tense individuals, bemoaning the multi-million dollar deals they forged and sometimes lost. She sought innocent relief, and that was all.

Liar.

She'd put clean underwear on and Tony looked at her as if he could see it, and smell it. Traders like them were master hunters, sensitive to the aroma of prey.

'Your wife?' she asked.

'Well, there's the thing. She kind of up and left me.' He closed the door and the grimace on his face told Carrie that it was a little embarrassing, but welcome too. He led her to the back of the house.

'You don't seem bothered,' she said bluntly, following him. She assumed that the kitchen was through the back, where the garden faced south, and she was right. Of course, someone of Tony's calibre would be wanting a full south-facing open plan modern kitchen, or at least his wife would. She'd once seen Monika in the gym, or at least she guessed it was her from Henry's description of her. Women like Monika were easy to spot. The jewellery, the gullibility and the stench of money. Carrie assumed that the marriage had ended because of her age. Men in their fifties should stay away from women twenty years their junior, unless it was just for sex. Marriage was plain stupid and she'd been surprised by his lack of judgement. Well, at least now she'd been proven right.

She admired the space.

'It's beautiful. Did you use the company I recommended in the end?'

'I certainly did, and he's done a fantastic job, I have to commend you on that. At first I wasn't sure about him, he looks like an ex-con to me,' he said, laughing. He stared at her expectantly as if waiting for her to either confirm or deny his assessment of Henry Nelson.

She tensed, but let it go.

'Ah, so that's why it looks so spectacular. He really is good, you shouldn't judge a book by its cover, you know, Tony.'

She looked around and felt unease at something nagging her.

'Monika had a new kitchen fitted and then left? That's weird. What woman does that?' she asked breezily. It was still unfinished and needed the keen eye of a woman to complete it. The space was beautiful and she regretted recommending Henry's company to Tony. For a fleeting moment, she recalled Henry's hands on her, as she lay back on her own marble island, testing the tap and spraying water all over her naked body as they both threw their heads back and laughed together. *Your pipes work well enough…* he'd whispered to her. Henry had been her little pup for a while. But then he'd met Monika.

Tony shrugged. 'White or rosé?' he asked.

'Rosé, please. It's hot.' The words tripped off her tongue as if she were a moderately casual drinker, one of those who take it or leave it; have one glass of rosé by the river Cam, then go home. As if she'd ever been that. People with pain to numb don't drink, they imbibe until blackout.

'Christ, I'm glad you've got a pool. I took the liberty…' she said, pulling a costume out of her bag. 'May I?' she asked. Sirens buzzed in her head, and red flags tried to warn her of guaranteed impending catastrophe, but she ignored them.

'Go out to the pool house and you'll find towels in the changing rooms. I'll bring the drinks. Thanks for coming, Carrie,' he said.

She looked at him and smiled. She turned and walked out of the kitchen's massive open bi-fold doors and across the lawn. She stopped midway and took off her sandals. The grass was warm underfoot and she was glad she'd brought a hat. The pool house was well kitted out, as she'd expected, and she chose a cubicle in which to leave her things. She changed into her bikini quickly, checked herself in the mirror, and said a silent thank you to Grace.

She left the changing room and made her way over to a lounger. Tony brought a tray over with drinks and nibbles and placed it on a table as she settled down in full sun. Behind the refuge of her sunglasses it was impossible for him to see her eyes follow his as he assessed her body. He stripped off his shirt and she returned his stares. He was in good shape.

'You take good care of yourself, Tony,' she said.

'So do you. I won't lie and tell you that I'm naturally fit. I did it for Monika, clearly. I can be honest with you, as you already appreciate me for the shallow man I am.' He handed her a glass and she took it.

'So, did you get bored? I warned you,' she said.

'You did not!'

'Didn't I? I should have.'

'To Logi trading,' he said.

They clinked glasses and she lay back with one arm behind her head. She held the glass in her hand, contemplating the bitter first sip. The last five years of sobriety screamed at her but she'd already made up her mind. *Protect your sobriety at all costs*, the voices clanged in her head, and her hand clasping the glass trembled. She could smell the liquid. She felt like a warrior huntress; the odour filled her mind with desire and instinct. Some people doubted that sharks could smell blood a mile off, but she knew it to be true.

'So, how much do you stand to make from tearing up Logi Trading and selling it off?' she asked, taking her first mouthful, hoping he wouldn't notice her grimace. It was remarkably sweet and pleasant. Expensive, clearly.

He drained his glass and she noticed him reach for the bottle and refill it.

'Come on, Carrie, let's not be crass. I intend to treat the workforce fairly and make sure they're looked after,' he said. 'Are you drinking that or just looking beautiful holding it?'

She took a few more sips of the liquor and was amazed at how warm it felt going down her throat. Her heart leapt. She knew she was on a precipice, but she jumped off anyway.

'Bollocks, you think I was born yesterday?' she asked.

'This excites you?' he replied.

'Because you know I can't trade anymore, the bank forbids it,' she said. 'I want to enjoy it vicariously through you.'

'Shame. Have you ever thought of going it alone? Working for yourself?' he asked.

'My pension is too good. I'm retiring soon, then I might think about it. I can imagine tinkering with this and that, from my pad in the Caymans.'

'Seriously?' he asked.

She laughed. 'Half serious. I'm thinking about it. I have no family here. No ties. Their tax package is excellent, and the weather is like this all year.' She swept her hand about her. She finished her drink and instantly wanted more.

'Fancy a lodger?' He looked at her.

There weren't many people who made Carrie struggle for words, but Tony managed it. Maybe that's why she'd come over here today. Because he intrigued her. And Monika was finally out of the way.

'I've remained single and child free all my life for a very good reason, Tony. You strike me as the romantic type who falls head over heels. That isn't my style.'

'Strictly sex and money then?' he asked.

'I'll think about it. I need a top up.'

He reached for the bottle but it was almost empty, so he went inside for another. She could already feel the alcohol in her bloodstream. She ignored the alarms going off all over her brain. She held her nerve.

The door to doom had been opened, and it was too late. She could blame it on the shock of earlier, but she'd dealt with more testing times over the last five years and not caved in. It was too late for reflection.

Tony returned and filled her glass. She gulped it, pushing her body's internal warning system into mute.

Tony turned the music up and it made her want to dance. She got up off the lounger and they spun around together. Tony moved well, and they laughed easily with each other. He filled her glass again and she downed it in one.

They jumped in the pool, glasses and all. He swam to the side and lit a roll-up. He took a long drag and passed it to her. She took it and sucked hard. The fumes burned her lungs. He swam to her and held her waist. She threw back her head and went under, down to the bottom. She smiled all the way down. The pool was deep and she opened her eyes to look around.

A figure swam towards her. It was an old man, and he had hate written all over his face. It was her father. Something grabbed her legs and she fought with it, because she wanted to stay at the bottom of the pool and tell her father all the things she'd kept hidden for forty years.

She punched the water and lashed out at his face, but the force was too strong and she was pulled upwards. A huge rush of air filled her mouth and she welcomed it, bobbing up and down on the surface.

'You nutter! What are you doing? Setting records?' Tony said, laughing. She laughed and swam to the side, where he'd left his cigarette. She sucked on it and craved another drink. She took a glass that was on the side, and took a mouthful.

'I'm so thirsty!' she said.

'I've got plenty,' he said. 'Come here,' he added. He pulled her towards him and kissed her and she let him. The vision of her father disappeared as quickly as it had come. This, here and now, was what she focused on. Today, not yesterday. Now, not then. Being alive not dead. Being free not incarcerated. Choosing her story, not being a slave to it. It was her choice to let this man in, she was in control; this was her moment to desire, and to take. Like everything in her life, she was in charge. The face of her father faded to nothing as Tony drew her close and took her glass out of her hand so he could pick her up and place her on the wide pool steps, underneath him. She felt the cool water lap on her body and the fuzzy cuddle of warmth in her head as she leaned her head backwards, to the sunshine, where the hot light blotted out unwanted faces.

He was surprisingly gentle for a cut-throat capitalist. His hands expertly sought out the places she kept hidden but which longed for love. She sensed his experience as he caressed her gently and slid her bikini bottoms over her muscle-defined thighs. The silent waves at the pool edge rose up and down her body and Tony's breath quickened. She expertly slid off his shorts with her toes and reached down to toss them into the water. Then he looked at her and, whether it was the wine, the weed, or simply that a man was between her legs, she arched her back and allowed him to take her power.

Chapter 21

Ewan took a free kick from just outside the box and it connected with his right foot, exactly on the sweet spot. It catapulted away and curled towards the goal mouth. The keeper stretched his full body length, but couldn't get to it, and it pounded into the back of the net. The boys cheered and ran around the pitch. Girls who'd come to support them fawned over him and Ewan revelled in being the saviour of the beautiful game. He'd scored. He was a success, the warrior of the moment.

Noah held up his hand, and they high-fived.

'She's looking over,' Noah told his friend. Ewan smiled and looked down at his feet. He'd been in love with Natalie since Year 4. She watched him as his teammates slapped him on his back. It was an impromptu match, disorganised and casual, but scoring a goal still brought with it a huge amount of kudos and attention. Noah whacked him playfully and reaffirmed that Natalie was watching. He risked a side glance and it was true; she was smiling at him from beneath her dark curls. Ewan was spellbound by her. Somebody bumped into him and he was jolted from his romantic musings. He looked over to the entrance to the field and tensed.

The mood turned stale and a hush descended on the teams as the air tightened around the rec. They watched as a group of boys entered the grounds, inviting stares from everybody there. Ewan looked over at Natalie, who no longer gazed at him. Her face had turned bleak and she gathered her things together, as did her friends. The fun was over.

Brandon Stand swaggered across the space, with his followers tightly grouped around him. He entered like a conquering hero. Ewan braced himself. Several huddles of girls pointed and gossiped, sticking in close formation, but didn't disperse, for fear of missing any action, even if it was to see Ewan Moore humiliated again. Ewan saw Natalie stick out her chest and flare her nostrils and he stood firmly rooted to the spot, entranced by her fierceness. He knew she hated Brandon Stand. He admired her sense of justice and how she was fearless in the face of impending menace, for that was what Brandon was: dangerous.

His eyes darted from Natalie to Brandon. She didn't move. He was reminded of something she'd said in Life Studies: something about men thinking they were in charge, but women knowing how to trick them into thinking they had the upper hand, proving that women were the real puppeteers, choosing the right moment to use their skills, which were infinitely more effective. The teacher had gaped, open mouthed, unable to come up with a retort, and Natalie had gained a round of applause from the boys as well as the girls. He hadn't really known what she'd meant, and neither had the others, but that wasn't the point; she'd said something controversial and different, and she'd stood up for herself.

Brandon paraded at the front of his group of hangers on. Noah walked to Ewan's side as the teams dispersed. The boys gathered their sweaters, brought along for fashion not warmth, as well as other items from the grass, and made their way towards the warehouses. The girls waited for Brandon's group to pass and then fell in behind. Except Natalie's group. The younger boys hung about the entrance and the older boys took over the football pitch, fooling around with the balls abandoned by Ewan's mates. There was a pecking order that everybody adhered to. A dominance hierarchy that made things tick along. It was unspoken and ingrained into everybody's habits. But Natalie constantly challenged convention and Brandon noticed. That was why Ewan feared for her. One day she'd go too far with her belligerence and Brandon would punish her for it. But Ewan's money was strangely on Natalie.

Brandon spotted him and grinned.

Natalie watched him. Ewan watched her.

Brandon walked towards the rec.

Ewan exhaled.

Inside, the usual Friday-night deals were being haggled over, but the coppers stayed away, because it wasn't worth their while arresting a load of kids for possession, when their time was better spent catching the big-league dealers. Everybody knew that getting caught with an ounce of this, or a couple of grams of that, would never see you wind up in court. The cops were after kilos, which led to processors and runners, generated by suppliers, which eventually steered them to factories in major cities like Manchester, Leeds and London, where gangs fought turf wars over the stuff. A few school kids smoking dope, and smashing up some crystals of ketamine to snort, wasn't even worth one shift of police work anymore.

Brandon spoke seriously to a few kids who came out of the warehouse. They exchanged words and went inside. Natalie walked in that direction.

Ewan noticed Noah catch her arm. No one stopped Natalie from doing what she wanted. She glanced round at him and winked. Ewan checked himself, not quite sure if his eyes were deceiving him. His heart scuttled to the pit of his stomach. He was desperate to protect her but he was rooted to the spot, unable to move. Noah said she liked him, but Ewan, faced with her following the boy who tormented him without mercy, wasn't sure at all.

He'd studied every movement of her body for the best part of six years, but every time she got too close, he froze like a dummy. Maybe that was why she was following Brandon, who was never short of words. Suddenly, he noticed her turn around and walk towards him. His heart pounded and his face turned pink. She came straight for him, not flinching, and never taking her eyes away from his. She stopped, just one foot away from him, and he looked into her eyes.

'Don't worry,' she whispered. 'It's not what you think. Brandon Stand is going to have the ride of his life tonight. I promise,' she said, taking a small plastic bag out of her jeans pocket and holding it up. It was transparent and contained dozens of pale blue pills. Ewan gazed at her with his mouth open.

'Where d'you get those?' he asked.

He looked around, worried that somebody would see. No one was interested in their conversation. The question about the bag was a relatively stupid one, given that he knew exactly where she'd got it. Everyone knew that Natalie's brother, Arch, was one of the biggest dealers in Cambridge. They lived in a massive two million-quid house, their parents were upstanding Tories, both Arch and Natalie were highly regarded students with fabulous futures ahead of them, secured with family money, but if you wanted the highest-grade skunk around, or the best trip this side of London, then Arch was the man to go to. His parents had no idea that he hid his contraband behind their walls of propriety and wealth. Natalie grinned.

'Leave it to me,' she said mischievously. She walked away.

'Don't sweat,' Noah said to him confidently. They watched her go. Ewan felt anger well up inside him, but it wasn't directed at Brandon Stand. Strangely, it was reserved for Arch Morgan.

Noah looked at him. 'She hates him,' he said, nodding towards the rec.

'You know what those pills are?' Ewan asked.

Noah smiled. Of course he did. Everybody knew what MDMA pills looked like. Then realisation dawned on Ewan and he forgot about Natalie's eyes for the briefest of moments. Arch Morgan had been known to supply heavily cut shit to people he didn't like. Dope laced with other chemicals that could cause untold damage to brain cells, on top of what the top-grade ecstasy did already. His mum had lectured him on it. But it was too late. Natalie was already inside, and what was he going to do about it anyway? The last thing Natalie would want to hear was what Doctor Moore thought. He said nothing.

Noah changed the subject.

'I'm going into a house tonight,' Noah announced.

'Like last time?' Ewan asked.

'Yeah,' Noah said.

Ewan began to breathe heavily and pace around.

'What is it with you?' Noah asked.

Ewan stopped circling and looked at his friend.

'We didn't get caught, did we? Come on, what else have you got to do? And besides, Natalie is up for it.'

'What?' Ewan asked. They both turned back to the rec as Natalie emerged without the bag, hands in pockets, looking very pleased with herself.

'Right, I'm ready, where are we going?' she asked, mainly to Noah.

She hooked her hand inside Ewan's arm and smiled at him. His heart skipped and he had no idea how his feet began moving, but they did, and he walked away, her hand tucked inside his arm, following Noah, as his heart began to sing.

Chapter 22

I used to think that Friday was the best night of the week: all that time stretching in front of me, with only good food, sex and frivolity ahead of me. I can't shake the sensation of Tony's arms around me and it takes me back to places I haven't visited for years. For good reason.

Now I try to find joy at the bottom of a washing pile. I fold my knickers and hold a pair up to the light, and recall when I wore a thong made from such little material that there was no room for a tuck and a gather, just the suggestion of nakedness. James comes into the utility behind me and I drop the underwear back into the basket.

'Are my white Calvin Kleins in there?' he asks. 'There are none in my drawer.'

'Have you looked on your floor?' I ask him.

He smiles and I wonder that Jeremy and I are responsible for his handsomeness. His face is tanned and full of mischief. He stands next to me and rifles through the neatly piled washing.

'James! I've just folded that!' I slap his hand.

'God, Mum, what are these?'

He playfully holds up my pants and presses them to his groin. I agree that they look more like wind sails than under garments.

'They're comfortable,' I say.

'For a whole family?'

'Sod off. Here, there's a pair of Calvins, do you need them now? I'll pop them in the dryer.'

I have a solution for everything. He kisses me.

'Do you think Ewan will go anywhere near the rec tonight?' I ask him seriously.

'I don't know. He wants to be like the other kids,' he adds.

'What does that mean?'

'You can't baby him just because he gets beaten up,' he tells me.

I sense resentment in his voice.

'Do I treat him differently to you, when you were his age?' I ask him.

He considers his answer before he replies. 'Yeah, you're more cautious with him.'

I turn away and get washing powder out of the cupboard. There are two more loads to put in. My Friday treat.

'Why are adults so serious? It's as if you have your fun cauterised at forty. I'm never getting married.'

I drop the washing and stand up to face him. I can't think of a comedic retort.

'See? Didn't you ever get stoned and do stupid things? I thought you both went to uni.'

'To be old and wise, one has to first be young and stupid,' I say to him. 'We used to get up to some crazy stuff,' I say, in my defence. It's unconvincing, even to myself.

'You don't have to stay with him, you know. Just because it's the proper thing to do. He's an arsehole, you have a right to kick him out. I would. And don't tell me he's my father and I should respect him, that's bullshit. Kids are always told that their elders know better but if that's the case then why don't I spend all day in bed after a session on the weed, feeling sorry for myself because I'm too scared to admit that I can't get a job as good as my wife's?'

The emasculation is complete. Jeremy has reduced himself to a foetus in their eyes: undeveloped, parasitic and suspended in the pose of a freeloader.

'Sorry,' he says.

'No worries. I appreciate your honesty.'

'Now I've got it off my chest we can go on pretending,' he quips.

It's one of my lines. He comes forward, and before I know it, his six-foot frame is bending towards me and he holds me. I allow him to overpower me with affection and sincerity. It's nice to be held for a while. Inside his hug, I feel curiously safe and it's his gift to me.

'Your pants will be twenty minutes,' I tell him after he's released me back into the big bad world. He disappears. I busy myself with the washing once more and try to remember how I became so miserable.

We were a foursome at college. Me, Jeremy, Tony and Sarah. The abandon afforded by the security of wealthy parents was lost on us then. The chosen few. Academia was imbibed alongside a pint of Guinness, next to the castle on the mound, steeped in history that meant nothing to us. Edinburgh wrapped us in a mantle of elitism preserved for those to whom tuition fees and monthly rent appeared trivial pursuits.

The bills were paid and our futures mapped out.

We took risks because there was no consequence. We were born to conquer and command. Smoking the odd joint and even taking LSD, we still followed the flock. The establishment swathed us in blankets of self-assurance and confidence that only money can buy. I look back on the abominable ignorance of the ruling class, and the precariousness of such a hold on the tide of superiority that we all took for granted slaps me in the face.

Jeremy has disappeared in all but name, Tony has been running all his life, mainly between women, I pretend to hold everything together because of my postcode, and Sarah… She never got to witness our combined failures. Now we're grown-ups, we can only hold on to the mirage of authority by doing what everyone else does: paying the mortgage, abiding by the law, and feeding our children to the meat grinder of education, so they can prop up the system too.

But my eighteen-year-old son has just told me that it all means nothing if you don't believe in it. Like the vision of an oasis in the desert: it's only there if you want it to be.

Chapter 23

Grace said goodbye to her last client of the evening with a high five. The gym was bursting with testosterone-filled males puffing their chests and flexing their biceps at her, readying themselves for their Friday night processions. Men stopped heaving as she walked by and congratulated her on her latest endorsement: Puma. The news came through this afternoon. The emblazoned tracksuit she'd been sent was another layer with which to cover her skin, because she hadn't learned to shed it yet.

It was her little taste of fame and she wasn't sure if it was welcome. She hadn't done anything differently. She hadn't won a Nobel Prize, or invented something important, or even written a book. She'd just been validated by yet more logos. She thanked those who were interested and keen for her best advice on topics covered in her latest video.

'When I took a day off yesterday, I felt so much better about going forward,' one young man told her. But then he smiled at her and looked at his gym shoes, which warned her that his interest in mental health was less to do with her videos and more to do with bagging a date. She sighed as she walked away.

It had taken six months for her to return to work after the incident. Vincent had been her most loyal client. He'd been training for a competition and he paid well. He looked like any other man training here tonight. Which is why she trusted none of them.

Occasionally she looked at the men peering at their own reflections in the huge mirrors, admiring themselves, pulling up their bodies, or squatting with ever-increasing weights, and considered herself a true survivor. To be able to work in this business again, after what she'd suffered, was a miracle. Doctor Alex told her so. Today's panic attack had taken her by surprise, but she figured it was the fear of the fate she imagined Monika had befallen. What were the chances of a woman going missing these days and for her not to turn up dead? Slim. Sexual predators were everywhere.

When she'd finally emerged from the toilet earlier, after she'd thrown up, Ignacio had been there, tenderly doting on her. She'd dismissed him brusquely and watched the hurt written all over his face. Now, as she came out of the staffroom, he was there again. She caught sight of herself in the mirror and felt her habitual repulsion. She didn't like looking at her body, and she hated other people peering at it even more. Ignacio approached her.

'You okay?' he asked.

She turned to him briskly. 'You've asked me that about ten times today,' she said.

'Sorry,' he said, looking hurt. 'Are you still upset?'

'Don't you have off days?' she asked him. 'I'm hungry and tired and the news about my client was a shock,' she added. It was the police who'd told her that Monika Thorpe was missing. But she'd been watching the Sky News reel on the giant screens. A body had been found by the river Cam, in Grantchester, and her gut churned over with scenarios.

Ignacio stood in front of her, unsure of what to do. She felt trapped. Suddenly her hands were clammy, and she felt weak and irritated that she hadn't kept any food down today. Purging was a choice and she did it on her terms. She still needed to retain some fuel. She was vaguely aware of Ignacio coming towards her and catching her as she fell. Noise and fuss surrounded her and she felt queasy. Ignacio felt her wrist and put his hand on her forehead as he laid her down gently. She pushed it away ungratefully, but she was too feeble. She was sat up, given water, mollified and told she needed to rest. She went to get up but her body was too fatigued. Ignacio held a nut bar in his hand and offered it to her, asking if everybody would stand back. People stared at her and she heard them theorise about why she might have collapsed, as if they were experts.

'She needs more carbs in her diet,' one said.

'She's overtraining, that's a classic sign,' another chipped in.

'She's pushing herself too hard.'

'I thought she was into wellness, not looking after herself...'

Then she saw Henry. He was a regular, friendly and polite, but that's as close as he got. He knelt next to Ignacio. Her queasiness dissipated and she felt awkward from all the fuss.

'Everybody seems to know what's best for you,' Henry said. He smiled at her and she rolled her eyes and took the nut bar from Ignacio, chewing on its chocolaty saltiness. It was just what she needed. Clearly the vomiting had got rid of the little nutrition her body retained and she had nothing left in the tank.

She hated drawing attention to herself, but the drama was coming to an end. Over the past two years she'd created an intimate relationship with her anxiety, and she could normally see it building. But tonight, like earlier today, it had taken her by surprise. That was twice in one day and it worried her. She got to her feet and thanked everyone for their concern, showing Ignacio the half-eaten nut bar. Ignacio and Henry took an arm each, as if she were some maiden in distress. The touch of their skin on hers was like lightning bolts.

There was an awkward moment between the two men, as to who was going to walk Grace to her car. Henry argued that Ignacio should stay in the gym. Ignacio argued that she was his responsibility because she was a colleague. Grace listened to them squabbling over her. Anyone interested in her fall had dispersed now, and headed back to their workouts. She backed away. Henry and Ignacio didn't notice her turn the corner and trot down the stairs to the exit, and out into the night, dumping the rest of the nut bar in the waste.

Chapter 24

The policewoman looked at Carrie disapprovingly.

It was the kind of look that could make a heatwave freeze. She wasn't used to being on the back foot. Here, in Tony's house, covered in the consequences of casual sex, no one knew her rank, importance or status. None of that mattered when the coppers marched into the house and sniffed around, like dogs chasing down street rats. She still had the remnants of cocaine on her breasts, where Tony had snorted it off, in between gulps of Pol Roger Champagne. Now, she was sobering up. She felt like death.

The doorbell had rung and rung, until Tony had finally checked the intercom and seen that the police were at his door.

'Shit!' he'd said in panic. They'd been upstairs, for some reason, Tony insisting they romp in his marital bed. She regretted it now and felt the heat of shame burning her semi-naked skin. They'd tried to clear up the coke, and the evidence of their lusty frolicking, but it didn't look good. She was still in her bikini, which was damp with evidence.

Carrie's five years of sobriety lay smashed before her. She felt like an imposter on the precipice of being caught out and exposed as a forgery. Every drop of self-loathing that she thought she'd had under control came back and assaulted her, fresher and stronger than it had ever been before.

Tony's wife was dead and her body had been found dumped near a tributary of the river Cam, by a field. As Carrie had been happily performing fellatio on her quarry, Monika lay bloated and abused, cold and lifeless. Murdered.

The police had called an extra squad car in to search the property upon witnessing the state of the victim's husband, and what he was up to during his period of intense worry over his missing – now dead – wife. Coppers had entered Tony's house armed with a hasty warrant, after it had been confirmed that the owner, the man they wanted to interview in relation to his wife's death, was suspected of being under the influence of illegal substances. The fact that it was also obvious that he'd been fucking about with another woman made Tony look like the most callous and heartless of suspects.

Carrie sat on a breakfast stool in the kitchen nursing her humiliation while the police searched the property, and she felt their eyes on her every time they passed through the room. She burned with scandal and absorbed the judgemental gazes of smug superiority.

She'd been allowed to throw on some dry clothes as Tony tidied up, but her wet bikini was soaking through them as she sat watching the police cast glances at her, and throw about their silent verdicts of a cheap bit on the side who'd been fooling around with a dead woman's husband. She'd already phoned her lawyer and the only reason that she hadn't walked out straight away was because she'd been breathalysed and was well over the limit, so she had to wait for a bloody taxi. She faced the further indignity of leaving her car here overnight. The police had tried to stop her arrangements to leave, of course, but she'd dealt with them before and knew her rights.

'Am I under arrest?' she'd asked them.

'No,' came the answer.

'I'm leaving then. Tony, I suggest you get a lawyer here before you say a word,' she'd said to him. But the cocaine was still working its magic on him and he'd giggled like a kid, babbling some shit to a female police officer about joining their party.

'Come on, you look like you know how to have a good time,' he'd said to the small bird-like officer. A burly six-foot male colleague had stepped in and warned Tony to behave himself, but had stopped short of cautioning him.

'Is he under arrest?' she asked.

'No, but—'

'But nothing, Tony, don't say a word.' He looked at her oddly and began to laugh again. He was knee deep in trouble and the stupid fucker couldn't see it.

The heightened sensory stimulation that she'd been enjoying had come crashing down around her and now she felt like a complete fool. However, ego aside, she had to think, and decide what to do. And that's what she'd been doing for the last hour. Only action could dispel the crushing sensation of inaction. Every feeling in the human body had to come and then go, otherwise it would be pent up forever and wreak untold damage. She breathed deeply and tried to rationalise her position.

She had to make this situation right, and the first logical step was getting legal representation for both herself and the man who was the prime suspect in a murder case. The police hadn't said as much, but Carrie knew that's what they were all thinking. That's what they did.

Carrie knew that for the police to reach such a speedy conclusion of homicide, Tony's wife's body must be in a hell of a state. It made her see Tony in a different light, for sure, but she had to believe he didn't do it. She'd known him for fifteen years. But the police wouldn't see it like that. She was caught red-handed, in his house, high and half naked. She was an unreliable witness from the get-go, and maybe even an accessory.

What if he did do it? Terrifying thoughts circled inside her head. Why did he invite her here tonight? Was it because he knew his wife lay dead in a field and he was creating some kind of alibi? She felt sick.

She'd refused when the police asked to search her bag. She knew that they were not able to do so without permission because she wasn't under arrest, even though they had a warrant to search the property. She also knew that if they found any drugs – which they surely would soon – then they would have a right to search her. She held on to her bag so tightly that the straps dug into her skin, protecting the last piece of privacy she felt she had in this dire situation. Her hair was quickly drying and she knew it was turning frizzy. Her make-up was no doubt smudged, and she was beginning to get a migraine. Tony kept talking.

'Shut up!' she breathed quietly, but he hadn't yet grasped the seriousness of his predicament. Her mobile rang and it was her taxi driver. She got up and was stopped by a young police officer.

'Let me go, you have no right to hold me,' she said.

The officer was a rookie and spoke into her radio. Carrie went to leave Tony to his fate. The next twenty-four hours would be crucial to get her story straight: she needed an alibi for every single hour before she'd driven here tonight. What a mistake that was. Tony was on his own, and there was nothing she could do for him. He had to sober up and get his own legal advice. Maybe she'd call him tomorrow or talk to him when she came to collect her car. She reached the front door and opened it, and was faced by another damn police officer who questioned her again. He was in plain clothes and she knew from instinct that this was the detective turning up. The man facing her was her true enemy.

'I'm not being held on any charges and it is my right to leave,' she told him.

'You're not going to stay and support your pal?' he asked sarcastically. She watched him. He wore a cheap suit, like they all did. Their morals were their Gucci. Condescending bastards. He had bad skin and a wolf-like smile. He stank of judgement. He looked her up and down.

Memories from decades ago flooded her brain. When the cops finally arrested her father for beating her to a pulp when she was nineteen, it had been the last straw of a litany of pain and abuse lasting more than a decade. The copper then had looked her in the eye and told her: 'I've got kids, it's tough, everyone argues. It'll be almost impossible to press charges against your dad, he's a respected member of the town council.' It had been 1989, when dads were the cocks of the family and the police were an all-white male institution, intent on protecting their own, because they drank pints together on a Saturday night. They'd had no choice but to arrest her father, because he'd struggled when they pulled him off her, but she was told he'd be released after he sobered up in the cells.

Sure enough, he was out in twenty-four hours, and after she was released from hospital it was Carrie who was charged with actual bodily harm for fighting back against a fifteen-stone monster. She'd hitched a ride to London, disappeared, and lived on the streets for five years. Being so close to the uniformed tribe now made her shiver.

Her fingernails dug into the palms of her hands and she was reminded of the work she'd done with Doctor Alex, who'd got her to expel her rage by hitting pillows, holding her breath under water, and taking long walks in the woods, carrying an axe with her to belt the shit out of a tree stump. But it was no substitute for hurting a real human being: one on the side of the law who had betrayed her.

She turned to leave.

'We'll be in touch,' shouted the detective, who was barely out of nappies. She reckoned he was in his early thirties, though his hair was thinning already and she assessed that men like him only worked such a thankless job for one reason: power.

But she wasn't scared of him.

'Detective Inspector Paul Hunt,' he shouted at her back, by way of introduction.

Hunt. She branded the name on her brain.

Her feet crunched on the gravel driveway, creating quite a different effect to the one earlier in the evening.

Hunt was an easy name to remember, and it probably rhymed with his character.

Whatever Tony's explanation was for his role in Monika's murder – innocent or guilty – she knew by the look of the detective that he had a battle on his hands, and she wanted no part of it.

Chapter 25

Two days before Monika's disappearance

Monika pulled away from the touch of her husband's hand on her hip as they went into Alex and Jeremy's house. They'd been invited for a BBQ and Monika had brought white lilies, which Alex took from her and placed in a large modern vase. She took them outside and beckoned them to follow. Tony turned to her and glared. Monika ignored him and followed Alex. At least for one afternoon, she could switch off from his suffocating suspicion.

'What a day! Thank you for inviting us, Alex,' Monika said breezily.

The children, who were no longer kids, were already in the pool, enjoying the heatwave with abandon. Monika wished she could strip off and join them but she'd worn her new Armani skirt, and heels, and she had on too much make-up. Besides, she wasn't drunk yet.

'Look at them! They've grown!' Monika said.

'They're not as angelic as they look, you know.' Alex gave her a drink.

She'd already had two glasses of wine at home to calm her nerves, but she'd declined the line of coke Tony offered her. Her heels sank into the grass as the conversation clung to the weather. Jeremy sidled up next to her and she moved away slightly, turning his offered greeting into an air kiss rather than the real thing. She pushed her dark hair behind her ear nervously, exposing her neckline, and she touched her hand to her throat. She tried to concentrate on what Alex was telling her about the children, and their school. She knew it was private and named after a famous man. In England, that meant it was expensive. All of Tony's friends had children and they all attended private institutions that Tony called 'stuck up', which she found curious because Tony had attended one of the most expensive of all.

The Moores' house was not as big as her own – Tony's house – but it was smart and well-tended. At home she had more rooms to escape to, should she need them, but here they all huddled on the grass, standing awkwardly, until Alex suggested she help with taking plates out to the table, which was set under an awning, covered in silver and crystal, as if this was their standard dinner preparation. Monika knew it wasn't. They didn't need to impress Tony, but Monika got the impression that Jeremy wanted to. The men's conversation turned to trading and bonds, a subject Monika knew little about, and she was glad to have something else to keep her busy.

Alex looked in control, as she always did. She wore her clothes effortlessly and her hair had been cut a little shorter, giving her more of an air of authority. She told Monika where to lay crockery and Monika followed her instructions exactly. Occasionally, between folding napkins and carrying platters of nibbles out to the table, she glanced at Tony, who always drank too much when he was with Jeremy.

Her eyes locked with her husband's friend's, who peered at her and smiled, but it came across as forced, and Monika suspected that Tony shared things with him that should remain private. She felt as though she might not be wearing any clothes at all.

Monika didn't see herself as somebody who was in a position to pity another, but she felt so towards Alex. It wasn't because Alex needed it – quite the opposite – but something about the way Jeremy looked out of place in his house made her unnerved.

'Wow, beautiful ring!' Alex said, picking up her hand.

Monika allowed her to hold it for a second as she admired the new bauble Tony had surprised her with. His standard apology.

'Emerald?' Alex asked.

Monika nodded. 'Colombian.'

Monika knew enough about precious stones to inform her of the value of such a trinket, and she saw that Alex did too, but she also noticed that Alex wasn't in the habit of receiving such gifts from her husband, and Monika felt silly, wishing she hadn't worn it. It was the size of Alex's thumbnail.

'Don't jump in the pool with that on, you'll go straight to the bottom,' Alex said.

A spray of water showered Monika's skirt and she stepped back from the poolside.

'Boys!' Alex admonished her sons.

They were growing strong and James looked like a man. But Tony saved his affection for the youngest, Ewan, whose jaw was developing and voice becoming lower in tone.

Tony emerged from the pool house in shorts and dive bombed the kids, making everyone laugh.

'Come in, Jeremy!' Tony shouted. But Jeremy made an excuse. He never took off his shirt.

Monika watched as Lydia swam to the steps and got out, saying she was cold. Monika understood that the pool was now crowded with testosterone and felt for the girl, who looked skinnier than last time. Monika smiled at her but Lydia scuttled past, into the house.

'Food!' Alex announced. 'You can go in the pool after.'

Tony had told her that Jeremy was cooking the BBQ but Monika watched as Alex tended the coals and turned the meat, checking it one last time before bringing it to the table. Jeremy simply stood around like a spare utensil, never letting go of his wine glass.

They took their places under the awning and the shade afforded some relief. Monika felt overdressed.

'So, skiing at Christmas?' Tony asked.

'Where can you ski in summer?' James asked Tony.

'Japan. Or the Andes. My God, yes, I'll take you there. Las Leñas. Those Latin women are to die for.'

James laughed and shook his head at the same time. Old men had no idea how repulsive they were to the younger generation.

Monika picked at her food, and watched Lydia do the same.

'How are those fencing lessons I'm paying for?' Tony asked Ewan.

He made the young boy blush and Monika glanced at Alex.

'They're coming on nicely, Tony, thank you. It was a thoughtful birthday present,' Alex said.

'Deal with those bullying pricks, eh?' Tony nudged Ewan. His speech was slowed down from the effects of the narcotics and booze, but nobody else seemed to notice.

The clatter of cutlery on plates jangled Monika's nerves suddenly, and the sun crept behind the awning onto her shoulder, turning it pink. She moved slightly and knocked over a glass of wine.

Jeremy jumped up. 'I'll get it,' he said.

His words slurred like Tony's. He mopped up the puddle of wine with a napkin and refilled her glass. She glanced at Tony, who glared at her.

James finished his food and said he had to study upstairs. Ewan followed him and Lydia took the opportunity to leave the table too, her food simply rearranged on her plate. Suddenly it was the four of them. Monika excused herself and went to the bathroom to breathe. She closed the door and checked her phone. She answered three messages and sat down on the closed toilet lid, allowing herself to slouch. A gloriously delicious sensation of freedom washed over her and she sat there for long minutes, wishing she was somewhere else.

She caressed the emerald ring and took it off, changed her mind and put it back on. It sat heavily on her finger, like a name tag, or the vintage details of a fine wine. A dog collar.

In the kitchen, Alex tidied up and smiled warmly when Monika reappeared.

'You okay?' Alex asked.

Monika nodded.

'You're not pregnant, are you?'

'God, no! Tony wouldn't have that.'

A shadow crossed Alex's face and Monika backtracked.

'We would have had children, but not at the moment. It's tricky.'

'Tricky?'

'Maybe I've got the wrong word.'

But it was too late. Alex saw through her attempt to use her second language as an excuse. Her English was perfect.

'Your children are a credit to you,' Monika said.

Alex looked at her oddly, and after a pause, said thank you, as if no one ever said it, and furthermore, she didn't believe it herself.

Their attention was drawn outside as Tony swore loudly, and the women peered out of the kitchen window. Tony's head was bleeding and Jeremy was laughing his head off. Tony joined him and fell to the ground, where they rolled around like children. Monika and Alex went outside and asked what on earth had happened. Monika went to Tony to examine his head. The blood wasn't stopping. It needed some form of dressing.

'Get off me, woman!' Tony snapped.

Chapter 26

Tony sat on a large couch under the bay window in the kitchen, remembering last Sunday when he'd been short with his wife in front of his friends. He didn't know if what he felt was grief or guilt.

Hunt found him and crouched down.

'Right, Tony. Your friend has gone. It's a bit fast to be fooling around, isn't it? So soon after your wife disappeared. Unless you knew she wasn't coming back, eh?'

Hunt rested on his bent knees and clasped his hands together. He was at eye level and Tony peered at him. He saw that the DI had huge sweat patches on his chest and under his arms.

'Carrie's gone?' he asked.

DI Hunt nodded. 'Did she have anything to do with Monika leaving? Did Monika know what you two were up to?'

Tony shook his head, trying to make sense of his reality. It had assaulted him without leaving him time or space to assess it. Now he was sobering up on a cognisant level, though chemically it would take much longer. He looked down to his body, as if it belonged to someone else, and realised that he was still in his swimming trunks. The velvet sofa that Monika had chosen for the huge bay window in the kitchen was wet, and he shifted uncomfortably. He began to shiver and rubbed his face in his hands.

'I think I'm going to be sick,' he said.

Vomit heaved out of him, right at the DI's feet. The copper moved out of the way and swore angrily, just avoiding the mess. Tony puked again and the DI shouted for help.

'Get him cleaned up, for fuck's sake,' Hunt said. Somebody grabbed cloths from the sink and Tony was helped upstairs.

'Don't compromise the scene!' Hunt reminded everyone.

'The scene?' Tony asked.

Hunt smiled at him but Tony knew it wasn't genuine. Then he realised what the instruction meant. His house was being searched, and he vaguely remembered being shown a warrant. Jesus, he thought in horror. Images and memories came flooding back to him; seducing Carrie, their embraces, the police at the door, and them trawling through the house.

Then he remembered his wife. She was dead and her body had been found at the edge of a field, near the river, close to Grantchester, by dog walkers. She'd been murdered. She wasn't just gone, but brutally attacked and dumped. And he'd been shagging Carrie. He paused on the stairs, holding on to the handrail, which, he saw, was covered in plastic. They were turning his house over and he remembered what Carrie said to him before she left more clearly now. She'd called her lawyer and urged him to do the same. Now she was gone, and he'd been a gibbering wreck, not listening to her sound advice. He rushed to his room, but was stopped at the door. The young PC escorting him told the officer that the gentleman was allowed to freshen up, if the bathroom had been processed. The uniform said he'd go and check. Tony waited in the hallway of his own home, freezing his nuts off, wrapping his arms around his body in an attempt to warm up. His house was crawling with police.

'Where is my wife?' he asked the young officer. The present caught up with him and he realised the stupidity of the question.

'I'm not on the case, sir. You'll have to ask the DI.'

Tony nodded.

'If you were to have knowledge of where dead bodies, possible homicides, were kept, then could you tell me?'

The officer looked at him and lowered his voice.

'I would say that the body would be stored at the hospital mortuary, sir.'

'Thank you.' Tony leaned against the wall. He looked around the hallway and saw his wife everywhere: the chandelier, the chaise longue, the paintings and the femininity. He turned away from the young PC, put his hand up to his mouth and cried silently. Hot tears warmed his chilled face and he rubbed his eyes.

'Sorry, sir,' the young uniform said.

Tony knew how it looked: like he didn't care, like he was a callous husband who'd clearly got bored of his young shallow wife, and got rid of her to make way for his mistress. It wasn't supposed to have gone like this. He wondered what Carrie was discussing with her lawyer. He needed to speak to her: they had to get their stories straight. The prospect of a plan forming calmed him, and he was able to bring himself to his senses and list in his mind what needed to be done next. Alex would know what to do.

The officer returned and said he could go into his own bedroom. 'Forensics have finished in this room,' he said.

Forensics? Jesus. He felt like a tiny fish on a huge reef, being watched by predators, which at any moment could strike from above to kill and feed. The sensation was a new one. He'd lost the initiative, if he'd ever had it, and cast his mind back to what he'd told the police so far. He scrabbled around for titbits of information about Monika's last day inside this house. Her house. He saw her new ring on the side of the jewellery stand by the window and picked it up. He hadn't even noticed it when he and Carrie had staggered in here earlier, giggling like school kids, searching for his stash of coke, which allowed him to get it up for a third time.

The emerald glistened deeply and he turned it this way and that, mesmerised by its beauty. Specimens like it were rare, and that was what made it so valuable. It was a one off.

Chapter 27

I've had plenty of drunken late-night phone calls from Tony but this one takes me completely by surprise. He's deep breathing down the phone and I hold it under my chin, rolling my eyes, pausing the Netflix series I'm watching. I'm following a true crime documentary because I'm a cheery soul, as if I don't have enough misdemeanour in my life. But it interests me. It never ceases to amaze me the amount of people who think they can get away with murder. They make basic mistakes and I love working them out before the big reveal. I've microwaved a huge packet of popcorn and I'm enjoying the luxury of solitude. Lydia came down earlier and she ate some strawberries, Cambridge Favourites, which are plump and juicy in season.

'Tony, slow down. I can't hear you properly. Are you drunk or high?' I give him the option because I'm an understanding friend.

'Monika's dead,' he breathes.

'What?'

The words finally break through the airwaves and I comprehend what he's saying to me but I don't fully take in the order of the words.

'She was murdered and they think I did it.'

The bowl of popcorn gently slides off my knee and it spills all over the floor.

'Who thinks you did it?'

'The police. They're here in my house. They're searching everywhere.'

His voice cracks and he sounds desperately alone. I've never known him like this but then I guess one of his wives hasn't been murdered before.

'Jesus. What happened? Where is she?' It's a stupid question but I can't seem to think of anything else to say. The enormity of it is overwhelming. My TV screen is paused on the face of a young woman who has was brutally stabbed and dumped in a storm drain in Texas, but it is appropriately distanced from me, on the other side of the world.

'She was found by the river, near Grantchester.'

'How do they know it's her? How can they inform you if they don't know?' I'm scrabbling around trying to fill in gaps because my head hurts with his pain and my own lack of understanding.

'Her tattoo. It's so distinctive. I told them about it when I reported her missing. They ask for that sort of information. It's got to be her. They want me to identify the body.'

The body. Now, Monika is sexless.

'I'm coming over,' I say as my body leaps into action after a delay of disbelief.

'No, there's no point. I'm going to the hospital.'

'I'll come with you.'

'No. I need to go alone. I don't want you to see her. She's…'

I fill in the gaps in my head and it remains unspoken. I've watched enough true crime programmes to know what he alludes to.

'What did you mean when you said they think you did it?'

'They haven't said it, but they're asking me all sorts of questions about our marriage and why I had somebody here when she was missing.'

'You did what? Who?'

'A woman I know. It was nothing, I swear, but we were…'

Tony's unfinished sentences irritate me but I know him well enough not to be left without possibilities. He means he was shagging somebody else, and likely getting high too. He never learns.

'You need to call Kingston,' I tell him.

Kingston is his barrister and if anyone is capable of getting Tony out of a scrape it's him. A sliver of doubt enters my mind and I question if Tony is capable of violence. It's not something I can stomach easily, but the truth, once planted, is hard to dig up and root out.

'I have, he's meeting me first thing in the morning. He's in Paris. He's on the next flight.'

'Good. Don't say anything. You have rights,' I tell him.

'It looks so bad.'

For Tony to admit this tells me only one thing. That Kingston is about to face the fight of his life. But Tony can afford it. He's paid for problems to disappear before.

'I have to go,' he says lifelessly.

We hang up.

I get up and pace the room, then clear up the popcorn and shove it roughly into the bowl, taking it to the kitchen. Jeremy is drunk in the pool house and sound asleep on a sofa in there. I've already turned off the lights and the TV and covered him with a sheet, not that he'll need it in this heat. The details of the autopsy of the woman who'd been murdered in Texas creep into my mind. England at the moment is about as hot as the Lone Star State and any decomposing body left on the banks of a river, vulnerable to the elements, would be reduced to a gruesome mess. I run to the kitchen sink and it catches my sick, which tastes of burnt corn. I run the tap and wash my mouth out. The puke burns my throat.

Just ten minutes ago, I was nodding off on the sofa, revelling in my seclusion. Now I desperately need some-body to talk to. James and Ewan are still out, not that I would seek counsel from either of my sons in a situation like this. Christ, I'll have to tell the kids.

Chapter 28

Ewan sucked on the skunk-laden cigarette. His shoulders immediately felt numb and the warm sensation spread through his body. He smiled at Natalie, who giggled. He'd never really been this close to her before, but now, armed with the courage of chemicals, he pulled her nearer. She held on to his hand and Noah looked over his shoulder and smiled.

'Come on,' he said to them. 'It's around this corner.'

The weather was cloying and even the teenagers, up to date in their fashion and swagger, took it slow.

They walked through an upmarket neighbourhood, dotted with luxury properties. Noah stopped outside one that Ewan recognised. It was Tony and Monika's house. His dad called them filthy rich and Monika a 'gold digger'.

Ewan didn't agree with many of his father's opinions. He liked Monika. She had read him bedtime stories when he was smaller, and she'd sung him songs to get him to sleep, which his dad never had. Even at twelve years old, he'd found comfort in somebody sitting with him at bedtime.

Dad called Tony a 'ballsy high flyer', but Ewan thought him fake. He'd caught him looking at his mother the same way he saw in movies, during scenes that made him feel uncomfortable. It was the same way he sometimes looked at Natalie. There were different kinds of lust, though, and the type he felt for Natalie fell into a category that was kind of harmless. There was also the kind he watched on YouTube, and that's how his dad looked at Monika.

'Woah, what are the cops doing there?' Noah sped up, past the two squad cars. Ewan and Natalie caught up.

Maybe Tony was in trouble. Ewan hoped the sight of the cops might put an end to Noah's plans, but it didn't.

Rich people don't care. That's what Noah said to justify breaking into their homes and robbing them.

They wandered around for another hour or so, but time was lost in a haze of Natalie's perfume.

'This one,' Noah said.

Ewan's heart sank as he was reminded of the last time they'd entered the same property, looking for stuff that was valuable. Anything really, as long as it looked expensive. Noah knew people who could get rid of high-value stolen goods, such as jewellery and fine silver. It was paraphernalia that meant nothing to Ewan.

'There's no one home,' Noah said.

'How do you know?' Ewan asked.

'I just know. Besides, she lives on her own,' Noah said.

Ewan looked at Natalie, who smiled encouragingly, and Ewan realised that, to impress her, he had to be brave. Courage came in lots of forms, and all he cared about was exciting her.

'It'll just be the same as last time, we'll turn the alarm off,' Noah said.

'You've been here before?' Natalie asked.

Ewan nodded. 'It'll be all right,' he said, more for himself than for her.

They walked into the driveway and their feet crunched on the gravel. Ewan could tell that Natalie was thrilled by the risk. He didn't know where Noah learned how to disable alarm systems, not ones that looked so expensive anyhow, but he didn't ask. He watched as his friend went to a box at the base of the wall facing the side gate and opened it. He took a tool out of his trousers and began fiddling with wires. It was Ewan and Natalie's job to look out for trouble. There was no doubt that the woman who lived here was rich, and that provided some kind of comfort: she wouldn't miss anything. He'd seen it for himself last time, the paintings, jewellery, fancy crystal, electronics and fine handbags. They didn't get a lot for it, and Ewan wanted none of it, but that wasn't the point. Noah seemed to be addicted to getting his hands on other people's stuff.

Ewan was more than willing to bail Noah out with cash, but he didn't want handouts. Something that was acquired legitimately wasn't worth losing sleep over; this was. Ever since Noah's dad lost his job, Noah had become obsessed with rich people.

The cannabis was still hanging around in Ewan's bloodstream and his senses were dulled, the edge of danger smoothed out. He and Natalie hovered about, alert to unwelcome attention, while Noah worked on the alarm. It didn't take long, and they were soon unlocking the back gate and sauntering down the side, along the wall, and into the back garden. The place was immaculate, like last time.

'She installed a new alarm, but it's a piece of shit like the last one,' Noah said. They all laughed. Natalie held on to Ewan's arm and he placed his hand over hers to reassure her, and it felt good.

Noah led them to the rear door which in turn led to the utility room at the back of the house, and he held the tool in front of him. He tried the door and they breathed a collective sigh of relief as it opened. Noah put the screwdriver away and they entered the property. There was soft music playing in the background and they tiptoed into the kitchen. They paused for a moment as they looked around and took in the grandeur of the place. They noticed the signs of affluence everywhere: the state-of-the-art fridge, with a digital control, the polished floor, a huge flat-screen TV on the wall and fresh flowers in expensive vases.

'Fuck! This place is amazing!' Natalie said.

'She's the bitch who sacked my dad,' Noah said, leaving the kitchen.

'Shall we leave her a little present then?'

Ewan and Noah looked at her questioningly.

She took a second bag of blue pills out of her pocket and held them up.

'Wouldn't it be hilarious if she reports a robbery and they found some gear? It would be revenge for your dad, Noah.'

Natalie stared at Ewan for support, and he shrugged, his heart pounding out of his chest.

'Right, then, that's settled.'

Noah led them straight through the back and up the stairs. Ewan held on to Natalie's hand, but she let it go as they went up the polished oak structure, quietly, hardly breathing as they glanced around. Noah seemed possessed and Ewan felt a knot of concern form under his ribcage. They watched as he opened a wardrobe door and a large metal safe sat there, beckoning them to take a look. They looked at each other and Noah was the one who stepped forward first.

He knelt down and fiddled with the handle. He tapped a code into the digital keypad.

Natalie and Ewan stared at him when it clicked open.

'How did you do that?' Natalie asked.

Noah smiled at them.

'Okay, there was a four-digit code written on the fridge board downstairs,' he said.

Natalie and Ewan looked at him. 'That's dumb,' Ewan said.

'What's in it?' Natalie asked. Ewan noticed that her chest was rising and falling as she breathed and her skin glowed like polished ivory in the late evening light, flowing through the upstairs landing.

'Fuck!' Noah said, standing up quickly.

'What?' Ewan asked.

Noah stepped back and Ewan moved forward to have a look at what had taken his friend by surprise. He put his hand into the safe and felt a cloth. He brought it out and unwrapped it as Natalie watched.

'Don't touch it,' Noah said. But it was too late. Ewan stood back, holding the item in his hand.

'What's she doing hiding that?' Natalie asked.

Ewan stared at his hand and Noah said they should go.

'Put it back,' Natalie said.

'Wipe it first,' Noah said.

Ewan wiped it with his t-shirt and his hands shook.

The knife was something that didn't belong in any respectable woman's house. It was long, perhaps the size of a school ruler, and the handle had finger indents, making it look like it should be used for hunting. Ewan leaned over and looked inside the safe, not knowing what else he was looking for. He felt around and brought out a fat envelope, which was stuffed with cash.

'Let's take it,' Noah said.

'Are you crazy?' Ewan asked. 'We don't want anything to do with this.'

'But she's hiding it for some reason,' Noah said, grabbing the envelope. 'She's loaded. She has all the money she needs, so this is extra and hidden for a reason. She'll never admit it was there, and so we can take it,' Noah said, staring at the money. 'Put the knife back,' he told Ewan. Who did as he was told, after wiping it a second time, more thoroughly.

'She won't report this,' Noah said, putting the money in his pockets. 'Let's go.' In some kind of warped sense, Ewan hoped that with this kind of money, Noah might stop burglarising houses for a while and give them all a break.

He banged the safe closed, and the door sprung back open. He backed away and Noah was the first to make his way out of the room. He watched as Natalie opened a drawer, pushed clothes aside, and left the bag of pills in there.

Ewan's heart raced.

They left the room quickly and headed down the stairs, just as a car pulled up outside.

Chapter 29

It was almost midnight by the time the police escorted a sober Tony Thorpe to the mortuary, inside Cambridge University Hospital. It was a short drive from his house to the sprawling facility on the outskirts of the ancient town. He was taken in a squad car and as he sat in the back seat, he listened to the police radio reporting petty crime from around the compact tourist attraction, famed for its university spires and colleges. They drove past busy restaurants on the edge of the river Cam and groups of people getting on with their lives, untouched by murder, laughing and embracing casually on a Friday night, unaware of the underbelly of villainy surrounding them. Tony stared, dead-eyed, out at the scenes as they whizzed by. He'd changed into dry, smart clothes to attend the formal identification of his dead wife.

Monika's name would be released to the press as soon as he'd identified her, but he knew already that it was her. The fat viper on her back, that he loathed so much, was a uniquely distinctive branding. The fact that she hadn't used her bank account, or her phone, or contacted her mother in Latvia also told him what he already knew.

So far, he hadn't been arrested, or charged with her murder, but he knew, just as sure as they looked at him with disapproving stares, that it was only a matter of time. His mind drifted to Carrie and he wondered if she'd given a statement. He knew he could count on her for one thing: she wouldn't compromise him if she had a choice. If she didn't have a choice, she'd just as surely throw him under the bus. To be fair, he'd do the same. They were identical creatures.

He hated hospitals. He avoided them, believing that illness was as much a sign of weakness as poverty. They parked in an emergency bay and a police officer got out of the car to open his door. Tony got out and felt the night warmth wrap around him, but it was anything but comforting. He was escorted to the entrance, and the driver sped off. He knew what they were thinking: woman goes missing, husband fools around, body turns up, and things get ugly. As time ticked by, all he could think of was how unprepared he was for this.

DI Hunt waited for him in the foyer.

'Evening,' Hunt said. Tony could tell that he was enjoying his smug superiority over his prime suspect. He saw the way he'd coveted his home and his cars, and Carrie's near nakedness.

Tony followed him.

He'd been briefed on the state of her body.

The gravity of what he was about to witness hit him, and he paused for a moment as they entered the busy reception hall. People came and went, some searching for signs to the right ward, others reading posters, and some trailing drips and oxygen tanks with them, looking forward to fresh air as relatives and staff escorted them outside for a cigarette. His desire for some chemical release gripped him and he began to sweat. The noises of a functioning hospital all merged into a low hum and conspired to make his head thump. He worried that people were staring at him, but some part of his rational self was still working and assured him this wasn't the case at all. It was simply a place of despair and, no matter how odd people looked, they were plainly suffering their own trauma, not reflecting his.

He recoiled from the sight of such sickness.

His escalating heart rate made his Garmin watch sound an alarm. His stress levels were through the roof and the watch told him to sit down and rest. Funny that when he was snorting coke off Carrie's breasts, the digital computer was quite happy that he was taking care of himself. He figured that if these were his last days of freedom, then such an activity was not a bad way to go out; she had spectacular breasts. But he checked his crassness and squinted against the bright lights, which were glaring at him conspiratorially. He asked himself absently why hospitals couldn't choose more soothing ways to welcome visitors.

He followed Hunt like an automaton, numb to any sensations apart from his own dread. His internal warning system was in overdrive and it told him to run away. He wasn't in control and his brain was at a loss as to how to process such an unusual eventuality. He had no idea where he was going. Private hospitals were small and homely places compared to this giant monstrosity of malady.

'Here,' Hunt said. They went through a door and took a lift, away from the main corridor, and Tony guessed that the route to the bowels of the facility wasn't something that was advertised. It was simply a metal door and a shaft down to the basement. He felt the cold now, so unused was he to anything less than thirty degrees for weeks. The cocoon of the lift cubicle was suffocating though, and he sniffed Hunt's stale body odour. He wrung his hands together and tried to wipe the sweat away from his brow and wished he'd popped a tablet of chewing gum into his arid mouth before they left. His back was drenched and he felt trickles of perspiration run down his spine, despite the coolness once the lift doors opened.

Hunt surveyed him like a hawk on the wing.

The corridor was bright and they stepped out into it. Down here it was quieter, but Tony still felt pressure in his temples. He followed Hunt and they were greeted by an older woman in a white lab coat. She gazed at him sympathetically and Tony took this as a bad sign. Was it because of the state of Monika's body? Had she already seen what he was about to behold? Or was he misreading her, and she thought he did it?

She introduced herself and he was vaguely aware of shaking her hand but he missed her name, or title. He remembered the last time he'd seen his wife.

'In here,' the woman said.

They were led into a room with no windows. She closed the door behind them and through the dim light he could see a window, beyond which was a gurney. On the table was a lumpy figure underneath a white sheet. He knew it was Monika. He turned to Hunt, who stared at him, expressionless.

'Ready?' he asked.

Tony nodded. He was on auto pilot.

'Take your time, Mr Thorpe. I must remind you not to touch the victim.'

Tony nodded.

'I'll lift the sheet when you're ready and all you need to do is nod or shake your head.' Hunt put on white plastic gloves.

They went into the next room and stood by the table. Tony's stomach tightened and he thought he might faint.

His hands began to shake again and he wished he had a gram of something to calm him. He regretted not accepting Alex's offer to accompany him. She was the most level-headed person he knew, though he didn't know many.

'Can I call someone?' he asked.

'Last-minute nerves?' Hunt asked him. 'I was told you wanted to come by yourself.'

There was a moment of ludicrous hesitation as his thoughts caught up with his body. Of course he could do this alone.

Hunt went round the side of the gurney and put his hand on one end of the sheet; Tony guessed the head end.

He lifted the sheet and Tony felt his knees give way.

Chapter 30

Two days before Monika's disappearance

Monika selected one of the bikinis from a pile in the pool house. They were Lydia's, Alex told her, so one of them should fit. Having not planned to swim, she now wanted to join in and fool around with the kids who'd come back downstairs. She was drunk and she knew it, but so was everybody else. She giggled as she and Alex changed quickly, stumbling over their pants. Alex seemed oblivious to any sense of body consciousness and Monika envied her confidence. For an older woman, Alex was slim and her skin taut and smooth. They stripped and whispered, laughing as they swapped string tops and bottoms, until Monika settled on one that she could tie tightly so it fitted her smaller frame. Alex admired her and told her she looked fantastic.

'Don't take any notice of Mr Grumpy,' Alex told her.

Monika laughed and shook her head.

'I know,' she said.

'You can stand up to him, you know,' Alex added.

Monika turned away and tied the strings. Her fingers fumbled carelessly.

'What's that?' Alex asked.

'What?' Monika asked, turning round.

'The bruise on your back.'

'Oh, nothing.'

They finished dressing in silence.

'Tony likes me to... dress up,' Monika said finally.

Alex smiled awkwardly, but it soon turned to a frown. 'What do you mean?'

'You know, he likes to play games. With me. It's all right, it just... it goes too far sometimes. Don't all games get out of hand?'

'No. Not ones with rules. It's none of my business, but if he hurts you—'

'No, it's nothing like that. Doesn't Jeremy do it? Tony said Jeremy likes to do it too.'

Monika's voice was hushed and her words faded away when she saw Alex's face.

'Please don't tell him I told you.'

'Monika, are you all right? Is this something serious? I know Tony's my friend but there are certain things that are not right. Just because you're married to someone, it doesn't mean that kind of thing is acceptable, or lawful—'

'No, it's nothing like that. I fell over. Don't tell.'

Alex looked directly at her so there was nowhere to hide. It was suddenly chilly in the pool house changing rooms and the opulent baroque décor, designed so tastefully and lovingly by Alex, appeared overpowering and gaudy.

'We've all got secrets, haven't we?' Monika said, and sniggered.

'What?'

Monika's smile waned a bit. 'You know, Tony told me a few things. I won't tell, honestly. It's not my place to, but if things get complicated, then I can always help.'

'Pardon?'

Monika hiccupped and held on to the doorknob. 'I don't feel well.'

'You've had too much to drink.'

'Are you mad?' Monika asked.

'No. Just sober. You know if Tony's hurting you, you won't find the answer at the bottom of a bottle. I should know, Jeremy lives inside one. You can take everything they say with a pinch of salt.'

'Pinch of salt?'

'Sorry, it's an English idiom. It means that Jeremy is a lying bastard and I don't believe a word he says.'

Monika's back was pinned against the wall, half to keep her upright, but half to distance herself from the older woman.

'It's not me you need to be afraid of, Monika,' Alex said, softening. 'Come on, you need some water.'

Chapter 31

Saturday mornings are supposed to be elongated moments of succour after a busy week, for all the family. A time to come together and rest. But at three o'clock this morning, I was still pacing around my bedroom, having moved there to try to get some sleep. Then James came home and woke me by rooting around in the fridge looking for snacks and then he put something in the microwave. Ewan wasn't far behind him but I was in no mood to argue, faced with what I have to tell them all today. I couldn't wake Jeremy, he was stuck in the middle of a deep blackout. Instead, I sat in the garden watching the sky turn from black to purple, like the bruises on Monika's body that I've been dreaming about.

I've set the table with the usual cereal and healthy granola, and muesli with yogurt, juices and various seeds, knowing it will go mainly untouched. Jeremy has fixed coffee and read the same newspaper a thousand times. His hands shake more than yesterday. I told him about Monika ten minutes ago and I'm amazed he hasn't poured vodka over his granola. I see death everywhere, from a bird crashing into the pool house window, to a slab of meat in the fridge waiting to be consumed.

The children are oblivious because I guess Jeremy and I always look as though somebody has been murdered.

James eats toast, perched on the windowsill, over-looking the garden. Apart from our soiree in the utility yesterday, it's the longest I've been in the same room as him for weeks, and I study how he's changing before my eyes. He senses something is up, but then discord is our new normal. He told me as much. I catch him eyeing his father and watching his hands shake.

'Can't you sit at the table like the rest of us?' Jeremy demands.

'Like the rest of who, Dad?' James asks back, indicating the lack of any cosy unity around the breakfast table, so lovingly laid by the lady of the house. If I didn't feel so wretched I'd do a twirl.

Jeremy looks to me for support, which isn't forth-coming, and then he tuts, going back to pretending to read the paper. James gulps juice and leaves, after kissing me. Then it's Lydia's turn to join the family get-together. She emerges, pale and waiflike, clutching a book, plugged into TikTok or some other electronic god. It might be my imagination, but she looks brighter than she did yesterday. And I'm going to destroy that shortly.

'Morning!' I say breezily. 'Muesli? We've got some of those strawberries left, they're so sweet.'

Lydia fills a glass with water and takes a dry cracker from a tin, and wanders off, chewing it.

Ewan appears as I'm washing pots, trying to find some-thing to do with my hands. I can't let everything fall apart because we've had dreadful news. I can't get a stain off a pan, and I rub it vociferously as if everything is all its fault.

'Sore head?' I ask Ewan, who Jeremy doesn't know crept in as it was getting light. He shades his eyes and squints and I can't help mourning his youth. If I hadn't been a seasoned drug-taker myself in my university days, I might think he was simply tired.

'I feel a bit tired,' he says, as if reading my mind.

'You were in late?' Jeremy asks. He has no idea. He's tetchy because I was able to answer the phone to Tony, and not him. Now the thunder from his missed opportunity to play a role has been stolen.

Ewan takes a piece of bread and smothers it in butter, then stops to watch the TV. The bread slips out of his hand, along with the butter knife, and I follow his stare. Jeremy hears the clatter of the knife and puts down his paper angrily. I forgot that the discovery of Monika's body might be on the TV and we haven't told the kids yet. But it isn't about Monika.

A report on a local boy is being played over. Police tape seals a field near the rec. My stomach hits the floor and I examine Ewan's face for tell-tale signs he was indeed there last night.

I turn up the sound.

'*Brandon Stand, the son of a respected Cambridge head-master, was rushed to hospital in the early hours of this morning, and died at around five a.m. of a suspected overdose of MDMA, more commonly known as ecstasy. The prevalence of the drug is a worry for local police, who have appealed for witnesses. They told us this morning that it is suspected that the drug taken by the young man was bought locally, and probably contaminated with other substances. Teenagers in the area have been warned not to buy suspect pills from drug dealers. It raises the question once more in our community about the scale of the problem in Cambridge, and local MP, Tania Foden, has been asked for comment. The parents of the boy have appealed for privacy at this very difficult time.*'

Ewan looks as though he has seen a reincarnated devil. I catch him as he falls and shout at Jeremy to get me wet cloths. Ewan's body is limp against mine and I lay him on the floor. I check his pulse. He rouses, embarrassed. Jeremy is glued to the TV, as is Lydia. James comes back in and whistles. The family rallies suddenly, but it's a fraudulent assembly.

'Holy shit,' James says.

Ewan holds on to me and pukes all over the floor. It stinks of booze. I use my dressing gown to wipe his mouth.

I stay on the floor, as the gravity of the news report hits us. Brandon Stand is dead. How do we break it to the kids now that Monika was found murdered? For a fleeting moment, I see my life as a giant puddle of sick.

Ewan struggles against me and gets up, then he darts away from the kitchen, followed by Lydia.

Jeremy and James are still watching TV.

I begin to wipe up the mess.

Chapter 32

'As you know, Mr Thorpe, at the moment, our inquiries are informal and we're recording this interview for investigative purposes. We'd like to build up a picture of your wife's last days, as you remember them.'

Hunt stared at Tony and sat back in his chair. Tony nursed the coffee that had been given to him; it tasted worse than piss. His barrister had briefed him before the casual chat, and they both knew that, in reality, it was about as relaxed as a Gestapo head count.

'How are you feeling, Tony?' Hunt asked.

It was a congenial opening salvo, laced with poison.

Tony smiled and picked up the piss, more for something to do, to gather his thoughts, than for refreshment. Tony had known his counsel for twenty-odd years. Kingston had been one of the first men of colour of his generation to be called to the bar. Tony had been one of his first customers. It was a universal truth that trouble followed trouble, and once Tony had experienced his first taste of it, he'd become hooked. More than a handful for his parents, he seemed to attract it, as easily as money. Both he and Kingston knew that the shit trail follows the cart horse, but often the perpetrator, and the spreader of the effluent, is not where you're looking for them at all. It was Kingston's job to find the source of the shit, at the same time diverting attention from his client. It was unusual but not unheard of for a barrister to attend a police interview. Normally it was done by defence lawyers, but Tony knew, and so did Kingston, that Tony was in the firing line here. Everything looked bad. His nonchalance, the age gap, and the fact that he'd been screwing Carrie on the day the police found Monika's body.

'I've been better,' Tony replied.

'Of course. My condolences, I didn't have time to offer my sympathy last night. Also, I'm not sure you would have remembered,' Hunt said. He let out a slight snort but Tony's face remained stony. He felt Kingston bristle. He'd already briefed him on what a prize bell-end the detective was. But Kingston was hopeful they could swing him around.

'I admit I was under the influence last night,' Tony said.

He'd discussed at length with Kingston what he should and shouldn't give away. They needed to start building a case against the prosecution, because Kingston agreed that it was only a matter of time until Tony was looking at a charge of murder, if they didn't come up with an alternative. When a female spouse is brutally dispatched, the partner is always the place to start, and the police clearly had nothing else yet. Kingston's experience with the police was that they were lazy: why find the real suspect when you have one sat here in front of you? It was Kingston's job to change their minds.

'Is that a normal Friday afternoon? Having a date over and getting high?' Hunt asked. 'Did your wife know you were having an affair with Carrie Greenside?'

Kingston glared at Hunt and Tony didn't reply.

'That's hardly fact-finding, is it?' Kingston said. 'Adultery doesn't a murderer make,' he finished.

'But it does encourage a healthy dose of rage for third parties. In our humble opinion, of course,' Hunt shot back.

'Are you suggesting that my client's wife beat herself to death because he was having an affair?' Kingston asked. Tony winced a little. But that's why he employed him: to ask uncomfortable questions.

Hunt looked at his notes and left the question hanging.

'We can overlook the possession charges. We found seven grams of cocaine and several ounce bags of pure-grade skunk. Pretty impressive stuff, Tony. Who's your dealer?' Hunt asked.

'Kids. They're everywhere, if you know where to look,' Tony replied. 'They all look the same, hoodies over their faces. It was a one off.'

'So how come you know so much about the supply chain if it was a one off?'

'History,' Tony said. 'I dabbled back in the day. Pushers hang out in all the same places, nothing changes, just their age.'

'Ah, yes. Your history. Let's talk about that, shall we? You got yourself into some scrapes, didn't you?'

Tony didn't react. He'd had brushes with the law, mainly for possession, but Kingston had smoothed them all out.

'Irrelevant, Detective. Let's move on, shall we?' Kingston interjected. 'Tell us about your case, just the facts, please.'

'I'll get to that,' Hunt said. 'So, Carrie Greenside. How long has she been your... help me out here. Lover? Mistress? Bit on the side?'

Kingston looked at his client and nodded.

'It was a one off. Monika took herself off for periods. I admit I was sick of it. That explains why I appeared so uncaring. But I'm not. I loved my wife. Carrie actually came over for a business matter last night but things got out of hand. I suppose, inside, I was angry with my wife for taking off again.'

'Do you often get angry with your wife?'

Kingston jumped in. 'Let us be clear, this was an open marriage. Sexually. Mrs Thorpe accepted her husband's dalliances, because she had her own. Maybe that's where you should be looking.'

It did the trick. Hunt looked genuinely interested. Tony watched him and, like Kingston had told him, as soon as the detective realised how much more work he'd have to do to build a case, they'd get him on side. Their tactic was to come across as willing helpers to the investigation.

'Do you have names?' Hunt asked.

Kingston had briefed Tony that, for now, mentioning the kitchen fitter too early would look desperate, they'd build up to it.

'I didn't check her appointments but you might want to start with her gym, perhaps,' Tony offered.

'Let's stick to facts, shall we?' Kingston said. 'What questions have you got that are pertinent to what happened to my client's wife? Last night was an unfortunate coincidence. A man whose wife disappears for stretches of time becomes used to it, immune, shall we say. So my client's actions after his wife's disappearance are only relevant if you think he had a direct involvement in how she came to harm, and you need proof of this. Also, until I have a copy of the autopsy report, and a summary of how you think my client's movements last night have any bearing on your case, if you have a case, then you're wasting our time. We agreed to attend this interview for informative purposes. We agree that the state of the deceased's marriage is relevant here, and my client is keen for the investigation to move forward, and so when you have new information, we'd like to see it as soon as possible. Do you have anything that might change his current position?'

Tony breathed a little easier as he listened to Kingston command the room. Hunt wasn't put off but he absorbed what Kingston was intimating, and was tempted by the worm on the end of the hook.

'I'm getting to that, counsel. Let's take a step back, shall we? Mr Thorpe, tell me about Tuesday evening, when you said that your wife was "drunk and delirious".'

Tony realised that the detective was now dancing to Kingston's tune, and it was impressively done. No wonder the bastard charged so much in fees.

Tony thought back to Tuesday evening. Monika's black hair, framing her beautiful face, watching as she danced around the chimenea. They'd lit it because it got chilly later in the evening, despite the unseasonal heat during the day. They'd talked at length about their future. But the night hadn't ended how it had started.

'Tuesday?' Hunt reminded him where he was.

'She wasn't herself. She'd drunk too much. It's difficult to keep count when she's in that mood. I was worried about her. Her small body couldn't take it.'

Tony paused and peered down at the table, which was stained with mug rings. Time stood still and he desperately wanted to get out of the tiny room. He forced his eyes closed and squeezed them with his fingers. Kingston had told him to show some emotion, but that kind of thing didn't come easy to him. It seemed to work and Hunt waited for him to carry on.

'When I realised she was intoxicated, I... After that, there was no point in trying to communicate with her. We argued.'

'About what?'

'She gets emotional when she drinks,' Tony said. He looked down at his hands. He sniffed.

'What was she emotional about?'

Tony shrugged.

'Forgive me, I'm an amateur when it comes to open marriages.' Hunt smiled smarmily. 'Is it possible that she wasn't as okay with your arrangement as you were? Did she know about Carrie?' Hunt asked. His hawkishness returned.

'How could she? It was the first and only time, and it was a mistake, like I said.'

'You didn't tell me it was a mistake, you said it was a one off. I presume you knew one another before? Did Monika perhaps suspect you had feelings for Ms Greenside?'

'Irrelevant, Mr Hunt. What's your point?' Kingston stepped in.

'Let me put it this way, how could you be so sure that she wouldn't walk in on you last night? After coming to her senses after one of her jaunts away, let's say?' Hunt asked.

'It was stupid,' Tony said. 'Like I said, I was used to her taking off.'

Hunt moved on.

'How long were you married?'

'Four years.'

'And how long did you know each other before that?'

'A year,' Tony said.

'Relatively, that's not long, is it? When did you decide to be sexually liberal in your marriage?'

Tony glanced at Kingston, who blinked, indicating that he should go ahead and tell Hunt what they'd discussed.

'I knew about Monika's past when I met her, I didn't think she'd carry on after we were married, but she did. It was always on the cards that I would never have her to myself,' Tony said.

'Come again?' Hunt asked. He sat up straight and his pen hovered over the piece of paper in front of him.

'My client's wife was a prostitute, Detective. She vowed to give it up when they married, but it's our suspicion that she did not.' Kingston answered the question.

Hunt paused and Tony felt examined as if trapped under a bell jar. His body begged him to run and opened his sweat glands as if to hammer home the point. He rubbed his eyes again, pretending heartache.

'Hold on. Let's play this forward. You're indicating that Monika was carrying on, in your words, selling sex, after she married you. Excuse me, Mr Thorpe, but you're not short of cash. Why? Also, if she went to meet a client on Tuesday night, you've just said she was intoxicated. Was she picked up? She certainly didn't use her car. It doesn't add up.'

'I'm just telling you what I know,' Tony said. 'I went to bed and she wasn't there in the morning.'

'Have you got proof that she was continuing in this profession after you were married?' Hunt asked.

'I hired somebody to do some digging about.'

'I can corroborate this,' Kingston added.

'And?' Hunt asked.

'We can put you in touch with the PI who was employed by my client,' Kingston said.

'That would be most helpful,' Hunt said.

They'd given him something else to think about.

'I haven't found her mobile phone, though, most of her numbers are in it.'

'The phone in a flamingo case, yes?' The description had already been given to the police.

Tony nodded.

'No, it didn't show up in the search of your house either.' Hunt tapped his pen. 'I need an alibi for you, Tony. Tentative examination of your wife's body has put her death at around midnight on Tuesday to midday on Wednesday. Let's go back to the argument. What time did you go to bed and leave her downstairs?'

'I went to bed about eleven. I was used to leaving her up on her own, drinking and listening to music, you know, romantic stuff that made her cry. She often slept in the spare room when she was like that. I thought I heard shouting in the street but I went back to sleep.'

'Well, you've got plenty of cameras around that fortress of yours. Maybe we'll find out what the strange altercation in the street was, eh? What about Wednesday morning?'

Tony had told Kingston that before Carrie came over, he'd disabled all of the CCTV cameras around his property.

'Mr Thorpe has informed me that there has been a problem with the security system around the property, they're wireless and I'm afraid they've been unreliable lately,' Kingston said.

Hunt glared at him and wrote something on his pad. Tony answered the question.

'I spent Wednesday morning trying to contact Monika. I spoke to several friends about her, trying to see if she'd visited any of them. I also know an excellent psychologist, who is a close friend. We discussed my wife's mental state.'

'And that's when you reported your wife as missing?' Hunt asked.

Tony nodded.

From the cocksure copper he'd been at the beginning of the interview, Hunt had become malleable and open to suggestion, just like Kingston said he would be.

Chapter 33

The senior pathologist doused her face in cold water. The heat outside was crazy, but she wasn't complaining. She had the afternoon off and intended to spend it sunbathing in her garden, and perhaps meeting a friend for a frappuccino by the river Cam.

Her assistants had done the prelim on the victim and she had all morning to perform the post-mortem operation. She'd read through their initial findings, and learned that the death had been a violent one. Murders in Cambridge were rare and so she planned to take her time on this; she didn't mind getting up early on a Saturday for such a case, as long as her afternoon wasn't interrupted.

The victim was young, healthy and in her prime. Keeping the body at an ambient two to four degrees in the mortuary preserved many things, including trauma, and this woman had gone through a brutal few minutes prior to death. People thought that death was quick, like in the movies, when a few gunshots or knife wounds resulted in the victim falling over, looking into the camera expectantly, and dying almost instantly. It wasn't like that at all. The human biome was incredibly resilient, and difficult to halt.

It took time.

The body bag had already been transferred from the chill room to the steel gurney by her assistants, and it lay like a lumpy rolled-up tent waiting for her attention. She'd scrubbed up and made sure she was sterile, not to protect the corpse, of course, but to safeguard herself against some of the more unsavoury bacteria found on rotting bodies. She'd been told that the woman wasn't yet in full bloat, and a forensic etymologist called to the crime scene had already estimated the time of death. It was her job to confirm it. The heatwave hadn't helped preserve the body and had contributed to virulent insect activity, but given all those factors, they were happy with their theory, working on Tuesday evening or Wednesday morning for her time of death. The timeline explained the stages of decomposition nicely, which fitted in with a three- to four-day exposure to the elements. If there's one thing that is a primary driver for decay, it's heat, and the thirty-degree ambient daytime temperature in the county of Cambridgeshire had cooked the woman's insides like a furnace. There wouldn't be much left of her internal organs to examine, and so she hoped she'd have some luck with the external and visible signs on the body.

She unzipped the bag, expecting the routine stench to fill the room. It didn't take long, but the mortuary workers were used to it and smeared perfume or Vicks under their noses. They also smelled the familiar whiff of bleach. Somebody had tried to clean up, and it was her job to assess how well they'd done. It was clear from her first cursory walk around the body that the woman had suffered terribly.

She took her time to walk around the body, placing goggles on her head to intensify the magnification levels. Before going inside the cadaver, which she expected would be pretty mushy by now, her assessment of the external form might prove critical in this case. She was well aware that, when this went to court, her notes might be pivotal in securing a conviction or not. But by the look of the woman's skin, she doubted she'd be able to find much forensic evidence now, especially with the presence of a common cleaning agent.

A female murder victim with this amount of trauma was always checked for sexual assault, but disappointingly, there wasn't much tissue left around the woman's genitals to say conclusively. The offspring of blowfly work quickly in this heat. She swabbed anyway and crossed her fingers. She liked to work in circles around the victim, moving closer on each circuit, making notes and speaking into her mic softly as she noted new details. She was trying to piece together a picture of this horrendously violent event by examining the bruising pattern and the photographs from the dump site. Absence of blood and matter around the body confirmed that the bank of the river Cam wasn't the location of her murder. Crime scene investigators had established that this woman had been killed before being dumped by the river. These cases were the most difficult to crack. Cleaning meant that vital evidence was lost and she'd already confirmed this without even touching the victim.

Her assistants worked silently around her. Music played gently in the background: after all, they needed some cheer in the place. It wasn't all doom and gloom. People died, bodies expired, and it was their job to pass on the final message to those who once loved them. In this case, those very people might in fact turn out to be the ones who'd killed her, but that was for the police and barristers to argue over. She, and anyone in this line of work, was well aware from talking to the many detectives she associated with that women who died in this way often did so at the hands of their most intimate partner: husband, lover, or ex.

The pathologist's post-mortem operations weren't usually drawn-out affairs, because her customers were typically atherosclerosis or stroke victims in their eighties, but today was different. The body would have to be meticulously scraped and taped for residue fragments and organic matter, like DNA, as well as taking samples from fingernails, toenails, teeth, eyes, hair and vagina, or what was left of it. Specimens would then be sent to the histology and toxicology departments.

The woman had once had beautiful black curly tresses and it seemed just as vital as it would have been the last time she'd laughed out loud and threw the mane back. She dug around in it, to see if she could find anything interesting tangled in it, like a foreign follicle or a manmade fibre. The skin, where it wasn't discoloured or bruised, was pale and perfect. She'd taken care of herself. Her fingernails were manicured and she still wore three pairs of gold hoops in each ear. One might expect them to have been ripped out during an aggressive attack, so it could be assumed that she was either overcome very quickly without struggle, or she was too terrified to fight back, like the impala's collapse before the final death bite of the cheetah.

The body had been stripped and so there were no clothes to examine, and there was little chance of getting prints off anything much. Swabs might prove inconclusive due to the state of the body, and she concentrated her attention on the huge head wound. She'd done experiments on pigs' heads, and hit them herself, several times, to ascertain how much force and how many sustained blows it took to collapse a skull.

It took a lot.

This was a rage-related death.

She intensified the magnification on her goggles and peered at the head area. The way the skin had broken, and the shape of the indentations, told her that either the instrument had been blunt, or that something had been placed between skin and weapon, perhaps so the killer didn't have to look at her. This was no rash decision. The bruises had begun to develop nicely, and this would aid in the dating of the blows. Tuesday night through to Wednesday morning matched her assessment.

'The crime scene must be covered in matter,' she said. 'But of course we'll probably never see it. Turn her over.'

The anterior of a corpse was less offensive than looking into the eyes of the deceased, and this woman's back was no different. In life, it must have been rather attractive. It was tanned and structured.

'Ah, this is interesting.'

The pathologist wasn't referring to the ugly tattoo that crawled up the cadaver's back. It was the back itself. To the right of her thoracic vertebrae, around numbers seven to nine, there was a large puncture wound.

'That will have ruptured her lung, and it looks to me to be where the most blood loss occurred.'

An examination of the ribs confirmed to her that the victim had either been attacked, or had fallen backwards during the assault, resulting in sharp-force trauma.

'This could have been the initial strike, with the head wound finishing her off. We'll see when we open her up.'

She went closer and requested her tweezers. She dug around inside the wound and finally pulled out a large splinter of wood. It was painted eggshell blue, and there were more.

Chapter 34

Carrie sat in a plastic chair, which she was already sticking to, thanks to the heat, and prepared herself by taking a deep breath. The detective smiled at her. The desire to punch him had not diminished at all from last night.

Hunt had entered the room like a grinning hyena. This was his patch. He wore the same cheap suit, which in the light of day was covered in stains. His shirt, presumed once to have been white, was milky beige from age. He sat down opposite her, spreading his legs and taking his time. She experienced the same sense of helplessness she'd encountered ever since the first time a man had pinned her down and overpowered her. Her father had been stunned when she finally learned to fight back. An ugly survival tactic she'd suppressed long ago threatened to emerge through her fists, which she kept hidden.

She'd brought her lawyer.

'At this time, Ms Greenside, we're conducting informal interviews as an information-gathering exercise on the victim, Mrs Monika Thorpe.'

He took his time over Monika's name and Carrie fixed on his mouth. He had bad teeth and a little spittle stuck to his gums when they moved, indicating to her that he rarely brushed them.

'The recording equipment is for investigative purposes,' Hunt said.

Both Carrie and her lawyer knew that this was no mere formality. Every word, every nuance, and movement perceptible on the recording, would be examined microscopically for clues later. It was little consolation that she wasn't under caution and so whatever she said couldn't be used in court. But perhaps that was part of the trap planned for her. An image of a young bear imprisoned inside a cage, in China, on a visit there years ago, flashed through her brain.

They had a narrative prepared. She'd gone through the whole story with her lawyer and was confident that it was watertight. She'd spent twenty years in male-dominated boardrooms, and knew how they operated. A conceited detective, cock in hand, wasn't enough to put her off her script, and yet her palms were sweaty and her heart hammered in her chest.

She looked into his eyes. He aroused a violent, visceral response in her, which she had to get under control. She reminded herself that it wasn't personal, and was just the system he represented challenging her darkest fears. His institution had damaged her, then failed to vindicate her. Merely sharing his air threatened her. Old wounds ran through her soul. Children like her remain mutilated forever, like stunted superheroes of survival, hypersensitive to danger and assault: perfect for capitalism.

But not so good in police interviews.

'Please state your full name for the interview,' Hunt said.

And so it began. Carrie tried not to allow herself to be transported back to the night she'd sat in a chair just like this one, over thirty years ago. Heat emanated from her skin under her loose blouse. The part of her brain that had formed millennia ago, fine-tuned for survival and to protect the organism from mortal danger, screamed at her to run.

The tap-tap of Hunt's pen focused her mind.

'How long have you known Mr Thorpe?'

'Fifteen years.'

'In what capacity?'

'Acquaintance. Train companion to King's Cross.'

'Lover?'

'It was a one off, I had no idea Monika was estranged or missing, I never would have done something so crass. I assumed – wrongly – that they were separated.'

'Did Mr Thorpe give a reason for his wife's absence?'

Carrie sat up straight and uncrossed and crossed her legs. The space in between them was wet with sweat.

'No.'

'Until last night.'

Hunt's smile threatened to derail her concentration, which was tenuous as it was.

'So, what gave you the impression that they were separated?'

'Tony told me his wife had left him, and that he was alone.'

Hunt wrote in his notebook and sucked air behind his teeth, in what Carrie described as the 'click-tut'. It was usually the preserve of a certain type of male who liked to show their disapproval or annoyance, but didn't have the balls to actually say anything. She glared at him.

'How well did you know Monika?'

'Never met her.'

'Last night, when you were in Mr Thorpe's *intimate* company, did he confide in you any details of where his wife might be?'

She let the salacious reference go. Her lawyer shifted in his seat.

'No, we didn't discuss his wife.'

'No time?' Hunt grinned.

'I'm tiring of the inference to my client conducting some kind of predatory affair at the expense of your victim. The tone is offensive and unhelpful, especially if you're expecting my client to voluntarily help with your enquiries. Shall we move on?' Her lawyer closed Hunt down, along with his vicarious masturbation over what she did or didn't do last night.

'How many times did you visit the Thorpe family home?' Hunt carried on.

'Like I said, last night was my first time, though I had been invited several times, and declined.'

'Did Mr Thorpe strike you as somebody who was missing his wife, or glad to be rid of her?'

'I didn't judge his emotions in those terms,' Carrie said.

'But he was pleased to see you and not grieving or worried?'

The grin.

'I couldn't possibly assess that.'

'But he was relaxed?'

An image of Tony on top of her in the pool, in his bed...

'Yes.'

'Where were you on Tuesday evening?'

'Training at the gym, working. I can corroborate all that with my appointment schedule. Why?'

'Is my client suspected of a crime?' her lawyer asked.

Hunt didn't answer.

'If not, this interview is over,' her lawyer said.

Hunt sat back and flicked off the recording. Carrie thought he couldn't get his legs any wider. Her lawyer gave a list of reasons, rights and precedents as to why they were leaving but they blurred into a hot buzz.

Hunt stared at her as she stood up and straightened her skirt. His eyes flickered to her thighs.

'But we've barely got started,' Hunt protested amicably.

'Have you got any factual questions for my client that don't involve aspersions about her character?' her lawyer asked.

'We'll be in touch,' Hunt said. He smiled, revealing his crooked teeth, and Carrie slipped through the door held open by her lawyer.

'Don't leave the country,' Hunt added.

Outside in the sunshine, despite the heat, Carrie breathed the air as if she'd been locked up for twenty years.

'I thought the force had changed,' she said, breathlessly.

'Don't worry, Carrie, the guy is old school. You've told me everything, you've got nothing to worry about,' he said. 'They're scrabbling around for crumbs. They still play bad cop now and again, they're trying to rile you, it's in their job-spec.'

'I feel as though they suspect me of something,' she said.

'The angle I think they're going for is that you knew Monika was missing and Tony couldn't wait to get you to his place, while his bed was still warm, as it were. It's bullshit, don't worry.'

'An accessory?' she asked.

He put his hand on her shoulder and patted it, not answering her.

'I'll be in touch,' he said. He walked away and she felt soiled. Her skin was tacky and her clothes suffocated her.

As she reached her car, she noticed a young man begging for money near the pay machine. He could have been in his early twenties but it was hard to tell, his skin was oily with dirt and his clothes were mere rags hanging off his body.

For the first time in her life, since being on the streets herself after assaulting her father and being charged with ABH, she stopped and handed the beggar a ten-pound note.

Chapter 35

I've invited Tony round here for the day. He'll likely get drunk with Jeremy, and I'll cook and nurse both of them, but it's the least I can do. I always pick up the pieces after his relationships end. I've been doing it for years. His track record with women is a wasteland of loss. I resign myself to the fact that I'll have five children to look after today, though the ones in their teens are infinitely less complicated. I recall Tony's torment when Sarah jumped off the library building in our final year at uni. It was then I decided to pursue clinical psychology as a career. Sarah's diseased mind and Tony's reaction both fascinated and horrified me in equal parts. She'd been growing too close to him and didn't understand that a man like Tony needs to be free. Four became three, and it's been like that ever since. Tragedy bonds us. I've watched Tony try to find other meaningful partnerships but they never last. And their spectacular endings are indicative of Tony's tidal magnetism.

Is he capable of murder though? I ask myself.

I don't know. He was interviewed by the police this morning, with the ever-present Kingston at his side. The man who magically makes Tony's issues disappear, keeping his life intact, just. Maybe Tony's luck has finally run out.

I'm making empanadas and as I roll out the pastry I listen to a playlist on Amazon Music called 'chill'.

It's having the opposite effect. I still haven't told the children about Monika. Ewan has gone back to bed, James is sunbathing and I can see Lydia doing laps of the pool. Jeremy is readying the pool house fridge and stocking it for his friend. He's happy because he's got a reason to drink today, and he has company. Tony will want to get plastered, and Jeremy would be a bad pal not to help him.

I pop the pasties in the oven and wash my hands. My phone rings and it's Tony.

'Hey, how did it go?' I ask him.

'Kingston was excellent, as always. It was bloody horrible, sitting there being scrutinised by some oik who thinks he can pin this on me, but Kingston is confident when they don't find any physical evidence they won't be able to charge me. It's a waiting game.'

'What sort of physical evidence are they looking for?' I ask.

'I suppose a weapon, some sort of forensics, I guess. God, I don't know how these things work, Alex. They're looking into her other relationships too, and her past.'

'Before you met?'

'There were plenty.'

I'm caught between wanting to believe him and a distasteful sensation in my gut. He's insinuating that Monika deserved what she got. I'm fully aware that my friend is a misogynist but that doesn't make him a murderer. But the reference to Monika's sexual history being at all relevant in a woman's murder, disturbs me. The idea that any woman is somehow responsible for a predator's behaviour because she is by nature alluring offends my senses. I think of Grace, and my own daughter.

I'm torn between the allegiance to my long friendship with Tony, and my own sex.

'What did the police say?'

'Oh, he understood, he's looking into it.'

A man-pact. It fits with what I know of Tony's ability to sneak his way out of reality.

I pick raw dough from under my nails. My hands feel tacky.

'I think the police will want to speak with you and Jeremy. I told them I spoke to you on Wednesday morning.'

I look out across the lawn to the pool house and imagine Jeremy as a character witness and doubt fills my head.

'Is that your alibi?' I ask.

'No, I was on my own, working.'

Flutters of hesitancy fill my stomach.

'So, you're expecting me to lie for you?'

'Or Jeremy.'

'Jeremy can barely remember what he *actually* did, let alone what he's supposed to have done. And I can't cover for you, I was at work on Wednesday. What about when you called me on Tuesday night? Won't they want to talk to me about that?'

'I didn't tell them.'

'Why? It corroborates you having no idea where she'd gone.'

He doesn't answer me.

'Tony?'

'I discovered she was having an affair.'

'Ah,' I reply. If I'm honest, I'm not surprised, just sad for him. I'm not going to smugly remind him that it was bound to happen; somebody like Monika was never going to be owned. But my theories are the last thing Tony needs right now. He's embarrassed. Monika has shamed him. If there's one thing he abhors more than losing money, it's losing women.

Chapter 36

Sunday 12 July

Two days before Monika's disappearance

Monika snuck out silently from the house. Tony was passed out on the sofa downstairs. They'd fought in the taxi on the way home from the Moores'. Tony had accused her of flirting with James. For God's sake, he was a teenager. It was a low blow. He was becoming desperate, especially when he'd had a few drinks and a couple of snorts of the white stuff. It was making him paranoid. He had no understanding of what she really needed, and it wasn't a boy. Nor was it an old man like Jeremy Moore, though he tried his best to push his way into her personal space and get a swollen sticky hand on her whenever the opportunity arose. She felt enormous pity for Alex, who was stuck in a marriage with a lecherous has-been. But then she realised that it wasn't only Alex who was trapped inside a loveless union.

She walked along the leafy boulevard adjacent to her home and welcomed the breeze travelling lightly on the night. Her skin clamoured for its refreshment and she relished its caress. The van was waiting for her at the end of the road. Henry wouldn't venture into the lights of the CCTV cameras guarding each of the establishments closer to the desirable residences of her neighbourhood. She saw it parked across the street, under bushes, away from the main drag, and giggled to herself at the illicit deliciousness of her liaison.

She climbed in and he drove away.

Henry knew the city. He took routes that she'd never come across before and she suspected it was because he liked to keep under the radar. He had a mysterious past and one which she wanted to unpick. In that, he was like her: running away from something and towards an alternative.

Maybe she could change his mind.

When he parked, he asked her if she was all right. He asked if Tony had hurt her. She shook her head gently, touched by his concern for her welfare but aware that his unease was more about her being in the company of her husband and not what Tony chose to do with that intimate time. She relaxed back into the seat and smiled at him.

'I just wanted to see you. I needed to see you,' she said.

'Yeah?' He looked at her, trying to read her face and held out his hand, to stroke her hair away from her face.

She read the power she had over him and glanced towards the back of his van.

'Here?' he asked, breathlessly.

'Yes,' she said, climbing over the back and into the cavern of Henry's work life. It smelled like her kitchen when the walls were stripped and bare, and of his body when he lay under her sink, twisting this way and that, battling with a copper pipe, trying to make it bend to his will. He followed her and she began to undress herself. He found her mouth with his and helped her undo her blouse, but they fumbled in the dark and she caught her foot on something heavy. She fell backwards and he climbed on top of her, finding something soft to prop under her body.

The interior of the van was furnace-like and cramped but she'd rather make love to Henry in here, surrounded by grime and dust, than to her husband in a penthouse suite overlooking Central Park.

She groaned as their bodies moved together and Henry pulled her hair softly. It was as if they were stuck together in the cramped space, inseparable and complete. Henry buried his head into her shoulder and she felt the van sway. She heard a slight tear in her skirt but she didn't care. Her clothes were mere vessels along for the ride, and the baubles at her ears and throat jangled sweetly with the rhythm, as if the links in jewellery were designed for just this.

Sweat covered their bodies and she fought for breath, as the weight of Henry's body seemed to her more powerful when pinned into such a confined space.

Images of Tony's face, as well as Jeremy's, bloated and urgent, melted away as she clung to Henry's back. They'd created their own existence, in here, in this moment in time. It didn't have walls, nor was it confined to a title or deeds. It was a thing one touches, like the glancing of Henry's grip as he held on to her.

It was something in and of itself all at once.

It was peace.

Chapter 37

DI Hunt reflected on the two interviews he'd conducted this morning. His desk had suddenly become busy and it was unwelcome. Two major incidents in twenty-four hours was something for the major cities, not leafy Cambridge. If he was to land his big promotion then he'd need to solve them quickly.

The forensic report from the search of Tony and Monika Thorpe's address was incomplete. These things took time to process, especially as the property was so extensive. He marvelled at how two people could need so many possessions around them. He did know at this stage that several DNA profiles had been collected, as well as a tonne of cash and a one-way air ticket to Latvia. But they still hadn't located Monika's mobile phone, and they might never. These days, people's phones were their life. They had everything on there. Facebook alone revealed so much about a person, as well as Google searches, likes on Instagram and shopping history. It was no longer just about the numbers stored on there, or even the phone calls. That tiny piece of Apple hardware was like a photo diary of the owner. Hunt, like other coppers, hardly used his mobile anymore. If people knew what they could extract from them, giants like Apple and Samsung would go under overnight. He'd trawled through Monika Thorpe's social media accounts, and felt sympathy for

Tony Thorpe. His wife was vacuous and entitled. She had all the hallmarks of a courtesan. She wore her baubles like medals, and smiled into a thousand camera angles, and Tony Thorpe – the man who paid the bills – was notably absent in them. Sat at his desk, piecing together the Thorpes' marriage, Hunt was warming to Tony Thorpe. The notion that Monika had several sexual partners was an angle that piqued his attention and might fit in nicely with a motive of a jealousy-fuelled rage of a lover, which the coroner had implied in her report, emailed over to him in the last hour.

He had to consider that recreational stimulants might also have played a part in the sordid life of Monika Thorpe, from what he'd witnessed of the husband last night. Too much money bred boredom and substance abuse usually trotted hot on the heels of excess in other things. For that, though, he'd have to wait for the toxicology report.

Then there was the spectre of the young man's death, last night, at the rec. Tony Thorpe had told him that his drugs were from provincial hoods and a search of local suppliers known to the police had thrown up some names.

Archibald Morgan's name kept coming up, and the guys in the drug squad told him that he regularly sold out of the rec on the outskirts of town, where kids gathered. Had Tony gone down there to score? After all, the rich normally attended to their dirty business in the more unpleasant areas of town. Brandon's mates had given statements testifying that the MDMA came from a dealer at the rec and Hunt planned to pay the lad's family a visit today. Archibald Morgan was eighteen, and no longer a minor, so Mummy and Daddy wouldn't be able to protect him. The drug squad had hauled him in last year, when he was seventeen, and some hotshot lawyer, hired by the father, had thrown the book at their enquiries. Archibald had left the station under his father's wing, grinning from ear to ear. It would be satisfying to get the lad back in and wipe the smile off his face.

On that note, he clicked open an email and saw that the toxicology and histology report from the coroner on Monika Thorpe's remains had arrived. He read it with interest. Her femoral blood showed a concentration of cocaine at 0.6mg/L. She also had a .24 per cent of ethanol in her system, which was almost at coma-inducing levels, which fitted with what Tony Thorpe said about her alcoholism. The combination of the two substances, at their current levels, the coroner had explained, was enough to induce stupor, but it all depended on what Monika had eaten and how used she was to being intoxicated to such high levels. He pondered if her supplier was the same as her husband's. It was certainly feasible that he paid for it.

No matter the detail, Hunt now knew she was wasted, not just giddy like her husband said. At least before he'd gone to bed. Another interesting development had piqued his interest too. The kitchen fitter they'd contacted when they'd been doing a sweep of last known contacts for Monika was an ex-convict, a violent one, and he'd also had contact with Brandon Stand's school, ostensibly as a reformed addict and preacher of a clean life. Likely story, thought Hunt. He'd read the file and learned that Henry Nelson was a nasty piece of work. Twelve years ago, high on a cocktail of illegal substances, he'd gone on a rampage looking for money, or anything he could sell. Holding up a general store, he'd been challenged by a member of the public and taken him out with a single punch; he'd later died in hospital. He'd got away with manslaughter because the victim was carrying a knife: no doubt planted by Nelson. It made his blood boil when people like that literally got away with murder. Eight years inside was no punishment for taking someone's life. There was a score ready to be settled there. A wealthy woman with a mysterious past might be a tempting project for an ex-convict.

He turned to the autopsy report of Monika Thorpe. He was used to gruesome crime scene photos and he didn't flinch as he bit into a sausage roll and flicked through Monika's wound profiles. He'd been there when they were taken. He chomped away as he read that there was a lack of evidence of sexual assault due to the state of the corpse, and that was disappointing. It looked like they were short on any forensic evidence at all, and he read with abject frustration about the presence of cleaning chemicals on her body. It indicated premeditation. The dump site interested him too. You'd have to have some strength to accomplish all of the above in one night's work. Tony Thorpe was a fit man, and intelligent, but somehow Tony's sophistication, the smoothness of his manicured hands, and his helpfulness with the inquiry didn't strike him as fitting the profile of somebody capable of the sort of violence wrought on Monika's body. Spouses strangle, they pummel in rage, and they don't tend to clean up after a crime of passion. It fitted better with the profile of somebody less refined. A kitchen fitter, perhaps, who also happened to be a violent ex-con, who also knew the kids at the rec.

Hunt closed the files on his computer, and those on his desk, and went to make a cuppa. Both cases bothered him. He looked forward to meeting Henry Nelson, who'd styled himself as a born-again reformist and found himself in the wrong place – or, more accurately, the wrong kitchen – at the wrong time, but Hunt didn't believe in coincidences.

Chapter 38

Henry lay on a bench and pushed weights. The gym was quiet, as it always was on a Saturday lunchtime. Sitting up and catching his breath, his eye wandered to the giant TV on the wall. He recognised the young teenager in the report and he sat up, putting down his dumbbells. He'd been at George Paget School only last week.

Two conditions of his probation were that he volunteer for a charitable cause, and that he attend professional counselling sessions, paid for by the state. For his volunteer work, he chose to visit schools and youth clubs, speaking to kids about the perils of addiction. He showed any of them willing to listen that prison wasn't a walk in the park, like it said on social media. Inmates didn't spend their days watching massive flat-screen TVs in huge lounges, and they didn't work out in state-of-the-art gyms, just like they didn't eat and drink like lords.

His stories scared them, and that was the point. He stopped short of the rapes in the shower block, where there was no CCTV. He didn't tell them about the blood running along the water gulley, and the screams of those who were held down by men twice their age, and subjected to humiliating torture. But he did share the stories of broken arms over bad debt, and he enlightened them on the horrific conditions at Her Majesty's pleasure.

The purging soothed his guilt.

A typical lesson might start with wise guys making jokes about getting high and streaming it live on Twitter, looking cool and in charge, owning time like a boss. Videos like it were widely available on the internet. Typically, the girls in class fawned over the tough boys saying they could cope inside. But after a while, when they shut up and listened about the twenty-three hours a day in a shared eight-foot cell, the suicides, the violence and, worse of all, the time spent inside one's own head, they quietened down a bit. By the time Henry was halfway through a session, he had thirty kids gazing at him, in silence. Even the brawny bully Brandon Stand shut up.

The knife edge between good and bad was flimsy and it only took one stupid mistake. Now, as he watched the TV, he figured that he hadn't hit home enough.

He buried his head in his towel. It had been a shit week and it was getting worse. The call from the police had left him going over the events from when he'd last seen Monika. He wiped his face and peered around the gym. He spotted Grace training a client and wondered if she'd heard anything. He'd changed gyms from one across town a year ago. He'd sought her out. But not for personal training. He saw himself as her guardian angel. She had no idea that he watched her drive home, especially in the winter when the sky was dark and hid terrible secrets. He knew that, despite the poise her name suggested, she was fighting a monumental battle. From the protection of her ivory tower, where she recorded her videos on mental health and espoused wellness, he knew that she faced the dark alone, and terrified, as if connecting with millions of strangers online would make the ghosts go away. All the money in the world couldn't do that. It had been the same with Monika.

He also watched Ignacio.

Part of keeping Grace safe was knowing where she was going and who she was seeing. But he trod carefully, as she was easily startled. Any sign of unwanted attention was batted away by her, like a dangerous bug. She guarded herself with exhaustive vigilance. She had no boyfriend to keep her home fires burning inside her million-pound flat bought by her parents, who couldn't protect her. He watched her YouTube channel and observed as she punished her body mercilessly. Henry saw what other people missed; his incarceration had made sure of that. He'd been annoyed at himself that he failed to notice her leave last night. She'd slipped out as he squabbled with Ignacio, and he was left deflated, and feeling that he'd let her down.

He lay back and settled under the bar, arching his back and grounding his buttocks and shoulder blades, and positioned his hands to lift a new personal best. Exhausting himself physically took away some of the monsters chasing him. He finished the set and sat up, and something caught his eye on the massive TV.

Other gym-goers gathered around the screen and he saw that Grace was watching too. But the piece wasn't about Brandon Stand. It was about Monika.

'*Next of kin have been informed… the body was found by the river Cam near a jetty… murder…*'

Henry felt sick. The exertion of lifting and his elevated heart rate, compounded by the shock, made him gag and he held his hand over his mouth. Then sense took hold and he realised that everything he'd worked for since leaving the nick was about to come crashing down around him. His phone vibrated at his feet, where he'd left it out of the way.

It was Carrie.

Chapter 39

I fear the trials of the day will never end. I've just sat the kids down and told them about Monika. How do you explain such a thing to teenagers? I did my best. She was in this house on Sunday and being so close to brutality has numbed them into silence. They've gone to their rooms, and even James is speechless. I'm struggling to pull myself in all the different directions today requires, and I realise I shouldn't have told Tony that he could come over. But the man is in a terrible state. He needs his friends. He's at the door.

He wears a white shirt and tan trousers, with Ray-Bans plopped on top of his head, and he's trying to be the Tony he was yesterday, last week, all his life, but he's not. I can tell by his eyes that he's broken. He's nervous as he comes in and gives me flowers. I take them and cuddle him. His body feels like home and I stay there for a while, holding him.

I feel him relax and he pulls away and looks into my eyes.

'I was a shit husband,' he says.

'Shush, Tony, stop it.'

'I'm an arrogant prick, and karma is coming to bite me on the arse.'

'Stop it, you're in shock, this isn't your fault.'

'Try telling the police that.'

I look furtively up the stairs to see if any of my children are listening and usher him through to the kitchen.

'You need a drink and some time with old friends,' I tell him. 'Did you hear about Brandon Stand? He was Ewan's bully at school.' I'm trying to divert his maudlin spiral.

'Who?' Tony asks.

I look at him oddly but can forgive him for not watching the news or listening to the radio at a time like this.

'A local teenager died of an ecstasy overdose in the early hours in hospital. He was the headmaster's son. Ewan had a bit of a meltdown.'

'His bully is dead – isn't that good news?'

The diversion works. Old Tony is back, if only for a moment.

Jeremy comes in from outside – he's been making the pool house lounge comfortable. We plan to spend the afternoon out there rather than in the house so the children don't overhear our conversation, which will inevitably be about Monika's gruesome death. I busy myself with locating a vase for Tony's flowers. The men slap each other on the back and I'm infinitely puzzled by the male ritual of physical prowess on display.

'Drink?' Jeremy asks Tony. 'I've got some fresh lemonade from Waitrose in the outside fridge.'

The chance of these two staying sober today is about as remote as Monika coming back to life.

'Great,' Tony says. They walk outside, asking me to join them. I nod and promise to follow.

'Anything to go with it?' Tony asks. They walk out together, shoulders hunched over, carrying the weight of the world, and I compare it to the two young carefree stags I used to know. How life changes and meanders like a great river bending against the rocks. I grab a cranberry juice because I've got work to do later, and walk over to the pool house.

'How is Ewan?' Tony asks, and I look away. Jeremy answers.

'Yeah, his reaction was intense. I guess he feels shame about wanting harm to come to him, but I've explained to him that it's what we all want for our tormentors, Brandon didn't die because Ewan wished him ill,' Jeremy says.

I marvel at his lucidity, but then he's using my words from how I explained it to James. I catch myself for almost believing that he could be intelligible. It's an easy mistake.

'Always psychoanalysing, mate,' Tony says. It's a moment of lightness and I settle into my seat. The pool house is shady and cool. I know I'm in for a long day. I'm itching to go and comfort my children and try to answer all their questions about Monika, but I need to at least listen to Tony, before he and Jeremy get totally inebriated, then I can leave them to it.

'Whiskey? JD? Or plain old vodka, mate?' Jeremy lists the intoxicating substances needed by the pair to drown their sorrows this afternoon. I stay quiet.

'JD will do, mate,' Tony says.

Jeremy busies himself with drinks.

'Thanks for having me over. I need it. Between the mortuary last night, and the police station this morning, my weekend is about the shittiest I can remember.'

'How was it?' I ask him. It's a simple, if trite question, but I want to at least give him the opportunity to get it off his chest. It must have been a horrific experience for him, viewing the body of his murdered wife.

'I don't need therapy right now, if that's what you mean. But I will say it was horrendous. She looked ghastly.'

'I'm sorry,' is all I can think of to say. The rest will come later, after his throat has been oiled by JD.

'I'm their prime suspect,' he adds.

I hear Tony and Jeremy's voices and they merge into one rumble as Jeremy drones on about what the police can and can't do. I know Kingston, and Tony doesn't really need legal advice, but Jeremy hasn't been this animated for months so I sit and behave myself. I look back to the house.

'What evidence have they got?' I ask.

They both stop talking and stare at me.

'Well, zero. I was asleep all night.'

It wasn't really what I was asking, but I let it go. Perhaps it's too soon.

'So, you've got nothing to worry about,' I say.

Tony sighs deeply. 'It's not as simple as that. Last night, when they came to my house I was… erm… with another woman.'

Tony looks at Jeremy for a reaction. I already know what a spectacular fuck up, even by Tony Thorpe's standards, he's made, but we don't share all our conversations with Jeremy. We never have.

'It looks bad,' he adds. 'I know, you can say it. I'm a total bastard.'

'Come on, mate, you need this,' Jeremy says, topping him up. Jeremy's answer to everything.

'Was Monika carrying on as well?' I ask.

Jeremy glares at me.

'Because that would be a good reason for you to seek comfort somewhere else,' I say.

Jeremy tries to interject but he's not keeping up. I'm crafting reasonable doubt for a potential jury. Jeremy is simply background noise.

'Yes, she was,' Tony says.

'So, do you know with whom? The police need to look there.'

'Kingston told me to leave that one until we need it.'

'Need what?' Jeremy asks, about three days behind the rest of the people in the room. I must go to Planet Jeremy some time – it seems infinitely simpler than here. But then I remember that he's on it, and it loses its allure.

'An alternative suspect,' I tell him.

Chapter 40

Natalie Morgan sat swinging her legs underneath the breakfast bar in her parents' kitchen, plugged into Apple Music. Mum was at her yoga class and Dad was at the golf club. The house was deliciously hers, for a few hours, until her brother appeared. There was nothing else to do on a Saturday lunchtime, in the heat, other than chill and drink cold fizzy sodas. Arch sauntered in and peered in the fridge, swatting her on the head as he went by. She caught his hand and they tussled playfully.

'Oh my God!' Natalie said, dropping her hand.

'What?' Arch asked.

Natalie took her headphones out of her ears and her mouth hung open.

'What is it?'

She turned her phone around and showed him a Snapchat message from one of her mates. He read it and the milk he'd got out of the fridge slid from his hand and it tipped over the edge of the marble island. Natalie jumped off her stool and grabbed a towel, trying frantically to contain the spread of the liquid. As she was holding the dripping towel over the sink, Arch turned to her.

'Is it a joke?' he asked.

'I don't know. Put the TV on,' she said.

He did, and flicked around the news channels. The story popped up straight away. It was hogging the headlines, and journalists, reporters and photographers were clamouring for airspace as piece after piece was reported about Brandon Stand. As well as some dead woman.

'*Brandon Stand's tragic death has shocked the small community… He was seventeen years old and the son of local headmaster, Terrance Stand, who received panicked phone calls from his friends shortly before midnight telling him that his son was in trouble. An ambulance was called to the botanic gardens at shortly before one o'clock this morning, and he was rushed to Cambridge University Hospital, where it was ascertained that Brandon had taken an ecstasy tablet. The drug is a recreational favourite amongst young people for the psychedelic sensations it induces… There is growing concern here in the city of Cambridge… Brandon…'*

'What did you do with the Molly I gave you?' Arch asked.

'I sold it,' she said.

'Who to?'

Natalie looked back to the TV screen, and began to shake, and then cry.

'Nat! What did you do with the gear I gave you?'

He pelted out of the room and she heard his feet on the stairs.

'Arch! What are you doing?' she shouted.

'Getting rid of my shit!' he hollered back.

She sprinted up the stairs to help him, at a loss of what else to do. She watched him empty boxes, flush bags down the toilet and hide rolls of cash in the flower boxes outside his window.

'Are you going to help or just stand there?' he demanded.

She got to work and it calmed her nerves but it was no easy task, Arch had shit hidden everywhere.

They froze at the sound of the doorbell.

It rang again. Natalie went to Arch's window and peered out of it. She saw a police car and ducked below the windowsill. 'Crap!'

'What?' Arch asked her.

'The police.'

They crouched under the window and Natalie begged him to tell her what to do, then they heard the door open downstairs.

'Archibald! Natalie!'

Their parents were home.

'Get off, Nat! You're pulling me!' Arch said. She hadn't realised she was holding on so tight.

'Archibald! Natalie! Come down at once.'

It was their father.

Arch went first and Natalie followed. The walk down the stairs was interminable and Natalie's heart beat out of her chest. The officers stared at her but it was the one in a suit she was most scared of.

'This is Detective Inspector Hunt, and he wants to ask you two some questions,' their father said.

They walked like men shackled on death row into the lounge and the officers were fussed over by their mother.

'I'd like to speak to the kids alone, sir,' Hunt said.

Dad glared at the man in the suit and Natalie pleaded with him inside her head for him to say no. But he didn't. One by one they were taken into the lounge. Arch went first. When he came out, he looked pale and beaten. He didn't look at her.

Then it was her turn.

The man called Hunt smiled at her and she sat down.

'Natalie, were you at the rec with your brother last night?'

Natalie was confused: had Arch told them he was there?

'I went there for a bit.'

'Did you see Brandon Stand?'

She nodded.

'Are you aware that your brother deals in Class A drugs?'

She shook her head.

'Did you see Brandon receive drugs from anyone?'

She shook her head.

'Who were you with?'

'Friends.'

'Names?'

'Ewan Moore and Noah Ashton.'

She felt like a traitor. She gave their addresses too.

Next, they showed her photographs of people she didn't know, until she came to one of Henry, the guy who came into school. He was funny, and all the girls loved him.

'Does Henry Nelson talk about his criminal past when he attends George Paget School?'

Natalie couldn't speak.

'Has Henry Nelson ever offered to get you drugs?'

She shook her head violently.

'Do you know what these are?'

The detective showed her a photo of a plastic bag containing tiny blue pills.

She shook her head.

'You don't have to protect Mr Nelson, Natalie. If he supplied them to Brandon Stand then you can tell us and we'll be on our way. Remember, a young man has lost his life. This is very serious, Natalie.'

A knock on the door saved her. An officer peered around it and informed the detective that her father had given them permission to search Arch's room.

Chapter 41

'I don't agree with Kingston on this. You need to lead the police to Monika's lover,' I tell Tony.

'You know better than a distinguished barrister, darling?' Jeremy slurs. He struggles with the assonance of distinguished and it sounds like *dish-gwings-dished*… It has too many syllables for him.

'Right, look. Let's work with what we've got. There's no point worrying about what the police might find. More importantly, you need to get your story straight about Tuesday night. What happened after Monika told you about her affair?'

They look at me as if I'm Inspector Morse. Tony gets up and paces up and down.

'The kitchen guy came round; he actually turned up at my house,' Tony says, as if he still can't believe it himself. I try to ignore an echo of recognition, and it puts me off track.

'Who?' Jeremy asks.

'She was fucking the kitchen fitter. I actually think she was going to leave me for him. He's got Nelson's Column on his van. I thought it was funny at the time, and quite clever. Nothing so solid, right? The best erection in town. Until he started screwing my wife. Henry Nelson, he's called.'

'Jesus,' Jeremy recoils in horror. I assess uncharitably that Jeremy is so indignant because it's not him that Monika decided to fuck. However, my more pressing dilemma is what Tony has just dumped on my already fraught nerves. Henry. This is news. I realise that Monika is the married woman he told me about and I feel the colour drain from my face. I know also that if there's anybody who can help us, it isn't Jesus. I keep my face straight, but my insides are turning over. I recover my faculties quickly.

'Let's start there. It won't be long before the police piece together the link between him and Monika, and you'll be in the clear. They'll have his van on CCTV somewhere, and that will be that,' Jeremy says. It's the most intelligent thing he's said all year. Or it would be if I didn't know that Henry has expert knowledge of the locations of all the CCTV cameras in Cambridge. I know this because he's told me that he actively avoids them, due to his criminal past. It's amazing what people reveal when they think their secrets are safe.

'What happened when he turned up?' I ask.

'I was upstairs. I heard them talking and he threatened to come and find me, she stopped him, then she left.'

'She left?'

Tony nods.

'With him?'

'No, on her own.'

'Where was he?'

'He came to the door, neither of us noticed her gone. He was doing his chivalry bit, and I found it amusing, but then we realised she was gone. He left then. Oh, God, it's a mess.' Tony sits back down heavily and spills his drink.

Jeremy fusses around him and goes to the house to get cloths. I turn to Tony.

'Who was the woman in your house last night, Tony?'

'Oh God, don't look at me like that Alex. She's a train buddy I've known for forever. She works in the city like me. I have no idea why I did it. We were high as kites, I suppose I just wanted a blow out.'

'Or blow job,' I say acidly.

He looks suitably contrite.

I say nothing. It's a problem we need to overcome if Tony isn't to be banged up for what happened to Monika.

'What's the copper like?'

'Who, Hunt? He's old school.' He sniffs. He's struggling with the gravity of it all, I haven't seen Tony this serious since…

'Do you think he believes you?'

'How the hell do I know that?'

'Come on, Tony. Think. That look between men, what's your instinct?' He looks at me and the penny drops. 'What did Kingston think?'

He recovers somewhat. 'He reckons they haven't got a shred of evidence and they know it.'

'So, you're allowed your panic attack, and your moment of loss of faith. Now, where's the Tony I know? Let's think this through rationally and give Hunt something to divert him.'

Jeremy comes back in and flaps over the spilt JD. He tops up Tony's glass.

'Everything is going to be all right, isn't it, Alex?' Jeremy asks me for help. I look at him curiously. I smile at both of them and am reminded that my two boys upstairs in the house, with all their immature fancies and habits, are more put together than these two.

'She was a mess.'

Jeremy and I freeze. I know what's coming, but he needs to get it off his chest. It will help him remove the emotion, and keep him sharp for the coming investigation, which will inevitably get rough, and so I encourage him.

'They let you see her?' I ask.

He nods.

'She was green and bloated, and the smell, dear God, the smell.' A sob escapes from his throat. 'Her face was still perfect, but the side of her head… well they tried to clean her up, but I could see how she died. She was like a broken doll. Oh God.'

We let him cry and we wait. Jeremy looks at me and I warn him with my eyes that we need to support him through this particular horror, it's the least we can do.

'Let it out. You're with people who love you,' I say.

'The smell…'

Jeremy covers his mouth as if he were in the room with her. I'm reminded of an abandoned cottage I found close to my house when I was eight years old. The walls crumbled and echoed with the sounds of children playing hide and seek. I trod on what I thought was a pile of twigs, but it was actually the fur of a rabbit, which melted away beneath the pressure of my foot, revealing a rotting corpse, alive with insects. It's a smell I'll never forget. The rabbit reeked of death.

Tony is still talking.

'I didn't see all of her, they wouldn't let me, just her face.'

I glance over at Jeremy, who has turned pale.

'They'll catch whoever did this,' I say. 'Forensic techniques are so precise now. They'll make sure every tiny scrap of evidence is collected. I work with the police occasionally, Tony, they have to be absolutely thorough to secure a conviction, you'll see.'

Jeremy nods.

'You need to ride this storm until the police get their real suspect. It was always going to start with you because you're the closest to her,' I tell him. 'We're going to get through this. Have your blow out tonight. Stay here, and in the morning, we'll put our heads together and, piece by piece, we'll work out where she went on Tuesday night.'

Chapter 42

Monday 13 July

One day before Monika's disappearance

Henry carried his toolbox inside the house and Monika followed him through to the kitchen. She wore shorts and a vest top but grabbed a cardigan from the hallway to cover herself and held it tight to her chest.

'Drink?' she asked.

She turned her back to him and popped the kettle on. Henry watched her and his body tensed. Normally, by now, she'd have flung herself at him, pressing her body onto his and forcing his t-shirt over his head. Like last night in his van...

The husband must be in.

He looked around but saw no signs of Mr Thorpe. The guy had lived a lot of life, you could see it around the house in the framed photos and furniture collected from afar. And he smelled of money. The tanned, clean skin and the shirts he chose to wear, open-necked, tucked into his pressed chino shorts, finished off with leather boat shoes for a casual at-home look, ready to jump on a yacht at any given moment.

He looked at her. It wasn't so much what women said that threw him into a blind panic, it was what they didn't say. The silence yawned between them. He stared at his toolbox and listened to the water bubble up inside the kettle. It seemed to take forever and she still hadn't turned around.

She walked to the huge American-style fridge and took milk out, still not looking at him.

'Is your foot okay?' he asked. She'd cut it last night when their concentration was otherwise engaged.

He dug around in the pit of the absence of an explanation for something to say, and it bounced off the walls that had been freshly plastered but had yet to be painted. Without the trinkets that make a room liveable – curtains, freshly hung pictures, the detritus of human movement – a new kitchen sounded like a morgue. The kettle flicked off and he jumped. She opened a drawer and Henry appreciated the craftsmanship in the soft close mechanism that he was so proud of. She rattled a teaspoon inside the sugar jar and it was like an orchestra of female scorn.

'Monika…'

She rounded on him. Her face was tired. She looked like she'd had a rough night.

'You know what I want,' she said.

She stirred the tea furiously, spilling a little on the side. The spreading brown liquid disturbed Henry's sense of order, because the marble worktop was porous and needed looking after. The seasons of a woman's moods were a mystery to him.

'Shall I—'

'No.'

She gave him his tea and he thanked her, cupping his hand around the fine china. His first cup was usually post coital, and accompanied by a wide grin, the warmth of the brew matching that of his newly spent loins, but he pushed the image away.

She looked at him directly for the first time now, and he saw the hurt in her big beautiful hazel eyes that reminded him of the horse chestnut conkers he'd lovingly polished as a kid.

'I need to get away, I can't stand it anymore,' she said.

Henry swallowed the hot tea and the cup scalded his hand. He put it down. He walked towards her but she shifted and pulled her cardigan tighter.

'I'm sorry. It's complicated. I can't just up and leave like you. I've built something from nothing and I have to work,' he said.

'I have money.'

'That's not the point.'

He didn't tell her that he couldn't breach his probation conditions…

Monika stared at him. Her hands relaxed a little around her cardigan, and it fell open.

He came closer and she allowed him to take her into his arms. A heartbeat's pause sat between them, then they both burst out laughing at the same time.

'I've wrapped my foot. I told Tony I banged it on a flower pot,' she said. The tension between them slid away.

'Hey, come here,' he said, pulling her closer.

She spoke into his chest. 'I'm not just another bored housewife.'

'No, you're not.' He kissed her.

'I'm ready to leave him, Henry,' Monika breathed into his shoulder, releasing his t-shirt from his shorts.

Henry reached his arms up over his head as his t-shirt slid off.

'Let's talk about it later,' he breathed heavily.

The kitchen was almost finished and he would no longer have an excuse to come here.

'Can I take you to bed?' he asked. 'Your bed?'

They'd explored every inch of the house entwined and eager for each other's pleasure, but never in her marital bed. He had no idea why he wanted to do it there, but he did. She nodded and led him by his hand through to the hallway and upstairs.

Chapter 43

Henry had a site visit to attend. He didn't feel like working, but he knew that it would take his mind off Monika. Business was booming. It was as if life was setting him up in a princely cabin in the sky, with everything he ever dreamed of: stability, money, and a beautiful woman; but then was planning to rip it all away, in a final plunge of the knife. And now she was gone. Murdered. He drove with a sense of foreboding.

The traffic was reasonable for a Saturday. He drove past shoppers laden with unnecessary rags and baubles, bought to fill a hole in their lives. One thing he learned in prison was that material stuff didn't matter. It was what was on the inside that counted. And that could be the most appalling place on earth, if you hadn't made your peace.

Now, his harmony was shattered. His whole body screamed at him to run, like Monika said. But that would make him look guilty as hell. He was reformed. His record, since leaving prison, was exemplary. He'd worked tirelessly for youths around the county. Surely any judge would see that?

But doubt rocked his mind cruelly, pulling it this way and that. *Stick to the facts*, he told himself.

He dialled Doctor Alex's number on his hands-free and waited. It went to voicemail. He left a short message.

'Hi, Doctor Alex, it's Henry Nelson. I'm sorry to disturb you at the weekend but I was wondering if I could get an emergency appointment? You said to call if I ever needed it. So, yeah... call me if you can. Cheers.'

He ended the call.

Between this job, and the one for the Thorpes, he'd filled his diary for twelve weeks solid. He'd even employed a labourer. His books looked healthy for the first time since he'd set himself up as a sole trader, two years ago. It had taken three years for him to claw his way back into mainstream life, after being banged up. He'd served eight of his sixteen-year sentence and had kept his head down. He'd seen more integrity inside than he ever did on the outside. He witnessed compassion and self-pride along those tiny cramped corridors. The problem was that the lessons learned were too late for most. He knew he was lucky to be given a second chance.

The man he'd killed had been lunging for him with a knife. His guilty plea to manslaughter had gone in his favour, else he'd still be rotting in there now. He got clean from drugs and booze the day he stepped into prison, and he hadn't touched anything since. When he stood in front of the kids in schools and told them his story, he said it with conviction and experience.

He considered Brandon Stand's class, and how they thought they were tough guys. Henry's time inside had given him a honed operative tool for seeking out idiots, and the headmaster's son was one. It didn't mean that what happened to him was deserved, it's just it came as no surprise. Henry reckoned whoever sold him his pills last night knew they were cut, or unusually high strength.

It was a tidal wave of bad shit that never stopped coming. One person, or even a hundred, walking the

219

streets, could never stop the incessant flow. All he could do was his small bit. He hoped that his work in the past couple of years would look good when the police came knocking, asking him about Monika Thorpe's last movements. The coppers would wet their pants when they found out he was an ex-convict, but he had to remain confident that the truth would win out. Monika was afraid for her life, but it wasn't because of him.

Carrie had reassured him over the phone, telling him to be vigilant but trust the process. The police were looking at the husband. She'd been evasive when he asked her how she knew so much, but then Carrie had a knack for finding out stuff that was well hidden. It's why he trusted her with his life. He knew she would be a character witness for him should he need it. She apologised for introducing him to Monika, he'd told her not to be stupid.

He parked the car and went to get his tool bag out of the back of the van. It wasn't closed properly, and a wrench fell out onto his foot. It hurt like hell and he swore loudly, picking it up and slamming it back into the bag, but as he did so, the wrench caught on some electrical wire, and his hand jolted with the sudden loss of forward momentum, slicing it on the top of a metal box. He swore and kicked the undercarriage of the van furiously. He looked at his hand and saw blood seeping out of the gash. Then a stinging pain engulfed his hand, and he realised that he'd done some serious damage. He fumbled around for a rag to wrap it, stilling the blood. After a couple of minutes, he checked it and saw that the bleeding had stopped, but a bruise was forming and he assessed the damage. A sinking feeling spread across his guts.

Chapter 44

Tony and Jeremy reminisce about the good old days and I know my part in this amateur production has come to an end. My need to stay sober today, not least for Ewan, who has had the shock of his life, overpowers my fleeting desire for booze. I can close the doors on Tony and Jeremy and get on with my day. The serious conversation of how to get Tony out of this mess is over. The rest of the afternoon will be a trip down memory lane that I don't wish to hear. Eventually, they'll turn maudlin and Sarah's untimely demise will come up. It's a conversation I don't need to be a part of. They were both in love with her.

I've had several missed calls on my phone and I excuse myself. They've forgotten that I'm not drinking and also how dull they have become because they are.

'Sorry, guys, I have to return some calls.'

'Nutters in need?'

Tony uses his pet name for my clients.

'Precisely. They don't stop being crazy just because it's the weekend.'

I walk towards the house and listen to my messages.

The first is from Carrie. She wants advice on something. She says she's had a shock and is struggling to control her triggers and she feels like using. It's a big deal because the woman has been dry for five years. The next one is from Grace. She tells me she's also had a shock and is suffering panic attacks. Henry's is the last I listen to, but like a typical man, he says the least out of the three. I hear his voice differently, armed now with what I know.

I take a deep breath and call Carrie first. She picks up, anxiously waiting for my call no doubt. I go into the lounge and close the door. No one can hear my private calls in here. It's nice and cool and it's one of the only rooms in the house where there isn't a need to assuage somebody's pain today. Until I listen to what Carrie tells me.

'Carrie, it's Doctor Alex. How are you doing?'

'Alex, thank you for calling me back at such short notice. I'm struggling a bit, if I'm honest.'

'Don't worry, I've made some time. Okay, start at the beginning. Take a deep breath, can you tell me a bit about why?'

'I did use,' Carrie said.

I wait. It doesn't take long for Carrie to fill in the details.

'It was shock, I guess. I freaked out when I heard noises in my house. I thought I was being burgled again. I was triggered, but I didn't see it coming. It got hold of me before I knew it. I went to a friend's house and accepted a drink, I didn't even think about the consequences. It led to other stuff and I'm so angry with myself.'

I can hear the anguish in her voice.

'So you made a mistake. Is anyone hurt?'

'No. Yes! Can I see you?'

It's a different Carrie I'm talking to, the one I met five years ago. It's a red flag.

'You said you thought somebody broke into your house?'

She's crying. I think I might have to see her today; the poor woman sounds broken. Something else has happened. I wait. It doesn't take long.

'My friend is in trouble. *I'm* in trouble. I'm caught up in something, Alex. With the police.'

'The police?'

'I went to the station in Cambridge this morning. They didn't delve into my past because I'm just a material witness at the moment, but if they do...'

'Why would they? What's your involvement in the case?'

'I'm not involved, it's just I know how the police work, remember? The way the detective looked at me, at Tony's house, I just know what he was thinking.'

'Tony?'

I close my eyes and a thousand pieces slot into place. *Henry screwing Monika... Tony screwing Carrie...*

'Just a friend, his wife is... dead.'

You're the train buddy that Tony was fooling around with last night when the police turned up. If it was DI Hunt I can only imagine what a smirk he will have had on his face. Cambridge just got even smaller. Carrie is still talking and I've never heard her like this before. She's terrified.

'You know how this goes, I'll be asked to testify. I'm involved now. Everything will come out. I'll be exposed.'

'Carrie, things have come on since the eighties. If it comes to that, I'll be your character witness. But it won't. Listen, why don't we meet tomorrow? I'll go into the office.'

My brain is whirring, I need to think.

'Really? That would be great, I feel... unhinged.'

'I can hear it in your voice. You say the police have already interviewed you?'

'Yes. I took my lawyer.'

'And are you in a relationship with this man?'

'No! It was a one off. I've caught the train to King's Cross with him for years. I don't even fancy him, Jesus Christ. He called me and stupidly, I went. I was panicking and I needed someone to talk to.'

'Come to my office at one p.m. tomorrow.'

· Carrie lets out a gasp. 'Thank you.'

We hang up but I hang on to my phone, as if it will give me the answers I crave. But there is somebody at the front door. I check the video intercom. A man peers back at me through the camera, and I press the mic and ask what he wants. He's probably a salesperson trying to flog cheap roofing.

He introduces himself as Detective Inspector Paul Hunt and I freeze.

'One moment please.'

I dart out of the lounge and out to the pool house to tell Tony and Jeremy to stay put. I will deal with Hunt. He can't snoop around without a warrant.

The colour drains from Tony's face.

I check my face in the hall mirror as if there is marker pen all over it telling him that his prime suspect in a murder case is sat in my pool house. I open the door.

'DI Hunt. Sorry about that, I had something cooking.'

'Ah, doc. We spoke over the phone.'

I make no move to invite him in.

'Lovely house.'

'Thank you.'

'Anyway, I thought I'd call round. It's a delicate matter.'

'Is this about Monika?'

Hunt's body language changes instantly and he apologises. 'No, not at all, I should have said. No, I'm here to talk about your son, Ewan. May I come in?'

Chapter 45

Hunt follows me into the lounge and I ask him if he'd like tea. He's checking out my house like a prospective buyer, but the ones who can't afford it and only come to peep.

'No, I'm good, but thank you. Is Ewan home?'

'Yes, but he's had a shock. It's not a good day.'

We sit opposite one another on armchairs, and I wonder what it'd be like to analyse Hunt. I have my opinions, of course. Like all humans, I judge within seven seconds of meeting somebody, and it's not good. Hunt reminds me of the hare in a hurry from the famous fable. He's keen to get answers, but probably hasn't got the mettle to commit to the race. He's under pressure, I can see that. He's been busy this morning, I'm not his only call – I know that from Tony – and with a murder on his hands, he's only just getting started. He'd probably rather be relaxing at home, watching *Match of the Day*, or down the pub with his other copper pals, talking shop. He's already got sweat patches under his arms, and his suit is tired. He wishes he'd gone to college and got a better-paying job, but he messed around at school.

'Like I said, Ewan's got a lot on his plate today. The boy's death in the news – he went to school with Brandon Stand, you see, and then—'

'That's what I'm here about.'

'Sorry?'

'Brandon Stand.'

'Oh. Is this to do with the assault on Wednesday?'

'No, sorry, I wasn't aware of that.'

'Brandon was Ewan's bully.' I let it hang.

'I see. That makes sense.'

'Pardon?'

Hunt takes one of those long sighs that coppers do when they think the layperson has missed something obvious, because civilians, to them, are quite simple creatures.

'There have been developments in the case of Brandon's death, and we've made an arrest this morning for supplying the pills that killed him. He had a lethal amount of MDMA in his system. Enough to fell a racehorse.'

'Crikey.'

I bet racehorses aren't so stupid.

'Does the name Archibald Morgan mean anything to you?'

'Yes, I know his parents. Ewan goes to school with his sister, Natalie.'

'Exactly. Well it's Archibald who has been arrested and Natalie has also been questioned. We think that Archibald gave her the pills and she sold them to Brandon, and I wonder if it might have been on purpose. Your son was with her last night.'

I can feel the cranberry juice from earlier gurgle in my belly and I think I want to rewind to sometime last week when my life seemed so much easier. It's acidic in my mouth. I'm fighting my instincts because I want to scream at him, but I need to remain calm.

'So you can see, doc, why I might want to speak to your son.'

Behind Hunt is a family photo, framed after a trip to the Serengeti. The children are pointing at a lioness and her cubs and I know what she is thinking. Ewan smiles back at me and my heart rate slows. I'm in control.

'Goodness. The day that keeps on giving.'

'Doesn't it?' Hunt says.

I read his body. He's uncomfortable. He doesn't want to implicate a well-to-do boy, the son of a decorated psychologist who offers no resistance to his questioning.

'I've just told my children what happened to Monika.' I let it sit.

'You must come across this all the time. The way families implode when something so awful happens. Monika was a family friend. Ewan was close to her.'

'I'm sorry.'

'Brandon Stand, on the other hand, was Ewan's tormentor for years. He's blaming himself for what happened to Brandon, but I know my son. This friend, Natalie, who says she was with Ewan last night – has she said that Ewan had anything to do with the drugs?'

'I can't really divulge—'

'I know. I work with the police all the time. I'm restricted by the same rules with my clients. We're bound by confidentiality. But sometimes, it's also good to share information and expedite, if you follow me.'

I can see his relief open his body to me. He's thinking how lucky he is to have a fellow professional to be technically smug with.

'Off the record, it looks like Archibald Morgan is a seasoned dealer. He's looking at manslaughter. The sister wants naturally to protect him and so she's willing to take the fall for him. She's swearing she took the pills and gave them to Brandon. But what we're really after is their supplier.'

I'm not really interested in the motives of other people's children. My allegiance is to my own.

'So, Ewan's physical presence at the rec last night might land him in the dock as a witness?'

Hunt nods.

'Can you give me time with my son? I need to speak to him and get to the truth. You know how a police officer can put people off.'

He smiles. His oral hygiene needs work.

'He's also a minor.'

'I'm not suggesting that I want to haul him in, if that's what you mean. I can give you time. You can feed back to me when you've had time to chat. Say, tomorrow? I'll give you my mobile number so you can contact me.'

I take his card and smile at him.

'Have you found who killed Monika?'

He sighs again but this time he's inviting me into his quandary with him as a fellow expert.

'We'll get him, that's for sure. I'm looking into several options. I don't want to brag, doc, but my background is in expert profiling, and I can say with certainty that we're looking for a narcissist.'

I almost regurgitate my cranberry juice, which is dangerously creeping up my oesophagus. He has no idea what he's talking about. However, his incompetence might work in my favour.

'A narcissist?'

'Yup. The feeling of power they get when they take control, and, you know, their sense of entitlement.'

I nod. He's way off the mark. Personality disorders are complex, and I've got one sat right in front of me, that's for sure.

'I have a feeling that your inquiries will lead back to me all in good time. I can save you the trouble,' I say.

'Come again?'

'I'm a therapist, Mr Hunt. I have some very wealthy local clients, and at some point you'll be asking me for a warrant to open my files, because this is a small town with a shortage of experts offering what I do. Monika's name came up in several of my case histories.'

'Is that ethical?'

It's a fair question, but one I've already looked into.

'As long as my clients aren't related, or connected to me in some way, I can treat them. There are certain scenarios when I might refuse treatment, for example, I can't treat my own family, or friends. Monika wasn't a client.'

'But you're telling me that you do treat one or more people who knew her?'

I nod. 'I'm sure you probably haven't even heard of them, and I'm sure it's nothing, but Monika meant a lot to us. If I can help in any way. Henry Nelson is one and Carrie Greenside the other. I also treat Grace Bridge, Monika's personal trainer.'

I can tell by Hunt's face that his bells are going off like Santa's sleigh on Christmas Eve and he can taste victory. Maybe he'll get a pay rise if he cracks this case quickly.

'I've already checked with my governing body. I haven't crossed any professional lines. They were distinctly separate cases. Until now.'

'Did you treat Tony Thorpe?'

'No. He's been a friend for many years. My husband and I were at university with Tony back in the day. He's a good example of somebody who I could never treat.'

'Your clients – the ones who you've mentioned – how well did they know Monika?'

He is well aware how well they knew Monika, but, like Ewan always tells me when we play Monopoly, he's on Pall Mall and I'm already on Mayfair.

'Can I suggest something? My priority right now is my son. I need to talk with him. Then, I'll gather together some information for you about when Monika's name came up in my sessions. Petition an emergency court order for my files. It might be helpful if you also request a formal meeting with me for this, so we tick all the boxes. Client confidentiality is watertight in my profession unless there is a crime suspected, of course.'

He raises his eyebrows because he didn't think I'd know how investigations work, but I do.

'Of course. I'll leave you to speak to your son. Call me tomorrow.'

'I'm sure you've got a hell of a day ahead.'

We stand. He sighs and I reckon he's replaced the air in my house twice over.

'Tomorrow.'

I show him out but once he's gone, I can still smell him all over the house.

Chapter 46

'Ms Greenside?'

'Yes.' The fine hairs on Carrie's arms stood up. She held the phone tightly as she stood in her hallway.

'It's DI Hunt. I'd like to ask you a few more questions, if I may. Can I pop over to see you?'

'Now?' Carrie asked. 'What's this about?'

'If it's convenient, I'll drive over right away. In fact, I'm close to your house.'

He hung up, not giving her a chance to even think. She could pretend she was out, but he'd called on her landline. Who did that? *Cops trying to catch you out, you dumb bitch.* She looked around her house frantically. What was she looking for? Anything incriminating. He wouldn't have a warrant: he didn't have cause, and he hadn't had time to secure one. But he'd turned up to Tony's last night with the right to search, how the hell had he managed to find a magistrate that quickly? Perhaps he was bent. They all were. She called her lawyer, but it went to voicemail.

She was nineteen again. The night her father sat bloodied and bruised in the back of a police car, bundled in there after they'd come to the house, when her mother called 999. But her mother hadn't done it to protect her daughter, she'd done it because Carrie was attacking *him*. She'd finally shown the courage to hit the bastard back and her own mother had called the police on her. She'd never spoken to her mother again after that night. That was the end of her years at home, if one could call it a home. She walked out and didn't look back, until she was arrested and charged with actual bodily harm.

Her hands shook. She dialled Tony's number. He answered, and she could tell straight away that he'd been drinking.

'Tony, can you talk?'

'Carrie? I'm with friends, wait, let me move into another room. Er, yes, how are you? I've been thinking about coming over, I need to apologise. And you need to collect your car.'

'There's no time for that. The police are on the way to my house, right now. That detective, Hunt, what does he know?'

'What do you mean?'

'Tony, listen to me: he's coming here, right now, I need to know what you told him this morning.' She sighed. 'When did you last see your wife?'

'Tuesday. She was drunk and she fell and hit her head.'

'What else?'

'I went to bed and left her ranting.'

'Ranting about what?'

'I don't know! The usual shit.'

'But you didn't say that to the police, right? You came across as a loving husband who made a mistake asking me over because you were grief-stricken and lonely?'

'Sort of, I told them she was a prostitute.'

'What?'

'I hired a private detective to find out about her past, you know, so I had something on her.'

'No, I don't know why you would do that.'

'Well it turns out I wasn't far off the mark, she was carrying on with other men.'

Carrie let the sinister irony go.

'Have they got anything on you?'

'Like what?'

'Evidence that you ever hit her, or cheated with anyone else? Fucking hell, Tony, have they surprised you with anything?'

'No. I don't think so.'

'Have they been snooping around any other friends?'

'Not that I know of. Oh, wait, they were interested in our kitchen fitter. In fact, I might have let on that she had a thing going with him.' He hiccupped and Carrie felt sick. 'I can't remember what I told them, I was exhausted, I identified my dead wife late last night.'

She closed her eyes. 'Henry Nelson? Are you talking about the kitchen fitter I recommended? Nelson? The one with Nelson's Column on his van? The one I recommended?' She repeated herself. He'd already confirmed that Henry did the work on her recommendation, when she stood in his kitchen admiring it. She needed it affirming again. She held her breath.

'Yes, him. Turns out she was screwing him all along.'

'What do they want with him?'

'No, wait, I didn't tell them about him, just a friend. Christ, Carrie, my brain is mush. I need to see you,' he said.

'Tomorrow. I need to think. Get some sleep. Where are you?'

'At a friend's.'

'Are you drunk?'

'Are you my mother?'

She hung up.

The doorbell rang and she jumped, dropping her phone. She ran into the hall and took the stairs two at a time. She sprinted into her bedroom and went to the wardrobe, flinging back her clothes, revealing the safe she kept in there. She froze. It was open.

The doorbell rang again.

She checked the safe. The knife was still there but the cash was gone. She slammed the door shut and punched in the code, and covered the unit with a thick coat she wore for formal events. Then she thought against it and removed the bulky garment, and opened the safe again, taking the knife and crawling under her bed. Under there, she unzipped her mattress cover from the underneath and ripped open the foam layer, stuffing the weapon inside it, zipping the whole thing back up again. It had been a stupid, momentary moment of madness. To hide such a thing for somebody who was a virtual stranger to her.

She crawled back out of the tiny space and looked in the mirror, straightening her hair and her clothes, and pinching her cheeks.

The doorbell rang again.

She ran down the stairs and went to the door, opening it.

'Sorry, I was in the bathroom,' she said to DI Hunt.

He stood with his hands in his pockets, examining her, and she had the same visceral reaction to him as she had at Tony's house. She wanted to punch his face and wipe the grin off it.

'Come in,' she said. She watched him cross her threshold and the tiny hairs on her neck stood up. Like vampires: once you let the cops in, they didn't leave until they sucked you dry.

Her heart had settled, and she showed no outward signs of panic. Despite being alone with a man she didn't trust, in a house that had been invaded once again: she was sure of it. She certainly hadn't touched the money; why would she? She didn't need it. Somebody had been inside her bedroom and her alarm hadn't sounded. Had she been in the house at the time? Or was it last night when she'd come home to the alarm disabled? She'd dismissed the noises as neighbourly cats, but panic gripped her and now she wasn't so sure.

This time she wouldn't report it to the police; she didn't need any more attention from them right now than she already had.

Hunt stepped into the hallway and looked around, hawkish, and Carrie felt as though he were assessing her whole soul. She closed the door and showed him into the kitchen at the back of the house. Instinctively she went to the back door and checked it was locked. It wasn't. She silently chastised herself.

'Can you give me a minute? I think I have a cat problem.'

She didn't wait for him to reply. She walked round the back of the house and went to the control box for the alarm, which was situated on the wall to the side. The flap was open and her heart sank. The whole system was down. No lights illuminated the panel and she swore under her breath at being duped by yet another incompetent company. They'd assured her that the console was impenetrable from the outside, but here she was, staring at it, wondering how anybody could have manipulated it so expertly. The master control was inside, of course, and only an expert, or somebody inside the company, could possibly know how the networked functioned. She cast her mind back to the last time she'd checked it, and it had been before she left for Tony's yesterday afternoon, so whoever had been in, it had to have been then. Her skin went cold despite the heat, and she shivered. She swore nothing else had been disturbed. She chastised herself for being an idiot, but she had been so thrown by the events last night that she hadn't checked the system properly before she went to bed, assuming it was another test. How remiss of her. She felt like she was losing her hold on reality. The fragility of her situation shocked her and she went back to the kitchen.

'Cats sorted?' Hunt asked. He'd made himself comfortable at the kitchen bar. Her chest felt tight, as if Hunt was sat on it.

'One of the locals likes to hang out here,' she said. She forced a smile. 'Can I get you a drink?' she asked, trying to delay whatever it was he'd come to say.

'Thank you, anything cold,' he said.

She got him a glass of ice and water from the fridge. She felt him staring at her as she moved around and he made her feel like a caged animal.

The fact was, she didn't have to let him into her home. However, she knew that he already saw her as a person of interest because she was sharing his prime suspect's stash of cocaine, and his bed. This was her opportunity to change his mind.

'So, how can I help you?' she asked, turning back to him. He took the water. She stood, leaning against the counter with her arms crossed.

'Great place you have here,' he said.

She didn't reply.

'You've come a long way.'

She felt her clothes tight on her body and wanted to adjust them but couldn't move lest she betray her true intentions towards him. She had a passing vision of plunging a knife into his neck and she tried to free it from her mind.

'I mean, from your record. I looked you up. You did a nasty job on your dad. And look at you now.'

Carrie froze. How the hell did he know about that? She thrust her memory into overdrive and went over everything she knew about DI Hunt's investigation so far. Then what Tony told her slammed into her conscious and made her stop breathing for a miniscule beat. An expert would have logged this unconscious action as a sign of stress, but she hoped DI Hunt was no expert.

Henry Nelson. The police would always look for somebody with a past, and Tony had just told her that he couldn't remember if he'd told the police about him or not.

'Why is my history interesting to you?' she asked.

'Well, here's the thing. I've got drugs popping up all over the place in my most pressing inquiries, not just the murder of Monika Thorpe, but the murder of Brandon Stand too. The kid who died last night. I reckon they got their ecstasy from the same dealer as your friend Tony.' He grinned like a wolf.

'Murder? I thought the child overdosed,' she said calmly. She'd watched it on the news, like everyone else in Cambridge. She hadn't known the boy, so why was Hunt bringing him up? Maybe Henry had. From his work at the school. The penny dropped. They were framing Henry.

She closed her eyes for what she felt was hours, but she knew was only half a second. In that time, she regretted ever meeting Henry Nelson. Falling for his brawn. It was as if she were drawn to him to help her bridge her present and her past. He massaged her ageing ego and healed her wounded inner child. A piece of frivolous fun with the kitchen fitter, but a momentary liaison that turned into a deeper connection. Until he met Monika. Maybe she recommended him to Tony on purpose, because she knew he was dangerous baggage. Just like she rid herself of all impediments in her life.

'Our enquiries have taken us in the direction of murder – or manslaughter, however you like to dress it up – because we think that Brandon might have been supplied dodgy pills on purpose.'

'I don't like your tone, Detective. I don't think I would ever "dress up" death. And as for Brandon Stand's drug supplier, I have no idea. I've been dry for five years.'

'Until last night.'

She felt her cheeks burn.

'Henry Nelson fitted your kitchen, right?'

'He did.'

'It's beautiful. He's very talented.' He ran his fingers along the marble counter, caressing it, and Carrie thought she might throw up. 'He fitted Monika's new kitchen too.'

'Monika, as in Tony's wife?' she asked.

He nodded.

'Just her kitchen, not Tony's?' Her sarcasm was lost on him, but his misogyny made her burn.

'I'm thinking Monika was quite taken by the young man. He looks after himself in the gym. She even wanted to leave her husband for him. The third wheel always knocks a marriage off balance.'

Carrie watched him slither his fingers along her counter and wondered if he was whispering lies into her ear, like all hissing fiends, just to get her to jump over the precipice. Henry hadn't told her that Monika was leaving Tony for him. But it made sense.

'But perhaps the feelings weren't reciprocated, I mean, to a young fit guy like Henry, she'd have just been a bit on the side. Drug her up and get rid of her when she got clingy,' he said.

Carrie took in what he was saying and saw where he was going. It wasn't so farfetched, but she still didn't believe it. Henry wouldn't hurt anyone. But he had. He'd been inside for eight years for it.

'I have no idea about that, but we no longer live in the 1970s and it takes more than a gym body for a woman to be "taken in", as you put it. Why would you under-estimate Monika? I didn't know her but she sounds like a discerning woman to me.'

'Not enough to earn your respect though? Didn't you feel uncomfortable having a mini party with her husband when she was missing?'

'I feel as though this conversation is more about my private life than your investigation, and if that's the case, you need to leave. You came uninvited and I've given you my time. What exactly are you getting at?'

He took a sip of water and the clink of the ice grated on her nerves.

'I'm piecing together a picture of my victim, and so far, I get the impression that somebody would be better off without her around. Who supplied the cocaine that you took with Tony last night? Was it you? Or was it Henry Nelson?'

Carrie had refused a blood test last night, as was her right. The detective's story of drugs and debauchery was at best circumstantial, but in court, with her past, it wouldn't look good. She'd beaten up her father, she'd lived on the streets as an addict, and her mother had testified that she was a liar. Society didn't like people who came good, not after all that shit; it liked to keep losers down, or else where did that leave everybody else? If you could climb up the greasy pole and triumph over adversity then it left no excuse for those who didn't make it. She felt trapped but, at the same time, her overwhelming sense of injustice fuelled rage. It was just like being hidden in her bedroom again, waiting for her father to find her and act out his self-loathing on the easiest target around: his defenceless child. Suddenly, the detective's face morphed into her father's and she saw him, red-eyed and full of hate, coming toward her, about to rip out her heart, again and again.

The noise of glass being placed on the counter jerked her away from the vile image and she saw Hunt getting up from his seat.

'How well did *you* get to know Henry Nelson when he was fitting you out?' he said. The upturn of the sides of his mouth made her shake inside.

She saw scores of faces behind his: all police, and all men.

'I've got daughters, it can be tricky.'

'Are you antagonistic?'

'Do you get on his wrong side?'

'Your bruises aren't that bad, did you fall over and hurt yourself?'

'Your school grades are pretty poor, did it disappoint your parents?'

Her eyes glassed over as she tried with every fibre of her body to keep control. Her fingernails dug into her arms; sweat trickled softly down her back.

'Are you feeling okay?'

It was Hunt who spoke and she was brought back to the present moment.

'There's my card. If you think of anything else, no matter how insignificant you might think it is, please give me a call. We'll get to the truth eventually. We always do. Henry Nelson is next on our list, so I'm sure he'll clear up any gaps for us.' He smiled again and flashed his stained, crooked teeth. He left the kitchen and went to the hallway. She followed him. He opened the door and turned to her.

'Your burglary five months ago,' he said. 'They've started up again. Kids looking for drug money. Keep everything locked.' And then he was gone.

She staggered into the kitchen, took his glass, and smashed it on the floor. Knife-like shards of crystal flew everywhere and she stood panting over the mess, her face contorted in stormy wrath.

Chapter 47

It's an hour since Hunt left. As he backed out of my driveway earlier, I watched him smile at me and nod confidently with collusion. It was a signal that told me we're in a secret conspiracy together, like two children who are planning not to tell their parents about a broken ornament. In the kitchen, I'm still peering out at the pool house, deciding what to do next. I need an ice-cold glass of water. The house is mausoleum quiet, and my children are more than likely plugged into electronics trying to forget the horror of two deaths in one morning – or at least the news of them.

Tony and Jeremy are jumpy when I go out to tell them all is clear.

'What did he want?' Jeremy asks me breathlessly.

I want to laugh out loud because they look as though I've caught them hiding like schoolboys and it reminds me of what they were like at university. Thick as thieves. I always used to dig them out of trouble then, too.

'Relax, it was actually about the boy, Brandon Stand. They're interviewing kids who knew him and might have seen him at the rec last night.'

'What's he doing on that case?' Jeremy asks me.

He does this. He thinks I have all the answers. But then later he hates me for it.

'Is Ewan in trouble?' Tony asks.

'No, I told the detective that I'll speak to him in good time, we've all had a shock. I'm going to do that now. I'm sorry, Tony, I need to make sure he's okay.'

'Of course. Please, he's much more important right now.'

Jeremy looks at us oddly and he seems out of place. He is. His best friend is more focused on his son than he is. But I don't have time for his feelings as well. I leave without saying anything else.

They'll no doubt get drunker and reminisce about the good old days. All Tony needs right now is reassurance from a pal, and that's what he's getting, he doesn't need me. He will when he's sober.

I'm relieved to be walking through the house and up the stairs to Ewan's room, because the conversation I'm about to have will be infinitely lighter than the one I've just left. To Ewan, it'll feel like his world is caving in, but he hasn't lived enough life yet to understand measure. It's tragic that a boy has died, but Brandon Stand was a vicious individual and these kinds of accidents happen all the time. To my son this is serious, and so I'll treat it as such. He's got me to make the problem disappear, unlike Jeremy or Tony, who only have themselves.

I knock, but there's no answer and I'm not surprised when I push the door ajar and he's under his duvet, head-phones on, neck in an awkward position, fast asleep. I steel a glance at him for a second because it's an opportunity I don't get often. He looks like his father.

I sit gently on the edge of his bed and touch his shoulder.

'Hey.'

He stirs. I take off his headphones.

'Hi, Mum.'

'Can we talk?'

'Yeah, sure. What happened?'

Fear haunts his eyes, which are red from crying. He wipes them, not wanting me to work it out. His room is that of a child; painted blue, with trophies and shields boasting his sporting prowess littering his table, scarves from football matches he's attended with Tony hanging on the walls, along with posters of beautiful popstars he'd love to meet, but wouldn't know what to do if he did.

'I need to talk to you about something important.'

He sits up. 'Monika?'

'No. Natalie Morgan.'

He shifts his weight in his bed and my body moves slightly with the motion.

'I had a policeman come to the house.' His eyes widen. 'I want you to do one thing for me,' I tell him.

'What?' he mutters breathlessly.

'Tell me the truth.'

'About the pills?'

'About what we will tell the police.' I place my hand on his cheek. 'Everything will be okay. Tell me what happened last night.'

Since he was a baby, looking into my eyes for his world, he'd been the one who clung to me, the one who was what the textbooks call easy. I know it's a label that's thrown around when a child is compliant, but the bond between us is simple. He begins to speak and I listen quietly, non-judgemental in my posture, to every word. He tells me about the girl who's dominated his school life for the last couple of years. His world with Natalie in it makes him feel as though he has a tribe. A world where he's important and accepted. His voice is steady and sure, and I bask in the glory of him opening his heart to me.

I don't interrupt. I let him finish. He tells me about the rec last night, and what Natalie said about the bag of little blue pills. Her wink. His body freezing in time.

'I knew what she was going to do, Mum. I didn't stop her.'

He buries his head in my clothes and I can smell him. It's an aroma of innocence. I hold him for a long time as he exorcises his anguish.

Finally, his sobs cease and I hold his head in my hands and take him to me, hugging him close.

'Am I in trouble? What will happen?' he asks. He's terrified.

'I don't know.' I'm telling the truth. Supplying Class A drugs at their age might land the girl a stint in juvenile rehab. If Hunt wants a head to roll and they're after someone for manslaughter, Ewan might be seen as complicit, if he ever takes the stand.

His life will be ruined. Even a caution on his record will stay there until he's eighteen.

'What about Noah?'

'He was there too, he didn't know either, Mum. That's not what he does.'

It's a curious defence and I'm keen to know exactly what Noah's hustle is if it isn't the same as Natalie's. I don't need to verbalise a question, Ewan knows he's rumbled. There's something else.

'Mum, I'm sorry, I...'

'Hey, look, the only way I can help is if you tell me the truth. What happened after Natalie gave Brandon the pills? Did you see him take them?'

He shakes his head. I exhale inwardly. He wasn't there when the lad imbibed the poison that would kill him, thank God.

'We went to a house. Noah does it sometimes. He likes to take stuff.'

My gut travels to my toes, like it does when I'm on Tony's yacht and he grins when he turns the mainsail so quickly that we all lunge to one side.

'Other people's stuff?'

A small nod.

'You went to a house and Noah likes to take other people's stuff. Are you telling me that you broke into a house?'

Ewan's pallor is pale green.

'We didn't really break in; Noah disabled the alarm.'

'You, Natalie and Noah were there? Who else?'

'Just us.'

'Did you get caught?'

He shakes his head.

'I wiped everything clean.'

My son is an honest thief. Still, my face doesn't change.

'The police didn't mention anything about a break-in. They're interested in the drugs, let's stick to that for now.'

'But won't they find out? Noah took a tonne of cash. We found a knife, it was a big one, but we left it.'

'Wait, what? A knife?'

'It was in the safe, wrapped up with the cash. It was some kind of weapon, Mum, it was massive.'

For a second, I fear I'm drowning and I can't save him, but I quickly pull myself together. The wheels on this cart began turning well before Ewan broke into a house and stole somebody else's cash. This was never going to be something that was sorted hastily.

'Where was this house?' I distract him.

He describes it and tells me that when he passed Tony and Monika's the police were there.

'Noah chose it because she sacked his dad. That's why he took the cash. Mum, I've got everything and he has nothing. That's why I hate the bikes. I don't want any more.'

I nod.

'What did you do with the money?'

'Nat hid it.'

'Where?'

He shrugs.

My body aches with exhaustion. Suddenly all I want to do is lie down. I smile at him.

'What will happen?' It's all he wants, like any child. Reassurance.

'Is there anything else?'

He shakes his head and I believe him.

'I'll talk to the police, everything will be all right, I promise. Brandon's death is not your fault. Let me worry about the burglary. They're two separate things.'

He looks at me oddly, as if he expects to be beaten, or locked away. His shoulders droop with the unburdening of anxiety, and my job here, for now, is done.

'You need to tell me exactly where you're going from now on and you need to stay away from Noah and Natalie until this is all over, do you understand?'

He nods.

'What will you tell the police?'

'Let me worry about that.'

I stand up.

'Fancy some ice-cream?'

He nods.

'I'll get it.'

I close his door gently and want to kick something hard, but then pull myself together and go downstairs.

The kitchen is a mess from breakfast and I decide that my anger is best taken out on the dishes. Jeremy and Tony will be no company now, and I need a clear head. There are leftover strawberries in a bowl and they're going brown and warm, their delicate life withering away already. They're so vulnerable to the heat. I can't save them and so I go to put them in the bin but I knock the bowl against a glass of cranberry juice and the damn thing falls onto the floor. There are pulverised strawberries and red juice everywhere and I gaze helplessly in horror at the mess. I stand still in the middle of a crimson puddle and don't know which shard to sweep up first. Juice drips off my fingers.

A distant memory from long ago jumps into my head.

Sarah, at the bottom of the library tower, broken and pulped on the concrete, making gulping noises, like a scared animal. Paramedics kneeling, trying to talk to her and tell her to hang on. A crowd gathering to ogle at the spectacle. A woman screaming. Tony and Jeremy, nowhere to be found.

'He loves you…' she'd told me two days before we were due to leave.

I push the apparition away and rush to the sink to get a cloth and start wiping up the chaos. Tiny shards of glass have been fired at speed like missiles, all over the kitchen, and the sparkling disaster seems endless.

I recall the police interview and the aftermath of Sarah's suicide. I also remember that it was pronounced a suicide by the coroner after the police ruled out the presence of someone else on the roof.

Chapter 48

Monday 13 July

One day before Monika's disappearance

Monika put the phone down. She'd called Alex to see if she'd left a necklace of hers in the pool house when she changed into the bikini she'd borrowed on Sunday.

Alex said she'd look.

They'd had a brief chat about the kids, who Monika always asked after.

Ewan was being bullied again and Monika knew herself, coming from a foreign country and being judged unfairly in all kinds of ways here in Britain, how it felt. Her heart went out to the boy.

A long time ago, when Ewan was about eleven, and they hadn't known each other long, Monika had played with the children, finding more in common with them than with Tony's friends. She'd read him bedtime stories. She recalled his small body under the duvet, waiting patiently for her to begin. She read him a story about a little cat who gets lost and is found by a small boy wandering alone in the night, in his pyjamas. Ewan loved it. She remembered his perfect face set in the soft light as he always drifted off before the end of the story. The moment of trust was all consuming and she took the opportunity to gaze around his room. It was as if being in it reminded her of her own home, and eased the pain of missing her mother. Ewan had everything any child could possibly want. There were gaming consoles, planes, model engines, hundreds of books, electronics and signed photos of Ewan with celebrities. Her eyes fell on one in particular. It was of Ewan, Tony and Alex.

Alex had a monkey on her shoulder and Tony laughed openly and warmly; the kind of authentic transparency she'd seen rarely in her husband in the time she'd known him. It was a testimony to the part of Tony that he gave to other people. Especially this woman and this child. She'd peered back at the boy and traced his jawline with her eyes. His hair, and the way it flopped, the shape of his head and the way his top lip curled. She'd studied other photos of his brother and sister. James had his father's forehead: strong and wide. Lydia had his eyes.

Ewan had neither.

After reading to him, she'd crept out of bed silently and tucked him under his duvet, and felt an urge to bend over and kiss him. It was a maternal, pure and simple desire, but it had been halted by a noise in the corridor. She'd got off the bed and picked up the photo and looked closer. Then replaced it. She'd closed the door quietly and turned towards the corridor, just as Alex was going down the stairs.

Chapter 49

DI Hunt hated working on a Sunday. One, because the football was on and it was Super Sunday, and two, he wasn't paid enough. However, it would go some way to helping his promotion to DCI should he be seen to be going above the call of duty to get these cases wrapped up. What Doctor Moore had told him had spurred him on. Meanwhile, he was making progress on the Brandon Stand case. Archibald Morgan was in custody, but the sister had been allowed home because she was a minor, and hadn't yet been charged. Her brother was looking at seven years for possession. If they could prove he intended to supply, then they'd go for more. Natalie would remain in the care of her parents until her testimony was needed.

Natalie Morgan's confession, admitting she'd supplied Brandon Stand with the MDMA that killed him, provided a potential link between this case and the murder of Monika Thorpe. And that link was Henry Nelson. He was sure that the kids were just protecting him. The Morgan kids were small fry; they had to have suppliers of their own. An ex-con, like Nelson, had ample contacts to set up such an arrangement. From what they'd seen of the brother, Arch Morgan, he wasn't the kind of kid who'd established a complex network of contacts in the last year or so. He was clearly getting his drugs from somewhere, and that, Hunt felt, was the key. Bringing Henry Nelson in for questioning was a priority, but tracking him down was proving difficult. A squad car was tasked with waiting outside his house.

Hunt felt the sweet trickle of success coming ever closer but as one case jumped right into his lap, the other confounded him. His team had been picking through Monika Thorpe's past for almost forty-eight hours now, but their picture of the woman was different to that given to them by Tony Thorpe. He'd chatted to his team of detectives about her.

'It says here that she was a grade-A student, boss. She flew through her law degree and got a double first. We spoke to her mother who said her daughter worked for a law firm in Riga, before travelling and saving enough money to study a conversion course in London, but she never started. Instead, she modelled and got herself on the front cover of several low-budget magazines, though there's no evidence of anything pornographic or glamour related.'

'So, nothing points to the sordid life she's accused of,' Hunt concluded. 'But it doesn't rule out that she might have been on the game, on the side, to earn a few quid,' he added. 'Though she didn't need it.'

'These rich types sometimes withhold cash from their spouse or keep it on a tight rein, to control them. Her own money might have been her way of breaking away from him,' one of his officers pointed out.

'It's feasible she led a double life, though we've found no evidence of punters. No trace of a website she used to advertise services, nothing like that. And we still haven't found her phone. The last known ping was around the area of her address on Tuesday night, before it was switched off. Vodafone have confirmed.'

'We spoke to the private investigator, sir, the one that Tony Thorpe gave us, and it's legit. He told us he travelled to Riga and chased down a few ex-boyfriends.'

'Anything sex-work related?'

'No, boss.'

'And the phone records from the house?'

'Regular calls to Latvia. All to her mother's number.'

The officer had spoken to Monika's mother this morning and she wasn't a fan of Tony Thorpe's. According to the mother, Monika was extremely unhappy and planning to go home. She indicated that the marriage was doomed from the start. Interestingly the wedding, a private affair, had only two guests, who were the witnesses: Alex and Jeremy Moore. Hunt already knew that the three had been tight since their university days.

Hunt had come across plenty of couples who overcame bigger differences in age, and background, and it often led to tension. He toyed with the possibility that Monika had played her husband for citizenship: a privilege she'd managed to achieve last year. She was in possession of dual nationality but she hadn't returned to Latvia in all the years she'd been married. So why now? Why the plane ticket they'd found during their search of the Thorpe's house?

Hunt had detectives contact local police in the suburb of Vidzeme, in Riga, on the Baltic coast, where Monika's wider family had lived since the Second World War. He'd never been to Latvia and knew nothing about it. Riga was a tiny city, with less than a million inhabitants. He imagined it as a cold and bleak place until he googled it and found that it was a World Heritage Site. The centre was full of old wooden buildings, painted every colour, surrounded by museums and places of culture. He warmed to the image of it and tried to imagine Monika leaving for the streets of London, on her own. With a law degree she never used, and then didn't have to because she met a cash cow.

Tony Thorpe was a man who seemed to live to work. It had never been the other way around. His private life was pedestrian. His previous dalliances with the law had been mere brushes, and related to recreational drug-taking. But battling with Tony's hotshot barrister just to gather intel on his private life, and dig up non-existent dirt, was perhaps unnecessary when he had Henry Nelson's involvement staring him in the face. The knucklehead already had a criminal record. Now, Hunt needed to find a motive, and some evidence.

Despite his tradesman's salary, Nelson was a member of a fancy gym in town, and it reminded Hunt that he still needed to speak to Grace Bridge, who was Monika's personal trainer. The doc had mentioned her. He knew from colleagues of his who attended such places of torture that PTs spent half their time chatting to their paying customers. Grace Bridge could be a goldmine of information.

As could Alex Moore. She'd make an excellent expert witness on the stand. She was professional, savvy and smart. He liked her. He'd requested the court order for her records, as she suggested. Getting to know these characters in Monika's life was the missing link. It was all about people in the end, when dealing with murder. Somebody who knew Monika wanted her out of the way, and somebody in her list of contacts knew it.

He called the gym and got through to member services, explaining who he was. It didn't take long for them to check their membership list and confirm that not only was Henry Nelson a member, but so was Carrie Greenside.

'What a web we weave,' he said under his breath.

An officer poked his head around his door and Hunt looked up from his desk expectantly.

'Boss, we had a witness statement come in from a neighbour of Henry Nelson's. Our officer was there trying to get hold of him, with no luck. I checked it out. There was a car parked outside the address late on Tuesday evening. It was a brand-new Merc, and it's registered to Carrie Greenside.'

Hunt grinned. 'Good work.'

He called Grace's number with a renewed sense of earnestness. She picked up and her voice was efficient and bright, typical of an open witness.

'Grace? It's Detective Hunt here from Cambridgeshire police. Have you got a minute?'

As he spoke to her, he entered her name into the police national computer database, and she popped up as a victim of a crime, two years ago. He sat forward and read the report as he spoke to her.

'I was wondering if I could drop into your work and ask you a few questions about Monika Thorpe as part of our inquiries.'

The young woman had been subject to a violent rape and the perp had received ten years. He'd be out in five, and he'd already served two; the woman must be at her wits' end. He wondered how her case had been handled. Coppers received a bad rap over rape cases because they were so damn hard to prove. Ten years was a stiff sentence, and Hunt figured the evidence must have been compelling. He read the details and concluded that Vincent Kemble was a violent thug.

'Why?'

He could smell the fear in her voice. No doubt any contact with the law brought back terrible memories.

'It's standard, Grace. I'm piecing together Monika's life and it seems that you were an important part of it.'

'I knew her a long time, well, by personal training standards. Most clients fall away after a few weeks or months, but Monika was dedicated.'

Hunt liked her babbling. It distracted her from what he really wanted. Most of the time when witnesses prattled on about nothing, they let go wonderful nuggets of information that cracked cases. Blatherers were good omens.

'Great. So could I come to the gym and get a feel for who Monika saw there regularly? You can give me a tour. I haven't been inside a gym for years, you might be able to convert me.' He looked at his watch. 'You on shift today?'

'No, but I am tomorrow, at three.'

'I'll drop by tomorrow, then. I'm not coming in Lycra, though.'

She laughed.

Bingo.

Chapter 50

It's rare I open the office on a Sunday but this is important, for me now too. I'm involved whether I like it or not. It's peaceful without Dora barking appointment times to me and bothering me with cancellations or enquiries. I fling open the windows with abandon and make a strong coffee. I sit heavily behind my desk, I've got work to do before they arrive.

Tony slept in the spare room last night, and by the time I put him to bed, with Jeremy already asleep on the couch in the pool room, he was blathering on about how much he really loved Monika. I told Jeremy and Tony I had emergency appointments today. They squinted lazily at me and I reassured them that I made fresh waffles. But looking after two drunken men was the least of my worries last night. Keeping Ewan occupied was my first priority and we watched a film together. Funny how a crisis brings him closer to me. Even Lydia was out of sorts, so much so that she ate some food and kept it down. I am used to the sounds of vomit hitting the toilet bowl, and there wasn't any. The death of Brandon Stand hit all the kids hard, and Monika's death paled into the background. I heard her once talking to my youngest son, in his room, privately and intimately. She read him bedtime stories, long ago, when he was still my baby. Even James stayed in last night, and watched some of the film with us, from under a blanket, laid on the sofa, close to me, as if I'm the one who'll keep us all safe.

I hear a lone car and watch as Carrie pulls up in her Mercedes. The car is like her: a roaring engineering masterpiece, covered in pretension. She wears a casual summer dress and shows off her figure. I hope not for me. I'm struck by her femininity but not disarmed by it. Carrie is no longer simply my client. The real work begins today.

I almost press the intercom to call Dora, but I remember that it's Sunday and I greet Carrie myself. I take a look around my office before she wafts in. It's a shrine to dignity and achievement but the trinkets of therapy – the candles, lotus symbolism, yin and yang room freshener, the eye of Horus – and the paintings on the wall, irritate me momentarily. Carrie removes her sunglasses and behind them I see puffy red eyes that don't belong there.

'Thank you for seeing me,' Carrie says with gratitude.

'Not at all, I didn't have anything planned.'

Only starting my own investigation into Monika's death.

'It's a beautiful day.'

She ignores me. Her mind is elsewhere.

Carrie takes her usual seat and I am reminded of the shelter the office affords me. My clients think I'm invincible, like a machine. I have a professional veil around me, and it cloaks Doctor Alex Moore underneath. I offer her a drink. She's changed, or maybe I have. I remind myself of my own routine. The first thing I do is wait. That's the easy part.

'I'm ashamed of something I've done,' she begins. It's a quicker than normal start.

I say nothing and she picks the skin around her nails. She's uncharacteristically jumpy and I pretend I don't know why.

'Like I said on the phone, I found myself in an awkward situation and it brought back so many negative memories.'

We're doctor and patient, she suspects nothing.

'What sparked it for you? Start from the beginning,' I soothe.

She walks me through the last forty-eight hours. How she wandered through her home, seeking predators. She explains how her guard was down when she made the rash decision to visit Tony. She doesn't mention his name.

'It's normal to have regressions.'

'I know, but so intense? Why now? After all the work I've done, and after all these years.' Her face is anguished.

'Tell me what happened after you realised there was no one in the house.'

'But that's just it: there was someone in the house, because later, the next day, I discovered something was missing.'

'What was it?'

'I keep a safe, in my bedroom. I'm terrible, I don't lock it all the time, but I had this time.'

'What do you keep in it?'

'Not much. I was given something to put in there. It's a long story. I know somebody who's had bad luck in his life. And I mean really bad luck. Shit just follows him around, and I was doing him a favour.'

'This friend. He's important to you?'

She nods. 'I guess so. I feel sorry for him.'

She's lying; he means more than that.

'Is that the same? Sympathy is an emotion, so let's go with that. You feel responsible for him somehow? Like a child.'

'He's a grown man,' she laughs.

'But you're close.'

'He fitted my new kitchen.'

She's not looking at me. She's focused on her own inner turmoil. I see Henry Nelson in her house as I imagine it. Ethically, I've crossed a line that I shouldn't, but I have to.

'And that's how you met? He fitted your kitchen?'

She nods.

I wait. I'm reminded of Henry's charisma. He's fooled plenty of women. Myself included. Or at least he tried. I peer at the flowers in the window box – if only they could give me some direction. They're party to everything I hear inside this office.

'He's a lot younger than me. I'm such a cliché.'

It's one of those moments where clients look to me to massage their ego.

'You're not a cliché at all, Carrie. Men are attracted to beautiful women no matter their age.'

'I was flattered.'

'And what wound was he shedding light on?'

Carrie has a habit of acting out with younger men. It's not the first time she's done it and it makes Tony – at fifty-five – an exception to her rule.

'Did it feel good to take power from an unconventional relationship?' I steer things back to Henry.

She blushes. It's rare but she doesn't seem to mind that I catch her out. After all, that's my job.

She nods.

'Okay. So, the relationship became one of guardian and trusting child? What did he give to you to hide?'

'A knife and some money.'

My heart races. Suddenly I want to take the framed photo of my children from my desk and hug it, so it can't come to harm.

'Have you any idea why he gave them to you to hide?'

'He works with disadvantaged kids and they fuck up all the time – excuse my language. He promised me that the knife hadn't been used for anything bad, and the money was to save this kid the aggro of it being found. God, I sound like a mug saying this out loud.'

'No. You helped somebody because they asked you. You were available to them, like a mother. Like your mother wasn't.'

Carrie puts her head in her hands and runs her fingers through her hair, like a lover might.

'You wanted to believe him.'

'I did believe him. He's straight. Clean. Reformed. I know he is.'

She thinks that repetition will make her words true.

'But you doubt why he gave you the knife?'

She nods.

'I believe him that it wasn't his to hide, but...'

'You feel used?'

She nods again. Her make-up and fake breasts seem slightly ridiculous in the harsh light, with the song of birds as a backdrop. Their melody is brighter when they're free, but caged birds still chirp, full of hope and life. If humans had that attitude, I wouldn't have any clients.

I let her think.

'So, the knife and the money were taken from the safe?'

'Just the money.'

'But you can't report it because it was there illegally in the first place.' I state the obvious. 'You've had quite a

262

weekend. I need to remind you of your declaration when we first met, that I have an obligation to report anything that might be linked to a crime.'

She gathers herself, stares and nods. Reality hits her.

'I haven't been involved in a crime,' she says convincingly.

'I believe you. What has this kitchen fitter to do with your actions on Friday night, with your other friend. You called him Tony?'

I need to tread carefully because it's not my style to delve too deeply into the detail. Specifics are like weeds. They suck oxygen from what is useful. I'm just distracting her from my fact-finding.

She takes a lungful of air.

'Tony is the husband of the woman who was found murdered. You must have seen it on the news. I recommended the kitchen guy to him, and I've got this awful feeling that Tony has something to do with it. Why else would he ring me, desperate to fill his bed with someone else?'

Her voice is like a machine gun on my nerves.

'I'm getting these flashbacks of shit that I thought I'd dealt with years ago. It's driving me crazy. I think I need some time off work and I was wondering if you could write me a sick note?'

She's closed back up but I have what I need.

'Of course, I told you I'd do that for you. This work is incredibly fierce. It depletes your energy. I'll sign you off for a month – is that okay?'

She smiles and her shoulders relax but her fingers still toy with themselves.

'You can breathe now. Tell me about your panic attacks.'

'It's tearing me to shreds. My shame and guilt have gone through the roof, I feel responsible for this woman and I didn't even know her.'

'So you think the husband had something to do with it?'

'That's what the police think, it's obvious to me. They were like smirking parasites, all over his house, and looking me up and down, like rubbish, satisfied that I'd been caught with him. I took drugs.'

I imagine Hunt finding Carrie in Tony's house, and vicariously gleaning satisfaction from the find: his suspect playing nicely into his hands. But it's a heavy admission, my opinions aside. I need to be transparent with her about disclosures.

'Carrie, I must stop you here again. Even though I'm bound by certain confidentiality laws, if there's a disclosure that concerns me, then the likelihood is that the police may eventually get around to a similar conclusion, once they delve into the history of this poor woman.'

I allow her to mull over the possibility. Clarity over-whelms her and she looks like she might have a full-blown panic attack, right here in my office.

'Oh, God, do you have to divulge information to the police because it's a criminal case? Even if I'm not involved?'

It's a curious habit of non-believers, invoking the Almighty. I do it myself.

'Why would the police ask me for your records? It's highly unlikely.' I throw the panic back her way.

'But they might? Oh, Jesus, Alex, can you help me? Please, I'm begging you, I can't go through all that again. I don't want to get involved.'

'Do the police have a valid reason to request personal information on you? If they do, they'd need a warrant. I've been asked to work on criminal cases before. We'd have to stop our work together.'

'Christ.'

There she goes again. As far as I'm aware, Carrie didn't experience religious repression during her childhood, so maybe it's an ingrained national hangover from puritanism. It's something that fascinates me. But I'm getting off track.

'The police have spooked you. They like to do that sometimes. But what about this young man asking you to hide something? That to me sounds like it was involved in something illegal. What is your gut telling you?'

I already know that simply by her sitting in my chair, opposite me, divulging to me her innermost fears, she's not far from crumbling altogether. She might even try to run away – why else is she planning to take time off work?

'I really don't know,' Carrie says. 'I just don't know.' She leans over and begins to cry. I have never seen her this vulnerable before. I pass her a box of tissues.

'Carrie?' I ask gently when I think she's done. 'You've told me a lot today about things that have happened. You've mentioned a lot of events. That's important because it anchors our timelines, but what's really important here is that you react as your authentic self and not the panicked child from long ago.'

But I know that's exactly what she will do. Because it's all she's got left when the trappings of success are blown to smithereens. Hunt intends to do just that.

Carrie's relapse is spectacular.

Inevitable fatigue is looming over her body. The session is almost over. I pass her the sick note.

'What will you do?'

'I'm looking after a friend's villa in Bali.'

Run, run, run.

'Does anyone know your contact details for an emergency?'

Carrie shakes her head wearily.

'You can give them to me.'

'Can I? Thank you. Thank you so much. Have you got a pen?'

Chapter 51

I'm on a precipice that I can no longer step back from.

Behind my closed eyes I see Ewan, on the Jeep, his eyes wide at the sight of the lioness. Lydia can't move.

'It's so much bigger than on TV!' they gasp. James puts his arm around his brother and forgets he's cool.

The lioness watches me, watching my children, and we connect over our mutual maternal ferocity.

The image disappears when Henry answers his phone after me calling it four times already. Maybe Hunt has got to him first.

'Henry, it's Doctor Alex here. How are you? I'm sorry it's taken me a bit longer to get round to returning your call.'

'Thanks for calling back, no worries, I didn't expect you to get back to me so soon, and on a Sunday. Sorry for interrupting your family time,' he says.

'You didn't. How can I help?'

'I was wondering if I could come and see you before my next appointment.'

'I've got a slot in my diary tomorrow, but I can talk now.'

'Right, erm...'

It sounds like he's driving. I can hear the tell-tale noises of traffic and the echo of hands-free. He's nervous.

Run, run, run.

'Or, I'm in the office now. I was actually working today anyway. You can pop in, if that suits you better?'

'Now?'

'I'm here.'

'I'm in Cambridge, I'll drive over now, thank you.'

'No worries, I'll see you soon, come to the entrance and just knock, I'm doing some paperwork.'

'I've been driving all night,' he says.

'Let's talk about it when I see you.'

I pace up and down my office. My mind races over what I should do. I don't know whether to call Hunt, or check with my governing body about confidentiality, or confront Tony, or just breathe and listen to Henry's version. He at least deserves a chance.

Wouldn't I want the same chance if it were me lying in the chiller at the mortuary? Who are my community? My inner circle? Can I trust them when I'm gone? What picture would the police get of my life from Jeremy and the kids? I have few real friends. Sure, we invite people over for dinner and Sunday roasts... but really, we don't even do that anymore. Sunday was a rarity. My isolation taunts me. I'm struck by how small people's realms are, and how they bump into each other and cross over. Jeremy is right: all I do is work. What would my clients say about me?

I take deep breaths and weigh up my options. I've already gone too far. I know I'm not legally obliged to pass on revelations secured in confidence, if I deem them to be benign, but that will change as soon as Hunt secures his warrant. Can I trust him? No. Oftentimes the police get it wrong. Hunt doesn't want justice for Monika, he wants the CPS to charge and convict somebody so he can claim glory. It's my job to make sure he focuses on the right person. To do that, I need to know more. And that's why I need Henry.

Sarah jumps uninvited into my head again. But I allow it.

She was one of the most vibrant and funny people I ever met. We were weeks away from our final results, and planning to travel through Europe on the Eurail pass. Kids these days have no idea how much of a big deal that was. It was akin to flying to the other side of the world and never coming home. Buying the ticket, planning the route, checking the overwhelmingly complicated bus and train timetables for ten different countries, and packing everything into a small rucksack: it was all part of the adventure. We were going as a foursome: me, Jeremy, Tony and Sarah.

But it never happened.

No one had seen that Sarah was so far gone. But I saw. Her suffocation of Tony, and her intensity. Three months in Europe would have been all-consuming. She had the ability to choke life itself and turn it to despair, a terminal spiral of depression.

She survived the jump and lived for seventeen minutes. Three medics held her together as she struggled to breathe through her crushed torso. Her legs ended up inside her shoulders and her guts spewed ten feet across the central square, which was full of students enjoying their beers.

It was the beginning of Tony's descent into self-destructive behaviour. Or maybe he'd been like that all along. It was also the beginning of Jeremy and I always watching out for him. Like a little lost brother, we overlooked his outrageous behaviour after that. I learned in the time it took for Sarah's body to plunge to the ground that nothing stays the same. Time changes in an instant and lives hang in the balance. But we got through it, and we'll get through this.

The noise of a car engine disturbs me and I see Henry in the carpark.

He slams the van door and I see the logo on the side. I've seen it a hundred times but today it doesn't make me smile. I know his prison time intimately and what led to it; I also know about – and participate in – his rehabilitation package and checks with his probation officer.

I go to the front door and buzz him in, smiling. He looks very tired. His lover has just been found pummelled to death and dumped near the river Cam. Plus he already told me that he's been in his van all night.

His face is that of a man who I am seeing for the first time. I open the door wide for him and welcome him in. He fiddles with his keys.

'Thanks for seeing me at such short notice,' he says bashfully, as if he's been running. He might be soon enough.

'Have you come from the gym?' I ask, breezily.

'No, I'm just hot and stressed, I've had some work on over the weekend, and lots to do.'

'What did you do to your hand?'

'Oh, I cut it yesterday at work, it's fine.' A chill travels down my spine.

'Come through. We've got the place to ourselves.' I wonder at the wisdom of being here with him alone. He walks behind me and I can hear my footsteps echo. I've told Jeremy and Tony where I am, but they're nursing hangovers, not considering me. I beckon him to sit down.

'I've put water out for you.'

'Thank you,' he says, taking a glass and filling it from the jug.

'Take your time to relax and let me know when you're ready.'

Henry leans over, and I appreciate his muscle power. He rubs his temples. I've never understood the lure of the gym but I have plenty of clients who do. Henry is a well-conditioned man, and he looks after himself. Monika would like that. And Tony would hate it.

'I think I might be in trouble,' he says.

I feel a moment of déjà vu, as if he's echoing Carrie's shame. My gut stirs.

'I've been caught up in something which I think is going to be very difficult to get out of,' he adds.

'Do you want to tell me about it?'

He nods. I omit to tell him about the police's right of search if they suspect a crime. If he's been in his car all night, he already knows they're after him. I give him time to make himself as comfortable as I think he's going to get.

'Is it material involvement or emotional?' I ask.

'Very much material, and that's why I'm worried.'

'So you feel in imminent danger?'

My powers of paraphrasing are needed here. Clients often splurge out garbled emotions and it's my job to put them into complete sentences, so we can both make sense of them.

'The woman I told you about, the one I was seeing...' Henry says. His chest beneath his t-shirt is pink, and it makes the tattoos look like ash against molten lava. 'She's dead.'

'I'm so sorry about that. It's a shock, I can tell.'

'She didn't just die. She was murdered.'

Like a typical man, he's plunged straight in. I need to halt him, or at least divert his premature discharge.

'Can I stop you there, Henry? I'm bound by law to report anything illegal. I have to ask you if this is a confession. I'm so sorry.'

'No, it's all right. I understand. No, it's not. I had nothing to do with it. But I'm sure at some point the police will come knocking, because I was in her house. In her bed.'

I keep calm because I have to, and Henry thinks it's because I'm a consummate professional.

'So you'll be a material witness, and possibly even a suspect.'

He nods wearily. I can tell it's been a long night for him and he's worn himself out. It makes him more malleable.

'I have to record that you understand that I might be asked to aid the police, in that case.'

'I understand. The thing is, I think it was her husband who did it. Monika told him about us and I went there the night she disappeared.' His face crumples and he buries his head. It gives me time to remember last Tuesday night.

Pandora's box is now fully open.

'As your therapist, Henry, you don't have to tell me details. It's my job to help you deal with the emotional fallout of whatever you're experiencing, but if it helps, you can start at the beginning and I'll guide you through.'

He takes a deep breath.

'Tuesday night, she called me. She was drunk, I could tell. We'd been having disagreements about leaving here, together. She wanted to leave him. She'd already bought a ticket to go home and she wanted me to go with her. I said I couldn't, not yet anyway. She went crazy at me and I think that's what led her to drink so much. Anyway, later she called me and said her husband had hit her. She sent me a photograph of her face. I drove over there and her cheek was all bruised and cut. I had to step in, I couldn't ignore it.'

'Was the husband home?'

I think my heart will pump out of my chest.

Henry nods. I recall Tony's version.

'There was screaming and tears, he looked proper broken, like he didn't expect it at all, but Monika had told me they were virtually separated already. To me, that was a lie. I could tell he loved her. I got in between them. I offered to take her to mine, but she refused, and then she got belligerent and violent.'

'Is that how you really hurt your hand?'

'No! I told you, I did this at work yesterday. Stupid, I know. The police will take one look at it and come to the same conclusion as you. I didn't hurt her, I swear. But it doesn't matter, does it? I can tell by your face. People like me will always be one step behind those who are protected by the system. The husband is rich beyond my wildest dreams, it's why I didn't really think Monika was serious about me. He's got a private yacht, and a chalet in Switzerland, for Christ's sake. The odds of the police believing me over him are zero. I'm a thug with a record, he's a pillar of the establishment.'

It's the longest monologue I've ever heard from him and it impresses me. But it also saddens me. He's right. The odds are stacked against him. Tony has Kingston, and Henry will have legal aid, when it comes to it.

'You haven't got to convince me, Henry. What case have the police got against you?'

'I have no idea. I guess my number will be on her phone, the husband might admit I was there on Tuesday.' He paused. 'I slept in her bed. We might have been seen together. She could have told friends. I don't know, it looks pretty bad. And now this,' he says, and holds up his injured hand.

'Have you got a lawyer?'

'Do I need one?'

'You know the score, you've just said it yourself. With your previous, the police won't treat you like an innocent anomaly.'

He already knows and that's why he's been driving around all night. He puts his head in his hands.

'Why can't crap just fucking leave me alone? I've done nothing wrong. I just can't get rid of my past. I don't stand a chance.'

I know I need to stop the session but I'm caught between this world and the next, and I need to make it to the other side, just like he does. For Ewan. For Tony.

'Do you have an alibi?'

'No, that's my problem. She disappeared. She just wandered off and then I spent an hour looking for her. I promised the husband I'd bring her back, but I couldn't find her. I tried, God, I tried.'

His prayer to above will go unanswered. But he already knows that, too.

'I went back to the husband to tell him I couldn't find her but he didn't answer the door. This is what I need to tell the police.'

'Have the police tried to contact you?'

'Yes, we had a brief conversation when they found out I fitted her kitchen. It was all very polite because then I was just somebody who'd been in her house. I told them I last saw her Monday.'

'So, you lied.'

He gazes at me and his face is crestfallen. He bends his face to his hands and I wait.

'Jesus, she was in my van.'

He's just filled the gap that Hunt will be looking for: concrete forensics. I feel dizzy with duplicity.

'What was she doing in your van?'

I don't need him to elaborate, his face says it all. My head fills with a vision of him and Monika in the back of his van and, in other circumstances, I might have congratulated her.

He looks up and his eyes meet mine.

'I didn't kill her,' he tells me.

I desperately want to tell him that I believe him, but Henry is a grown man; gone are the days when he needed a matriarch to tend to his wounds. He knows what's coming and there's little I can do to stop it.

Chapter 52

I'm hoping that Tony has left by the time I get home, but he hasn't. He and Jeremy are sat at the breakfast bar, both nursing what looks like buck's fizz out of our wedding crystal champagne glasses. We only have three left. The rest were smashed years ago.

'Somebody's not happy,' Jeremy says, when he sees my face.

They giggle like school children.

'I'll go and check on the kids,' I say.

'Before you do, the police called. They want to speak to Ewan,' Jeremy says.

I stop at the doorway and turn around. 'What did you tell them?'

'I said I thought you were sorting it out.'

I don't know whether to laugh out loud or walk up to Jeremy and punch him in the face. Tony is the first to stop smirking.

'Alex, why don't you call them back and buy some time, I'll call Kingston, he can be here within the hour.'

He's always got an answer. Tony, the great fixer, has delivered his solution to the problem – money – and he looks at me as if to ask why I'm so stressed. Next they'll be telling me, from the top of their clinking rims, to calm down.

'Who did you speak to? Was it DI Hunt?'

'No, some constable.'

'Right, they're probably behind time. Hunt assured me it could wait. I'll call him.'

'Alex works her magic,' Jeremy grins and gulps his drink. Sadly, he doesn't choke.

Tony gets off his bar stool and comes to me.

'Let me take your bag,' he soothes.

Jeremy eyes me with suspicion. He's a charlatan, caught in the act of forgery.

'If you find a better solution at the bottom of a glass, do let me know,' I fire back.

It's childish, unnecessary and inflammatory, but I don't care. I'm tired, scared and I have dead wood dragging me into the murky depths.

'Alex, come on, I've got your bag. Tell me what the detective said,' Tony distracts me.

I've already explained what Hunt said to me yesterday, but they were inebriated, and he's obviously already forgotten. He ushers me into the hallway.

'Whatever trouble Ewan's in, Kingston can sort it.'

'Tony, he's a minor. This could sit on his record for years, at least until he's eighteen. Do you want that?'

'Until who's eighteen?'

We swing around and look at the stairs, it's Ewan.

'Nothing, darling.'

'Don't treat me like a kid, Mum.'

James appears behind him and trots down the stairs.

'Trouble brewing?' he asks breezily, then seeing my face, he raises his eyebrows and slides past us into the kitchen.

'Woah, Dad, on the sauce already?' I hear him say.

Tony looks at me and reaches his arms out. I let him hold my shoulders as Ewan walks past us to join his big brother. I hear Lydia's voice. She must have been outside sunbathing. It's a full house and I wish it was under better circumstances. I imagine a home teeming with life, with happy well-adjusted children wafting around the kitchen extension, fixing pancakes and maple syrup for their Sunday brunch. Instead, I feel the crack of timber, before it gives way, burdened by too heavy a load.

Tony pulls me gently and I take a deep breath and we join them in the kitchen. I watch my children move around and their bodies glide around the space, avoiding Jeremy, like shoals of fish instinctively knowing to part before the lunge of a tiger shark.

'What's with the adult voodoo?' James asks, waving his hands up and down in the chasm of silence between the grown-ups. His perceptive humour is normally welcome and cleverly satirical, but not today.

'This is about the police, isn't it?' Ewan said.

Jeremy freezes. Even his drinking hand stills.

'Why are the cops after my little bro?' James asks.

'It was about Natalie Morgan,' Jeremy says.

'Who's Natalie?' asks Lydia.

'*The* Natalie?' James smiles. 'The drug dealer who gave pills to the lad who died?'

Chaos erupts. Jeremy shouts at James. I shout at both of them. Tony gets between us. Lydia stands, mouth open, and I notice that she was about to eat something.

'I'm on drugs too,' Ewan announces at the top of his voice.

Everything stops.

I knock a champagne glass over and it smashes on the floor. It's Jeremy's so it was empty. Now we have two. I bend over to gather the pieces of broken crystal.

'We're all on drugs, aren't we, Dad?' James says.

'Wait a minute, James,' Tony says.

'Can we all calm down and take a breath,' I say.

'Wine is a drug, isn't it, Dad?' James continues. He glares at his father, but he's also smiling. He turns to his little brother. 'Don't sweat, bro, the whole of society lives numbed-out.'

Jeremy seethes. I get the dustpan and brush from the utility and start sweeping up broken shards.

'Natalie Snapchatted me from the police station yesterday, she was in jail,' Ewan says.

I stand up. His innocence makes me want to laugh and cry at the same time.

'Jail? Woah, that's dramatic. So the cops want to chat to my little brother?' James says what the adults don't dare to.

'What?' Lydia asks, and begins to cry.

'Sex, drugs and rock and roll,' James says. 'I'll take brunch upstairs, thank you,' he adds, walking past me.

'Ewan, do you want to talk about it?' Tony asks.

'Talk? Yeah, that'll make it all better. It'll stop Ewan getting high and Dad drinking, and Lydia throwing up. Talk will solve everything,' James says on his way out. His parting salvo.

'James, what has got into you?' I plead with him.

'How dare you speak to me like that!' Jeremy's face goes purple and he stands up and puffs his chest out towards the disappearing rear of his eldest child.

'That's enough!' I shout.

'C'mon, Ewan, let's go shoot up together, and get your story straight,' James says from the hall. He leaves and Ewan follows him.

Lydia leaves her bowl on the side and runs upstairs and we hear her door slam.

'Tony, can you call Kingston?' I ask him.

Jeremy sighs and walks out into the garden. He shades his eyes from the glaring sun and I can see him sweating under the intensity. I throw a thousand pieces of a wedding gift into the bin and lean against the counter. Tony comes to me.

'We'll sort this. I'll protect Ewan.'

'What if you go to prison for murder, Tony? Have you thought about who will protect Ewan then?'

Chapter 53

Henry rubbed moisturiser into his skin. He paid particular attention to the tattoos that covered his body. Memories popped into his head of the stories behind each one. He didn't take body art lightly, even the ones he'd tried to cut off. Generally, his clothes masked most of them. The spider's web on his elbow was his nod to prison time. He had various animals too, as well as some stupid ones he'd got when he was a young idiot, but still they reminded him of how far he'd come. But now that was all unravelling. He kept telling himself to calm down and stick to his story.

Doctor Alex had told him that the truth would surely redeem him, but her demeanour told Henry otherwise. He was on his own. He had no one to rely on. Even the doc had her defects. Everybody had secrets. Why end up a therapist? But it was easier to throw mud where it was already stuck. If push came to shove, she wouldn't protect him. She was just as much part of the system that failed him as the coppers. Prison was society's waste bin, where they discarded everything they didn't like, and threw it away to bury. Integrity was relative, and he didn't have letters after his name. He wasn't her typical client with millions of pounds behind him. His therapy was paid for by the state. It was a peculiar truth that the institution turned a blind eye to the quality of professional he chose, and thus the cost, but that wasn't his problem right now. Monika was.

He'd spent another night in his van, avoiding CCTV cameras, like he'd once told Doctor Alex, as a joke really, but now he feared it could be used against him. Only an ex-con did such things.

His thoughts burdened him and felt heavier than any weight he'd lifted at the gym. He'd dropped in at home to change and grab a few items that would see him through, on the run. He'd been careful. The street was quiet and he'd come in the back, over the neighbour's fence. Locking the door behind him, he climbed into his van and set off, pulling out into oncoming traffic. A few horns jarred his mind and he pulled on his seatbelt. He hadn't even gone twenty yards when he saw blue lights behind him and he looked in his rear mirror quizzically. A siren sounded and he was flashed. Shit. He pulled over and his hands began to shake. The spectre of metal bars, the jangling of keys, being told when to piss and when to eat, the smell of incarceration, all conspired to hijack his nervous system and make him do something stupid. But this time, he knew the game was up.

The police car slowed and parked behind him. His heart sank to his belly. He watched as an officer approached. He looked around, and noticed a small crowd gathering to see what the fuss was about. He spotted a couple of neighbours and splayed his hands, as if to say he had no idea what was going on. They gave him the thumbs up but still watched, like spectators of a blood sport. Everybody loved a good sacrifice. The officer reached the car and Henry lowered his window.

'Henry Nelson?' the officer said.

'Yes.'

'Can I see some ID, please?'

'What's this about?'

'Let's just get the ID, shall we?'

Henry didn't like the fella's tone. It reminded him of the screws in prison: all power and no respect. He knew his rights but he didn't much feel like having an argument in front of his neighbours. He opened his wallet and took out his driver's licence, showing the officer.

'Can you step out of the car, sir?'

'What's going on?'

'Just step out of the car, sir.'

Henry took his keys and put the window up. He got out of the car and stood in front of the officer. Another stayed in the driver's seat of the squad car. Memories from years ago rose up in his belly and he had a feeling of impending injustice.

'Henry Nelson, you're under arrest for the suspected supply of Class A drugs to minors, resulting in the death of Brandon Stand. Please turn around and face the car. You have the right to remain silent…'

It wasn't the charge he was expecting, and he almost laughed at the farcical charade. He stared at the officer and glanced at his neighbours, bereft of feeling. He turned around and allowed the guy to put hand ties on him. The restraints were tightened with force and he winced as the pain from his injured hand travelled sharply up his arm. The neighbours pointed and whispered.

'Henry, what's going on?' one shouted.

He shrugged.

'We'll take you now, sir.'

'What about my van?' he asked.

'We'll take care of that.'

He was led to the vehicle behind and his head was lowered by the man's hand as he got in the back seat. Recollections of being sent down from the courthouse, being led to the waiting vehicle – the ice box – and sitting in the back of the van on his way to prison came flooding back.

The back of the police vehicle was cramped, taken up by all the technological kit, and the officer sat close to him didn't say a word. Voices chimed in his head from the radio, and lights flashed. The air conditioning kicked in as they set off and he saw the faces of his neighbours, already making up stories about the young man they'd thought they'd known. The officer beside him had tightened Henry's seatbelt before his own and it seemed to crush his chest and his arms behind his back.

'Are these really necessary?' he asked.

'Just until we get to the station, then I'll take them off.'

'But I'm not a risk, I've done nothing.'

The officer said nothing except to speak into his radio. Henry was transported back in time, to other police car rides he'd enjoyed at the cost of the taxpayer, but then it had been totally justified.

It didn't take long to negotiate the Cambridge traffic and they parked in front of a police station. Henry hadn't been inside this one before. His crimes had been committed far away in central London. He'd believed he had the best chance at staying out of trouble in a tame suburban town like this one: how wrong he'd been. The officer beside him got out first and went round to Henry's side of the car to help him; he could say that this was the most humiliating situation he'd ever endured, but that would be incorrect. He was led up the steps to the entrance and recognised the familiar set-up that was inside every police station in the country. He was checked in and he confirmed his name and details, knowing the procedure well. His wrist ties were removed and he rubbed his flesh. The restriction of blood flow made his recent wound throb and blood seeped from the bandage he'd wrapped around it carefully this morning. The admin officer behind the desk looked at it and Henry couldn't read his face, but he didn't have to; he knew what was coming.

His belongings were checked in and itemised. He hadn't been charged and so he didn't have to enter a plea. He simply acknowledged the arrest. Then he was led to a cell and the door was closed behind him. The bare walls taunted him. They were white, and the floor was blue. There was a single cot bed, covered in a solitary blanket, and he sat on it and put his head in his hands. He stared up at the camera in the corner. The cell was silent, but it was the din inside his head that sapped his resolve, and it took all his strength not to totally lose it and freak out. The smells and lights sneered at him, teasing him about his inner badness. The rot had always been there, it mocked, and would never disappear simply because he spoke to a few kids about keeping clean and looked out for a damaged girl. His father was banged up, as was his brother, and countless uncles and grandparents before them; he hadn't broken the cycle, that wasn't how it worked. The sins of generations felt heavy on his shoulders and the weight of it made him lie down on his side. He closed his eyes to still his mind: if it couldn't see, then maybe it couldn't think.

Chapter 54

The day of Monika's disappearance

Monika assessed her face in the mirror. Her cheek was red but could be covered with make-up. Her black hair curled around her oval face and her large brown eyes stared back at her like portals of warm fur. Her lips were full and rounded; Tony had said he loved kissing them. He still did.

She had her mother's eyes. She stared at them now and disappeared into them. She wouldn't cry. People here treated her as if she was stupid, because she was beautiful. She had an honours degree in Law from the University of Riga, in Latvia, which she'd never used. Instead, she was the embodiment of the stereotypical younger woman who seeks a rich, older husband, and she hated it. She wished she could, for a moment, step out of her skin, and surprise everybody.

In a few short years her life had been reduced to the status of Tony's trophy wife. She turned up on his arm at parties and she talked to his friends. She suffered the lust of his friends and associates, like Jeremy Moore, and she decorated her husband like the baubles on a Christmas tree. Everything was prettier with lights on, even a bastard like Tony.

286

Her body froze when she heard his voice downstairs. He was on the phone. No doubt to Jeremy, his appeaser and partner in everything. She knew this because of the way his voice changed. In the short time she'd got to know her husband she'd learned to read him like a book. His voice, and all the tones and oscillations therein, depended upon whom he was addressing. And the only people on the planet who Tony fawned to were Jeremy and Alex. Everybody else he spoke to like chattels.

It was a pity that Jeremy was so shallow because his children were charming. They were young enough not to be totally screwed up by their parents, though they all showed signs of it. It was one of the reasons she remained childless. Anybody with the arrogance to think they could create another human being, in their image, must be crazy.

Until she met Henry.

Even she couldn't get over the cliché of a bored housewife falling for her luxury kitchen fitter, but it had happened that way and nobody would ever understand. Of course, at first, any woman faced with Henry Nelson's physique, in their kitchen, all muscles, blue eyes and blond hair, stripping cupboards and building things, would stop to enjoy the view, but it was when he opened his mouth that the magic happened. He was kind, intelligent and gentle.

She took a picture of the mark on her face and sent it to Henry, then waited.

Chapter 55

'Grace, nice to see you. I'm sorry we didn't catch up over the weekend. I did call your number but it went to answer phone.' She's sat in my office, a tiny slip of a thing, and if I fancied a flutter, I'd wager that any second her body was about to implode before me. She relaxes a little bit when she seeks her usual place on the sofa opposite me. I watch her gaze around my office, like she often does. She casts her eye over my personal photographs on my desk, placed there to give clients a sense of familiarity and homeliness. Her eyes settle on my hands and she examines my wedding rings. I wonder if she realises how tarnished they are underneath the gilded exterior.

'How are your videos going?' I ask her. I need to make her comfortable before I address the real reason she's asked for an urgent appointment.

Grace is an entrepreneur, but then she can afford to be. I watch her uploads, because I'm interested in what is out there in the ether about wellness and self-help. It's a minefield. My profession is being hijacked by amateurs who churn out wisdom without responsibility or consequence. It's dangerous, like any harmful substance, and comes at no cost. Online mental health gurus analyse out loud, and quote sayings riddled with inaccuracies about the human condition. The vast majority of bilge I read is uninformed and woefully under researched. Most of it is diagnostic speculation at best, and should be left to the experts. Even Newton said he could calculate the motions of heavenly bodies, but not the madness of people.

However, I don't see Grace's offerings as hazardous, just naïve, and innocent information-giving for people to better themselves. She's a survivor, who has endured severe trauma. Now she wants to save people. It's common. Only this morning, before she came into my office, I watched a piece she'd recorded about deep breathing offering relief for acute anxiety attacks. I reckon if I'd have suggested this to Grace when she first walked through my door, she'd have run a mile. One needs to tread lightly.

'I got half a million views on my last one.'

'That's amazing. You're reaching so many people,' I tell her.

I think it's terrifying that young women like my daughter are being told how to live by armchair aficionados, but my parents' generation thought that pop music was an abomination, so it's all relative.

'I don't know if I'm making a difference, though,' she adds.

'I can see that's important to you. It's difficult to quantify. Define the difference you'd like to make,' I suggest.

She can't, because it's an itch under her skin that she can't scratch.

'Maybe look at it in terms of contributing to something rather than solving it for people.'

She takes her time to think and smiles.

'I like that.'

I've made her feel useful. I wait. She looks at her hands. Her fingers appear raw, as if she's been pulling the skin off in ribbons. Still, I wait.

'You must have heard about the woman who was found murdered in Grantchester?' she asks, finally.

'Yes, I did, I think everyone knows about that. It was shocking. Her poor family.'

'I know.'

Grace pauses. I've made her stop and think about Monika's family and their suffering. She's toying with her compassion. My eyes wander outside. I'm dog tired. I spent last night trying to pull together the disintegrating parts of my life at home.

'I trained her. Monika was one of my clients.'

'So you knew her well. That's shocking, Grace. Is that what triggered you this weekend?'

She nods.

The air in here is stifling, even though the windows are open. I toy with locking out the birds and suffering the soulless sterility of the air-conditioning unit.

'I can't help but think that when a woman is harmed like that, it's because she's... well, a woman.'

I wait.

Her body releases a great sob, and it takes me by surprise. She isn't big enough to store such a sound. It's all consuming and violent. I push the tissues close to her.

'God, I'm sorry,' she weeps.

'Not at all, let it out.'

'She was so beautiful. Why do men think they can do that?' she sobs. 'I've had dreams about her.'

'Do you want to share them?' I ask softly.

She takes her time and gathers herself.

'I see her body, bruised and cold. She's all alone on the riverbank, no one to protect her, and the man who did it is free to brag and feel all big about himself, as if that's what it means to be strong and manly.'

It's a fair assessment of toxic masculinity, I suppose. She blows her nose.

'I see them all day at the gym, strutting about like big strong men, puffing out their chests and looking at me as if...'

'They're displaying their sexuality in front of you, and it threatens you?'

'Yes! They never stop. I know what they want.'

'They want you?'

Grace stares at her hands and at the tissue, which is damp and disintegrating. She reaches for a fresh one and blows her nose again. The noise makes my nerves jangle. I concentrate on the birdsong from outside.

'I'm sure they don't but that's how it makes me feel.'

'Why do you say, "I'm sure they don't"? It's perfectly feasible that men will want you in that way. Gyms are intensely sexual environments, like you say, all that huffing and puffing, and showing off one's body. Do you know most of the men who frequent your gym? Are they predators? Are they aggressive?'

'No. I know most of them and they're not like that at all. Ignacio is the gentlest person, he's like a brother.'

'Ignacio?'

'He's a colleague.'

'Right, and who else?'

'They're all lovely, really.'

Now we're getting somewhere. I'm beginning to think that Grace really can't help shed any light on Monika's last days on this earth, so I might end up being able to carry on her therapy after all. I'm glad, because she's a tender soul. I feel as though I can really help her.

'So, they're not all monsters who harm innocent women?'

The tears flow again and I wonder if Ewan is coping at school. We decided he should go in, to show he's got nothing to hide. He's a warrior and I'm proud of him. I called DI Hunt and he agreed that I could dictate Ewan's statement over the phone. He reassured me that their suspects are the Morgan children. And Henry. It's unlikely Ewan's testimony will be required. But unlikely isn't good enough for me, I need to make sure.

Grace is still crying.

'Good, let it out,' I soothe.

I can see her mind whirring and suddenly she begins to smile. It's soft, as if she's been taken by a recaptured memory. A good one.

'You're smiling,' I say.

'Am I? God, I must look a mess.'

'Healing is messy. What were you thinking of when you were smiling just then?'

She fiddles with the tissues in her hands, which are red and raw, and I picture her recording a YouTube video just as she is now. I wonder how many likes she would get. But the truth isn't palatable in the world of make-believe.

'You just made me realise that Ignacio is actually a lovely person,' she says. Her face beams with the honesty of infatuation, but then a shadow clouds over it once more. 'Monika was in a couple of my videos.'

I know this because I've seen them.

'Her husband wasn't happy. I think he controlled her.'

'What makes you say that?' I ask her, bracing myself for what she might tell DI Hunt about Tony.

'She told me. She said he didn't want her to retrain in English law. She desperately wanted to. She was so bright and clever. He stifled her. He made her so unhappy, I saw it in her face every time he was mentioned. He picked her up once, from the gym, and he looked at me as if I was a threat.'

I'm careful to control myself.

'Did she ever tell you that she was scared of him?'

'No, but I think she was.'

'Do you think it's something that you should tell the police? You said they called you.'

I hold my breath.

'No. It's none of my business. My father makes my mother feel exactly the same. It doesn't mean he wants to kill her. It just means that I'll never marry a rich man. They have too much power.'

I smile at her wisdom.

Chapter 56

'Time is ten thirty-five a.m. Interviewing Henry Nelson in connection with supplying Class A drugs to a minor, under caution. The witness has declined legal representation.'

Experience told Henry that lawyers were only interested in one thing: money. They trained for years to sit next to desperate souls who hoped they'd defend their rights to the letter: wrong. He looked at the detective, who was a classic dick-swinger, just as Carrie had told him.

In his cell, where he'd been for more than twenty-four hours now at the approval of the CPS, he'd been over and over his last conversation with her as she packed for Bali. His arrest was drug-related and so that told him that they had nothing on him for Monika. But it was only a matter of time before they pinned that on him as well.

'I haven't touched drugs in ten years,' Henry said.

'So the testimony of seven pupils of George Paget School is lies?'

Henry glared at the detective and Hunt smirked back at him. Carrie had been correct: the guy's cheap suit and bad teeth made him look like a failure, but Henry could see that, underneath the mud, there was an enemy diving for pearls. He stood no chance in the war of words, and intended to say very little. He wanted to know exactly what they had on him. Testimony from kids was surmountable. He didn't blame them. They'd say anything to please adults. They'd clearly been coached, whoever they are: Brandon Stand's cronies, no doubt.

Hunt was a bedrock of the system. Sat in this small windowless room, on cheap plastic seats, he wasn't looking for the truth. He was looking for a fall guy. Henry's mouth felt dry. Denying basics like refreshments was a police tactic that was difficult to prove was done for malicious gain.

Hunt pushed a photo towards him. It was of a small clear plastic bag, filled with little blue pills. Those blue birds used to be his lifeline. He'd do anything for them. But not anymore. He'd heard that some bad shit circulated on the market these days and he was glad he was out of the game.

'So, like I said, Henry, we have reason to believe that you supplied at least one bag of these to minors from George Paget School, with the intent to make a profit. Unfortunately, one of these little blue pills killed one of their students on Friday night: Brandon Stand.'

'Yeah, I know Brandon, the school bully. I don't deal drugs.'

'He was the headmaster's son.'

'So what? He terrorised the younger kids and the headmaster knows it. He's reported – he *was* reported – regularly but, surprise, surprise, nothing was ever done.'

'Are you suggesting that Brandon deserved to come to harm?'

'Not at all. You asked if I knew him, and that's how I did, I'm giving you context. I never dealt drugs to school kids, or anyone. I haven't touched an illegal substance since I was banged up, but you already know that. What else have you got?'

'I don't know why you would suggest that I know your comings and goings, Henry, this is why you're here today. We rang you on…' He checked his notes. 'Friday. About an unrelated incident, as we thought then, and you told us that you'd last seen Monika Thorpe on Monday of last week, in fact exactly a week ago. What were you doing on Friday?'

Henry watched Hunt shuffle pieces of paper, flicking and fiddling, trying to catch him out. The mention of Monika ruffled him but he kept his composure. Hunt had dropped a crumb and was letting him stew on it: another police tactic he was familiar with.

'I was at the gym, then I went to work, like always.'

'And Friday night? Did you visit the recreational ground over near Coulter Park?'

'No, I've never heard of it.'

'So why would Brandon Stand's friends implicate you in offering pills to them and suggesting meeting there?'

Henry snorted. 'That's bullshit and you know it.'

'Look, Henry, it would be a lot easier if you just told us the truth. We have several pupils from George Paget telling us that you educated them in the use, handling, sourcing and cost of illegal substances. Can you tell us why that may be?'

'Because you told them to?' Henry said. His outward bravado was waning. He was tired, hungry, thirsty and desperately hostile toward the system that was about to stitch him up. He began to sweat and a wave of prickly heat spread over him. His back became sticky and he would kill for a gulp of fresh air.

'How did you hurt your hand, Henry?'

'At work, yesterday morning, on a tool. It's fresh, you can see for yourself.' He unwrapped the bandage and showed off his damaged hand. The swelling had begun to go down, and the blood had coagulated and stuck. It was a mess.

'Wounds don't behave in such a convenient manner in my experience, Henry. That could have been done at any time over the past week. What were you doing Tuesday night?'

Henry's stomach sank to the floor. *Here we go.*

'Nothing.' His hand throbbed.

Hunt shuffled papers again and the noise was getting on Henry's nerves.

'Do you recognise this?'

Hunt showed him a photo.

'It's the field behind Grantchester, by the river.'

'Indeed it is. Note that the witness positively identifies the dump site of Monika Thorpe's body.'

'What? What's this about? What have you got? This is bullshit!' He stood up but two thick hands, the size of bunches of bananas, pressed on his shoulders, and he realised that he'd have to keep his cool should he want to get out of this.

'Look, I don't know what you're piecing together here, but it's rubbish. Everybody who goes for a walk out of the city knows that field.'

'Have you heard the name Grace Bridge?'

'What?' A tingling feeling crept up Henry's spine. The colour drained out of his face.

'We've been looking into your record, Henry. It's protocol, don't worry. But we notice that you changed your gym membership to the same one where Grace

Bridge is a PT, shortly after the incarceration of your brother, Vincent.'

No, no, no…

'I look out for her,' he whispered. His voice seemed a million miles away from his body.

'You "*look out for her*". Hmm.'

'I have nothing to do with Vince, he's my half-brother anyway. What he did was vile. I wanted to make sure she was okay. He's a low-life bastard, I have nothing to do with him.' He felt himself descending into a dark pit.

'Brother, half-brother. Potato, tomato. Bad apples falling from the tree, and all that. I guess that's why the victim never made the connection? I trust she doesn't know?'

Henry stared at him.

'So, your relationship with Carrie Greenside is one of the reasons you're here today. You fitted her kitchen too?'

Hunt was all over the place, as if he was digging into his body with a hundred knives all at once. Henry had no idea where the next attack would come from.

'Yes,' Henry replied. His throat constricted, making his voice crack.

'You know who we're talking about? The very close friend of Tony Thorpe. In fact, a bit more than that, eh?' The detective smirked.

Henry felt sick. What the hell was he saying? He remembered that it was Carrie who recommended him for the job on the Thorpe home. No? Surely? Why? His head scrambled and fogged up.

'So, we have Carrie Greenside's car parked outside of your house, positively identified by a neighbour, around one a.m. and two a.m. in the early hours of Wednesday fifteenth of July. What have you to say about that?'

Henry stared at him blankly.

'Social visit?'

Henry couldn't speak. He'd called her, not knowing what to do... who to turn to...

'Discussing kitchen worktops?'

Henry didn't answer.

'So, back to business. There were significant amounts of cocaine in Monika Thorpe's blood from her toxicology report. We were wondering if you knew where she got it from. This is your opportunity, Henry, to describe the exact nature of your relationship with Monika Thorpe, because we're searching your house and your van as we speak. You know how this works, Henry, I've read your file.'

'It's the husband you should be looking at, not me. He hit her and I saw the bruises.'

'Hmm. So, Tuesday night. Where were you between the hours of eleven o'clock at night and three a.m. on Wednesday morning? I presume you and Ms Greenside were together?'

Chapter 57

DI Hunt wasn't used to fitness centres. He hated them. Not only did they remind him how unfit he was, but how inadequate as a man. They were full of testosterone-fuelled muscle-junkies who watched themselves sweating in mirrors. He knew he didn't fit in, and it made his intense feeling of failure even worse.

Grace had said she'd meet him inside the gym. He took the lift, which had a sign inside it that offered priority use for vulnerable and physically recuperating clients. Great. The doors opened and he was assaulted by pop music and bright lights. People grunted and gyrated, and he looked around, lost, like a child taking their first steps. He knew what Grace looked like because he'd looked her up on the gym website; he'd also read her police file. He saw her and she waved. She was talking to a very attractive man who looked of Latin descent. His skin was the colour of honey and his hair was jet black. He had the natural grace of a jaguar. She pointed to him and smiled. He felt even smaller. He caught sight of himself in a huge mirror and looked away again.

Grace walked over to him and they shook hands. He was aware that his palms were sweaty, to match his forehead, and hers were cool and gentle. She was tiny. He wondered if he smelled of body odour and it reminded him of the hurtful comments at school. He was known as

Bobby Orange on account of his BO. His armpits began to feel sticky as if the mere memory sparked a storm of stink.

'Should we get a coffee?' she asked.

'I was going to ask if there was somewhere a little more…' He was lost for adequate words.

'Less busy?'

She strode towards an office at the back of the gym and he admired her body. She was clearly blessed with those genes that made everything look in place. He remembered the transcript from her trial, and Vincent Kemble's defence trying to argue that she'd come on to him and made him confused as to her intentions. He'd also read her medical records, and the detail of her internal injuries, and felt disgust that a barrister could ever argue that it was her wish to have sex with her attacker. But he watched her now and understood why any man would want to be in that position. It was a controversial assessment but women had to be careful, he believed. Someone in tiny not-really-there shorts, being overly friendly, could lead to misinterpretations. If only women understood the power they held over men, they'd be more prudent, perhaps, and make his job a lot easier.

She led him inside an office and closed the door, which said 'Assessment Room 1' on it. It was air conditioned and he felt some relief. She beckoned him to sit down and fixed two coffees from the machine. She handed him one.

'I thought you fitness people didn't drink coffee,' he said.

'That's a myth,' she said. 'I don't eat lettuce all day either.'

'Good, I was worried there for a while.'

'Do you go to a gym?' she asked.

'Do I look like I do?'

'It's never too late to start. You might like it.'

He fumbled around in his briefcase and brought out some notes. 'You're aware I'm here to ask you some questions relating to the murder of Monika Thorpe?'

That wiped the smile off her face. Never too late to start...

'Yes.'

'So, your relationship with Monika was as client and trainer?' he asked, waiting for her response so he could make notes. He was disorganised at the best of times and often started a new pad of paper only to lose it for hours, or even days, before he could write up his findings. Another reason to get on board with current technology, but he never quite did.

'Yes.' She sipped her coffee. He felt as though he'd levelled the playing field a bit and felt a pang of guilt as she retreated into a quiet shadow of the confident trainer he'd seen out in the main gym. It passed.

He asked her about Monika's mindset in the weeks running up to her murder, as well as anything that she'd confided in her. Grace painted a picture of an independent woman who came across as frustrated and lonely.

'She talked a lot about her husband, I think she was scared of him,' she said. 'I think they might have fallen out. I got the impression that he was very controlling.'

He noticed that Grace spoke protectively of her client. She became jumpy and he could either put it down to being involved in a police investigation or because he'd possibly hit a raw nerve. He saw that her décolletage was reddening and she restlessly played with anything she could get her hands on; a pencil, a tiny model of a skeleton, a computer mouse. She also tapped her foot. It changed the atmosphere inside the room.

'We have a man in custody,' he said.

She stopped her jittering and looked at him squarely. 'Really?' she asked.

'Do you know this man?'

She looked at the photograph and her jaw set in an open position. 'Well, yes. He's a regular here.'

'How would you describe him?'

'Is he in trouble? Is he the man you have? That's impossible, Henry wouldn't...' Her words tapered off. He continued to hold her stare but she looked away, then back to him.

'How well do you know him?'

She faltered; torn, no doubt.

'Pretty well, I mean, as well as you can know someone here. He comes a lot. He's a nice person.'

Now she was defensive.

'And this man?' He showed her another photograph.

'Is this some kind of joke?' She stood up abruptly, knocking the chair over behind her, and her anger bubbled up. Her face changed into a grimace and her body was poised to fight, or run. Hunt didn't move.

'Do you?'

She turned away and walked to the other side of the room, then back again. 'Yes, it's... I do know him... I know his name, I...'

'Grace, it's important.'

'Is he out of prison?'

'Vincent Kemble,' he said.

'Why are you doing this? What's this all about?' Her voice reached a pitchy crescendo. There was a banging at the door and it opened suddenly: it was the tanned, good-looking trainer.

'Grace, are you okay?' he asked, throwing the detective a threatening stare. His accent was Spanish or Italian. Hunt didn't reply. Grace stared at him.

He introduced himself and asked the trainer to join them.

'No! It's all right, he doesn't need to stay,' Grace said.

Hunt ignored her and showed him the photograph of Henry Nelson, and asked if he recognised him.

'Yeah, he works out here,' Ignacio said. He stood in front of Grace, but the aggression had gone since the detective had told him who he was, and why he was here.

'Vincent Kemble is Henry Nelson's brother,' Hunt said. He omitted the 'half' for effect, and he got what he wanted.

Grace turned pale and backed into a corner.

'What's going on? Who is Vincent Kemble?' Ignacio asked, looking between the policeman and Grace.

'I can't breathe…' Grace whispered.

'What's going on?' Ignacio's voice grew louder.

'I can't breathe…' Grace repeated. Her legs collapsed and she fell to her knees.

'Get some help, now!' Hunt barked at the trainer. He couldn't tell if the girl was play acting. Ignacio fled the room and called for help. Grace was hyperventilating. Hunt knelt down and held her head. She was fully on the floor now, and panting. Her eyelids had drawn back and she was muttering. There was nothing of her and she reminded him of the girls who hung around gang members: all skin and bones, and drama.

'Grace? Stay with me, breathe, come on, you got this.' Hunt held her as she shook and fought her demons. Maybe he'd gone too far?

Another man entered the room and knelt beside Grace, putting her into the recovery position; somebody else wheeled in an oxygen tank. A mask was strapped to Grace's face and she sucked the pure O2. Hunt stood up and observed. He'd seen plenty of people fake such attacks but he realised this one was genuine. If he ever needed a witness to testify against Henry Nelson, he had one now, right before his eyes, seething with betrayal and reeling at the duplicity. He could see her mind whirring and he had no doubt that she was replaying all the times she'd stood next to him, here in the gym, perhaps even helping him with his routine – or whatever they did in here – and reliving the moments in real time, but on this occasion feeling the full force of revulsion and treachery. It never ceased to amaze him what he saw in people. He'd read that rape cases could have flashbacks but he'd never seen one with his own eyes. It was quite a thing.

It didn't matter what Grace Bridge thought of the detective now, and he didn't care. What he did know was that he had a perfect prosecution witness.

Chapter 58

Carrie sipped Champagne from a crystal flute in the first-class lounge at Heathrow. Her nerves had steadied, but she felt the nagging warning of peril. Only when she was on the plane would the doubt subside. Getting away geographically was imperative, even if the shadows followed inside her head. She felt slightly guilty at leaving a grave situation, but her emotional and mental wellbeing was her only priority. Everybody made their own way in this life and if she was to heal properly, she had to stop saving people. Including Henry.

Two men, both of whom she'd bedded, were prime suspects in a murder case. The fact that she saw neither as capable was irrelevant. She didn't trust the law, and she didn't believe in fate. A few weeks on a beach in Bali would sort her out. She wasn't entirely sure she'd return. She'd made it her lifetime's work to be unattached. It was safer that way. But now she'd left herself vulnerable. Distance was the only thing that mattered.

She sat back in the comfortable armchair and closed her eyes. She recalled the first time she'd met Henry. She'd opened her door in a rush, late for the King's Cross train, expecting an overweight builder to be stood there, unshaven and unkempt. But the vision of Henry when she flung open the door took her by surprise, and in the split second she hesitated, he saw it. Three days later they were shagging in her pool house. He'd surprised her with his knowledge of what a woman of her years might crave. She knew that experience like that came with practice, and she smiled as she recalled thinking how many bored housewives he'd serviced over the years. Carrie was neither, and she kept him intrigued. Her energy levels were that of a woman half her age and he kept coming back for more.

Visions of Henry's naked body filled her head. She sipped Champagne and allowed her mind to wander. She hadn't had sex like it in a long time. It worked for both of them. She could smell his aversion to commitment the first time he smiled at her. And it suited her just fine. Nowhere in her house escaped contact with what turned out to be a short but intense liaison. The kitchen table, when she'd cracked her head on the oak and they'd howled with laughter as he hopped around trying to find something to put under it, his legs pinned together with his trousers around his ankles. Or the time on the stairs when they'd crawled from step to step, aiming at making it to the bedroom, but not quite pulling it off, as they remained on the fifth step, ending up knocking three paintings off the wall, worth ten grand each.

Then he gave her the knife and the cash.

She opened her eyes and got herself a refill. He told her the kid was innocent, which is why she'd agreed to hide the stuff for him. But what if they weren't? Her desire to keep a child safe, like no one had done for her, would be her undoing. The opportunity to give a child something she'd never had was overwhelmingly alluring. But she'd broken her life rule: let no one in. She felt a crushing fear around her ribcage and had the vision of buildings falling on her.

Then she'd recommended Nelson's Bespoke Kitchens to Tony on the train one day, over takeaway coffee and FTSE predictions.

She went to the bar and poured another glass, telling herself that in Bali she'd give up again. It was just a setback. She looked at the departure board and checked her flight to Abu Dhabi, which was her first stop. It was on time. She was flying with Etihad because they were the best, and she could afford it. No one could get to her in the air. If she could choose, she'd probably spend her whole life up there. Everything down on earth became insignificant when she was up in the clouds, safe and timeless, with nothing to worry about.

She'd tidied up her life on the ground. Her finances were comfortably secure, offshore in the Cayman Islands. Her house was paid for and expendable, and she'd packed her full allowance of suitcases covering all seasons. She was eager to board.

She poured another glass.

Tuesday night, when he'd called in sheer panic, she'd known that she'd become a big sister to him. There to turn to in tough times, no longer a lover. She'd been usurped months ago. Not that she thought it would ever last. She wasn't that stupid. She'd driven over to his house to comfort him. It was probably the most reckless thing she'd ever done in her adult life, and she realised that it was because she had feelings for him, which is why she was right to get away now.

She tried to relax and closed her eyes again but every time she did, another flaw in her narrative presented itself uninvited to disturb her peace. She tried to concentrate on the hum of coming and going around her. She followed the blur of voices and a few announcements, and took some deep breaths, willing herself to calm down. One voice, though, got louder, and it was joined by others.

She opened her eyes and saw two uniformed police officers talking to the receptionist at the desk. Attention surged through her body, making her fingers tingle and spark to life. Her hairs stood on end and her palms began to sweat. They were coming over to her. One spoke into his radio and the other locked his gaze onto her face. The receptionist trotted behind them. Carrie's ears were full of ringing bells and her vision narrowed. The officers' vests bulged with menace and their hips jangled with cuffs, gadgets and keys. If there was ever a metaphor for warning, it was this. She couldn't move.

All she could do was pray they passed her, on their hunt for someone else.

But they didn't.

'Carrie Greenside?'

Words failed her. The officer repeated his question, clearly impatient and keen to get his task completed. She nodded.

'Stand up, please, ma'am. I'm arresting you for supplying Class A substances to minors and for obstructing the course of justice. You are not being charged at this time, and so you do not have to reply, but anything you do say...'

She wasn't aware of standing of her own volition, but she found herself upright, spun around and plastic ties attached to her delicate wrists. Suddenly, her innate sense of injustice roared upon her and made her body jerk away from them.

'What is this? Get off me! I've done nothing,' she screamed. She caught a glimpse of the receptionist's face, who was horrified.

'Calm down, ma'am. Don't struggle or I'll have to restrain you. I weigh over two hundred and thirty pounds. I don't want to have to force you downstairs.'

She struggled.

It took both officers to carry her to the elevator and down to a waiting squad car. They cable tied her feet as well and she tried to bite one of them. She caught him unguarded on his forearm and he squealed.

'Fuck you!' she screamed.

'Shit! That's assault added to your list, lady. As well as resisting arrest.'

'Fuck you!'

She was bundled into the back of the vehicle and was aware of a small crowd watching her.

'Fuck you too!'

There was a metal cage in the back space of the car, and she was thrown in. There was nothing for her to get hold of to damage: she only hurt herself as she writhed like an ensnared beast. The door slammed but the car rocked with her physical fury. The door opened again and something was sprayed into her eyes. Jesus, it burned, and she howled in pain. The door was slammed again.

She never saw where she was taken because her eyes were scorched. The agony was so great that she lost control of her senses and wet herself.

By the time they arrived at their destination and she was carried out of the car, her body was limp and she was silent. And she stank of piss.

Chapter 59

The day of Monika's disappearance

As Henry's van pulled up, Monika raced outside to warn him. It had been a mistake, texting him the photo of her bruised cheek. She closed the door quietly, hoping Tony wouldn't hear. Their argument had ended how it always did: with them going to separate areas of the house. But she knew she'd gone too far this time. She'd questioned Ewan's paternity and she'd never expected Tony's reaction. She realised now that Ewan was the most guarded treasure he had, and all the investments, shell companies, deals, assets and contracts meant nothing compared to his one true love. His son, Ewan, and his mother.

She walked towards Henry's van and met him marching around it as he slammed his door.

'Are you okay? Where is he?'

'No, Henry, listen, I shouldn't have told you—'

'Of course you should. He's got you trapped here and look at you, now you're making excuses for him. Monika, it's time to put him in his place.'

'No. Things are different now. I need to handle this.'

'Your eyes… have you been snorting?' Henry asked.

Monika looked away. Henry ran his hands through his blond hair and kicked the wheel arch of his van.

He heard a stumble and turned to Monika just in time to catch her.

'Get off me! So what if I had a pick-me-up? Men can act how they please, it's not fair.'

He caught her shoulders in his grip and stared at her. Tiny crystals clung to her nostrils.

'Jesus Christ,' he whispered.

She wriggled one hand free and struck him with a hard, glancing blow to his chin. He grabbed her hand before she could do it again.

'What's wrong with you? I came here because you asked me to.'

'No, I didn't. It was a mistake. Get your hands off me.'

The door opened behind them.

Tony stood in the grand entrance, surveying his property. Monika froze. Henry puffed out his chest and let go of Monika.

'A bit late to be measuring up, Henry?' Tony asked. But it wasn't a question.

'I don't take it lightly when a woman is mistreated,' Henry said.

Tony looked between them. Monika closed her eyes and held her hand out to steady herself.

'I beg your pardon?' Tony asked.

'Her face.' Henry stepped towards the door. 'Lay another finger on her and I'll slap you around a bit, shall I?'

Tony laughed so hard that his body bent double. Henry raged and clenched his fists. But by the time Tony recovered, it wasn't Henry who caught his attention, but Monika. She wasn't there.

Henry swivelled around, following Tony's gaze.

'Welcome to my world,' Tony said. 'She does this. By the way, she fell on the chimenea, by the pool. I've never hit her.'

'Sure thing, pal.'

'I'm not your pal. Could you remove your van from my driveway? And consider your contract terminated. I do hope Monika learned something from her experiment with a bit of rough from her side of the tracks. You stay where you belong, and I'll do the same, eh?'

Henry backed away.

'You're not all that. It just goes to show that your fat wallet isn't enough when it comes to making a woman like that happy. She'd rather someone her own age.'

Henry got back into his van and pulled away, screeching out of the gate, past Monika, who'd hidden herself in a bush. Cocaine often made her believe that she could disguise herself and she even smiled as she stepped out of her cover, but as she watched Henry's van disappear, and Tony close the front door, she had no idea what to do, apart from get some fresh air for a while.

Keeping to the shadows, the warm night air kept her wrapped in a counterfeit jacket of wellbeing. For now. She felt herself abroad, on a Riviera somewhere, strolling along a promenade, from bar to bar, before she was caged by the blindness of love and marriage. The streets were empty. In suburbia everyone goes to bed on time. Headlamps from a distance threw shadows beyond the mighty trees above and light danced across the road as she continued to wander. She realised she was lost. Not geographically, but universally.

When a vehicle slowed down beside her, she thought she might be asked for directions, but then a friendly face peered out of the open driver's side window. A mixture of relief and guilt flowed through her body and she realised that she was tired. She got into the passenger side and closed her eyes as they drove away.

Chapter 60

DI Hunt stared at the DNA results from Tony Thorpe's house.

They'd collected genetic material from those he knew had been in the house, except for Henry Nelson, but he had that to hand already, thanks to his prison time. The case was coming together, but not how he'd expected.

First, he had Henry Nelson all over the place; the master bedsheets, the bathroom, Monika's toothbrush, her underwear and three towels. It was, as expected, all over the kitchen but that was virtually irrelevant, given his job. But a kitchen fitter's seminal fluid shouldn't be in the bedroom. However, it would be difficult to argue in court that Nelson had harmed Monika simply because he was in her bed. DNA didn't last long on organic matter, it degraded fairly quickly, and so the assumption was that Monika had sexual contact with Henry Nelson relatively soon before she disappeared.

Then he moved on to Carrie. Back in 1989 the police didn't routinely collect DNA, but Carrie Greenside was a Leicester girl and some bright spark, no doubt inspired by the arrest of Colin Pitchfork a couple of years previously, had instructed his department to start taking it as procedure, until everybody realised how expensive a hobby it was. They'd had her on file for over thirty years. Ms Greenside had not only been in the Thorpes' pool house and the kitchen area for a quick martini. Her DNA was in the bedroom too.

He read her file.

Over thirty years ago, an angry and aggressive young woman had attacked her father with a frying pan. She'd said he was beating her to death and it was self-defence. The mother hadn't corroborated her story and Carrie had been charged with actual bodily harm. As he read on, he wondered if perhaps he'd underestimated her. A big-shot city worker, with loads of cash and a smart-mouthed lawyer, was distracting. He knew that it was trendy these days to forgive so-called trauma survivors and what they'd been through. Now, he questioned if Carrie was the abuser and not her father. He found it hard to believe that a grown man, allegedly beating his nineteen-year-old daughter to death, could be overpowered with a frying pan. Likely story. At nineteen, Greenside had been given a second chance and let off with a suspended two-year sentence for hospitalising her father. Maybe that was a mistake. He searched her probation notes and read that she'd gone off grid after that, moving to London and living on the streets. She'd fallen into the cycle of selling her body for cash to put up her nose or inject into her sorry veins. It was a typical tale of a girl who felt sorry for herself, but also revealed her true colours. He remembered colleagues of his, all male, gradually too scared to doubt the word of these so-called victims, as the idea of child abuse became trendy. Fathers became afraid to discipline their kids and anyone who lifted a finger against a child was viewed with suspicion. In his book, where there's smoke there's fire, and he was glad that his nose had sniffed her out before she left for Bali. That, and the doc's tip off.

Carrie Greenside was a violent criminal.

She'd been transported to the station from the airport, like a howling alley cat, so he was told, and he wished he could have seen her face when they walked into the first-class lounge. He loved seeing the high and mighty get their just deserts. She was in a cell three doors down from Henry Nelson, but he'd sit on that little gem until he started working on her. Nelson was being gradually broken down and he had the same plan for Carrie. She was dressed in her going-away clothes and there was something supremely satisfying about watching the CCTV from her cell as she paced up and down in her white suit and heels; no phone, no food or water, and no dignity. For someone like her, it would be a levelling for sure. The piss stain on her pants wasn't even dry. He'd secured a warrant to search her home.

His initial suspicion – that the husband killed Monika Thorpe in a fit of jealous rage – was wearing thin. The more likely story was that Henry Nelson went to the house, egged on by his spurned lover, took Monika for a 'drive', and ended up getting rid of her. Moving and disposing of bodies was always easier for two. Carrie Greenside had been hanging men out to dry all her life. She had balls of steel.

Tony Thorpe, in love with a younger woman who took him for a fool, and cheated on him, had understandably gone on a bender to cope. Meanwhile, Carrie Greenside, green with envy over her lover's new squeeze – a younger, sexier version – set about planning to get rid of her. No doubt, Carrie was in Thorpe's bed to make it look like she was part of his recuperation, rather than the plot against him. The court order for Doctor Moore's files had been pushed through and had arrived this afternoon. It was time to give her a call.

'Doc, I hope I'm not disturbing you, I'd like your professional opinion on a matter,' he said.

Hunt knew Alex Moore would make a damn fine witness.

She had a soothing voice. It was sexy. He liked listening to her. Ostensibly, for a complex case, it was always a good idea to get an expert on board who was as affable as this psychologist was. She had the kind of manner that convinced him she sought the truth. His case was shaping up nicely.

'I'm filling out background on some of our persons of interest,' he said to her.

Hunt didn't deem it necessary to bother her with an update on his case. It could sway her against him; after all, she must have bonded with his two suspects. He omitted the fact that they were both in custody.

'Go on,' said the doctor.

'We received the court order today, I can access your files on Henry Nelson, Carrie Greenside and Grace Bridge, but I'm not a fan of formality. I've got some questions for you, if you don't mind. I can send over the order if you need to see it.'

'Of course, if it helps. They're complex cases. Send it over for my records, but I'm happy to answer your questions.'

'I know all about Carrie's father.'

'You do?'

'Do you think she made it all up?' he asked.

'I beg your pardon?'

DI Hunt sensed the doc's surprise. She'd naturally want to protect the work she did with her clients, he guessed. But maybe even she had been manipulated. Master opportunists had talents that even the police found difficult to grasp. They dealt with them all the time. Nine times out of ten, it was the flaws in human testimony that stalled results. People lied, all the time, and got away with it. The law was really there to be interpreted, that was all. He'd been a copper long enough to know that. It's why they didn't bother investigating certain crimes. If there wasn't enough gravitas in a person's personal projection, then there was no way in hell they'd convince a jury. On the other hand, perpetrators could sway even the most carefully selected cross section of the public. Look at Bundy. Hunt knew that Carrie Greenside in the dock, if they got her there, would be a tricky customer, and he needed leverage to convince the CPS to charge her.

He changed his approach.

'What I mean is, do you think it's possible that someone with her backstory could be over-dramatising things? I'm getting victim-this, victim-that, but did anyone actually look into the facts? I mean – with respect – it's your job to listen to one side. Is it possible that you have patients who come to you and fabricate things, to get your sympathy?'

There was a pause and he gave her time.

'The short answer is absolutely yes, but Carrie Greenside has all the hallmarks of complex PTSD.'

'What's that? I thought war vets got that?'

'You're confusing the different types of PTSD. When somebody experiences something terrifying, like a bomb dropping on their house, or hand-to-hand combat in war, they can get debilitating flashbacks that render them helpless in specific situations, like lightning or thunderstorms, for example. However, complex PTSD is the result of sustained terror over a long period of time, and child-abuse victims fall into this category.'

'Oh.'

It was news to Hunt. God, there was a tagline for everything these days.

'I'm not saying that it can't be faked, but it would be highly unusual. Her story is very convincing.'

'Could she have read about it?'

'Detective, what are you getting at? All symptoms of PTSD are almost impossible to sustain convincingly if they're faked.'

'What about a narcissist? You see, I've been reading up on it. A shrewd player makes it their life's work, don't they? To get people like you on their side? All I'm asking is if it's possible.'

'Anything is possible. May I ask where you're going with it?' Doctor Alex asked.

'Well, her behaviour is flagging up more questions than it's answering, in my book, and I think a story like the one she's down on record as having would certainly be... how shall I say? Convenient.'

'I don't think there's anything convenient about Carrie's situation. She suffers terrible flashbacks and panic attacks in ordinary situations that wouldn't affect most of us.'

'So, she's mentally ill?'

'No, I didn't say that. PTSD is a condition, not an illness. It's a very understandable reaction to things that children are not supposed to experience on a daily basis.'

'So she's got huge anger issues and hasn't developed normally. That would make her pretty unstable.'

'Maybe it would help me if you told me exactly what Carrie is supposed to have done?'

Hunt sighed. This wasn't exactly going the way he'd envisioned. But he needed to get the doc on board.

'Her history of violence bothers me. I have reason to believe that she was jealous of Monika. Isn't part of this whole thing about children being raised wrong that it leaves them emotionless? She has all the traits I'm looking for, and her boyfriend comes from a nasty family.'

'I see.' Doctor Alex paused again. 'Her boyfriend being Henry Nelson?'

'Exactly. Look at Fred and Rose West. The perfect storm.'

'In my capacity as their therapist, I really need something concrete to work with to give a proper assessment of what they might be capable of together, if that's what you're asking me.'

'I'm sorry to drag you in on this, doc, but, like you said, I would have got around to you eventually, even if you hadn't have approached me like you did. You could be crucial for us getting to the bottom of this.'

'Right. I follow you.'

'You said yourself that Ms Greenside accepted stolen goods from her lover and perhaps Monika got in the way.'

'Perhaps.'

'Well, doc, thank you for your time, it's been… educational. Oh, one more thing. I paid a visit to Grace Bridge yesterday and had to be the bearer of some terrible news. She might need your help. I'm afraid I dumped it on her. I'm not a counsellor, I leave that sort of thing to you guys.'

'What was that?'

'It turns out that Vince Kemble, the guy serving time for her brutal rape – now there's one woman who I know told the truth, I've read the file – is Henry Nelson's brother. Can you believe it? He said he moved to the area to protect her. Some warped sense of chivalry there, if ever there was.'

The doc went quiet.

They hung up.

Hunt smiled. The case was a virtual wrap.

Chapter 61

Hunt caught me off guard. It's amazing when a snowball begins to roll, and it gathers extra weight at an alarming rate. Hunt has been busy. I never even contemplated Carrie's potential involvement in all this. I open her file on my computer and go all the way back to when we first met, and I'm searching for an answer to Hunt's question. Not for him. But for me. Could she have made it all up?

DI Hunt reminds me of my husband. Jeremy always rushed his work. Which is why he never practised. Results don't come quick enough when you have to treat a patient for years. Just like Hunt, Jeremy is in the ride for the finish line, not the race. He's in the wrong job, but that's not my concern.

I deal in what I see, which is exactly what a good detective should do. But Hunt is eager for a suspect to send off to court, and my testimony is the backbone of his case. The problem is that my facts are undeniable, but this time the water is muddy. It's almost impossible to dredge through years of client appointments and separate facts and opinions; the subjective from the objective. But I must. It'll take me hours, and I buzz Dora to tell her to cancel all my appointments for the rest of the day.

But I've also been doing my own digging. About Hunt. An old colleague of mine, who owes me a favour, has sent me a copy of the psychological profile of several police officers. Hunt was treated seven years ago, when he was a lowly constable, as part of a general institutional push to clean up ingrained misogyny in the force. Hunt volunteered because it gained him some free therapy. And he needed it. It's written in black and white in front of me. Grandiose egotist. It reads like a disease but isn't one in the strictest sense. However, it's the type of condition that is almost impossible to treat, because narcissists like Hunt never recover. And it's common for them to accuse others of their own failings. As long as I massage his ego and play the feeble woman reliant upon his superior experience, he'll likely look for the answer that gives him the best chance of looking like a hero. His hunger for attention pervades every aspect of his life, and I'm about to make him look like all the things he craves to be. If I want it.

I put my faith in my detailed casefiles. I've always been meticulous with my notetaking. The answers I seek are somewhere inside these pages in front of me on my screen. There is no doubt that I'll be called as an expert witness, I'm all Hunt's got. So I have to be rock-solid in my attestations.

Hunt got one thing correct. Clients are selective with what they let slip. The human brain is supremely clever: it stores only what it needs to protect the host. Memory is highly unreliable, however, coming from an accomplished authority like myself, juries tend to think that, for some reason, my memory is better. My clients purge what they need to and nothing more. Like Lydia evicting her breakfast. They sit on my comfy couch, potentially fabricating narratives, merely to tolerate life. It's a *form* of truth; a version that's invented to fit their individual egos and needs. It makes me a facilitator of fabrication, but this is beyond a working jury: a selection of fourteen civilians who are desperate to get back to their families.

Hunt wants me to make his suspects fit his case, Jeremy-style, omitting the hard work. It's up to me to decide if I can do it. For Ewan. For Tony.

I have affection for Carrie and Henry, but they're not my children. The worst nightmare of a trauma survivor is not being believed. Should I deliver Hunt what he needs, and testify that my clients are potential liars? It would destroy them, like being abused all over again. The alternative is I let the case destroy my own family. I have the unique opportunity to re-write my son's narrative and protect him from harm, and keep him and his father clean. There's no contest.

If Ewan were to be implicated in the crime of supplying drugs and breaking and entering, at the age of fifteen, he won't stand a chance. A criminal record at that age will screw him for life. Just look at Carrie and Henry.

I rub my tired eyes and remember the day Ewan was born. The baby wasn't supposed to live. I had been warned not to get pregnant a third time but it happened. Ewan had been starved of oxygen for almost five minutes, and survived. He is a miracle.

My expert judgement is never sullied with emotion. Yet it is. I wear my cape of psychiatry like a metal jacket, and it causes people to believe that my conclusions hold more weight. Probity is relative.

And yet I need reassurance.

I ring Tony.

'Alex, it's good to hear from you, I'm glad you called. The police seem to have gone extremely quiet, or am I just being optimistic?'

He sounds remarkably calm.

'Maybe they're looking elsewhere. Finally, Hunt could be getting his act together and doing his job.'

'Do you really think so?'

'Perhaps.'

'Alex, I was wondering if I could ask a favour.'

He catches me off guard because I've called him for the same thing. I let him go first, awarding me the upper hand.

'The woman I was with on Friday night.'

'Yes?'

'Carrie Greenside.'

'Yes.'

'I knew her for fifteen years, she told me a lot.'

'Go on.'

'Like you were treating her.'

'Ah.'

I think I know what's coming.

'Won't the police want to talk to you?'

'And you think what I tell them might sway Hunt?'

'Crikey, Alex, I… erm… yes, actually. You could sell snow to Eskimos.'

'You want me to do a sales pitch on Hunt?'

Tony laughs, but I don't.

'You should have come to work for me, Alex.'

'Don't go over that again. I'm perfectly happy getting inside people's heads and not their wallets, thank you.'

'Ah, but you do both, and that's why you're dangerous.'

I could tell him that Hunt has already got access to my files and that I fully intend on being his star witness. However, Tony has a loose mouth. Besides, he pillow talks too much, I should know, and I have no idea who his latest squeeze might be. It's too much of a risk.

'Did the police find all your phones?'

'No. Not the one I use to call you.'

I pause.

'In return...' I ask.

'Anything. What do you need? You know I'm always here for you, Al. Is Ewan okay?'

He hasn't called me that in years.

'That's my point. He might need a new start. In fact, we all do.'

'I'm listening,' Tony says.

'Away from Cambridge.'

'And you want me to pay for it?'

'Yes.'

'He's my son, Al. I'll always look after you. Can I ask about Jeremy?'

'I'll take care of Jeremy.'

'Name your price, Al, and consider it done.'

It was that easy.

'Al?'

'Yes?'

'You haven't asked me if I did it.'

'Did what?'

'If I killed Monika.'

'I don't have to.'

Chapter 62

'Ms Greenside, we've been over this many times. We have found, inside your house, in the stuffing of a mattress, a large knife that we know, from fingerprint analysis, was used in a serious offence. Now, why don't you just tell us why you hid it?'

Carrie wrung her hands. Her body seemed awkward, like a teenager's, and her brain was foggy. Her clothes were alien and she felt the eyes of the detective searching her secrets. She couldn't seem to make her thoughts stand up in order. Her foot hurt from kicking the interview room door, repeatedly, until she'd been restrained once more, adding to her misery. Smog shrouded her vision and she lost sense of where she was. She was aware that a man in a suit was sitting beside her and the policeman referred to him as her assigned legal representation, but she couldn't join the dots and they were both tiring of her vagueness. Her wrists and ankles stung from the tightness of the cable ties, which had, once again, been removed after her promise to behave herself. The aroma of urine choked the air and she picked at her fingers.

She'd already been charged with assaulting a police officer, and resisting arrest.

'Carrie, you're going to pull the skin off, and you won't find the answers there.'

Hunt's voice.

'Stop calling me that!' she snapped. The lawyer jumped, and she felt the draught from the shift in his excessive weight. He was fat, and took up more room than his chair could offer. He'd been supplied by the CPS because she hadn't been able to call her own. Her privileges had been denied her.

She was surrounded by men.

'We also have witness testimony that puts you at the address of Henry Nelson in the early hours of Wednesday the fifteenth of July, for at least an hour.'

'I had no idea that he was going to give me a knife. I just put it there because he told me to.'

'Carrie, you're an intelligent woman. Do you really expect me to believe that? I assume you mean Henry Nelson gave it to you?'

She eyed him with suspicion.

'Did you hide anything else for him, Carrie? A heavy tool, like a wrench perhaps?'

The lawyer remained silent. She saw her mother's face, disappointment written all over it. *Carrie is a difficult child…*

'No.'

'What about these?' He held up a clear bag full of tiny blue pills. 'Found in one of your bedroom drawers.'

'What? I've never seen those before in my life.'

'And your DNA in Monika Thorpe's bed, from your hurried liaison with her husband? An act of revenge, perhaps, after Henry killed her?'

Carrie registered snippets of sentences, disjointed and noisy in her already crowded head.

He slid a photo her way. It was of a white sheet, with stains ringed in red. It was, she was told, exhibit C. He showed her another one.

'A hair follicle belonging to you.'

The lawyer sucked his teeth. The noise grated on her nerves. It was the universal noise of a man's disapproval of a woman. *Click-tut*. A memory of Tony convincing her to go upstairs... romancing her better judgement away from her. Tricking her with lust.

'He planted it!'

'Who planted what?'

'Tony!'

It was Hunt's turn to click-tut.

'He didn't have to plant anything, though, did he? We already know you were a willing lover, it's not news. It's your motive I'm interested in. I suggest that the business meeting turning into something more amorous was planned by you, to make Mr Thorpe appear the heartless husband.'

The room sucked her in and the walls closed down on her head. She scratched her scalp and rubbed her face. She was aware of a hand over hers, trying to force it away from her mouth area.

'Carrie, you're scratching your skin, you're going to hurt yourself.'

She looked from the lawyer to Hunt. They were plotting against her.

'The way I see it, Henry moved on to a younger woman, and you hated Monika for it. Then when Henry decided to get rid of her because she wanted to run away with him, you encouraged him and helped dispose of her body.'

'No!'

'So tell me your version.'

'What? Shut up!' She rocked back and forth and ripped at her blouse. She searched around the room for answers. Her skin was hot and itchy.

'We have your phone records, and we know Henry called you late last Tuesday night. What did he say? Did he ask for your help? Why did you go to his house shortly after?'

Hunt's mouth moved but his words were jumbled mumbles.

'We've found men's clothing, Henry Nelson's size, in your laundry. Did you take home his bloody clothes and wash them for him? You seem to like making his problems go away.'

Movement behind her melted into one. The hand on hers became two and suddenly she was unable to move. She saw plastic cable ties and realised they were restraining her again. A face lunged toward her in a dream-like sequence, and it was the face of her father. His eyes were red with fury and she froze, terrified of what he might do if he got really mad. She saw his fists curled up, ready to strike, and she cowered, shielding her head from him. She covered her face and struggled with a body.

'Carrie?' Somebody was shouting her name.

'We understand how unresolved anger can manifest itself even after years of supposed dormancy, in cases such as these. We will take the assessment for mental capacity.' It was her lawyer talking but she couldn't see his mouth move. *Mental capacity...*

'What did you do to your thumb?' Hunt asked her.

She stared at her hand and remembered the broken vase.

Hunt gathered his papers, pleased with himself. He was leaving. But she hadn't been released.

No.

Not again.

She managed to get her bound hands away from those holding them and held them up in front of her eyes, to confirm that she wasn't going mad. But they were covered in blood.

Hunt stood up. 'Get help in here, now!' someone shouted. She didn't know if it was the detective or the lawyer. What was the difference?

She lunged across the table and went for the detective's throat.

'*Carrie!*'

They landed on the floor. Her fingers wrapped vice-like around his neck and, even with her wrists bound together, she managed to keep a tight hold, with her full weight on top of him.

Her lawyer's voice boomed. Carrie couldn't tell who was on her side, if anyone. She held tight and felt hands all over her, but still her grasp held strong.

'Get her off!'

Knees, elbows, God knows what, attacked her from all angles, but she couldn't be budged. The blood vessels pumping oxygen to her biceps felt engorged and she tightened her grip. The detective's eyes reminded her of her father's. He was turning purple, and it felt good.

'Carrie!'

A waft of air momentarily interrupted her concentration and she glanced sideways. A figure rushed towards her, holding something. Burning hot rods shot through her and she convulsed, falling sideways, hitting the ground.

Her head shut off and her vision went black.

Chapter 63

'Henry, why don't you just stop wasting everybody's time?' Hunt asked. 'We've got CCTV footage from a neighbour of Mr and Mrs Thorpe, showing you pulling up outside their house, at speed, on the evening of Tuesday the fourteenth of July, at eleven forty-five p.m. You then leave, in fact screech away, at eleven-fifty-nine p.m.'

'So you can see where Monika went?' Henry asked. His throat was raw and his head felt like a mixer. He'd lost sight of what was real and what wasn't. He couldn't remember what he was accused of in what order. He knew they'd found ecstasy pills in Carrie's bedroom, and his clothes in her laundry.

'We've also got Monika's DNA all over your van, Henry. Her hairs tangled in tools, her blood on the corner of a toolbox, and a gold necklace identified by her husband as belonging to Monika, who was last seen wearing it on Sunday the twelfth of July, two days before her murder.'

Henry stared at him blankly.

'We've also got you speeding out of Cambridge on the A603, which is on the way to Grantchester where Monika's body was found dumped, at twelve thirty-two a.m. on the morning of Wednesday the fifteenth of July, shortly before you headed back with Carrie Greenside, so she could collect her car.'

'I couldn't find her. I tried.' His voice was a whisper.

A knock on the door interrupted the interview and an officer bent over to tell Hunt something. He smiled hawkishly.

'Henry Nelson. The CPS have decided that, on top of the charge of possession of banned substances with intent to supply, we have now passed the threshold to charge you with first degree murder. You do not have to say anything, but anything you do say...'

Henry sat forward very slowly and put his head in his cuffed hands.

'It is now the view of this department that you willingly entered into an agreement with Ms Carrie Greenside to entrap and entice Mrs Monika Thorpe to a place of your choosing, with the intent to take her life. You drove Mrs Thorpe to a secluded spot and murdered her with a tool from the back of your van. You then sought the help of Carrie Greenside to dispose of the body. Do you have anything to say?'

Henry looked up at the detective, whose face was covered in triumph. Henry's guts fell to his toes. The police had their story; the case was as good as solved. He didn't stand a chance. He had a violent history, he consorted with criminals, he supplied and used drugs, and he was conducting an illicit sexual relationship with the victim, as well as his supposed accomplice. Their motive was lust-fuelled jealousy, and their alibis were each other.

'How's Carrie?' he asked lamely.

'Ms Greenside has been charged with accessory to murder and unlawful disposal of a body.'

The years he'd spent studying the locations of CCTV cameras around cities, and avoiding them, learning the back roads, had gone out of the window in a moment of recklessness because Monika had wandered off. By his own admission, he'd confronted the victim's husband on the night of her murder, and Monika had been in his van, many times. His fate was sealed. His injured hand was a further physical testimony to recent violence. It was over.

'Mr Nelson?'

He looked up. DI Hunt was a little man in every sense of the word, but it didn't matter. In the world of law, Henry couldn't win. He didn't have enough fingers or toes to count how many times he'd told young lads inside prison that justice always prevails. But it didn't.

'Mr Nelson?'

Hope seeped out of his body.

He felt a tear slip down his cheek. Was it worth it? Should he give a statement to be read out in court? Just because it was his truth? No one else would care, but did he care enough?

'I didn't do it, and neither did Carrie.'

'You've said that, but we know that's not the case, is it? Will you at least comfort the family by passing on why you did it? Give them some solace to allow them closure? A confession might make the judge go easy on you for sentencing.'

Hunt waited.

This was how it was done. He felt the wheels come off the engine inside his head and felt everything stop. He could have jumped over the table and landed a punch, easy, but he'd given up, and he knew that Carrie had already done it. He recognised her howling voice as she'd been dragged back to her cell. It was only then he'd truly realised what was going on. Now, the detective's face told him everything he needed to know: the bruises around his neck and the scratches down his cheeks.

Good on you, Carrie. We'll never win, but we won't go silently.

'Violence obviously runs in your family, like it runs in Carrie's,' Hunt said.

Rage bubbled up in Henry, but it went nowhere. Hope was a fool's game. He grinned.

'Something funny?' Hunt asked.

'Not at all. Face hurt?'

'You'll be transferred to the nick on remand, where you'll await trial. Goodbye, Henry. Take him down.'

They were three little words Henry thought he'd never hear again. Snapshots of life inside taunted him. His shoulders sagged forward and he imagined himself already in the witness stand being taken down the steps to the ice box, and the long journey to incarceration. He had no fight left. As officers escorted him out of the interview room, he thought of Grace. He'd kept her safe for almost two years since Vince went down. Who would look out for her now?

His cuffs clicked open and he was shoved roughly from behind, into the cell, as the door slammed shut. He sat down heavily on the plastic-covered bed. Bile burned his throat. He stared at his tattoos. He ignored the ones he'd had done inside; they were immature and irrelevant. It was the ones he'd had since then: the lotus, symbolising being born into shit, but growing out of it, regardless. The unalome, symbolising the path to enlightenment through chaos and transition. And the arrowhead, symbolising his future.

No future. He began to scratch them, gently at first, rhythmically rubbing as if trying to find some grounding in the bedlam. Then the first slivers of skin came away, stinging his flesh, but not enough to stop. The pain distracted him. His nail broke more soft skin and soon, a patch two inches long had completely rubbed away. The petals of the lotus flower disappeared, and his arm swelled with tension as blood trickled down his arm. The blood oozed along the tributaries of his physique, purging the shame all over again. It joined the bloody bandage protecting his wounded hand – a wound that would clinch the case against him, when they told the jury that Monika fought back before he smashed her skull in.

Chapter 64

Friday 7 August

It's been over two weeks since Carrie and Henry were arrested and charged. They were both denied bail and are remanded in prison until their trials, which will take months to come to court. The thought of them behind bars haunts me. It's not fair, and I'm still not convinced that I'm doing the right thing testifying for the prosecution. For now, the drama has dissipated and life has chugged back to some form of normality. Jeremy has continued to decline, physically and mentally, and has fallen into a deep depression since Monika died. He sleeps downstairs most nights. I wake him in the morning with a strong coffee, and he climbs the stairs wearily to our bed, where he stays for the rest of the day. He has begun to display signs of alcohol dementia. Experts also call it wet brain because his grey matter is literally soaked to death.

This morning, he went to put a bottle of milk away and opened the oven, where croissants were baking, and placed it in there, melting the plastic and causing a catastrophe, which I cleaned up. There are other times he'll stop mid-sentence and look blankly at one of the children, as if seeking clarity for where he is.

The disease is underdiagnosed, because it presents the same as Alzheimer's, but I've lived with Jeremy for thirty years and I've seen the steady decline to full-blown aphasia, apraxia and agnosia. It's a living hell for the rest of us. Unless he's asleep, which he is now.

The house is quiet. Lydia is at a therapy session and it takes me all my strength not to get involved because she's being treated by an amateur. Ewan is at school. The sensational press interest over the death of Brandon Stand continues to cause a stench in the corridors. The headmaster retired early on health grounds. James comes and goes, like my faith in the system.

My dealings with DI Hunt are sporadic. He struts around, triumphant and masterful, promoted on the back of my clients, which I delivered to him. Ewan was spared a police interrogation. His friends entered plea arrangements against Henry, and Hunt informed me that their testimony clinched him as the instigator of Brandon Stand's death too. He's looking at manslaughter, plus murder, in separate trials, if he makes it to them. I know intimately how Henry will fare in prison for a second time. Carrie is facing an accessory charge. As a witness for the prosecution, I cannot find out how they are holding up on remand.

Tony has been more than generous. He was dismissed as a suspect. I've seen a practice in Windsor that I like. My plans don't involve Jeremy.

I follow the news closely. The last photos I saw of Henry and Carrie, on the front pages, were shocking. The disintegration of their bodies and their reputations have stripped them of everything they had. But I also have to be able to believe that the two of them could have planned this all along, using me as a testing ground for their stories.

My ego should be wounded. I will say on the stand that I counselled both but didn't spot their delinquency.

Hunt's evidence is convincing. But my testimony is important. So is Grace's. It isn't personal. Henry was the last person to see Monika alive, and his car, phone and own testimony put him at the scene. His injured hand wasn't a coincidental accident after all. The cleaning of the body proved premeditation; and dysfunctional adults, plagued with childhood misfortune as a result of maltreatment, are more likely to be capable of the cold-heartedness associated with such acts. Both the accused scored seven out of ten on the ACE (adverse child-hood experiences) scale. It doesn't mean they necessarily committed the crimes; just that they're more likely to have done. Circumstantially, Hunt's on thinner ice. The prosecution will argue that Monika had become clingy and fixated on Henry Nelson, and thus inconvenient to him. Then there was the knife found under Carrie's bed, proving she'd be willing to commit criminal acts for her lover. They'll say Henry is a narcissist who is obsessed with unavailable women, especially married ones. They'll say that Carrie is a sociopath and a control freak who had violent intentions towards women because of her mother. Together, they're a couple who acted out their damaged backgrounds by inflicting pain on others.

The press can't yet report them as Monika's killers, just the suspects as charged, but already their characters have been destroyed. But every night when I see Ewan's face, I forgive myself a little bit more.

I try to concentrate on the job at hand, to distract me from my racing mind. I'm looking for something. I've never employed an accountant – they're overrated – but every year, when I file my tax return, I regret it. I'm rifling through receipts, trying to sort them into date order. I detest the task. I work through my diary chronologically. The big stuff, the clients' fees and the bills, are already entered onto spreadsheets and filed, by Dora. It's the detritus of one's life, the day-to-day running of one's own business that makes all the difference to my turnover. Everything is saved, even the kids' receipts from places like Tesco and WH Smith. We've got into a habit of throwing them into a bowl in the kitchen, and from there, they get chucked into a box, in my study, to be sorted in late summer.

I come to the receipts for July and stop at one. It's from 15 July. It puts my daily business of buying notepads and staples into perspective, and I see Monika's skull being bashed in. A few more receipts have the same date and it makes my hands tremble. I calm myself and allow the banality of the task to refocus myself. Two items stand out, and I have to cross reference them with my bank account on my Mac.

One is a carwash facility, which I match with a card transaction on the joint account. The other isn't a receipt at all. It's a queue number docket for the recycling dump, downtown. Both are dated Wednesday 15 July.

I stare at the screen, and then to the photograph of my children on my desk. Ewan's smiling face beams back at me and I realise that no matter how much money Tony gives me, and regardless of how much I continue to protect them, I won't find peace until I've done the right thing.

I go back to the queue docket and the carwash receipt, and I relive the morning of 15 July. Jeremy was proud that he'd performed a domestic chore and he wanted praise for getting my car valeted. I call the number of the recycling plant, which is on the slip. It's answered on the fifth ring by a breathless man with a gruff voice. I garble something about tracing equipment, asking if they have CCTV.

'Head office has it, it's all digital. I can access it on the computer here, but, love, we're crazy busy at the moment, a dickhead just dumped a truckload of hard-core rubble in the wrong skip. Are you police?' the voice asked.

'Yes,' I cough.

'Good, it's only ever police who want it. More thieving?'

'Yes, lots of it going round, I'm afraid. Can you send it to the usual email?' I ask him, impressed by own capacity for smoothness.

'I have no idea what that is, my love,' he says.

I give him an email address, trying to be as breezy as possible. It works and I stare at the phone in my hand. The blind trust of law-abiding citizens is truly beautiful. I give him the date of the docket and we hang up. Seconds later, an email pops into my inbox and I stare at it.

I open it breathlessly; it's an easy-to-work Mpeg and I navigate around it quickly. An image appears on my screen and I press play. I note the date and time of the footage. The guy has sent me the recording for the whole day and so I forward to when the ticket says Jeremy was there. The voucher says he was in the queue at nine o'clock in the morning: before he had my car valeted.

Then I see him.

I watch Jeremy, in my car, pull in and park. I recognise his clothes. I've washed them for three decades, and I know every fibre of them. He gets out of the car and goes to the boot, taking out something large. I identify it straight away, and I know it's the blue wooden coat stand that I ordered from a bespoke company in France.

Once, it had complemented my nod to the hedonism of the seventeenth century, with which I chose to decorate the new pool changing rooms. There are gold mirrors in there and padded seats, and a chaise longue. Silly really, now I think about it, but Monika loved it.

I return to the footage and watch Jeremy throw it nonchalantly into a skip. Then he goes back to the boot and lifts something else out. It's another piece of the coat stand, and I recall the argument we had over it. I accused him of blacking out and falling over it, probably breaking it in temper. He said I must've moved it. The argument was never resolved.

I close my computer and I know that I must tell Hunt. Reasonable doubt only takes one person to stand up for the accused, and present new evidence, which could force the whole case to be reviewed.

I sit back and sigh. Allowing a spouse access to a private computer is like sharing a bank account: never a good idea. He's regularly accessed my client files, to glean ideas, presumably. I know his passwords, and he's lazy so he never changes them. I retrieve his files, which I've been collating over the last couple of weeks – preparation is key if you want to be the victor in divorce proceedings – and begin organising them into one, for Hunt. The dozens of photos of Monika stare back at me. He believed I'd never find them, or the paper he was working on. In one of his fantasist and addled stupors, he'd called it 'Chosen Suspects in a Murder Case, by Doctor Jeremy Moore, BSc, PhD, APA Award for Outstanding Lifetime Contribution to Psychology'. Jeremy has never been awarded anything by the American Psychological Association.

Chapter 65

Hunt sits back on a cheap plastic chair and it creaks and gives way, sending him backwards a few inches, with a loud crack. He tries to recover himself and I keep my face straight. I give him a few minutes to sort himself out. He fiddles with the lever and shuffles back into an upright position. He's flushed.

His arrogance during this investigation has perturbed me, but also buoyed me, because I know he'll be easy to sway.

'Rest assured, we've got our killers,' Hunt tells me, after I say I have concerns about Henry and Carrie's guilt.

'How can you be so sure?'

'I can't reveal my sources, but I'm convinced that Henry beat Monika to death and Carrie helped him dispose of the body.'

I recall Monika's tiny frame and reckon this won't stand up in court. Neither will all the other holes, once a barrister gets their hands on the actual evidence.

'The case is proceeding nicely, don't you worry.'

'Look, Detective, I'm not worried because you might not get a conviction, and that somehow my reputation will come under the spotlight. This is about the truth.'

'The truth?'

He almost smiles but he knows me well enough to stop himself. He sees me as serious, to a fault, and consummately professional. In fact, when I've thrown spanners at his prosecution he's reciprocated with daggers and a mystical shroud of jargon to try to put me off.

'Yes, the truth.'

'I have to protect the integrity of my informants, otherwise they wouldn't be informants now, would they?' he says. I let it go. His smugness irritates me. 'There's a lot more to this than you know. It'll all come out in court.'

I raise an eyebrow. 'And what if I told you that I'd discovered new evidence?'

He shifts uncomfortably in his seat. The room is small and I hear the hum-drum of the workings of his office coming and going outside his door. His workspace is a disaster zone, just like his mind, I suspect. He's trying to belittle me.

'Look,' he says, as a father would when reprimanding a child. 'You said yourself that Nelson is a narcissist.'

'No, I didn't – they were your words,' I tell him. His attempt at amateur profiling has dogged his whole investigation. 'You said all along that you were looking for a narcissist.' I recall how he'd regurgitated the definition triumphantly straight from Wikipedia, and given me a self-congratulatory grin, as if he'd just been awarded a DPhil from Oxford. Or a lifetime achievement award from the APA.

That stops him. He sits up straight, closing his legs for once. His face becomes grave and a flicker of concern crosses his brow.

'I've found some disturbing new evidence, and I'd like you to at least take a look at it.'

'What type of evidence?'

'Evidence that might give you a different suspect and exonerate my clients.'

He sighs and the puff of air travels my way.

'It's impossible to go in a different direction now,' he says. 'The evidence is virtually wrapped up; it's too late.'

Sweat beads have broken out on his brow.

'What if I withdraw my testimony?'

He panics. 'You can't.'

'Yes, I can. It'll make me a hostile witness and the prosecution won't want to touch me, especially if I reveal I submitted crucial new evidence before the case was concluded against the defendants. Information which, by right, should go to the defence team.'

'Are you a lawyer now?'

'No, but I know a good barrister.' I've spent an hour on the phone to Kingston and he's given me all the answers I need.

'There's nothing you can tell me that will change my mind on this,' he says. 'I've been doing this too long – believe me – to fail to recognise when someone's guilty. I can smell it. What we've got here are two very sophisticated killers who tragically stumbled upon somebody in their way. Your friend, may I remind you – Monika, God rest her soul. Think about her mother. She's flown in from Latvia to repatriate her daughter's body.'

Nice try. His invoking of the Almighty tickles me. I've hit a nerve.

'If you change your testimony now, because you feel sorry for your ex-clients, which is understandable – we in law enforcement see emotions get in the way all the time – then you could be held in contempt of court. Do you want that?'

'Will you at least look at what I've brought, and humour me with your experience, professional to professional?'

He sighs again and spreads his legs. Finally, he nods. 'What have you got?'

I reach for the envelope in my bag. I've printed everything, except the Mpeg, which I've uploaded onto a USB. It clatters onto the table as he empties the contents.

'The investigation has been travelling in the same direction since you dismissed Tony as a possibility. But all the time, this has been under your nose.'

I wait as he examines the documents, the photos, the Google history, and watches the CCTV from the tip.

'I remember the morning well, now it's in context: he insisted on taking my car. I like it valeted regularly but on that morning he was adamant that he'd get it done.' My lie is a tiny one, but, even so, I need to make sure that justice is done. It's clear that Hunt is unwilling to accept the evidence. 'I drove his car to work. There were several heavy black bags in the boot, which I threw into our commercial waste at work. Their collection day is Wednesday. I noticed the coat stand missing that evening when I came in, and when I asked him about it, he said he couldn't remember. We argued about it.'

Time seems to freeze Hunt's breathing and he rewinds the CCTV footage over and over again.

The blood has drained from his face.

'What colour is it?'

'Pale blue, it's French baroque—'

'Jesus... How did you get this?'

'I asked them for it, how else? I was going through my tax receipts and found the docket, and noticed the date. It sent me into a blind panic and I looked into it for myself. I didn't expect to find anything important.'

He covers his eyes with his hands and sits back. He looks like a man who has just had some devastating news.

'What is it?' I ask him.

'Do you have a photo of it? The coat stand. When you first bought it?'

I search my phone. I'm proud of my interior design forays, and I keep photos in files there. I scroll through the one entitled 'Pool House' and find some close-ups of the coat stand. I'd forgotten just how beautiful it was.

'What is it?' I ask him again.

He doesn't answer me. He's mesmerised by the coat stand. He moves my phone this way and that, zooming in and out.

'Please, tell me what's going on.'

My plea is all it takes to soften him and bring him back to life. His face is full of sympathy for me and it begins to dawn on me that he's confirming my worst fears.

'You've got a part of it, haven't you?' I ask him.

'Not so much a part, but pieces. Very small pieces.'

'You said yourself that the case's weakness has always been evidence with which to convince a jury. You never found a tool in Henry's van with Monika's blood on it. Just the box. The blood could've been from any of their encounters. Henry and Carrie have previous proclivities to violence, and they showed capability of collusion and opportunity, they knew the victim, and they have motive. But there's still something missing, isn't there, Paul?'

He looks up at me. I know what he's thinking.

'You're accusing your own husband of murder?'

'I don't know my husband anymore. He's secretive, distant and haunted by something. He was obsessed with Monika – look at those photos – he was jealous of her lovers, and I have no idea what he was doing on that Tuesday night because he often sleeps downstairs.'

'These are grave allegations.'

'No graver than the ones facing Henry and Carrie. I saw your face when you saw that coat stand. What is the procedure for the admittance of new evidence?'

I already know the answer because Kingston has explained it to me. Hunt now appreciates that I'm not going anywhere without his promise that he will at least consider the possibility that they've got the wrong suspects.

I've floored him. He gives the impression that he's shocked and disgusted by what I've given him, but the reality is that what I have actually done is compromised his integrity. I've shown him up. We both know that the only thing he wants is for me to go quietly and leave the envelope with him, so he can either destroy it, or use it. It's his choice, but he knows if he makes the wrong one, he's lost his most valuable witness for the prosecution. Me.

Chapter 66

'Interview with Jeremy Moore. Time is…' Hunt looked at his watch. 'Three fourteen p.m.'

Hunt shuffled a stack of papers. Jeremy's whole body ached. He sat still, trying to focus on the man facing him and the questions being asked of him. His body was rapidly letting him down. The stillness of the room, along with its plainness, challenged his nervous system. Hushed immobility was something that eluded Jeremy in his day-to-day life. Normally, the ping of electric signals travelling around the cavern of his brain was enough to keep him moving. Even the simple path to the pool house was sufficient to distract his degenerating biology. Every organ in his body had begun to corrupt, years ago. But Hunt couldn't see that.

On the outside, only a specialist would have spotted the fine layer of moisture that blanketed his clammy skin. Untouched by the sun, thanks to him not being able to sit still for long enough for it to seep through the exterior, he remained pasty all year round. The swollen face wouldn't be noticed by anybody who hadn't known him ten years ago and had nothing to compare it to. Some might assume that the puffy softness indicated a kindly ageing. However, the dilated pores, choked with the task of detoxification, told another story. He kept his hands in his pockets to still the rhythmic tremors, and his sunken eyes and blood-shot sclera, slowly fading to yellow, could be put down to tiredness, worry and stress. Should Hunt have asked Jeremy to stick out his tongue, a furry, grey carpet would have awaited him. However, this wasn't a health check-up and Hunt was no doctor.

Jeremy's feet and knees tapped up and down underneath the table, and he kept his focus by looking at the clock above Hunt's head.

'Mr Moore, it's been explained to you why you're here. We'd like to ask you some questions as part of the investigation into the death of Monika Thorpe.'

Jeremy felt a shift of the air in the room and realised that Hunt was waiting for a response.

'Yes, I understand.'

He wiped his brow with the back of his hand. Hunt's furrowed and Jeremy could identify only one emotion on the detective's face: pity.

'Your relationship with Monika Thorpe?'

Hunt pushed something across the table, and he saw haunting visions of Monika's face – dozens of them. He peered at them lovingly.

'You were in love with her?' Hunt asked.

Jeremy's stomach growled, but he'd become accustomed to ignoring it.

He wanted a drink.

'Sorry?'

'Your feelings for Mrs Thorpe?'

'Oh, yes, she was pretty perfect.'

'Perfect? That's a grand accolade. Here, drink some water.'

Jeremy looked at the plastic cup in front of him but declined to take a sip. The blandness of it was disappointing even as it sat there, transparent and pure.

He needed a proper drink.

'These photos: why did you collect them?'

'She was a project of mine.'

'A project?'

'Yes, you wouldn't understand.'

'Try me.'

Heat welled up from the floor and settled in Jeremy's mouth like a desert.

'Mr Moore, can you tell me where you were on the evening of Tuesday the fourteenth of July?'

'I can't remember.'

'You can't remember.'

'Why do you keep repeating my sentences?'

'I'm trying to get some answers from you. It's simple, really.'

'What was that last one again?'

'It was about Tuesday the fourteenth of July. We know what you did on Wednesday the fifteenth; you got your wife's car valeted – inside and out – and you got rid of a broken coat stand.'

'Yes.'

'Why?'

'I think Alex asked me to.'

'You *think*?'

'I don't know. I can't remember.'

'Had you used her car on Tuesday the fourteenth?'

'Yes.'

'To go where?'

'Tony's.'

'So, you remember now?'

'Yes.'

'So, did you see Mrs Thorpe on Tuesday fourteenth?'

'Yes.'

'What time?'

'I can't remember.'

'Did you hurt her?'

'No.'

'But you can't remember.'

'Yes.'

'Did you kill Monika Thorpe?'

'No.'

'But you can't remember.'

'I'm sorry, what are we talking about now?'

Jeremy knew he was helping with inquiries about Monika but couldn't recall the context.

'The death of a woman you saw on the evening she died. A woman you were obsessed with. A woman whose body had shards of wood lodged in her back – wood from the coat stand you got rid of on Wednesday the fifteenth.'

'Right.'

'Right – you killed her.'

'No… I didn't. I just can't answer your questions. I'm sorry, I need to get some air.'

Jeremy stood up.

'What was your reaction to Monika taking lovers?'

'What? Who?'

'Anybody but you.'

'I need to—'

A large uniformed officer blocked the door.

'Jeremy, why did you write this paper?'

Hunt showed him something.

'It's clever, I'll grant you that, suggesting that certain people suffering from psychological problems could be framed in a murder case.'

Jeremy sat down but stood straight back up again, and paced up and down. Hunt watched him.

'I really need to—'

'Jeremy, you're not going anywhere until we've got some answers.'

Jeremy twisted away from Hunt and stared at the wall. He avoided the shaft of sunlight. He threw a glance over his shoulder and fished around in his jacket pocket.

'Sorry, what was that?'

Jeremy pointed to the table and Hunt picked up the photos to rearrange them. In the three seconds it took, Jeremy had whipped out a hipflask and taken a gulp.

Hunt glanced up at the camera in the corner of the room and back to Jeremy, who'd put the receptacle back in its hiding place, and was up and pacing again.

'Mr Moore, do you have blackouts from drinking?'

Jeremy clamped his mouth closed, fearing the fumes would reveal his hand and expose him as a fraud. He shrugged.

'Is this you?'

Hunt pointed to a photo. It was grainy, but Jeremy could still make out his trilby hat on the head of the driver, though the face was blurred.

'Looks like it. I drive my wife's car all the time.'

'Note the suspect has identified himself as driving the vehicle KU22 4OA, on the night of the fourteenth of July.'

Jeremy scratched his head. 'When?'

'I put it to you that when Monika Thorpe rejected your advances, you got angry and the two of you fought. You attacked her inside your own pool house, didn't you?

You used the wooden coat stand to do it. The coat stand which disappeared, or so we thought. Then you drove, with her body in your wife's car, to Grantchester jetty, where you beat her with a tool from the boot – like this. A tool which is now missing from the boot of your wife's car.'

'Have you finished?' Jeremy asked.

Hunt shrugged. 'Have we?'

'I'm not having some amateur sleuth analyse me and make up stories from some receipts, photos and whatever it is you think you have there in your file.'

The long sentence exhausted him. He swished his hand across the desk and the exhibited evidence floated to the floor.

'Do you deny the allegations?' Hunt asked.

'That's what you want, isn't it? To triumph in your cheap suit.'

Hunt sat further away, pushing his chair back. Jeremy had transitioned from edgy, scatter-brained and vulnerable, to arrogant, threatening and unpredictable in a matter of seconds. As long as it took to swig some strong liquor.

'I'll leave you to think.'

Hunt left the room.

Chapter 67

'Interview with Doctor Alex Moore...'

Alex straightened her skirt and coughed gently.

Hunt nodded to her.

'Doctor Moore, can you tell me in your own words your routine on Tuesday the fourteenth of July?'

'Well, I've checked my work notes and—'

'Sorry to interrupt, but can we start from when you woke up?'

'Oh. Of course. Jeremy wasn't in bed when I woke. He was asleep in the pool house. He's been doing that for a long time.' Alex clasped her hands together and cast her eyes down. 'I left him to sleep because I was in a rush. I fed the kids, then I left for work.'

'Did you have any communication with your husband at all?'

'No. My car was blocked in, so I took his.'

'Carry on.'

'I had a full day of clients and I didn't hear from Jeremy all day. When I came home, my car was back so I had to park in front of it. I remember it was around seven in the evening.'

'Do you know where he was?'

'He was in the pool house, but I was cross he hadn't spoken to me all day so I didn't go out there.'

'But you knew he was in there?'

'Yes.'

'Alone?'

Alex looked up.

'As far as you know?'

'I presumed he was.'

'And the children?'

'I said goodnight to them around eleven. Ewan was already asleep. Lydia was in the bath listening to music and James was out at a friend's overnight. The lights in the pool house were still on.'

'Did you tell your husband you were going to bed?'

'No, I locked up and went to bed. I figured if he didn't want to talk to me in four hours then he wouldn't begin at eleven at night. I gave up.'

'And did you hear anything after that?'

'No.'

'As far as you recollect, had you noticed the blue wooden coat stand missing before then?'

'No.'

'So when did you notice it gone?'

'The next day when I went to check on him.'

'Tell me about the morning of the fifteenth of July.'

'I got up early, because I heard James being dropped off. Jeremy wasn't in bed when I woke up, so I checked the pool house. He'd slept in there again.'

'Can you describe his appearance? Anything out of the ordinary?'

'Well, he was naked under some towels. But I was worried about him because I smelled bleach. I thought he might have been sick.'

'Where were his clothes?'

'I don't know. They weren't in the laundry when I got home.'

'Did it not strike you as odd?'

Hunt waited as the doc collected herself. It was a tough gig, implicating one's husband in such a crime. Even for the doc.

'I'm used to it, I guess. Jeremy is, erm… Not well.'

Hunt passed her a box of tissues and she took one.

'Indeed. What about when you received the news of Monika's death, did his behaviour not raise any red flags?'

'When my friend Tony Thorpe told me Monika had gone missing and he'd last seen her on that Tuesday night, I had no reason to suspect my husband's behaviour or connect the two.'

'And was it that Wednesday, the fifteenth, when you noticed the coat stand missing?'

'Yes. It was usually in the pool changing rooms. There were towels missing too. I assumed he'd used them to clean up the mess. We argued about the coat stand, but he can't remember things during blackouts.'

'Is this it?' Hunt showed a photo from the CCTV footage from the tip, as well as a copy of the photo Alex had taken when she'd first ordered the stand from France.

'Yes.'

'Has your husband ever been violent?'

The doc stared at him and he felt wretched having to put her through this. She sniffed and wiped her eyes.

'Yes. He has, when we've argued about Monika.'

'When was that?'

'Many times.'

'When you discovered the photos on your shared computer, what did you think?'

'I thought it confirmed that he was obsessed with her, but she rejected him.'

'Did you witness this?'

'Yes.'

'And the paper he wrote, entitled "Chosen Suspects", and the use of your confidential client files?'

She was back on familiar territory and gathered her composure.

'In my opinion, Jeremy fantasised about being published and celebrated. It reads like an academic study. Like somebody constructing a crime scene.'

'And in this paper, he creates a scenario where a murder occurs and the two suspects most suitable for the crime – in his opinion – could potentially be clients of yours?'

'Yes. I knew he read my client notes, but I had no idea what he wanted the information for. I changed my passwords as soon as I found out.'

'And the conclusion of the paper, for the record?'

The doc coughed and took a deep breath.

'How to get away with murder. Only somebody suffering from clinical narcissistic personality disorder would believe such a thing possible. Add to that a brain addled and confused by addiction… Sorry, this is very difficult for me.'

'Take your time.'

'It was obviously planned for a long time.'

Chapter 68

I'm waiting for the fallout of Jeremy's arrest but it's taking forever. My phone rings and it's Hunt.

'We had to let him go. We've had him for twenty-four hours, and the CPS haven't made up their minds. We had no choice.'

'Where is he?' My hand tightens around my mobile phone and I run to the back door and lock it, then I rush through to the garage and close that too, then I head to the front.

But I'm too late.

'He's here,' I say.

'Doc, I'm sending a car over just in case.'

'Bit late for that.'

I hang up.

The gravel on the front drive crunches as Jeremy pulls in slowly. He's out of the car and at the door before I can think what to do. His face is thunderous and I know he's sussed out my collusion, because of what Hunt had from my Mac. He comes in through the door and slams it shut.

Ewan is upstairs, Lydia and James are out.

Jeremy stops when he sees me, and he looks at me with deadly loathing. He's more awake than I've seen him in months.

'Darling,' he says, and I feel caught in a spider's web. His words drip with acid.

'Ewan?' he shouts.

My son doesn't answer so Jeremy takes the stairs and I follow him. He bursts into Ewan's room and goes in. I run to keep up.

'Mum?'

Ewan's voice is small and terrified.

'I'm here. Jeremy, leave Ewan out of this.'

Ewan looks between us. He shrinks back on his bed.

'Jeremy, leave him out of this. Come downstairs and we'll discuss it like adults.'

'Shut up, you bitch.'

'Jeremy, the police are on their way. You need to think carefully. Don't be stupid. It's over, they know everything.'

'Dad,' Ewan says meekly.

'She called me stupid,' he says to Ewan, pointing at me.

'No, she didn't, Dad.'

Jeremy launches his body at Ewan's chest of drawers and swoops everything off it in one go. He roars, and the sound coming out of his frail body is primal.

'Mummy's been to the police, Ewan. I'm a murderer, and I'm going to kill Mummy too, and it will be your fault forever.'

I close my eyes. There is no way out without my son. Ewan glances at me and I try to give him the reassurance he needs, just in a look.

Ewan starts to cry.

'Cry baby, just like you did when Brandon Stand got the better of you. You're no son of mine.'

'Jeremy,' I implore him to stop. These are words that kids never forget, but he doesn't care.

I take a step towards Ewan, and Jeremy warns me to stop.

'Fuck you, Jeremy,' I say, and I go to comfort my son. The blow takes me by surprise, and I see Ewan's expression of horror too late. In the distance, beyond the ringing between my ears, I fancy I can hear police sirens.

'Stay back, whore,' he says. As he grabs me, and I fall off the bed, my head bangs on the floor.

'I'm not a whore, Jeremy,' I tell him. I don't know where my strength comes from but I have to defend myself in front of Ewan. 'You know that.'

He faces the window and I look up to Ewan and mouth 'RUN! RUN!' He pauses for half a second then springs out of bed and bolts for the door. Jeremy isn't quick enough to catch him. Drunks are slow. We're alone. Jeremy is unsteady on his feet, and I'm amazed he was able to drive, but that will only add to the prosecution's case. I will testify that it's normal for him to drink and drive, if I survive the day. My head is bleeding but he's going to have to come up with something more imaginative to get rid of me than purely physical power, of which his body is depleted.

'Jeremy, think,' I say. I'll do anything to buy time.

He lunges at me, and in trying to wriggle away, my foot catches on the corner of Ewan's gaming chair. I feel him on me and I fight with him as hard as I can. He's a millisecond behind my reactions and we struggle to exhaustion, but he's banging my head up and down on the floor. The carpet doesn't save me. I can feel blackness spreading over my vision. His tenacity surprises me. My brain rattles in my skull and I feel my fingernails ripping with the force of my desperation to get him off me.

He straddles me and puts his hands around my throat and begins to squeeze. The police sirens are getting louder. It's not my imagination. His eyes are glossed over with hate

362

and booze. His breath is stale and sour. I don't want this to be my last vision on earth. I claw at his hands. His face is bursting with hatred and I feel as though I deserve it, but I can take it. It's worth it.

'Ewan isn't your son,' I manage to whisper.

He releases his grip and then slaps my face.

'Ewan isn't your son,' I repeat. 'He's Tony's.'

His body freezes. I've articulated it and it can never be undone. Of course he suspected before. But now it's undeniable.

The pain inside my body dissipates as I read the final tragedy unfold across his face. It's supremely satisfying. The shock is total. I cough and fight for breath, but his dead weight still pins me down. Metallic liquid fills my mouth. I hear the police enter the house.

His hands tighten around my throat once again. Spittle drips from his mouth. He's an animal, at the moment of the kill.

This is it.

I smile, and prepare for the inevitable. I will surely pass out, but I may be revived if he can be dragged off me within the next minute. Then he slumps on me and I know the police are in the room.

But they're not.

Ewan stands in front of me, holding a spade. Jeremy doesn't move. He's a dead weight on top of me and Ewan helps me get him off. Bodies enter the room and take Ewan outside, gently taking the spade away from him. A medic bends over me.

Everything goes black.

Chapter 69

The evening of Monika's disappearance

Monika climbed into the passenger seat.

'How did you know?' Monika asked.

'Tony called me.'

'Oh.'

'You need somewhere to stay?'

'Thanks, Alex.'

They drove to the house in virtual silence. Alex didn't ask intrusive questions and Monika didn't offer explanations.

'Let's go in the pool house. The kids and Jeremy are fast asleep.'

'I'll be quiet, I promise.'

The treble-glazed sliding doors shut out the night, and the heat, and Alex fixed Monika a drink from the fridge.

'I'm not sure that's a good idea, I've had enough.'

She was unsteady on her feet, Alex had already noticed walking from the car, but she gave her the drink anyway.

'I'm leaving him.'

'Why don't you cool off and sober up.'

'Don't do that, Alex.'

'Do what?'

'Be so superior, and judgemental. Your own husband is an alcoholic right under your nose, I wouldn't be too quick to assume I'm the only one who needs to cool off. Everybody needs a release.'

'Don't pretend to know Jeremy, Monika. He's got no excuse. He's lazy, self-indulgent and has been depressed for a decade.'

'No wonder, really.'

'What?'

'You sit in judgement, all high and mighty, but never look at your own family falling apart under your nose.'

'Stop it.'

'You know what?' Monika stood up shakily. 'I'll get myself home. The last thing I need is to take charity from you so you can play mediator for Tony again.'

She staggered and Alex caught her.

'I know how perfect you really are. Does Jeremy?'

'Shut up, Monika.'

'Ouch, you're hurting me. Get off. I'm sure Jeremy doesn't know that his perfect wife got pregnant by his perfect friend. Does Ewan know who his real dad is?'

'Shut up, Monika.'

Alex pushed her with full force and she clattered into the baroque coat stand, which snapped underneath her weight. In slow motion, Alex tried to reach out and catch her, but the stand toppled over and Monika with it.

The sound was like gravel under foot, and Monika struggled to move.

'My back,' Monika whispered.

Alex rushed to her and examined Monika's back, trying to see in the dim light.

'I can't breathe,' Monika gasped.

Alex saw the blood on her hand and broken shards of the coat stand, and realised that Monika's lung had in all probability been punctured. She was struggling to breathe and blood spread over her blouse underneath her. Alex ran around the side of the house, grabbing towels, opening the gate and checking for signs anyone was awake inside.

She sprinted back to the pool house and moved Monika, who was terribly pale, and was unable to move on her own. She managed to get her to her feet and wrapped towels around her torso tightly to stop the blood loss. Her weight wasn't onerous to support and Alex managed to get her to her car, but when she tried to bend over, Monika cried out.

'Get in the boot. I need to get you to hospital.'

Alex helped her and laid her out on a blanket. It wasn't a long drive to the university hospital. She slammed the boot down and ran back to the pool house, looking back over her shoulder at the car.

It was deathly quiet.

It didn't take long to clean up the mess and throw bags into the back seat of Jeremy's car. She could deal with the coat stand tomorrow. She shut off the pool lights, locked the doors and put together a bag of cleaning products, gloves, cloths and then, thinking at the last minute, rushed back to the house and grabbed Jeremy's coat and trilby.

She'd already made up her mind that she wasn't taking Monika to the hospital.

'Tony, calm down, she'll come back,' she soothed over the phone as she drove to Grantchester.

Monika had stopped moving by the time she got there.

Chapter 70

October

I'm not one to over analyse.

I'd like to think that it was my stoic intervention that brought the drama finally to an end. And I've also been credited with preventing a terrible miscarriage of justice. Carrie and Henry are both free. They're traumatised – understandably – but that just means a little more work is needed. They never lost their faith in me, even when faced with the worst demons from their past, as they awaited their trials.

Hunt has been awarded his longed-for promotion, and Jeremy has a new home, on remand, At His Majesty's pleasure, while the CPS put together their case against him. He was denied bail due to the attempted murder of his wife.

Ewan is playing rugby again and he's stopped wetting the bed. He's also joined a gym. Lydia has put on weight, and James spends more time at home. Tony visits often. He feels guilty about his friend. It's a natural response to the major trauma that we've all been through.

I have my work to keep me focused. With my help, Henry has been fully exonerated and will no longer face charges for the supply of the drugs that killed Brandon Stand. Archibald Morgan is facing manslaughter for that.

His family moved away. Ewan's heartbreak over Natalie leaving outweighs his horror at what his father did. I suspect he overheard what I said to Jeremy in those final moments. He's never asked.

He and Tony have grown close.

The delay to the prosecution has meant that vital evidence was lost, such as the rubbish thrown into the commercial waste bins at my office, and the lack of any search of my pool house at the time. Despite the vigorous cleaning, the police still found traces of Monika's blood, though who spilled it remains the job of the barristers to prove beyond a reasonable doubt. They've got their perpetrator now. This is the way these things go sometimes.

There were variables. I can't take credit for everything. I've learned from unpredictability. Jeremy's paper on a perfect murder, which I wrote, of course – but the police believe Jeremy did – has been a project of mine for some time. It started innocently enough. But it grew. The broken minds inside my files, and the real potential of average humans to snap into pieces at any moment, and commit murder, led me to theorise about my patients, but also those close to me, including my own husband. His slow fragmentation to utter dysfunction makes my clients look veritably sane. Any number of them could be capable of it, but the answer was there staring at me all along. The paper was not only my method, but also my proof. It's genius.

Book-worthy, or so I'm told. With the blessing of Carrie and Henry, I've accepted a publishing deal. We'll split the royalties fairly. I receive daily emails from all over the world asking for my opinion on unsafe convictions. I've been invited to speak to human rights groups and forums about miscarriages of justice. I'll do my first TED talk next year.

I've even managed to get Grace to forgive Henry. Life is all about perspective. I've repackaged her emotional avoidance and turned it into a positive mindset, which she responds well to, and it allows her to feel as though she's a warrior, moving on. She's accepted that Henry's intentions were virtuous. He only wanted to protect her. Carrie has been prescribed an experimental drug for psychotic episodes; it was touch and go with her for a time. Even I never expected her to implode so spectacularly. It's contributed hugely to my work. Henry has turned out to be quite the writer. He's good to have on side. I may need a scrapper from the wrong side of the tracks again one day. He's suing the Cambridgeshire Constabulary for damages and abuse of process. Like David, he's taken on the Goliath of the establishment, and with my help, he might win. If he does, he'll be the champion of the oppressed, and forever in my debt.

I leave the study and find Lydia in the kitchen checking Ewan's suit. Even James acquiesced when I asked him to consider letting me buy him one too. They look terribly smart and grown up. Today is Monika's memorial. Her body has been repatriated to Latvia. She was escorted by her mother on a private charter from Luton Airport, paid for by Tony.

Poor Monika. What a terrible way to go. It was an accident. A fatal mishap. But all calamities can be turned into opportunity, especially when the stakes are so high. Monika tried to force me to reveal myself, like a bully. But she underestimated the force of a mother protecting her young. Moments in life can change one's whole trajectory, undoing destiny with one seismic shift. Life is really just a series of turning points and you can learn from them, or not. Like Sarah. Her face as she fell over the edge of the tower roof, after I pushed her, was unforgettable. But instead of allowing it to define me, I used it to grow. Tony understands how much he needs me now more than ever.

I've moved the photo of the family on safari in the Serengeti to the kitchen, because it's a constant reminder that what I did was for my cubs. The lioness is always alert. Instinct always true.

I didn't break the rules, I just used them to my advantage.

I'd do it again in a heartbeat.

Acknowledgements

I loved writing this book. Watching it come together from a tiny whisper of an idea about complex PTSD to the finished product has been a great joy. Thanks for this must go firstly to the whole team at Canelo. Their fantastic encouragement and belief are what keep me writing. The incredible work of my editor, Katy Loftus, merits special mention, who pushed me to realise possibilities which started as abstract conversations.

Thank you to my agent, Peter Buckman, and the Ampersand Agency, whose loyalty, belief and commitment remains my solid foundation. I like the lunches too.

Thank you to Verity Lewis, my friend and lovely human, who helped me with the boundaries of psychological therapy. I know your mum would have loved this book.

As always, to Adrian Priestley, who answers all my random police procedural questions, even when on holiday for much deserved rest and recuperation. Thank you for your continued support of the Kelly series.

I would like to thank my closest fellow crime buddies for their friendship, candour and hilarious WhatsApp conversations, which to anyone who spends a significant amount of time stuck inside their own heads with murder, are priceless. Sheila Bugler, Marion Todd, Sarah Ward and

Jeanette Hewitt, you make me laugh out loud when I'm about to pass out with self-doubt.

To Team Lynch, Mike, Tilly, Freddie and Poppy, my biggest fans. Your passion and giddy excitement for my ideas is my central source of encouragement to keep producing stories about the more disturbing flaws in all of us. I'm sorry if I scare you.

I've taken liberties with the geography of the beautiful city of Cambridge and hope I can be forgiven for them in the name of a good story. Any inaccuracies are entirely mine, and of course, fictional in their inclusion.